CARVING SHADOWS INTO GOLD

CARVING SHADOWS

INTO

GOLD

BRIGID KEMMERER

BLOOMSBURY

LONDON   OXFORD   NEW YORK   NEW DELHI   SYDNEY

BLOOMSBURY YA
Bloomsbury Publishing Plc
50 Bedford Square, London WC1B 3DP, UK
Bloomsbury Publishing Ireland Limited
29 Earlsfort Terrace, Dublin 2, D02 AY28, Ireland

BLOOMSBURY, BLOOMSBURY YA and the Diana logo
are trademarks of Bloomsbury Publishing Plc

First published in the United States of America in 2025 by Bloomsbury YA
First published in Great Britain in 2025 by Bloomsbury Publishing Plc

A catalogue record for this book is available from the British Library

ISBN: PB: 978-1-5266-5218-8; eBook: 978-1-5266-5219-5; ePDF: 978-1-5266-5220-1

4 6 8 10 9 7 5 3

Book design by Jeanette Levy
Typeset by Westchester Publishing Services

Printed and bound in India by Thomson Press India Ltd

MIX
Paper | Supporting
responsible forestry
FSC® C010615

To find out more about our authors and books visit www.bloomsbury.com
and sign up for our newsletters
For product safety related questions contact productsafety@bloomsbury.com

For sale in the Indian subcontinent only

For my dear friend, Jim Hilderbrandt,
who's never afraid of a little magic

Syhl Shallow

IISHELLASA
ICE FOREST

THE
FROZEN
RIVER

THE
CRYSTAL
PALACE

BRIARLOCK

WILDTHORNE
VALLEY

N

BLACKROCK
PLAINS

THE ROYAL COURTS
OF THE ALLIED NATIONS
SYHL SHALLOW AND EMBERFALL

TITLE	NAME	RESIDING IN
Queen of Syhl Shallow	Lia Mara	Syhl Shallow
King of Emberfall	Grey	Syhl Shallow
Their Daughter	Princess Sinna Cataleha	Syhl Shallow
Queen's Chief Adviser and Sister	Nolla Verin	Syhl Shallow
Royal Physician	Noah of Disi*	Syhl Shallow
Counsel to the King	Jacob of Disi*	Syhl Shallow
Brother to the King	Prince Rhen, Acting Regent	Emberfall
Princess of Disi, Rhen's Beloved	Princess Harper of Disi*	Emberfall
King's Courier/Queen's Envoy	Lord Tycho of Rillisk	Both

*"Disi" is not a real country, though the people of Emberfall and Syhl Shallow both believe it to be the birthplace of Princess Harper. In truth, "Disi" refers to Washington, DC. When a curse tormented Prince Rhen years ago, Harper, Noah, and Jacob were magically trapped on the grounds of Ironrose Castle in Emberfall, with no way home aside from breaking the curse . . . but that's a different story.

CHAPTER 1

TYCHO

I should start keeping a list of all the ways fate hates me.

This ride to Ironrose Castle was supposed to be easy. Enjoyable. After the battle in Briarlock that nearly killed the king of Emberfall and overthrew the queen of Syhl Shallow, I've been desperate for easy and enjoyable.

And it was—for the first few days.

I normally make this ride alone, but when we left Briarlock, I had a small group for company. Prince Rhen, of course, returning to his home in Emberfall, where he acts as regent while Grey is in Syhl Shallow. We also had a small group of Emberish soldiers who assisted in the battle.

And then there's Jax, the blacksmith who carried treasonous notes against the king in exchange for silver to save his home. Jax, who later protected the king in battle, and likely saved his life.

Jax, the young man who's been slowly stealing my heart.

Not that anyone should know that part. I'm *well* acquainted with the way rumors and gossip can fly among a group of soldiers, so I've maintained focus and discretion. Traveling with a group means the going is slower, with plenty of time for others to observe and whisper. My reputation as King's Courier has been in question for weeks, which is part of the reason I've been ordered to return to Ironrose Castle at all.

But for those first few days, Jax still laid his bedroll near mine at night, and he would sit with me for every meal. Some of that was due to necessity, because he doesn't speak Emberish, and not many of the soldiers speak any Syssalah. But some of it was due to *want*. I'd catch Jax watching me when I'd volunteer to ride a patrol or take a turn sitting sentry. It would spark warmth on my cheeks, and I'd have to turn my attention elsewhere—only to glance back and find him blushing, doing the same thing. My heart would thump and I'd swallow a smile and I'd count the minutes until we could be at Ironrose.

Easy. *Enjoyable.*

Or it *was*. But a few days after we left, King Grey sent half the army contingent to join us, carrying word that such a large force wouldn't be needed in Syhl Shallow. Suddenly, our lighthearted, small group turned into twelve dozen. With more men and horses to feed, more equipment to carry, and more duties to assign, our slow pace dragged to a crawl. The gold-and-red livery of the Emberish army was suddenly everywhere, impossible to escape: jostling for food at mealtimes, crowding under cover when it rained, looming in the dark when we laid out bedrolls.

Sleep grew challenging. When I'd finally drift off, nightmares haunted me, reminding me of a childhood where soldiers tormented my family. Every time my eyes fell on the colors, I began to feel a tiny pinch at the back of my neck. I found myself shying away when soldiers met my gaze, flinching if they drew close. Forbidden magic would flicker in my blood, sparks and stars responding to my flare of panic. I'd force myself to stand my ground, but sometimes their presence was too much to bear, and I'd skip a meal or lie awake for hours.

By the end of the seventh day on the road, I'm surly and snappish. Instead of wanting to cower, I'm spoiling for a fight.

It doesn't help that most of these soldiers are wary of Jax. Within the larger group, speculation has clearly run rampant, and I can see their glares and hear the muttered whispers. They think he plotted against the king.

But if Jax understands their muttering, he ignores it. He keeps his head down and works when we stop, fixing horseshoes and repairing tack. He rides in one of the wagons when we move, and he doesn't complain. He does his best to parse out Emberish when no one is around to translate, and I know he must be frustrated, but he doesn't let it show.

Lately, I've seen him seek out the few friendly soldiers from that first group for company when I've volunteered for duties. There are so many soldiers with us that I don't *need* to volunteer, but I'd rather walk lonely loops as a sentry than lie anxious and awake on a bedroll. But my sudden absence is creating a distance between me and Jax that shouldn't be there, and I don't know how to undo it.

By the seventh night of our journey, I've hardly seen Jax all day. Once we stopped, there was the busy setting of the camp, which is always loud and chaotic, so I avoided it in favor of tending to the horses. Then the mad rush for dinner, which I skipped. Again.

So now I'm clinging to the shadows, brushing the sweat marks out of Mercy's fur, wondering if anyone would notice if I just laid my bedroll out *here*, when a recruit brings word that Prince Rhen has asked to see me.

I sigh, give Mercy a pat on the shoulder, and get on with it. As I walk, I avoid eye contact with every soldier I pass. I keep trying to shake off my discomfort, but it *clings*, like claws that have dug in and found purchase. I'm no stranger to traveling with an army, and it shouldn't bother me so much. I served in the Syhl Shallow army for years.

Then again, that was never enjoyable either.

Just as I break free of the main part of the camp to approach the prince's tent, my shoulder slams into someone heading the other way.

My head is down, so I don't know whose fault it is, and it's barely a glancing blow. Any other time, any other *place*, and I'd say, "Forgive me," and move on without thinking about it.

Tonight, I'm coiled like a spring ready to snap, and magic waits under my skin, ready to flare. I whirl like I've been poked with a branding iron. "*Hey*."

It's a soldier, of course, because they're everywhere. He was in the process of saying an offhand *sorry* over his shoulder, but the belligerence in my tone stops him—or maybe it's whatever expression is on my face. He draws himself up, and his eyes go flinty.

The camp was bustling with activity, but the air around us suddenly goes quiet. Nothing draws the interest of bored soldiers like the promise of a fight.

But a man calls out from somewhere to my left. "Samson, that's the King's Courier. Pick a fight with him, and the captain will have you riding back in chains."

Samson's eyes flick up and down my form, taking in the black armor, the dual crests on my breastplate that show my allegiance to both countries. He scowls, then backs right down. "Forgive me, my lord."

He doesn't wait for me to say anything; he just turns away.

A part of me is relieved.

A darker part is disappointed.

Motion around us resumes, and I look for whoever called out to stop the fight. It's one of the soldiers who was with us from the beginning. He's a first lieutenant named Kutter, and he's sitting by a fire, fletching arrows with two other young soldiers named Sephran and Malin.

To my surprise, Jax is with them.

I shouldn't be startled, but I am. The firelight bounces off his eyes, and his long, dark hair is bound into a tight knot at the back of his head. His crutches are on the ground beside him. They're far enough

4

away that I can't hear what the soldiers are saying, but Jax's eyes are on me.

I feel like he's picking me apart.

He's noticed the shift in my mood over the last few days, but there's no privacy here, so he hasn't pressed. I don't even know what I'd say. He's one of the few people who knows everything about my past, but it was so long ago. It shouldn't matter anymore. Besides, I'm the King's Courier. I can't exactly admit that I hate the king's army.

All of this makes me feel so weak, and I scowl. No wonder I want to punch someone.

Jax sees my expression shift, and he frowns.

But then Sephran gently pokes him in the arm with an arrow and says something that makes Jax look over and smile.

That gives my heart a firm tug. I wonder what Sephran said, whether it was something Jax understood, or if it was just a tone he was responding to.

His smile turns into light laughter, and the tug in my heart turns into a clench.

When he glances back over, I've already looked away. But I feel his gaze follow me all the way to the prince's tent.

Prince Rhen is the only person in the camp with a private tent, and though it's not large or well lit, he's *alone.* The sudden muffled silence is welcome, and when I step inside, I feel like I can breathe for the first time in hours. The forbidden magic that was pulsing under my skin finally seems to settle.

The prince sits at a small table, going through a stack of stained and folded parchment. We're close enough to Ironrose that he must be getting reports from point-to-point runners now.

"Tycho," he says, without preamble. "We should arrive by sundown tomorrow."

5

This isn't a surprise. I could make this trek with my eyes closed. "Yes, Your Highness."

"The army couriers have reported that Lord Alek has already been escorted back to Syhl Shallow. I thought you should know."

Lord Alek worked with the Truthbringers to trap the queen and execute the king. I'm a bit surprised they're sending him back, honestly. I thought Grey would just leave him in the dungeon at Ironrose—but I suppose he wants to interrogate the man himself. I snort. "Are they dragging him behind a horse?"

"No. He claims innocence. He states that there is absolutely no evidence tying him to these attacks—and he's not wrong." Rhen's voice is grave. "You should be aware that he'll likely be questioned and released. At least for the time being."

This news hits me like an arrow, sharp and true. Of anyone in the two kingdoms, Lord Alek is the last person who should be walking free. After the last few days among the soldiers, I didn't think my spine could grow any colder, but apparently it can.

"Again," Rhen says, more quietly, "I thought you should know."

I frown. "Why?"

The lantern light flickers off his blond hair while he studies me. It falls across his face, drifting over the patch that covers his missing eye. "Why not, Tycho? We've become friends, have we not?"

He says this like it's a genuine question—and maybe it is. Maybe he's really . . . not quite sure. Considering everything he did to me, I should probably hate him. I know Jax does, and he's only seen the scars Rhen's guards left on my back.

But the prince has a dark and tortured past, just like I do. He doesn't know my entire history, just his part in it, but over the past few months, I've developed a kinship with Rhen that I never saw coming.

Maybe he didn't either.

I let out a breath and run a hand through my hair. "Yes," I say. "We have. But . . . can you send word? He shouldn't be released. He was obviously plotting against the royal family. Grey interrogated Jax. And Callyn told the queen herself—"

"I'm not sure the testimony of a blacksmith and a baker who *were* proven to be working with the Truthbringers—at least in a small way— would hold up in front of Syhl Shallow's Royal Houses."

I scowl.

Rhen continues, "When the attack took place, Lord Alek was here, in Emberfall. We were all *with Grey* when news of the attack was delivered—you included. Lord Alek claims he had nothing to do with it—and none of us can prove otherwise. He claims he's being persecuted for speaking out against the king's magic, so locking him up will make him look like a martyr. It would give the Truthbringers *more* power. Fear of the king's magic has been growing, and Grey is on shaky ground with the rumors that have already been spread."

My fists are clenched at my sides. "I *told you* Alek was politically tricky."

"Indeed you did. Trust that Grey will make sure he's kept on a very short leash."

I hate this. I hate *all* of this. I've been worried about the soldiers *here*, but now I'll worry about Alek finding a new way to kill everyone I care about. I remember little Princess Sinna screaming in the woods, blood running in a thin stream down her throat while a soldier threatened her life.

"Fine," I say, and the word is sharp. "Any other good news?"

Rhen's eye widens marginally at my tone, and he sits back in his chair to study me fully.

I wince. I might've been ready to pick a fight with one random soldier, but I'm not about to do it with the king's brother. My anger isn't with Rhen anyway. "Forgive me. I shouldn't have snapped. It's been . . . a long journey."

He studies me for another moment. "You're not usually so irascible. I've sensed that there's a problem with the soldiers—"

"What?" My eyes snap to his face. Have I been obvious? "*No.* There's not."

He frowns and finishes his statement. "—and their perception of Jax."

Oh.

I force myself to swallow. I need to get it together. "Just camp gossip. About the battle in Briarlock. It will pass."

"They're suspicious of him?"

"No. Well—not really. Maybe." I make a frustrated sound, because I remember how that same gossip and suspicion followed *me* right into court in Syhl Shallow. "The king was attacked. The soldiers are wary."

"If it's causing discord, Tycho—"

"It's not."

He stares at me, and I realize I've interrupted him twice. But if Prince Rhen feels that bringing Jax back to Ironrose is more trouble than it's worth, I'm not sure what I'd do—especially if Lord Alek has been freed.

Alek would kill Jax for turning on him. I know he would.

I bite the inside of my cheek to stop myself from talking. The silence in the tent swirls around us, and I can see the prince thinking.

If he were Grey, he'd demand answers—and he'd probably get them, because I'm loyal and I'll yield when pressed. It's part of the growing edge of resentment between us. But Rhen isn't Grey, and I've discovered that he's savvy and patient. He gets answers in his own way, in his own time.

So I'm not surprised when he simply says, "Very well. What of your magic?" His voice is very soft, so there's no danger of anyone outside this tent overhearing. "Is *that* causing a problem?"

I frown, thinking of how often the sparks and stars flicker in my

8

blood now. But we'll be back to Ironrose in a day, and I'll be away from the soldiers. "No, Your Highness. I'm just tired. Truly."

"You've said nothing to anyone?" he presses.

Like I'd talk to anyone here. "No. Here in Emberfall, you and Jax are the only two who know."

"Good. Has there been any indication from the scraver Nakiis that he would be making his claim?"

I frown. Yet another band of tension tightens around my heart. My vow to Nakiis is a large part of the conflict between me and Grey. I promised the scraver one week of service where I would fight in his defense—at the time and place of his choosing.

I have no idea when he'll collect.

I have no idea who my opponent will be.

"No," I say to Prince Rhen. "I've seen no sign of him."

He studies me again, and for a moment, I'm worried he's going to dig for more information, or ask more questions about the soldiers and their agitation, or anything that will make me *irascible* again.

But he doesn't. "Good." His eye flicks toward the flaps to the tent. "You're dismissed, Tycho."

I give him a sharp nod, then duck through the exit, surprised how quickly my relief at being inside turned to relief at being allowed to *go*.

CHAPTER 2

TYCHO

By the time I head back across the camp, it's almost full dark. Jax and the other soldiers were gone when I exited Prince Rhen's tent, their fire banked and left to embers. They were fletching arrows, so I wonder if they went shooting.

That tug in my heart refuses to go away.

I'm being ridiculous. I'm glad he's found a few friends when so many people here look like they're waiting for a chance to leave him bleeding in a ditch. But I don't recognize the emotion that keeps pulling at my heart every time I see Jax with them. Is it longing? Jealousy? I'm not sure.

Either way, he's not here. He likely followed Kutter and Sephran wherever they went.

That clench in my chest doesn't loosen one bit.

Across the field, soldiers are laying out bedrolls and starting card games. Bottles of liquor are pulled from hiding spots, whispers calling warnings whenever an officer is spotted.

I head back toward the horses, where I won't be alone—at least, not yet—but it's easy to lose myself in the shadows.

When I get to Mercy, Jax is waiting there, feeding her an apple, his eyes gleaming in the fading light. A few tendrils of hair have pulled loose from his knot to fall around his face, and there's the faintest hint of beard growth along his chin. He smiles when he sees me, but it's a quiet smile, a private smile.

"Jax," I say. My heart gives a little skip, because I just want to grab hold of him and not let go.

But then I consider the soldiers, the meeting with Rhen, the way fate seems determined to take every moment of my life and make it as difficult or painful as possible. My skipping heart stumbles and falls.

"I thought I might find you here," he says.

I'm not sure what that means, and I can't read his voice. "Yeah?"

He nods, shifting on his crutches to lean against Mercy's shoulder. "I remember what you said about soldiering. I can tell you don't want to be traveling with the army."

That's a little too astute, and I almost flinch. I hate that I'm so easy to read. It's a good thing I'm being sent away from the king, because if Grey sensed my discomfort, he'd order me to spend every second of every day in the center of a formation. He's more the type to face any challenge head-on, without fear. I've always admired that. Aspired to it.

Envied it.

I shake off these thoughts. "What did I say about soldiering?"

"That you loved training and sparring," he says. "But the actual soldiering . . . not so much."

There's weight in his voice, and I frown. I know it wasn't his intent, but the way he found me here makes me feel vulnerable, like I was hiding.

That's probably what makes me say, "*You* don't seem to mind it much. I saw you with Kutter and Sephran."

The words come out sharp, like a challenge. A line appears between his eyebrows, and Jax straightens on his crutches. "Oh, so you're trying to pick a fight with everyone you meet tonight."

Maybe I am. But as with Rhen, I wish I could reel the words back into my mouth. I run a hand across the back of my neck. "No," I say with a sigh. "Jax—"

"Oh, stop. Here." He pulls a wrapped square of muslin out of the pouch at his waist, then holds it out to me.

I stare at him for a moment, flummoxed.

"Take it," he says, thrusting the fabric at me. "I know you skipped the dinner call. I'm willing to bet you missed the midday rations, too."

I take the muslin, and it's heavier than I expect. When I unwrap it, I discover six dried strips of beef, a wide slab of cheese, and an orange.

My heart gives another clench, and my eyes flick back up to his. I swallow hard. "You brought me dinner?"

Mercy is nosing at his fingers, looking for another apple, and he runs a hand down her face. "You nearly drew your sword when that soldier bumped into you. I figured you should eat something."

I flush. "I wasn't going to pick a fight."

He makes a noncommittal sound and turns back to the horse. "Eat. You'll feel better."

The sad thing is, he's probably right. Now that the food is in my hands, I can smell it, and I'm *starving*. Mercy is stretching her neck out, reaching for the orange, her nostrils flaring as she whuffles for the fruit. I smile and duck under the tether lines to keep out of reach. "I'm sure Jax already gave you my apple," I tell her.

"She asked nicely," he says.

I take a few steps back from the horses so I can sit in the grass. Jax seems to hesitate, but then he drops his crutches in the grass and sits down beside me. The sky is darkening overhead, and several stars are already visible, gleaming among the purple and pink of the few clouds that linger. It's warmer here than in Syhl Shallow, and now that it's late spring, we've begun to reach the days when I'm grateful for the fading sunlight, because it means the weight of leather and weapons won't be such a burden.

He's quiet while I eat, so I'm quiet, but I'm very aware of how close he is. Our knees are almost touching. I think of everything Rhen told me, the way he wanted to know if the soldiers have a problem with Jax being here. A tight knot of worry forms in my gut, joining the dozen others that never seem to loosen. The sky keeps darkening overhead, and we haven't said anything in so long that I nearly jump when Jax's fingertips brush over mine.

It's just a faint touch, a light reminder that he's here, and I look over to find his eyes sparkling like the stars. Everything we have together is new and untested, but he's one of the few people I know whose presence always seems to . . . to *unwind* me. Sometimes, like now, I want to grab him so badly that it aches.

"You haven't been sleeping either," he says.

I don't know what to say to that, so I shrug.

"You're the King's Courier. Surely you warrant a private tent."

I scoff. "I'm not going to ask for a private tent. My reputation is already in the gutter."

He's quiet for a moment. "Because of me."

"What? No."

"It's all right. As I've said before, I know who you are. I know who *I* am. The king told me there were tensions at court because of our . . . involvement."

I go very still. A breeze cuts across the fields, slicing between us.

"When did he say that?" I finally ask.

"In Briarlock." Jax looks at me as the shadows lengthen across the grass. "When he was asking me about Alek and everything he did. The king explained how you risked your role at court."

"That wasn't because of you, Jax." I finish the last piece of dried beef and attack the orange peel a little too aggressively. "I mean—it was. But Alek made it seem like I was the one working with the Truthbringers, instead of *him*. He did it to get a target off his back. Grey shouldn't have said that."

If he were here right now, I'd be risking my role at court again, because we'd have words about it.

"I've hardly seen you these last few days." Jax looks out at the sky, and his voice turns careful. "You asked for discretion before we left. I thought that might be why."

Oh. I frown.

I remember the moment he's talking about, when I pulled him into the shadows beside the forge on the morning we were due to leave. "We'll be traveling with the prince and a handful of guards and soldiers," I said to him, pressing my hand to the warmth of his cheek. "You've been given a new role, and I've been given new orders. I don't know any of them well, but I do know how soldiers think. I don't want rumors following us back to Ironrose Castle."

He nodded, and I leaned in to kiss him—just as Prince Rhen's soldiers rode into the tiny courtyard beside the forge and we were forced to break apart. It was the last time we shared more than a glancing touch.

Until this moment, I didn't consider how my words would combine with Grey's warnings to fill Jax's head with doubt. I didn't consider how my actions would lead him to think he'd done something wrong. I've spent days with my own thoughts so tangled up that I didn't realize the same thing was happening to Jax.

I set down the orange and look at him, but his eyes are fixed on the stars.

"Jax," I say softly.

"It's all right. I understand." He reaches for his crutches. "I likely shouldn't be sitting with you in the grass for so long."

14

I put a hand on his crutches and hold them there. "Stop," I say softly.

He stops, but he's not looking at me now.

"When I asked for discretion," I say, "it was because I have a position at court, and I know how soldiers talk." I roll my eyes a little. "And that was before we had a hundred of them to worry about."

"I know." He still hasn't let go of his crutches, and they're tight under my grip, like he'll flee the instant I take my hand away. "And I might not speak the language, but it's no secret that most of them resent me. I know you have to keep your distance."

"No—Jax—you don't understand. I'm not worried about *me*. Well—not much, anyway."

He finally looks at me. "You're worried about me?"

A bit of warmth crawls up my neck. "A bit."

"Why? I expected it. I know what I did." He snorts. "Honestly, the bigger surprise is that *any* of them are nice. I'm sure it's just because they know the prince himself hired me to work in the forge."

"*Exactly.*"

He blinks at me. "Exactly?"

I forget that he has no experience at court, no history with rumor and gossip and how quickly it can spread like wildfire. His experience is only from the other side, the filtered stories that would make it all the way to remote villages, usually far from any sort of truth at all.

"You defended the king when it mattered," I say, "and you supported the army when they arrived—without question. Grey knows that. Prince Rhen knows that. You were offered the position at Ironrose for your skills in the forge. You *earned* this, Jax." My cheeks are growing warm, and I drop my voice, abashed. "So . . . I don't want anyone to start thinking the King's Courier just brought you along for your skills in his *bed.*"

"Oh." His eyebrows go up. "*Oh.*"

"Yeah. *Oh*." I pick the orange back up and begin pulling apart the pieces.

We sit in silence again, staring out at the darkening sky, but now my thoughts are on what I said, and my cheeks refuse to cool. Any soldiers who were lingering with the horses have moved off, and some of the tension that was clinging to my shoulders begins to ease.

Jax finally looks over, and he smiles mischievously. "So you think I'm skilled?"

I choke on the orange. "Silver hell, Jax."

He laughs softly, and it's a low rumble of sound that tugs at my heart again, but in a different way. A warmer way—because now I'm thinking about the exact skills he's talking about. We're so close that I can hear his breathing, and it's full dark now. Moonlight finds his eyes, and I feel a clench in my belly. My hands want to touch him so badly. I'd pull the pin from his hair so it would spill loose, and then I'd drown myself on the taste of his tongue.

I realize Jax is gazing back at me, his lips slightly parted, waiting for me to yield.

I shouldn't. I meant what I said.

But the night is so dark, the only sound coming from the horses casually stomping at flies. In the distance, the camp has mostly gone quiet as card games settle and others drift off to sleep. Another cool breeze blows between us, lifting those tendrils of hair around his face.

Maybe I *am* weak, because I can't take it. I reach out and pull the pin.

His hair falls around his shoulders, and Jax lets out a breath. Despite the chill in the air, warmth fills my chest, a flame flickering to life. Out here, we're alone, and we could be back on the other side of the mountain, the soldiers and my worries and Rhen's warnings all a distant memory.

But a man coughs somewhere nearby, and then I hear a low rumble

16

of another man's voice, saying something about his stash of sugared spirits.

We snap apart so roughly that some of the nearby horses snort and throw their heads up before settling. Then we sit stock-still as two men, practically invisible in the darkness, dig through some saddlebags before their boots retreat through the grass to head back to camp.

I don't know if they saw us. I don't even know if it would *matter*.

"What did they want?" says Jax, his voice barely louder than a whisper.

My heart is pounding so hard, and my entire body is practically vibrating with tension. Sparks and stars flare in my blood again, my magic ready to face a threat that isn't there. I have to run a hand down my face.

"One of them had a stash of liquor," I tell him. I take a rough breath, and it sounds ragged. "Forgive me. Now you see why I've given you distance." My hand is still curled around the pin from his hair, and I hold it out on my palm. "Here."

Jax glances down, but he makes no move to take it. His eyes hold mine devilishly, and he says, "Keep it."

I don't know what it is about the words, but I feel them all the way to my core. I close my fingers around the slim piece of metal and fall back in the grass, closing my eyes.

Jax laughs, the tone low and sultry.

"Stop laughing," I murmur. "You're killing me."

"Stop lying there. You're killing *me*."

I flush again, and I open my eyes. He's so beautiful in the moonlight that it's almost heartbreaking. "I didn't mean to leave you alone, Jax."

"I haven't been alone. *Lonely*, because this is the longest conversation I've had in days, but not alone."

I wince, thinking of the soldiers he was with earlier, wondering how they got along, because only Malin speaks any Syssalah at all. "I'm glad some of them are friendly."

His eyes trace my expression. "You could have joined us."

That chases some of the heat out of my body, and I look back up at the stars. On the first few days out of Briarlock, I *would* have joined them. I would have played cards or dice, and we might have shared stories around a campfire, with me translating for Jax.

But I think of the press of soldiers at camp, the nightmares that have haunted my sleep, the way that man brushed against my shoulder and I was ready to draw blades.

I shake my head.

Jax's fingers brush over mine again. "Too much soldiering."

He doesn't say it like a question, but I nod anyway. It's not the whole truth, not quite, but it'll do. Something about the silent darkness makes it easier to admit fears in the middle of the night, even with my magic waiting right under my skin to respond to dangers that don't exist. "Yeah."

His fingers are drifting away, and I twist my hand to capture his before he can let go. I keep my eyes on the sky, because otherwise I'm going to pull him down to me, and I don't want to risk another soldier seeing us. But I can't sit here like this without touching him at *all*.

His fingers wind through mine, and we sit there for the longest time, just letting the wind wash over us as darkness cloaks the fields.

"Tycho," he murmurs. "We shouldn't sleep."

My eyes flutter open, and I'm startled to discover I *was* beginning to fall asleep. The breeze whipping through the grass is ice cold now. There must be a storm coming. Clouds obscure the stars overhead, and I wonder if we both drifted off for a time.

"Sorry," I say roughly.

He grimaces. "After everything you said . . . I figured we shouldn't be found this way."

"No, you're right." And our bedrolls shouldn't be the only ones empty, either, but I don't say that.

I hate this. The chill in the air suddenly matches my mood.

"Come on." I uncurl to standing, then hold out a hand. "Let's go."

He takes my hand, but when I pull him upright, he grabs hold of the front of my armor. At first, I think it's for balance—but then he presses his mouth to mine.

I inhale sharply, but I don't protest. Maybe it's too much or maybe I'm too weak or maybe I'm just dreaming, because I'm lost to the sudden taste of him. My hands tangle in his hair as the wind whips around us, biting at my skin. That fire lights in my belly again, sending heat through my veins. I should let him go, but I don't. I should stop, but I won't.

This is reckless and foolish, but right this second, I don't care.

Maybe fate doesn't hate me after all.

But then I feel a spark in the wind, and it tugs at my awareness. I pull away, breaking the kiss. Our breath clouds in the air between us like it's midwinter, the air so biting it makes me shiver.

It doesn't make sense. We're a few weeks shy of summer.

"Tycho?" Jax says, and from the alarm in his tone, I know he sees it, too.

But he's not looking at our shared breath. He's staring at my arm, at the sheathed knives along my bracer, where the hilts are exposed by the leather.

Frost forms on the steel, ice crystals gathering with alarming speed.

"Scravers," I whisper.

I look up to the sky, but it's too dark now, especially with clouds covering the moon and stars. All I see are flickering shadows. Wings? I'm not sure. The wind burns my eyes, and I shiver again.

Then an inhuman voice finds my ears, carried on the wind.

—*Find the magesmith.*

I remember Rhen's question, about the scraver Nakiis. I owe him a week of service, and he said he'd collect when he was ready.

Is this it?

A wild screech tears across the night, followed by another, sending the horses into a panicked frenzy.

"*Tycho*," Jax says urgently. "Is it the one you know?"

Soldiers are shouting from the camp, woken by the sounds, and the screeches overhead intensify. There have to be at least three of them, maybe more. My blood goes cold.

"Tycho!" Jax demands.

"I don't know," I say. "Jax, I don't know!"

I look up at the night and inhale a breath of frigid air, ready to call Nakiis's name.

Before I can, a winged creature slams right into me. We crash into the ground and roll, but those claws have gripped tight. I can't reach any of my weapons, but it doesn't matter. It feels like my arm might be ripped right off my body. Men are shouting, and scravers are shrieking. It sounds like a lot more than three.

Then I can't focus on anything else.

All I can feel is pain.

CHAPTER 3

JAX

A few minutes ago, I was glad we were alone, cloaked by shadows and silence. It took me forever to find the nerve to grab hold of Tycho's armor, to press my mouth to his, but I've hardly seen him in days. He sat there speaking of concern for my honor. He pulled the pin from my hair. The sky was fully dark, the soldiers were tucked away at the camp, and Tycho was right in front of me, smelling like oranges and leather. We were alone, and I was no good.

Now I'm regretting the solitude. I'm regretting my inexperience. Because a *real* soldier would be a hell of a lot quicker with a bow and arrow.

As it is, the scraver rips Tycho away from me, and I lose a moment to shock before I remember I'm armed. Tycho is swearing, struggling against the scraver's grip, and the creature makes an inhuman sound that hurts my ears. The scent of blood flares on the air, causing a visceral reaction in my gut. Soldiers are shouting near the camp, but I have no idea what they're saying. They're too far to help anyway.

Then I have an arrow nocked on the string, and I'm drawing back to shoot.

It's so dark. All I see are wings and shadows, and I can tell they're rolling, fighting, tussling. Tycho's voice breaks off on a sound I don't ever want to hear again.

But I hold the arrow. I can't see. I don't want to hit *him*. I don't know what to do. I might have the gear, but I'm not a soldier. Sweat erupts between my shoulder blades.

Then they come to a stop. Tycho isn't swearing anymore. He's not moving at all. The scraver has him pinned to the ground, and it rears back, claws ready to swipe through his throat.

I shoot.

The arrow snaps off the string and goes right into the scraver's chest, hitting with enough impact to shove the creature sideways. In the dark, they could almost look human, those dark wings barely more than a shadow. But the screech that comes from its throat is so inhumanly shrill that I want to cower. Several horses break free from the tether line and bolt.

I have another arrow nocked already, and I shoot again. This time the scraver collapses to the ground, silent.

I'm breathing hard, my heart pounding in my ears. Tycho still hasn't moved, and I've completely lost track of my crutches. I have to crawl to him.

Blood is everywhere, on his armor, on his face, in his hair. His armor seems to be hanging loose at the shoulder. I don't think he's breathing.

Then the clouds shift, and a bit of moonlight peeks through. I can see the reason for the blood. Claws have ripped across the side of his head, tearing through his ear, his cheek, into his mouth. His other arm is a shredded ruin where it wasn't covered by armor. The scent of blood is so thick in the air I can taste it, hot and metallic.

I choke on a sob. "Tycho. *Tycho.*"

He doesn't move.

He's forbidden to use his magic, I know. Does that mean he might not have used it in time to protect himself? Could he be dead?

The thoughts are too terrifying to contemplate, and I don't have time to think about it anyway. Another screech pierces the night above me, but I'm ready. The wind feels like ice against my skin, but I don't care. An arrow is nocked, and I'm firing as soon as my eyes lock on the motion. One shot, two. *Swip, swip.*

This scraver drops with a heavy *thump*, landing somewhere distant in the grass.

But then I hear words on the air, and the sound is odd, almost like a thought instead of a voice.

—You heard Xovaar. Find the magesmith.

Xovaar. Is that a name?

Find the magesmith. Are they looking for Tycho? Or the king?

More screeches erupt overhead, but now soldiers are responding, and the shouts have drawn closer. More arrows are firing from the other side of the tether line, the screeches of the scravers cutting abruptly short. Winged bodies fall to the grass.

I look down at Tycho and choke on a sob again. I turn my head and shout for soldiers.

"Help!" I call. "Help me!" But I realize I'm shouting in Syssalah, and of all the words they've taught me, *help* hasn't made the list.

I look down again and press a hand to Tycho's cheek, which is wet and tacky with blood. "Please," I whisper.

And then I notice that his cheek is *whole*, when a moment ago, it wasn't.

As I stare, the rest of the injuries begin to heal as well, his arm knitting back together, the gash through his scalp sealing over, leaving nothing but blood, his magic responding to put him back the way he was. After a moment, he draws a ragged breath, and his eyes flutter open.

23

His expression twists with fury, and he shoves me away with surprising strength, flinging me to the side. Claws graze my cheek, then my shoulder, and then I hit the ground, just as Tycho draws a blade and slams it into the scraver that was descending on us both. The creature collapses on top of him, claws digging at the grass, but I can tell it was a killing blow. The efforts are futile.

Tycho grunts underneath its weight. "Help me, Jax."

I shove it off him, but it takes longer than it should. My left arm doesn't want to work. Tycho is gasping, but he pulls the blade, then stabs the creature again.

This time it goes still for good.

He pulls the dagger free again, then wipes it in the grass. Wind is still whipping across the fields. Half the horses are panicking, dragging at the tether lines, while dozens seem to have broken loose. The clouds have shifted again, and moonlight reveals the wash of blood across his face, the streaks through Tycho's blond hair. We're both on our knees, breathing hard, looking in all directions, waiting for another attack. The wind might be ice cold and brutal, but the screeches have gone silent now, the only sound coming from the shouting soldiers who seem to be heading this way.

Tycho's fingers brush my shoulder. "One of them got you." Without warning, pain flares in my arm, and I nearly jerk away.

"Wait," Tycho murmurs. "It only takes a moment. You remember."

I do. In fact, the pain is already subsiding, easing away as my own injuries heal and dissolve into nothing. I swallow, and the touch of his fingers turns into a caress against my arm.

"Where else?" he says, eyeing me critically. His hand lifts to my face, where the claw marks are already beginning to sting.

I try not to flinch when I feel another flare of magic. "But—but you're not supposed to use—"

"Jax." He gives me a look. But the shouts have gotten closer, and soldiers are suddenly pushing past the tether line, carrying torches and weapons and enough righteous rage to fight a war right here. Tycho's hand drops away from my face before he heals much of anything at all, and he shoves to his feet, holding out a hand, all brusque duty now. Just one man offering another a hand up from the battlefield.

I can't lock away emotion so quickly, and it doesn't help that I can't understand half of what the soldiers are saying.

They're afraid, though. Afraid and angry. I hear it in their voices, see it in the flickering shadows that dance across their eyes. Some of them are splattered with blood, too.

They see the bodies of the scravers we killed, and the blood sprayed across Tycho's armor. It's all over *me*, too. Voices raise, men looking to the sky, pointing at me, at the camp, at the loose horses. I don't see anyone I know, and I can only pick out random words, and nothing makes sense. We're not under attack by scravers anymore, but nothing seems *better*.

"What are they saying?" I say desperately. "Tycho, what are they saying?"

"They don't know why the scravers attacked." He speaks quickly, his voice a low rush, because soldiers are moving closer. "But three men are dead. Maybe more. They think the creatures might have followed you from Briar—"

A soldier snarls something, cutting him off, and Tycho takes a step forward, blocking the man from getting in my face.

Then, in a move that surprises me but shouldn't, Tycho puts a hand on the man's armor and shoves him back.

I don't need to speak Emberish to know it's a little too rough, a little too *much*, especially right now. I forgot how keyed up he was when I saw him walking toward the prince's tent, when he looked ready to pick a fight with anything upright and breathing. He all but growled at *me* when he found me waiting with Mercy. As soon as Tycho puts his hand

25

on this soldier's armor, I can *feel* it, the snap in the air that predicates a fight. There's an indrawn breath, a ripple of tension that spreads. Tycho has drawn himself up, and my own shoulders go tight. There are so many of them. I have no time for fear, just action.

But just as quickly, shouts erupt from the back of the group, the clear sound of orders being given. Soldiers begin to fall in line, snapping to attention.

These words don't need any translation, because I've heard them a hundred times by now.

Make way for the prince.

Even the men who seemed ready to brawl are falling back, expressions washed clean. No anger, no fury, just readiness.

It's a skill I don't have. Too much has happened in the last ten minutes, and I can't unwind all my thoughts yet. But Tycho has ducked to fetch my crutches from the grass, and he's all but shoving them against my armor. By the time Prince Rhen reaches us, even Tycho looks sharp and ready, while I'm barely steady on my crutches, my jaw tight and my shoulder stinging.

The prince is backed by two guards and six soldiers. Four of the soldiers have arrows nocked, and their eyes are on the sky. Another two carry lanterns, and the light gleams where it finds Prince Rhen's weapons, throwing shadows across his face. He wears a leather patch over one eye, but still, some scars are visible where they escape the covering, and the flickering light seems to accentuate them. I know from Tycho that the prince lost the eye in a battle with a magesmith years ago, when Prince Rhen and King Grey were fighting over who was the rightful heir to the throne in Emberfall.

I also know Prince Rhen is responsible for the dozen whip marks on Tycho's back, so every time I see the patch or the scars on his cheek, I don't feel one single ounce of pity.

In fact, every time I see him, I want to punch him right in his stupid face.

I shouldn't feel that way. I *know* I shouldn't. He's giving me a new opportunity in Emberfall. If I knew nothing about their history, I'd be on my knees, groveling with gratitude, because the prince doesn't *seem* like the kind of man who'd chain a boy to a wall to have him flogged. Tycho has made his peace with it, so I should, too.

But I think about Tycho hiding out here with Mercy, his ready tension that nearly made him brawl with all these soldiers, and I wonder if he's made peace with anything at all.

Too much soldiering.

It makes my heart hurt.

The prince looks across the sea of faces, then settles on Tycho, who's still slicked with so much blood that half his vibrant blond hair is almost blackened. The lantern light reveals huge gouges across the leather of his armor. Prince Rhen is questioning him, and though I can pick out a few words, I haven't learned anywhere near enough to follow their entire conversation.

But the key concept is clear, and I don't need translation for that. Scravers attacked. Tycho doesn't know why. Nakiis wasn't one of them.

Most of the closest soldiers are looking at the prince and Tycho, listening to everything they say, and I'm sure word will spread the very instant the prince is gone. But some of them are looking at *me*, and I consider what Tycho began to say before we almost fought.

They think the creatures might have followed you from Briarlock.

I have nothing to do with scravers. Until the battle that nearly killed the king and queen, I'd never even *seen* one.

I think of that odd voice in my head while these scravers were attacking.

You heard Xovaar. Find the magesmith.

27

They definitely weren't after me.

"And you, Jax?" Prince Rhen's voice breaks through my thoughts, and I can't decide if I'm more shocked that he's addressing *me*, or that he's doing it in Syssalah. "Tycho said none of these scravers were familiar. Did you recognize any of them?"

I suppose I shouldn't be surprised about the language. Even though we've hardly exchanged words, I heard him speak it in Syhl Shallow. The king is his brother, after all, married to our queen.

Prince Rhen is nowhere near as fluent as Tycho and King Grey, though. He talks like he's learned from a book, all slow, careful pronunciation and perfect grammar.

Like everything else about him, I hate it.

"Jax." Tycho flicks the back of my hand with his fingers, and I realize the prince asked me a question and I haven't even answered.

"Ah . . . no, Your Highness," I say quickly. "It was very dark. I didn't know any of the scravers in—"

"Slower," Tycho murmurs, and I realize the prince is frowning slightly, trying to make sense of my words.

It makes me want to speak faster.

But I don't, because this man *is* the king's brother, and I'm not an idiot. "I didn't know any of the scravers in Briarlock," I say slowly. "They arrived to aid the king." I hesitate, thinking of that odd voice in my head. "But one of these said . . ."

My voice trails off as my gaze fixes on the soldiers gathered around us, how so many of them seem to think this has to do with me, or with Briarlock. Few of them speak much Syssalah, but they're still focused on this conversation, listening to every word. Many of them speak a *little*, and I have no doubt my parts will be remembered and repeated. I've never had to consider rumors and gossip and how quickly one piece of information can spread like wildfire and bring down an entire kingdom.

I don't know why these scravers might have been looking for a magesmith, but if winged creatures are suddenly hunting anyone with magic, I'm not sure it should be announced to the entire army.

Especially if they're hunting the King of Emberfall.

Prince Rhen is waiting for me to continue, and I glance between him and Tycho.

My voice drops. "I . . . I don't know if I should say this in front of everyone."

The prince's expression sharpens. He turns his head and says a few words, and the gathered soldiers fall back almost instantly, at least twenty feet. Even the royal guards drop back ten. But to my surprise, Tycho falls back, too, and I realize Prince Rhen took me at my word. He ordered *everyone* to give us space.

I'm suddenly alone in the grass with the prince.

My heart thumps hard, and my mouth goes dry. Despite my feelings about him, Prince Rhen is intimidating. This *moment* is intimidating. As if what I wanted to say won't be worth all this trouble, and he'll have the soldiers shoot me or drag me behind a wagon for wasting his time.

The wind washes across the fields again, whipping between us. It's not cold now, but I shiver anyway.

"Tell me," the prince says, and I swallow.

"One of the scravers spoke," I say, keeping my voice low despite the distance. "It . . . it wasn't like a voice." I watch him work these words out in his head, and I remind myself to go slowly. "But I heard it. It said, 'You heard Xovaar. Find the magesmith.'"

"Xovaar," he repeats. "Was that one of the scravers in Briarlock?"

I shake my head. "I don't know."

"Were they looking for Tycho?" he asks. "Or the king?"

"I don't know that either. But I heard the words *after* it tore into Tycho—which makes me think it was still looking."

"Tore into Tycho?" Prince Rhen echoes, like my phrasing is unfamiliar. His eye widens, and he glances from Tycho to me. Tycho is closer to the lanterns now, the blood on his face and armor even more apparent. I'm sure I'm not much better.

The prince looks back at me, and awareness lights in his gaze. His voice goes very, very quiet. "You were both badly injured."

I freeze, realizing what I've nearly admitted. Tycho is forbidden from using his magic. Would he have been allowed to use it to save himself? To save me? What about the soldiers who died?

It's too many questions, and Tycho is already under enough strain—most of which he doesn't deserve. If he wants to admit to using magic, it can be his choice, but I'm not adding more challenge to his life.

So I keep my voice level and even. "No, Your Highness. He was able to stop the scraver before it got past his armor. I shot the first one. Tycho stabbed the second. Blood went everywhere."

I'm not a bad liar, and I might've been able to fool my father, but Prince Rhen is too savvy. He stares back at me, and for a moment, the weight of my lie hangs in the air between us. He knows. I *know* he knows. My heart keeps pounding, and I set my jaw, waiting for him to challenge me.

He doesn't. "What made you keep this private, Jax?"

"I didn't mean for you to send Tycho away, too." I hesitate. "But what the scraver said . . . it felt important."

He gives me a nod. "It is." Then he turns away and begins issuing orders again.

I let out a heavy breath. My palms feel slick on my crutches.

Tycho returns to my side. "They're striking the camp. Prince Rhen wants to return to Ironrose tonight. He doesn't want to risk being out in the open any longer than we have to. I'm going to fetch my bedroll and saddle Mercy. You should get your things."

"Wait." I move close and take hold of his arm, and the knives on his bracer are cold under my fingertips. I desperately want to put a hand against his cheek again, to reassure myself that he's really all right. Using magic to heal himself is exhausting, I know, and he was *already* exhausted.

He glances down at my hand, and he goes still. When he looks back up, his eyes hold mine, and he doesn't pull away.

Before I can say anything, a soldier breaks apart from the group to approach us. Tycho straightens, and my hand falls off his arm. I brace myself, but it's only Sephran, one of the young men I was sitting with earlier. I know he won't be coming to start trouble.

"Sephran," I say—though our conversation will probably end there, because he hardly speaks a word of Syssalah.

"Jax," he says with a smile—but then he draws close enough that he must take in the blood and the state of our armor. The smile drops off his face. He pats his shoulder, then points to mine, then asks a question, glancing at Tycho for help.

"He wants to know if you were hurt," Tycho says, and his tone has gone a bit cool. He doesn't even wait for me to respond; he just says something in response, and Sephran gives us both a nod, then turns to follow the other soldiers.

I start to frown, but Tycho glances at me. "Come on. I told him you're all right, but we've been given orders to move. That means us, too."

Oh, of course. I stick close to his side as he moves back toward Mercy. "Tycho," I say softly. "The scravers were looking for a magesmith. I heard one of them say it."

He grimaces. "Me too. I don't know if any of the soldiers heard it— or if they understood. It was in Syssalah."

My eyes widen. I didn't consider that—but of course I should have.

"Do you know who Xovaar is?" I say.

"No." He pauses. "I only know Nakiis. The scravers in Briarlock left before I could learn *any* of their names."

"Do you think they're after you?" I say. "Because of your vow to Nakiis?" I pause. "Or are they looking for the king?"

"I don't know. Is that what you wanted to tell Prince Rhen?"

I nod, then hesitate. "He knows you used your magic."

Something in his gaze tightens, but then he glances after the prince, who's nearly back to his tent already. "It's all right." He pauses, and his expression falls. "I would've used it to save the others, too. I didn't know. And because I've been ordered to keep it a secret, none of them know I have magic that might've helped."

There's resignation in his voice, and I frown.

"This wasn't your fault," I say softly.

He laughs without any humor. "I'm the first one who let Nakiis out of a cage, Jax. Some of it is."

We've reached Mercy, and he begins pulling her gear from where it's stashed along the line. Nearby, dozens of other soldiers are doing the exact same thing. It's pitch-black, and no one says much, but the heady tension hangs in the air. I can't get away from it.

That means I should be packing up my things, too.

"I'll be on the wagon," I say, because those are the only parting words I can offer.

"Hey," Tycho says, and I turn. His eyes find mine in the moonlight, and they speak volumes without him saying a word. I want to stride back through the grass to hold him, but I can't, so I simply look back at him until my throat tightens dangerously.

"Thank you," he eventually says. "For dinner. And . . . everything."

Always, I think, but that feels like too much. Too big. A word I shouldn't say to the night air. Something I couldn't say without revealing every ounce of my feeling to everyone around, regardless of language.

But I give him a nod, and I say it in my heart.

CHAPTER 4

JAX

Normally, the soldiers are full of talk while we ramble along, but the commanding officers have ordered everyone to be silent so we can listen for another attack. They didn't need to bother. All eyes have been on the sky for hours, the air humming with tense anticipation. Every single soldier is on horseback, their bow unstrapped and ready to fire. I've got mine on the bench beside me, but the supply wagon rattles along too fast, jarring my body with every bump and rivet in the road. I wish I could be on horseback like the others. If I had to shoot like this, I'd never be able to aim.

The soldiers are in a wide formation that covers a lot of ground, Tycho riding at a distance to my left, some of the others I know somewhere off to my right. Before we left, I took a minute to exchange my torn and stained tunic for a fresh one, but blood streaks the breastplate of my sparse armor, and my fingers are still a bit tacky. No one has spoken to me since I left Tycho's side. They've hardly *looked* at me.

Hints of pink appear on the horizon, and an officer ahead shouts an order. We all draw to a stop near the crest of a hill. A low murmur goes up among the soldiers closest to me, and I sit up straighter, searching shadowed faces for emotion, trying to pick out phrases I understand. They don't sound concerned, but it could mean anything.

I go to my knees on the bench, straining to see, but the hill is too high, and there isn't enough sunlight to see much. I make a frustrated sound and wonder if it's worth standing on the bench with my crutches or if that's just asking for a broken neck.

"Hey, Jax."

I turn to find that Sephran has ridden his horse over, and I smile. Malin is beside him. Much like the others, they don't seem concerned that the officers have called a halt.

Unlike the others, they're willing to talk to me.

They're obviously experienced soldiers, but I don't think they're too much older than Tycho. Sephran is the taller of the two, with ruddy cheeks and sand-colored hair, along with broad shoulders and a muscled frame that could be intimidating if he weren't so quick to smile. At his side, Malin is leaner, more compact, with thick black hair, tan skin, and sharp eyes that remind me of a fox. The language barrier makes it tough to be *entirely* sure, but I think they're close friends. Between the two of them, only Malin knows any Syssalah, but we've made do. I appreciate that they try *at all*.

"Malin." I point ahead, at where the prince and the officers have stopped. "Did something happen?"

He shakes his head. "No. Prince Rhen sends soldier to look . . ." The words trail off as he runs out of words he knows. He points ahead and makes a circle with his hand. "To *look*."

"To look at what?" I say.

"To look at . . ." He blows a breath out through his teeth, then swears, then turns to Sephran, asking for help, searching for a word.

This is how every conversation goes. I keep waiting for them to run out of patience with me, but so far, they haven't.

Malin finally looks back at me. "Big house? House for king?"

"Castle?" I guess.

He snaps his fingers at me and nods. "*Castle.* Look at castle. For scravers."

"Are they there?"

"Don't know. Look first." Then he taps his chest and points again. "We go after. Yes?"

I nod fiercely, because every time we reach this point in a conversation, it feels like we've solved a puzzle. "Yes. I understand." But my heart is pounding, and I want to stand up on the wagon bench again. Everyone is wary of the scravers and whether the attack is a warning of more to come—and I am, too. But my own thoughts are also fixed on what's to come for *me*.

"Are we that close to Ironrose Castle?" I say.

Malin nods. "Over . . ." he begins, then frowns, miming the motion of going over something. "Over mountain?" He points ahead.

"Over the hill," I say.

Some nearby soldiers are paying attention to this exchange, and one of them calls something snide, and the others laugh darkly. I frown, wondering how this will go. But Malin rolls his eyes and offers them a rude gesture.

A little glow flares in my heart. I've never really had any friends beyond Callyn. Aside from Tycho, I thought I'd be so alone here. When another soldier calls something else, Sephran scoffs and tells him to stop being an asshole, and it makes me smile.

Sephran notices, and he smiles back. "Oh, you understand *that*," he says in Emberish.

When I say, "Yes," his smile turns into a grin.

The sky is gradually lightening overhead, and at the top of the hill, some of the soldiers begin to separate from the others. It takes me a moment to realize that Tycho has disappeared, but I search the shadowed sea of soldiers to find him retrieving one of the spare horses from the back of the supply line. Eventually, he trots back to where I'm waiting, leading the second horse alongside Mercy. Blood still clings to his armor, but he splashed water on his face before we left, because his skin is clear, his blond hair only bearing a few streaks now. He takes in Malin and Sephran by my side and gives them both a nod, but his gaze settles on me.

"They've sent a scout down to Ironrose," he says, confirming what Malin told me. "But Prince Rhen doesn't suspect anything. We've had no sign of trouble for hours, and it would've been easier to attack when we were out in the open, especially in the dark. The castle grounds are surrounded by sentry stations with lookouts. It would be challenging for even a lone scraver to approach unseen. Now that it's sunrise, the soldiers will head for the barracks, but I'm to take you to the Shield House so you can get your bearings."

I don't know what the Shield House is, but before I can ask, Tycho rides close to the wagon, and holds out the reins to the horse he's brought me. Behind me, officers must be receiving orders, because shouts call down through the waiting soldiers, and they begin to move into formation again.

I inhale sharply, because I wasn't prepared for such an abrupt change in course. But everyone else is moving, and I don't want to cause a delay. I use the side of the wagon to climb onto the waiting horse, then tie my crutches to the saddle where a bow usually hangs. The horse must feel my tension, because he sidesteps anxiously, and I grab hold of the saddle, worried I'll fall.

"Steady." Tycho takes one of the reins back. "Just let your legs hang. I'll lead."

I flush, wishing I didn't look incompetent on top of everything else. "Sorry."

"Don't be sorry. You'll learn." He clucks to the horses and they start forward.

At my back, there's a low rumble of conversation, and then Sephran calls, "Hey, Archer."

He's called me that before, and the nickname makes the glow in my heart grow warmer. When I turn, he's got a friendly smile and a hand lifted in a gesture of farewell. But instead of saying anything close to *goodbye*, Sephran carefully and clearly pronounces the words in Syssalah to tell me to suck a piece of horseshit.

If anything could distract me from the scraver attack and my new position, it's that. Tycho jerks the horses to a halt and whips his head around.

Sephran's not an idiot, and his face falls as he realizes he's said something wrong. He turns murderous eyes on Malin, who bursts out laughing.

"It's a prank," Tycho murmurs to me, already gathering up his reins again. He calls something to Sephran, which must be a translation, because the soldier steers his horse over to punch his friend in the shoulder.

Malin is grinning at me. "I teach him, too."

Despite everything, that makes me smile. I lift a hand, too. "*Goodbye*," I emphasize in Syssalah. "Not you, Malin," I say, because I know he'll understand me. "*You* can suck a piece of horseshit yourself."

He laughs, and I expect Tycho to laugh, too, but he clucks to his horse again and turns away. I remember the way he was ready to draw blades last night, and I wonder if he thought the prank was real, if he was worried Malin and Sephran truly meant me harm. There's an odd hum of apprehension clinging to him, and I'm not sure how to ask. When Mercy starts walking, my horse starts alongside without any urging from me.

At my side, Tycho is quiet, so I glance over. The sun has risen enough for me to see his features more clearly now, the brown of his eyes, the few days of blond beard growth sparking along his jaw. I wonder if he still feels guilty about the attack, or if he's just exhausted—or if Prince Rhen said something while they were riding. His hand with my horse's rein rests on his knee, and I could reach out and touch him. My fingers long for it.

But we've got a hundred soldiers watching us depart. I consider what he said about *discretion* when we were sitting in the field, so I don't.

"The soldiers weren't nervous," I say quietly. "But you are."

"I'm not nervous."

There's an edge in his voice, and I think of how he was when he *first* found me waiting near the horses last night. He acts like the soldiers are the ones looking for a fight, but I'm not sure that's true. I think *he* is.

I look over at him. "You're something."

He frowns. "The soldiers aren't nervous because they think it was a random attack. Or that the scravers followed us as some kind of retaliation for what happened in Briarlock. Either way, they think we were victorious. That we chased them off."

"And we did."

"Maybe. But they don't know the scravers were looking for a magesmith. We have no idea how many there are, or if more will come looking." His tone turns darker. "If they come looking for *me*, I could be responsible for an attack on all the people living at Ironrose. There are families. Children—"

"Tycho! You are not *responsible*—"

"But I am!"

"How? How on earth are you responsible for this?"

He blows out an angry breath between his teeth. "Because I'm the one who made a promise to Nakiis. You *know* that."

"I do know that," I snap, because my own temper has a limit, and I seriously can't take one more second of this. "I also know you made that promise to save the *king.*"

Tycho's frame is tight, his eyes locked on the horizon. "Enough, Jax."

"And you didn't steal the king's magic," I growl, fighting to keep my voice low. "He gave it to you."

"He didn't know what it would do."

"I don't care. You weren't born a magesmith; he made you one. And because of that, you were able to make that bargain to save his life. He should be here, by your side, *defending* you. Instead, he's sending you off to live in exile. I almost watched you die last night, and now you think it's all your fault? Bullshit."

Tycho sets his jaw and doesn't look at me. I wish I had the skills to ride on my own so he weren't leading me like a child on a pony. I have half a mind to yank the rein out of his hand and give it a shot anyway.

But I don't. We ride on in silence.

Great. I suppose he got the fight he wanted.

I glance over my shoulder at the soldiers we're leaving behind. I've lost Sephran and Malin to the crowd, and now it's just a sea of gold-and-red livery.

The air between me and Tycho crackles with tension. I won't take back what I said, but I can't take the silence for long.

"Where did you say you were taking me?" I finally say.

"The Shield House." His voice is just as cool as mine is. "It's beside the forge, not too far from the stables. It used to be an armory, but when the king had army barracks built beyond Ironrose, it was repurposed. Now it houses many of the forge workers and the groundskeepers." He pauses. "And you."

And me. I feel unprepared. Untethered. I knew I'd be given a place to sleep, but until this moment, I honestly hadn't given it much thought. I didn't expect much. I thought maybe it would be a cot in the forge, or in the loft over the stables. Maybe that was foolish.

But Tycho said *many*. *Many* forge workers. My heart gives a little uncertain kick. If a lot of people live in this Shield House, that means I'll likely be sharing a room with someone. Probably a lot of someones.

I've never lived with anyone but Da.

I doubt any of these people will speak much Syssalah. From my experience with the soldiers, it's mostly broken phrases and halfhearted greetings—basically the extent of my Emberish. I won't have Malin and Sephran anymore, because they're being sent back to the barracks. And Tycho . . .

I have no idea where he sleeps. He's the King's Courier, so I doubt he rooms with the tradesmen. Surely he sleeps in the castle proper. I wonder how far away that is.

Right now, I don't want to ask.

As we ride up the hill, my chest has grown tight, and my horse prances, feeling my tension. I snatch for the reins before remembering I'm not supposed to do that, then grab hold of the saddle. For a breathless moment, I'm worried the gelding is going to bolt.

"Easy," says Tycho, his voice quiet and low for the horse, and then I realize he's got a tight hold of the rein. The horse blows out a snort and paws at the ground, but he doesn't run. I murmur a soft word of apology to the animal and unclench my fingers.

I expect Tycho to say something sharp or critical, since the air between us is so weighted, but he doesn't. Instead, his voice is just as quiet for me. "Look up, Jax."

I look up and find his eyes, full of color now that the sun is beginning to rise, painting gold in his hair. He holds my gaze for a long moment, and so much emotion is there. But none of it is anger. None of it is resentment. It's longing. It's regret.

Too much soldiering. Like before, it makes my heart ache.

But then he says, "Not at me. Look down *there.*"

So I turn and look, and the sight of Ironrose Castle quite literally takes my breath away.

I knew the castle grounds would be vast, and they are, easily spanning a hundred acres. I want to memorize every inch of it, because I'll have to describe it in a letter to Callyn later. The castle itself is massive, constructed of cream-colored bricks that glow pink in the sunrise, with countless sparkling windows, numerous cobblestone walkways, and at least a dozen outbuildings situated around the grounds. Flowers are in bloom everywhere, in pots and on trellises and strung from glimmering archways, arranged in rows in perfectly tended gardens. Gold-and-red flags and pennants hang at regular intervals, bearing the crest of Emberfall—the same gold-and-red crest that appears on Tycho's armor beside the green, black, and silver crest of Syhl Shallow. Shadows still cling to the sprawling grounds, but I can make out a massive courtyard, what appears to be a training arena, a huge stable and carriage house, as well as guards and soldiers stationed everywhere.

Well beyond the castle, near the back half of the grounds, stands a wide, squat building with two chimneys billowing smoke. I can see a glowing forge, but we're too far to hear any familiar clanging. I wonder if the forge runs all night. Beside it, there's a much larger two-story structure with a few lit windows, but I can't make out much else.

Though I can just identify a large black shield shape emblazoned on the front of the building, cut with gold-and-red stripes across the center.

The Shield House. My eyes skip back to the castle, which looks gargantuan by comparison. It might as well be a hundred miles away. My days of using crutches to quickly make my way down the dirt lane to Callyn's are gone.

The gelding must feel my tension again, because he stamps a hoof, shifting restlessly, tugging at Tycho's grip on the rein. Down near the castle, a series of bells ring out, faint on the breeze.

"What do the bells mean?" I say, and I hate that the words sound too quick, too anxious.

"It means it's time for breakfast." Tycho lets go of Mercy's rein, and I expect him to cluck to his horse again, but his fingers brush over mine, lingering for a moment.

I look up and meet his eyes, and I see that same longing. That same regret.

I realize we're not fighting. Not really. Not at all.

I turn my hand to give his a squeeze, the way he did in the grass last night.

A blush finds his cheeks, and his voice is husky when he pulls away. "Let's go."

CHAPTER 5

JAX

The gardens in front of the Shield House are just as lush and well tended as everywhere else on the castle grounds, roses and peonies in full bloom. The cobblestones are freshly swept, and there's not one single spot of chipped paint or rotted wood anywhere. When we dismount to tether the horses, I can smell baked bread and cooking meat, which should be appetizing, but my stomach is churning.

Breakfast with my father was always simple: just the two of us, him usually reeking of ale or sweat or both. We'd eat boiled eggs or dry pastries that Callyn had left over from the bakery, along with some weak tea because Da never liked it too strong. Even with the soldiers, breakfast was quiet in the early morning darkness, just hard bread and dried strips of beef that were passed out while everyone took care of their horses.

From the sound of clattering dishes and the low rumble of conversations, breakfast in the Shield House will not be simple or quiet.

Beside me, Tycho is unbuckling my pack, which means I've been staring too long. He tugs it over his shoulder, then holds out my bow and quiver. "I'm sure you're hungry. Let's go find Master Garson. I'll take the horses to the stables when we're done, so you can take your time settling in."

I don't know if I'll ever be able to settle in here. I've never doubted my skills as a blacksmith, but looking at the pristine conditions of the grounds is making me doubt everything. Tycho is waiting, so I hang the strap of the quiver across my chest and slip the crutches under my arms.

Tycho leads me up the steps and through the doorway, and suddenly we're in a massive room with two long tables. At least a dozen men and women sit at each table, and two serving girls are carrying trays of meats and sliced fruit from another room on the opposite side. A boy of about twelve is feeding logs to a low fire in the hearth on the back wall. Everyone looks bright and clean and well-fed, and I want to walk right back out the door—especially when they spot us and the lively conversation dwindles into nudges and whispers.

My hair is a wild tangle from the journey here, and I want to twist it back into a knot, but I've got nothing to use. There's probably blood and dirt on my face, too. It's definitely on my hands and armor.

I glance at Tycho. He's in the same condition, bloodstains and all, though he looks like a warrior returning from battle, while I surely look like . . . well, like a poor blacksmith dressed up like a soldier. Half a dozen pairs of eyes snap to my crutches, and then to my missing foot.

One of the serving girls sets down her platter and whispers behind her hand to a young woman seated at the table closest to her. My heart is pounding, and I jerk my eyes away before any warmth can crawl up my neck.

At the other table, a man rises from his seat to approach us. He's broad-shouldered, taller than my father, with dark eyes set in deeply tanned skin, thick gray hair, and a trim beard. He's not too far past middle age, but he still looks like the kind of man who could pull a tree out of the ground bare-handed. He's in trousers and boots and a clean tunic, but his hands are heavily callused, and I recognize the tiny burn scars from working around a forge. This must be Master Garson.

"Tycho!" he cries, and I can immediately tell he's someone who booms every word he says. He claps Tycho on the shoulder, then launches into a sentence full of words I can barely understand.

While Tycho smiles and responds in kind, I find myself automatically listening to see if Master Garson is slurring. Inhaling to see if he's the kind of man to down a pint of ale before breakfast. Wondering if he's going to hold my hand in the forge if he doesn't trust me to—

As soon as I realize what I'm doing, I tell myself to stop.

This man isn't my father. I'm not in Briarlock.

Before I can shake off the memories, Master Garson claps me on the shoulder like he did to Tycho, and it makes me jump. I'm glad I have a good grip on my crutches. My fingers tighten anyway.

"Master Jax," he booms.

Master Jax. I've never been called that in *any* language, and I'm not sure what to make of it. I have to clear my throat so I can speak the few words I *do* know. "Master Garson. Hello. I . . ." I've learned what to say when I meet someone, but I'm too tired and too rattled, because my brain goes blank. For a terrified moment, I think I'm going to repeat what Sephran said.

Eventually, I manage, "Thank you?"

Master Garson looks somewhat amused by this, but he nods. "Welcome."

At my side, Tycho speaks to me in Syssalah. "I told Garson we had to ride hard through the night," he says. "He knows you need to rest. He'll have Molly—one of the serving girls—bring a platter of food to your rooms, along with some boiled water so you can wash. The tradesmen will be heading out soon, so it'll be quiet. You can sleep."

I wonder if Molly is the one who was whispering about me.

45

Everyone is still staring, so I nod to Master Garson. "Thank you," I say again, and he blinks, and I realize I've said it in Syssalah this time. I grimace and hastily repeat it in Emberish. Then I nod at the others and say it again.

A few nod back and murmur, "*Welcome.*"

A few look away and go back to eating.

A few exchange glances and mutter. I try to ignore it, but I remember the way the soldiers treated me. Uncertainty has already gathered in my gut.

Master Garson calls across the room to one of the serving girls, presumably Molly. She *was* the one who whispered about me. I snap my eyes away, trying to keep a scowl off my face.

But she must like Tycho, because she offers him a bright smile and a curtsy, then loads a platter with food. We follow her down a short hallway, my crutches clacking with every step. She's chattering away, but despite the whispering, her tone is upbeat and cheerful. I think she's only talking to Tycho until I realize she's said *Master Jax*, and we've stopped in front of a door.

"She says these are to be your rooms," Tycho clarifies for me.

Rooms. I know boarding houses have long rooms with pallets for sleeping. Maybe this is like that. I wonder if other people are still here, if Tycho means to leave me among strangers.

Molly is staring at me expectantly.

"Sorry," I say to her in Emberish. That band of panic around my heart goes nowhere. "Thank you?"

She smiles at me, which takes me by surprise. She's a bit younger than Callyn, I think. Pretty, with fair skin and dark hair wrapped up in twin braids. She glances between us and says something. I expect Tycho to repeat it in Syssalah for me, but he doesn't. He takes the tray of food and responds in kind, because she nods quickly, bobs a curtsy, and says, "Yes, my lord," then dashes off.

I want to ask what she said, but Tycho pulls the latch on the door—and it's not a room full of sleeping pallets at all.

The room beyond is large, with wood-paneled walls and a wide, multicolored tapestry hanging to my left. I immediately spot a small hearth set into the opposite wall, two plush chairs with a low bench between them, and a larger table in the corner. Another door is past the hearth, but it's closed. Tycho steps past me to place the tray of food on the table, then drops my pack on one of the chairs beside it. I follow him in, and the door closes behind me, but I don't move beyond that spot.

This space is larger than the main room of the house I left in Briarlock.

I glance at Tycho and then at the closed door near the hearth. "Who else shares this?" I whisper.

He follows my gaze. "No one." He frowns a little, then opens the other door, and I see the edge of a bed beyond. "These are *your* rooms, Jax."

I fall back a step, and my shoulders hit the door.

There's no possible way I've been given this space to live in. It's too big, too grand. My eyes travel over the walls again, scanning the hearth—which I can see now has a grate on the other side that allows it to heat the bedroom as well. Through the doorway, the bed seems larger than I could ever imagine needing, and I think there's a wardrobe as well.

The door is pressing into my back now, which hurts a little bit from what happened with the scraver—but I can't move. I don't deserve any of this. This is a room for a skilled craftsman, not a village blacksmith.

"I thought . . . I thought I'd have a cot in the forge," I say, and my voice is rough.

Tycho comes to stand in front of me, his eyes searching mine. "Prince Rhen wouldn't offer you a position and leave you without *lodging*, Jax."

That makes me frown. I don't know what to say.

47

"Do you want to explore?"

I shake my head briskly, because I'm content to stand here against the door until my heart stops pounding.

Tycho *tsks*, then reaches out to take hold of the bow across my chest. He gently gives it an upward tug. "Up and over," he says, like I'm a toddler learning to dress for the first time.

It makes me feel sheepish, and I smile.

Tycho feigns a gasp as he pulls the bow over my head, mindful of my crutches. "A *smile*?" He reaches for the quiver strap next. "That was easier than I thought."

My eyes flick to the room—the *rooms*—at his back. "This . . . this is too much," I say, and the words come out like a secret.

"It's not," he says, but his words are just as weighted. He tugs at the quiver strap.

I let go of a crutch to pull the quiver over my head myself. "You don't need to disarm me."

"Well, someone needs to. You can't stand here barring the door all day. I do need to report to the castle at *some* point."

His eyes are shadowed with exhaustion, but his tone is light, and I can't tell if he's teasing or being serious. A little of both, I think.

When I don't move to disarm any further, Tycho reaches out, his fingers hooking under a strap of the breastplate that sits by my rib cage. I'm tense and ticklish, so I draw a sharp breath and bat his hand away.

To my surprise, he bats me right back. Like his tone, I can't entirely tell if we're playing. The movement is a little too aggressive, a little too belligerent. When I shove at him, he catches my wrist, and we scuffle.

Then my back hits the door, his weight pinning me there, and it draws a different kind of gasp from my lips.

His fingers go still, one hand keeping hold of my wrist. The room is so quiet that I can hear him breathing, and I suddenly can't tell if he's pinning me or if he's holding me.

His thumb brushes against the base of my hand, and it sends a bolt of warmth through my body. There's nothing aggressive in the air now. Tycho is close enough that I forget this massive room that I don't deserve, I forget the fact that we're on the grounds of Ironrose Castle. My world has centered on nothing more than the warmth of his brown eyes and the weight of him trapping me against the door.

Tycho reaches up with his free hand to push a lock of hair out of my eyes. My breath catches when his fingers tug at the strands, tracing along my cheek to tuck the hair behind my ear.

"Jax," he says roughly. "What you said. When we were riding. I'm—"

A sharp knock sounds at the door at my back, and I jump a *mile*.

He swears under his breath and draws back. A girl speaks in Ember-ish from the other side of the door, and Tycho responds in kind, then looks at me.

"Molly has delivered boiled water for your bath," he says. The spell is broken, and any roughness has vanished from his voice. He ducks to fetch the crutch I dropped, then holds it out for me. "I'll bring it in. You really should disarm and eat. I'll stoke the fire in your washroom so the water won't go too cold."

I've moved aside so he can open the door, but my thoughts are still tangled up in the feeling of his thumb against my hand, and I'm barely processing what he's saying.

Tycho keeps talking as he carries steaming buckets past me. "I know you've picked up some common words from the soldiers, but I'll leave a list with the kitchen girls that might be helpful. You'll find clothes in the wardrobe, too. Master Garson will show you to the forge tomorrow. He'll have you start with horses, because Prince Rhen sent word that you worked with the soldiers when they were in Briarlock. I've heard you around the camp. You know a bit of Emberish when it comes to shoeing horses, right?"

His voice has grown more faint, so I move into the second room.

The bed coverlet is softer than anything I've ever touched, even softer than the downy feathers on the baby chicks that Callyn has in the barnyard every spring. The fabric is a faint blue that matches the morning sky outside the window. I was going to open the wardrobe to see what clothes I might find, but a mirror is bolted to the wall beside the archway into the washroom, and I catch a glimpse of myself.

I almost do a double take. Specks of blood and dirt everywhere. My hair is a wild mess of tangles.

I do not belong in this room.

"Jax."

I blink and look over. "Yeah."

"Do you mind if Master Garson asks you to start with horses?"

"No. Yes. Horses are fine."

I must sound unsettled, because he stops in front of me again. "You'll feel better once you've had time to rest. You need to eat, too." He leans in, and for a breathless moment, I think he'll finish whatever we started against the door—but he inhales and whispers, "And take a bath."

I grin and shove him away.

I half expect him to tussle again, but he doesn't. He takes a step back and stops by the table where he left the food. He hesitates, and his expression turns the tiniest bit uncertain. "And . . . if it pleases you, I'll return before sundown to fetch you for dinner."

He sounds so formal. As if I'd say no. As if I won't be counting the minutes until he returns.

But I match his tone and nod sagely. "Why, yes of course, Lord Tycho. But only if it pleases you similarly."

For the first time, a hint of a blush finds *his* cheeks, and he frowns, glancing away. I can feel his unease, his distress. I want to tackle him and beg him to stay, to let his demons settle and go quiet. I want to wrap my arms around his neck and not let go.

But I think of what he said about needing to report to the castle.

I think about what he said about *discretion*, and how people will talk. We've probably been alone in here long enough.

Regardless, he's already moving toward the door. He pauses there, looking back at me. "Be well, Jax."

I have to force myself to remain still. "Be well, Tycho."

And then he's gone.

CHAPTER 6

TYCHO

I thought everything would be easier when we got to Ironrose.

Imagine my surprise that it's not.

Despite my exhaustion, I hardly slept. Every fiber of my being is urging me to stride out of the castle, cross the grounds, and rap on Jax's door. I want to chase the worry out of his hazel-green eyes. I want to lead him onto the training fields and teach him everything I know, so he'll never have to worry about anyone hurting him ever again. I want to find every single person who might mean him harm so I can show them what a mistake that would be.

I want to inhale his breath and listen to his heartbeat and pretend the world doesn't exist for a while.

The king should be here, by your side, defending *you.*

His words stoked a flame in my heart that hasn't dimmed—and my loyalty to Grey nearly made me turn it into an argument. My chest feels tight, resentment sitting in my gut.

It's making it difficult to pay attention to what Prince Rhen is saying. We're in his strategy room, late afternoon sun beaming through the windows. He's been making notes along a slip of parchment while he talks. He looks better rested than I am, but he was already awake and working when I finally made my way in here.

"I've started preparing an accounting of what happened for Grey," Rhen says. "I've also sent word to the nearest cities for reports on whether there have been any other scraver attacks. I will wait for a response, but I will not detain you longer than a day. If there is a chance that violent scravers seek a magesmith, my brother needs to know as soon as possible."

I go still at those words. My blood turns to ice.

I will not detain you longer than a day.

If he didn't have my full attention a minute ago, he does now.

Prince Rhen intends to send me back to Syhl Shallow.

Of course he does. The worst part is that I agree with him. The king *does* need to know.

I force myself to nod. "I understand."

"Grey and Lia Mara were to have the second part of the Royal Challenge in Syhl Shallow this autumn, but they will need to weigh the political ramifications of hosting an event after such a bold attack on the throne. Canceling could send a message of fear—but hosting one could be a risk. Even still, it would do well to continue their vision of unity between the countries. A sense of accord is very much needed right now. Lord Alek should be in the Crystal City by now. Once Grey interrogates him, he and Lia Mara will need to make a decision about how to proceed."

Lord Alek.

The last time I rode courier between Emberfall and Syhl Shallow, he tried to kill me. I sure hope Prince Rhen was right about Grey keeping him on a short leash.

And I'll be riding right back to a palace where the king doesn't want me.

So much tension is coiled inside me with nowhere to go. The prince keeps writing and talking, but I've stopped listening entirely.

I saw the look in Jax's eyes when I left him in the Shield House. Now I have to tell him that I'm leaving Emberfall.

Prince Rhen looks up from his paper, and I realize he must have said something that requires a response.

I have no idea what it is, but I nod dutifully. "Yes, Your Highness."

Rhen's not a fool. He regards me for a moment, then sits back in his chair and sets aside the parchment entirely.

My shoulders tighten, and I expect a word of rebuke, as that's all I've gotten from Grey in recent weeks. Something like, *You should be grateful, Tycho. You are the King's Courier. You've already put the kingdom at risk. Jax could have found his fate at the end of a rope.*

Rhen only says, "Should I send someone else?"

His voice is quiet, lacking recrimination, but I scowl and look away. I know my duties. I don't even want to consider how Grey would react if Rhen sent a guard or a soldier with a missive like this. I'm in enough trouble already.

"No," I say.

"I could. I know you expected to remain at Ironrose until you received a summons from Grey."

That snaps my head back around. "*No.*"

"I've considered that it could be dangerous to send you, if there *are* scravers lying in wait to attack a magesmith."

That nearly gets me. I hate how very badly I'd like to claim this excuse—but it sits a little too close to fear, and Grey would never allow it. If I want to keep my position, I need to be the one to deliver this message to the king.

"If there are scravers lying in wait," I say, "it would be unfair to send someone else. At least I have magic to protect myself."

"Ah, yes. Your *magic.*"

The way he says that makes me go still.

Rhen doesn't look away. "I asked Jax if you used magic, and he denied it. Did he know?"

He's asking if Jax lied right to his face.

I think of that moment in the tent, when he asked if Jax was causing a problem with the soldiers, and I brace myself. "Yes," I say, "but you must know—"

"Tycho."

"—he's simply trying to protect me. He's not causing a problem with the soldiers either. They're worried about his involvement with the Truthbringers, but you know how gossip flies. Some of them think he had something to do with the scravers, but—"

"*Tycho.*"

I stop. My hand is tight against the edge of the table.

But then I *can't* stop. I rush on, heedless. "I'll do my duty. I swear it. Whatever you need. I'll carry your message to Grey. But please—Your Highness—please don't send him back to Briarlock. If Alek is loose, he'll kill him. I know he will. Jax can't run. His father is dead. Even Callyn is gone. He'd be alone. He'd have no defense. *Please.*"

This time he waits until I've finished speaking, and I'm a bit breathless. Rhen hasn't moved, and he's just looking right back at me.

"Are you done?" he says.

I frown, abashed. I feel warmth crawling up my neck.

A line appears between his eyebrows. "Why would you think I'm sending him back to Briarlock?"

"You said you noticed problems with the soldiers," I say, more quietly this time. "And I know he lied about the magic, but . . ." My voice trails off.

"He's very loyal to you. I wasn't looking to censure that, Tycho. I admire it."

That makes me flush fully.

He continues, "When I mentioned the soldiers, it was because I do not want them sowing discord over Jax's presence here. Tensions are high enough. We are at peace with Syhl Shallow. If there is a problem to be solved, tell me, and I will solve it." He pauses. "I know you and my brother have yet to come to terms over your differences, but you offered me your trust. I'll do my best to be worthy of it."

On the day we left Briarlock, I refused to tell Grey what I'd sworn to Nakiis. But later, Rhen asked if I trusted him enough to tell *him*.

And I did. When it comes to the king, I seem to have nothing but the capacity for failure anymore. But Rhen defended me against Alek, and more than once. He spoke up for me to Grey. He offered Jax the position here, and I have no doubt that a good part of his reasoning was as a kindness to *me*.

"You are worthy of it," I say quietly.

"Thank you." He pauses. "So tell me truly. Should I send someone else?"

I consider Grey's reaction if someone else rode up to the gates of the Crystal Palace. I consider that remaining here might make Ironrose a target, if I'm the one the scravers are after.

I consider the sound of Jax's breath when I pressed him up against the door of his room this morning. I consider how badly I want to stay.

I have to look away. "No. You shouldn't send someone else."

Rhen is quiet for a long moment. "Very well. But if scravers seek *you*, sending you alone might leave you too vulnerable. With Truthbringers plotting against the king, I don't want to make you a target for anyone *else*. Scravers aren't the only thing we have to worry about right now." He sighs, considering. "One of the soldiers we first left with spoke some Syssalah. Do you remember which one?"

I think of the young men playing a prank this morning. It should have made me smile—but it didn't. I was too eager to get away from the soldiers, my thoughts about Jax too wound up and complicated to process. But I nod. "Malin."

Rhen makes a note on his parchment. "Take Malin, and wear army livery. You can be soldiers delivering orders across the border. Stick to the main roads, and ride through the day." He looks down at the table and moves some papers until he reveals a map of Emberfall. "If you leave by midday tomorrow, you should be able to reach Redcrest by sundown."

Wear army livery. I feel like a nail has been hammered into the side of my rib cage.

I force myself to nod, because I just swore that I would do my duty, and I can't exactly walk it back now. "As you say."

"The Truthbringers may have been stopped in Briarlock, but I hold no illusion that they were *all* eradicated. Any who remain will be more cautious. I know the scraver Nakiis helped you in battle, and I know you swore to fight at his side when he calls. But Nakiis was once bound to the magesmith Lilith—and she nearly caused the downfall of this entire kingdom. You must be wary, Tycho. If there are more scraver attacks, it will lend weight to the Truthbringer cause that magic is a threat. This will not go well for the king."

"I know."

Rhen looks back at his letter and writes for a while, and the silence builds between us again. It's so different to sit with him instead of Grey. I don't know when it changed, but all my time with the king seems to make me feel like I'll never measure up.

Rhen speaks into my silence. "Was Jax satisfied with the Shield House? You didn't say."

I can't help but glance at the window. I think of the way Jax would glare at Rhen's tent every time he thought I wouldn't notice.

He's honestly lucky the *prince* didn't notice.

Prince Rhen said Jax was very loyal for lying to protect me, but I'm willing to bet at least half of it was sheer belligerence.

"Yes," I say. "Overwhelmed, I think. He's grateful for the position."

Though I'm not sure how much gratitude will be left once I tell him I'm leaving again.

"Make sure he knows he's welcome to call at court if it suits him. I don't think Harper will forgive me for not bringing him around this morning, but I know you both needed to rest."

I doubt Jax would willingly go anywhere near Prince Rhen, but I nod. "I'll tell him."

Rhen looks up, and I'm not sure what he sees in my face, but there must be longing in my voice, because he says, "Go, Tycho. You have less than a day of liberty. I know you don't want to spend it in *here*."

I sigh, but he's right. I shove myself out of the chair.

Rhen goes back to his letter, all business once again. His golden hair falls over the patch covering his missing eye, and I think of the way he asked about trust. I think of the way he asked about *friendship*, as if he wasn't sure.

I would never call him lonely, but just now, I'm the one who isn't sure.

I've stopped in the doorway, but he doesn't look up, and his pen doesn't stop moving. "Don't linger," he says lightly. "It's unbecoming."

"Do you care to spar tomorrow?" I say. "We could meet in the arena before I have to leave."

His hand goes still, and for a moment, there's a sudden weight in the room.

I instantly realize why, and I wish I could undo it.

Rhen *hates* the arena, the way I hate the soldiers, or the gold-and-red livery, or the memories of my childhood. He has just as many demons as I do. His are different, but just as haunting, formed by years of torment. I don't know *all* the details—but I know he and Grey used to be tortured in that arena.

"Forgive me," I say immediately. "I only meant—we could meet in the courtyard instead—"

"I know what you meant." His voice is a bit hollow, and he looks back at his paper. "And the courtyard torments *you*, does it not?"

Silver hell.

Rhen still hasn't looked up, and now that feels very deliberate.

I let out a breath and turn away. He offered friendship, he asked for *trust*, and now I worry that I've unraveled it.

"Forgive me," I say again. "I meant no harm. I thought you might enjoy the swordplay." I don't wait for a response; I simply turn for the door.

But the prince speaks at my back. "Tycho," he says. "I admire your loyalty, too. I'll do my best to make sure Jax faces few hardships until you return."

I hesitate. He's already done enough, and he shouldn't have to trouble himself with that. But it's like we're *both* stumbling through the concept of friendship, and with Prince Rhen, it's odd to consider him stumbling through anything.

"Thank you," I say, looking over my shoulder.

"And I would enjoy a bit of swordplay," he says, without looking up. That hollow note is back in his voice. "But I haven't drawn blades in that arena since Emberfall was trapped by the curse."

I frown. "Your Highness, I swear to you. I didn't intend—"

"I know," he says. He finally looks up at me, and the hair falls back from the patch over his eye, leaving the scars that peek out from behind it fully visible. "But maybe it's time to leave old wounds behind. I'll meet you in the arena, Tycho. Two hours past sunrise. Don't be late."

CHAPTER 7

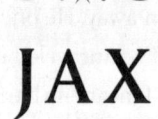

JAX

A distant, rhythmic clanging wakes me, and for a moment, I think I'm back in Briarlock, my father working in the forge, waiting to clip me on the ear for sleeping late.

But this bed is much too soft to be the one I left behind, and the clanging is far too muffled. My eyes open to find late afternoon sunlight peeking around the heavy woolen curtains of my new bedroom in the Shield House.

It's real. I'm here. I rub at my eyes and stare at the ceiling as if I have to prove it to myself over and over. My skin and hair don't even feel the same. They definitely don't *smell* the same. We had buckets from the well and the heat of the forge at home, so a hot bath was never really a luxury, but the only soap we had was made from tallow and ash. It never fully got rid of the soot that would cling to our fingers, and everything always smelled faintly of woodsmoke.

My washroom here in the Shield House is stocked with jars of creams and lotions and perfectly cut squares of soap, all of which smell like oranges or lilacs or melted caramels. After Tycho left, I soaked in the warm water until I was worried I was going to fall asleep.

The clanging from the nearby forge continues, but as Tycho promised, the Shield House itself is quiet. I haven't been truly *alone* in weeks, and it's odd to suddenly have so much space to myself. The light around my curtains seems fairly bright, so it must be a while until sundown and Tycho's return. I think of the way he pinned me against the door earlier, and heat crawls up my neck.

But then Molly knocked on the door and we snapped apart. It reminds me of what he said when we were sitting in the grass.

I don't want anyone to start thinking the King's Courier just brought you along for your skills in his bed.

Perhaps I should have considered this earlier. He gave me every sign on the journey here. Even before, every time he visited the forge, he spoke of how he longed to just be Tycho.

When we were alone together in Briarlock, he could be.

Here at Ironrose Castle, he can't.

The thought puts a little steel in my spine, and my cheeks cool. I should dress and explore before he returns so he doesn't think I expect him to hold my hand through every moment.

In the wardrobe, the clothes are like the room: far too grand. I find linen tunics and leather jerkins and belted jackets. There are a few belts for swords and daggers, though no actual weapons. It all feels too generous, and I want to leave it untouched—but my only other options are the blood- and sweat-stained clothes I wore to get here.

Everything is too big, but I make do with a belted jerkin and a pair of trousers that have a cinched waist. I turn the pants inside out to knot the bottom of the right leg so they don't catch on the crutches, then buckle and lace my soldier boot over my left. I don't have a nail to pin my hair in a knot, so it hangs in loose waves over my shoulder—but at least it's not full of blood and tangles like before.

When I finally find my way down the hall, the large dining room is empty, but feminine voices carry from the kitchen beyond. I mean to slip out the door without being noticed, but they must spot me anyway. The lively girlish chattering turns into hushed whispers and abrupt giggles. After a moment, there's a *bang* and a *clatter* and suddenly Molly appears in the doorway, followed by another girl, slightly older, with olive skin and shiny black hair.

Molly offers a quick curtsy, which takes me by surprise. "Master Jax," she says, then elbows the girl beside her.

I'm less rattled than this morning, but I'm not an idiot. I can see their nudges and whispering. But I had a week of that nonsense with the soldiers, and at least these girls aren't armed.

"Hello," I offer. "Molly."

To my surprise, she smiles brightly in response, looking genuinely delighted that I remembered her name. The other girl gives me a curtsy, too, which makes her the second person to *ever* offer me a curtsy. Her cheeks are faintly pink, and she taps her chest and shyly says, "Lola."

"Lola," I repeat. "Hello."

Molly reaches into her apron pockets and withdraws a slip of parchment and unfolds it. "Are you hungry?" she says slowly in Emberish, which is a simple enough phrase that I know. Then she bites at her lip and glances down at the paper. "*Tahrah*?" she says, carefully pronouncing the word in Syssalah. "Hungry?"

For a moment, I'm stunned. I know Tycho said he'd write some things down, but it's an unexpected kindness that she'd attempt to use my language.

The tense band around my heart eases a bit. I think of Callyn's sister, little Nora. She'd be poking and whispering, too, but it would be curiosity, not malice. Maybe this is the same.

I venture a smile. "No. Thank you."

"You're welcome." She glances back at the paper, more confident now. I watch her eyes skim for another phrase, and I wonder how much Tycho wrote.

"Ah . . . do you need help?" she says, again repeating it in Syssalah.

"No. I want . . ." I search for a word I know, but everything I want to say is too abstract, too complicated. *I'm going to wander around. I want to see the forge. Explore for a little while.*

"Lookout," I finally guess, a word I know from the soldiers, but then I grimace because that's not quite right. "Walk?" I make a circle with my hand and gesture toward the door, then at my eyes. "See?"

"Oh," Molly says, but she glances at Lola, who frowns.

So *I* frown.

But then Lola's eyebrows go up. "Look around?" she guesses, pointing to her eyes and then making a circle with her hand like I did.

"Yes! Look around."

Molly smiles like they've solved a riddle and looks at the paper again. "Dinner," she says, "is at sunset." She translates it again, but she points at the window. "Two hours?" She holds up two fingers.

"Two hours," I repeat, and nod. I knew the increments of time from working in the forge, so at least that isn't new.

In two hours, Tycho will be back. My heart gives a little skip.

But I remember how much has changed, and it stumbles back into a normal rhythm.

"Thank you," I say to them both. I close my fingers on the crutches and make my way out into the sunshine.

I expected the forge to be large, but it's downright massive, at least ten times the size of what Da and I shared at home. Calling it a forge *at all* seems too simple, as it's really an open structure composed of multiple forges, with the *clang* of hammered iron sounding from every direction and a haze of smoke in the air. Men and women move about with practiced efficiency, pulling iron from fire and pounding glowing metal everywhere I look. A low rumble of chatter carries over the noise, with the occasional burst of laughter. A few dogs wander among the people, too, waiting for scraps of hoof from the blacksmiths who work with horses. The animals are tethered on the far side of the structure, soldiers and guards standing alongside, some waiting more patiently than others. I don't recognize any of the soldiers, and after what happened, I don't know if I *want* to, so I keep going.

Near the opposite end of the forge, a loud *clang* blares over everything else, followed by a *crash* and a shout and a plume of smoke. I peer through the haze as a new voice starts yelling, the tone thick with anger. It's Master Garson, his face red from the heat of the forges, sweat threading his hair. I have no idea what he's saying, but his fury is all directed at one of the blacksmiths on the other side. For an instant, I'm frozen in place, trapped by memories of another man's anger.

Then some of the smoke clears, and I see him reach a middle-aged woman who's fallen beside one of the forges. She's coughing, and he's helping her up. A younger boy nearby is speaking rapidly, and a few other people have gathered. I try to listen for words I know, but there's too much commotion.

As I watch expressions and mannerisms, I begin to realize that the boy is apologizing. The woman was hurt somehow, but seems to be all right. She claps him on the shoulder.

So does Master Garson. He smiles, then moves away.

I misunderstood his emotion. It wasn't anger at all, but *worry*. The thorn in my heart eases a little bit.

But then a man mutters to my left, and I glance over to see that he's glaring at me. He looks away before I catch his eyes, and I have no idea what he said, but I can *feel* the animosity.

That's enough time in the forge, then. I tighten my fingers on my crutches and head for the path.

Across the sprawling fields, the castle gleams in the late afternoon sunlight. I can make out archers on a training range in the distance, and I step off the cobblestone path to see if I can find a better view. My fingers itch for my bow, but I doubt I could join them. They're probably soldiers engaged in an exercise, and the archery field would take a long time to reach on my crutches.

A new thorn of worry replaces the first. Everything here is far.

A familiar voice interrupts my thoughts. "I knew I'd find you near the forge."

I turn to discover Tycho behind me on the walkway, and the pulse of relief in my chest is profound. The battle-worn soldier from this morning has been washed away, leaving a dashing young lord in his place. He's bright and flawless in a loosely laced vest and calfskin trousers, and I'm stunned to realize that for all the months I've known him, this might be the first time I've ever seen him without his armor and weapons. He looks casual and elegant all at once, with hints of privilege everywhere, from the silver buckles on his boots to the glimmer of gold filigree in his buttons.

If he'd shown up like *this* in Briarlock, I would've stumbled over every single word. Honestly, I'm not sure I'm going to be able to speak right *now*.

"What's wrong?" he says, and I realize I'm staring.

The first thought that pops into my head is that I wouldn't *mind* being brought along for my skills in his bed.

Focus, Jax. I flush and jerk my eyes away. "Ah—you're so early."

"I would've been earlier, but Prince Rhen wanted to speak to me." He jerks his head at the path. "Come on, let's walk. I wanted to show you around."

"All right." I have no idea where we're going, but I'm still tongue-tied, so I wrap my fingers around my crutches and fall into step beside him. Then, right when I'm in the middle of chastising myself about lusting after him, Tycho reaches up to tug at a strand of my hair.

My heart stutters. My voice? Gone.

So much for discretion.

But almost immediately, he lets go. "You left your hair loose."

"I—ah—" My thoughts keep refusing to organize. "I . . . I gave you the nail I was using," I say. "I didn't know how to ask for another one."

"Oh." He winces. "I should have thought. I can help. Let's head for the forge."

I wish I could read his voice. It's warm, but also so polite. So genteel, like he really is a young lord I happened to cross paths with.

Maybe that's on purpose.

It's the first thought that's given me a measure of composure. He just touched me, but then he immediately let go. Perhaps brief touches and simple friendship are all he can offer now.

The thought tugs at my heart. Not only for me, but for *him*. When I first met Tycho, he had the bearing of a fierce soldier, skilled and fearless, trussed up in armor and weapons that warned of violence at the first sign of trouble. It wasn't until later that I discovered how much vulnerability he keeps locked away behind all that leather and steel. The first night we spent together, he was so tense, so hesitant. Too many people had taken advantage of him in too many ways. It was like he'd never been able to find a moment of happiness for himself.

I hate that my presence here could mean he won't be able to again.

He's begun to change course, heading back toward the forge, but I think of the man who scowled at me and I shake my head. "I'll get a nail tomorrow." Then I shrug. "Or maybe not. I'm in a new place here. I should just cut it all off and be done with it."

"*Jax.*" Tycho draws a sharp breath. "Don't you *dare.*"

I look at him in surprise, and now it's his turn to look abashed.

A flush finds *his* cheeks this time. "I mean . . . do as you like, of course."

He's slowly killing me. The most primal part of my brain doesn't care what our roles are. We have a week's worth of tiny touches and secret glances between us, and despite the fact that I can still feel that hum of tension radiating from him—to say nothing of the fact that I literally *just* convinced myself that he might be restricted to simple friendship—I also want to grab hold of his vest, press close, and remind myself of the taste of his skin.

Then I realize what he said. *I would've been earlier, but Prince Rhen wanted to speak to me.*

With my next step, I very deliberately put a few inches of distance between us, and I keep my eyes fixed on the path.

I don't think it's noticeable, but Tycho lets out a sigh. "There's something I need to tell you."

"It's all right," I say, and I mean it. I allow another few inches of distance, just for good measure. "I know who you are," I add. "I know *where* we are. I won't complicate things for you."

"That's not—"

"It's fine!" I insist. "I know I'm a commoner."

"Would you shut up? That has nothing—"

"Tycho." I catch myself. "*My lord.* If Prince Rhen has ordered you to keep your distance because of political maneuvering—"

"*Jax!* Prince Rhen has ordered me to *leave.*"

The words hit me like a fist to the gut.

It seems like they've hit him equally hard, because his breathing is a little quick, and he's stopped short on the path.

"Tomorrow," he adds, and it's another strike I'm not ready for.

I turn to face him. "Why?" I say darkly.

"Because of the scravers. If we were attacked by a magical creature seeking a magesmith, the king needs to know. As soon as possible."

67

I'm staring at him as if the words don't make sense, but they do. I hate it, but they do.

This shouldn't even be a surprise. I should have figured it out myself. I literally just said it to him.

I know who you are.

He's the King's Courier. It's his job to bring confidential news to the king. It's his duty to risk his life for the royal family.

I turn and start walking again. I don't even know what to say.

Tycho falls into step beside me. Maybe he doesn't know what to say either, because he's equally silent. For a while, the only sound is my crutches against the cobblestones, and it reminds me of the moments after we argued this morning, when anger hung in the air, but his loyalty was clear.

As soon as I have the thought, I wonder if this is why he came early. He came to tell me his orders, and as soon as we get back to the Shield House, he'll take his leave. He'll climb on Mercy tomorrow morning, and it'll be . . . what? Weeks or months before I see him again?

And I'll be stuck in a place where I can't speak the language and half the people hate me.

No wonder he was so emphatic about discretion.

I was so foolish. I knew his role. I *knew* it.

So I give him a nod. "Thank you for informing me of your duties, my lord. You don't need to trouble yourself with showing me the grounds. I can make it back to the Shield House on my own."

I only make it one step before he catches my arm, and there's absolutely no give in his grip. I'm ready to smack his hand away, but then I make the mistake of looking up to find his eyes.

Like before, they're full of longing. Sorrow. Regret.

Want. Need.

"Jax," he says softly. "Please."

68

Ah, he's going to break my heart. I yield to his grip and sigh. "As always, I know what you're sworn to do. I just . . . didn't expect you to have to do it immediately." I scowl and glance away. "I don't know how anyone here believes in fate when it only seems to offer misery."

"Fate brought me to your forge."

I snort. "Well, it brought Alek, too."

He sighs and moves to let me go, but I lift a hand and let my fingers rest over his. It's tentative, and a part of me expects him to pull away.

But he waits. It's always startling to consider that he has the skill and strength to fend off an army, but a gentle touch has the power to hold him still.

I brush a thumb across his knuckles because I can't help it. I'm gratified to hear *his* breath catch.

But he *is* the King's Courier and I *am* just a blacksmith, and despite everything else, there's still a distance between us that won't be solved on this pathway.

As if to prove the point, I let go—and so does he. I swallow.

For a moment, we stand in the sunlight, and regret fills the air between us. I think I could ask him to return me to Briarlock right this instant, and he'd do it.

A part of me wants to. But there's nothing there for me. Not anymore.

And our positions would be no different. He'd still be putting himself at risk, working in service to the king. I'd still be longing and lonely and waiting, just somewhere else.

I turn back to the path and start walking, because one of us has to.

"How does your expression go?" I say. "Fate has already drawn a path beyond this moment, right? So we have to follow it through."

Tycho's eyes light with surprise, but then he gives me a rueful look. "Did Grey say that to you? He says it all the time."

"Yes." He said it in battle, when we faced dozens of armed Truth-bringers and everything seemed bleak and hopeless.

"You don't believe in fate, Jax."

"I don't know what I believe," I say honestly. "But he was right."

Tycho glances over, and he nods. "As you say." His fingers brush against mine again, then drop away. "Let's follow it through."

CHAPTER 8

TYCHO

Every time I'm with Jax, it seems destined to end too quickly. I thought we would have weeks to move past this weird distance that's formed between us—and now it's a matter of hours.

After a week on the road with the soldiers, seeing him with shining hair in the sunlight nearly made me forget my own name. When he touched my hand, I had half a mind to tell Rhen to get on his own horse if he wanted to send a message to Grey so badly.

But of course I won't.

Jax is right about fate, though. All we can do is follow this through.

I'm determined to show him everything I can, so I start by leading him to the cool dimness of the stables between the army barracks and the Shield House. Mercy is kept in the royal stable beside the castle, so I'm not as familiar with this one, which mostly shelters horses reserved for the army. We're nearing the dinner hour, so the aisles and court-yards are busy with soldiers coming off patrol. Anyone we traveled with is off duty now, so no one here looks familiar, but the sight of their gold-and-red livery throws tension back into my spine.

I shove those worries away. There are too many others to focus on. Jax and I weave between people and horses until we get to the stall of an aged gray gelding.

"This," I tell him, "is Teddy. His real name was Iron Hammer or something like that, but he hasn't seen battle in at least ten years, so you can honestly call him whatever you want. He'll be yours until you're ready for something more."

"Mine!" Jax says in surprise.

"Yes. Not forever, of course, because he's old and slow, but he's a steady mount for learning. Prince Rhen arranged for it."

Jax clamps his mouth shut at that.

I want to remind him that the prince he *hates* isn't going to leave him at a disadvantage, so of course he'll have a horse. Knowing Rhen, Jax will probably have anything else he could want, too.

Jax's eyes have gone cool, so I keep my eyes on the horse and continue. "I wanted to introduce you to Master Hugh, but he's seeing the miller tonight, so you'll have to meet him tomorrow. He runs the stables, and he trains the recruits who can't ride. His daughter married a soldier from Syhl Shallow a few years ago, so he actually speaks Syssalah fairly well—"

"Someone else here speaks Syssalah?"

The eagerness in his voice drives that spike of tension a little deeper. I remember what he said about needing a nail and not knowing how to ask. "Yes," I say. "I saw him this morning and told him I've taught you a little on Mercy. He said you can come every night after dinner and he'll put you in with the recruits."

Jax was stroking a hand along Teddy's muzzle, but at this, he goes still. "*Every* night?"

I nod. "You'll learn quick. Recruits are usually riding point-to-point after a month."

His eyes widen a little at that, but he runs a hand down the horse's

72

face, and Teddy presses his head against his chest. Jax murmurs a soft word, rubbing under his mane.

I watch, transfixed for a moment. He's always so kind to horses. It was one of the first things I noticed about him. Jax seemed brusque and petulant, but when it came to Mercy, his touch was so gentle, his voice so soft.

His eyes flick up to find mine, and my heart gives a tug. I want to pull him into this stall and bury my hands in his hair and forget every oath I've ever sworn. He's so close, the air between us buzzing with warmth.

Down the aisle behind me, the last two soldiers are being raucous and loud as they untack their horses. They're the only ones left, and they're not happy about it. Jax frowns, his eyes skipping past me to see what they're doing.

"They're angry?" he guesses.

"They're hungry," I tell him. "They were delayed getting off the field, and they're saying that whoever's last will only get scraps."

Stall doors slam, and some of the nearby horses jump, but Teddy doesn't move. I want to tell the soldiers to knock it off, but I remember what it was like to be the last man to the mess hall at the end of a long day. Jax's expression turns wary as he draws back into the stall, and I realize he's remembering the hostility of the soldiers on the journey with us.

"It's all right," I say. "They just want their dinner."

The soldiers draw close, and I hear one of them muttering behind me. "Apparently they have too many traitors in their own country, so now they're sending the broken ones here."

The other one snorts. "Raglan said one of them lured another monster over the mountains." He spits at the ground at our feet as he passes.

I whip around, but at first, I'm more *shocked* than anything else.

"Hey," I snap.

They barely turn, but the first one smirks. "Why don't you take your trash back where you came from?" Then he keeps walking.

I don't recognize either of them, but they're young, with no stripes on their livery. I'm not in my own armor, so I'm sure they have no idea who I am, but I still can't quite believe the blatant disrespect.

Actually, I can. I lived through it in Syhl Shallow.

My shoulders are so tight. I inhale to call after them, to force them to attention, to threaten to have them stripped of their rank and duty.

What I really want to do is draw a sword I'm not carrying and find some kind of release for all the anger and frustration I'm carrying in my heart.

"Tycho." Jax's voice cuts through my fury. He's still beside the horse, but he's pulled back fully into the stall. His hazel-green eyes are dark and shadowed.

"Don't pick a fight," he says.

I scowl. "I'm not going to pick a fight."

I just *want* to.

But when I look back after the soldiers, they're already gone.

A quiet falls over the stables, only interrupted by the soft sounds of horses moving about their stalls, rustling hay and straw. Jax has laid a crutch against the stall wall, and he's leaning against Teddy now, still stroking a hand under the horse's mane. In the shadows, he's beautiful. Striking, really, especially with his hair unbound.

He's studying me carefully, and I wish I could read his thoughts.

Jax reaches for his crutch. "I'm discovering you have a temper."

"No, I don't."

He gives a little laugh, but not like anything is funny. "Well, those soldiers won't be the last, and it's not worth risking yourself." He shifts to move past me.

I put a hand on his arm, and he goes still, waiting.

"You're worth the risk," I say, my voice low.

He looks up, his eyes finding mine. We're closer than we were on the path, trapped together by the narrowness of the doorway. I think of the way we scuffled in his room this morning, how it was the first time we were alone. I wanted to confess all my thoughts and fears to him right there. His arm is a heavy weight under my hand, and he's so still that I want to do it *now.*

But he's right; those soldiers won't be the last. He has his own challenges. It's unfair to burden him with anything more than that.

"If they hassle you," I say, "tell Master Garson. Or tell Prince Rhen himself."

Jax says nothing to that. His eyes drop to where my hand rests on his arm, but now there's a tightness in his jaw.

"He would put a stop to it," I add. "The prince said you're welcome to call at court."

Still nothing.

I move very close, and keep my voice low. "Jax," I say softly, and he doesn't look up.

Do you really hate him? I want to ask.

But I can't. I'm afraid of the answer. I'm afraid to leave him here with soldiers who resent him and a prince he won't ask for help.

Jax finally lifts his eyes to find mine, and for a moment, I can see the answer in his gaze, as clearly as if I've asked the question.

Yes, I hate him. I hate what he did to you. I will always hate him for doing that to you.

It's an intense look. A burning look, both protective and vengeful. No one has ever looked at me like that, and it steals my breath.

He told me not to pick a fight, but that look in his eyes could start a war.

But then he blinks it away, and he pulls free of my arm to give Teddy a final pat. "Come on," he says hollowly. "Surely you have more to show me."

CHAPTER 9

TYCHO

We saddle Teddy and fetch Mercy, and then I take him everywhere I can think of, from the archery fields to the armory to the cobbler to the tannery. We spend so long exploring that we miss dinner at the Shield House, so I show him where he can request meals from the kitchen that opens to the back side of the castle. That's where we get sweet cornbread and a bowl of stew before riding across the fields to see the granary and the carpenters' workshops.

Emberfall has been allied with Syhl Shallow long enough that some people speak a bit of Syssalah, enough to offer greetings and maybe a little more, but the king and queen don't spend enough time here for it to be very widespread. Rumors about the scraver attack have already been whispered, and I hear a few murmurs about whether dangerous magic has returned to Ironrose—and whether the new blacksmith has lured it here. Jax doesn't understand everything they say, but I see the tense worry in his eyes, exacerbated when people give him a cool glance or mutter under their breath when they don't think I'll notice.

Though I do.

As the hours pass, the distance between us shifts into something different, unspoken words put away for later. Or maybe we're both just tired and sad, and holding on to tension feels like too much effort. Either way, his presence at my side has become more comfortable. Our conversation flows, skipping away from difficult topics, drifting along the here and now.

Eventually, the sun drifts below the trees to leave the moon hanging alone overhead, but I try to ignore the fact that time keeps marching forward. As darkness spreads through the sky, we ride back toward the forge and the Shield House and the stables where we first fetched Teddy. The sentry stands surrounding Ironrose are all lit with torches, blazing against the night. I stare at the stars, thinking of the attack, wondering if it's a mistake to be out after dark. But the air is temperate, barely any breeze this time.

No sign of scravers.

"Is the Crystal Palace so vast?" Jax asks. He's staring across the fields at the castle, which gleams in the moonlight now. Several windows flicker with candlelight, and more torches are lit beside the guards that stand along the parapets.

"You've never seen it?" I say in surprise.

He shakes his head. "I told you I've never left Briarlock before."

That's right. He did tell me that once. I wonder what it must be like, to see the king's castle in another country before seeing the queen's palace in his own.

"The Crystal Palace is massive," I say. "But it's built along the mountains and faces the city, so the grounds aren't open like this. There's a wall, with one set of main gates." I shrug. "It's just . . . different here. The castle itself is heavily guarded, obviously, but on the grounds, people are free to come and go."

As I say it, I realize I've never really considered *how* different they are. The Crystal Palace is very closed off, all but barricaded from the city proper. Here, an ordinary citizen could quite literally ride straight up to the castle. They'd be stopped at the steps, of course, but they could make an inquiry. They could leave a message, in the hopes it would get to the king—or to Prince Rhen, I suppose, since Grey is so rarely here.

In Syhl Shallow, no one can reach the palace unless they have reason to.

I think about the Truthbringers and all their grievances against Grey. As much as I hate Alek, he always spoke about protecting the queen. For the first time, I wonder if the Crystal Palace gives the illusion of isolation. I wonder if Lia Mara seems trapped by the king and his magic.

She's not, but it likely wouldn't take much convincing for people who wanted to believe it.

Jax glances up at a guard stand as we pass, then ahead at the Shield House. The paths are almost too difficult to see, but I don't want to admit it.

"When I get back," I say, "I bet you'll have learned to ride well enough that we can take the horses out to Silvermoon Harbor. They have a huge outdoor market, and it's really quite grand—well, if you don't mind the scent of cooked shellfish."

"I've never eaten shellfish."

"That's a crime. Grey and I used to race each other across Rillisk for steamed crabs. It makes me want to take you right now."

Jax looks over, and the breeze lifts his hair a bit. "Is it far?"

A note of intrigue hides in his voice, as if he'd go right now if I said we could. My heart stumbles, and I wish I hadn't said anything at all. "Two hours on horseback."

"Oh." He looks at the sky. The moon is high, stars everywhere. "It's very late."

It is, and I hate it.

I nod anyway. "We should put Teddy back before the stable hands douse the lanterns." My chest is tight as I say the words.

When we get to the stables, the lanterns are already doused, the doors latched. Luckily they're not locked. I find a lantern and strike a match, then tether Mercy in the aisle so I can help Jax tend to Teddy. It's not enough light, but I don't care. If I meet his eyes now, it'll be my undoing. The dark and the quiet press around us from all directions, and we say nothing while we strip the horse's gear and brush the sweat marks from his coat. It reminds me of when I was younger, when I worked in the tourney with Grey. It would be late and dark and quiet just like this, and I would be so grateful that the night was over, the crowds gone, leaving no one but us and the horses.

I haven't thought of those days in years—but as soon as the memories form in my mind, more join them. Some are pleasant, like when Grey first confided in me about his magic, how he was hiding. Or the way he taught me to hold a sword, the way we'd practice in secret. How it was the first time in my life I'd ever felt a glimmer of confidence.

Some memories aren't pleasant at all, like the times the soldiers would be loud and aggressive and scare me into the shadows of the tourney grounds. Sometimes the nights would grow long and the scent of ale would be thick in the air, and Grey would find me hiding under the stands, tracing lines in the dust. I always worried he'd scold me for being lazy, but he never did.

I have to force my thoughts away from all this, because they won't go anywhere good. Not right now. Not with all the voices of angry soldiers wrapped up in my mind, tangling with terrible memories of my past.

Instead, I focus on the sound of Jax's breath as he stands on the other side of Teddy, rubbing the sweat out of his coat. I think of sunlight gleaming on his hair. I think of his hand brushing mine, or the way we scuffled in his room before I pulled away.

I think of the sound of his gasp when I pinned him against the door, and something inside me clenches tight.

But instead of bringing relief, these thoughts also turn somber.

Because I'm leaving. And this night is about to end.

Welcome to Emberfall, Jax. I'll see you later.

My chest goes so tight that my hand stops against the horse's ribs. For an instant, I don't think I can breathe. I'm glad the shadows are so thick, that Jax can't see my face clearly. The brush drops silently into the straw, and I press my hands into the horse's coat, burying my fingers in his mane. A moment later, I press my forehead against the crest of his neck.

Straw shifts underfoot, and I think it's Teddy, moving away from my nonsense, but then arms slip around my back and Jax pulls me against him.

It's a simple embrace, but also *more*, as if I were falling and he caught me. Or maybe it's like we were *both* falling, because I've held him like this once before—on another day when I was due to leave him.

I have to chase that thought out of my head, because his weight is against me and his breath is warm and sweet along my neck.

"I'm sorry," I whisper. My voice almost breaks. "Please forgive me, Jax. I'm sorry."

"Hush."

"But I am. Not just for the leaving. For—" This time my voice does break, and I swear, then growl in frustration as I have to pull away to swipe at my eyes.

He draws back a few inches to watch me, and I duck my head away.

"For all of it," I finish.

He puts a palm against my face, and I go still. His thumb traces along the damp line of my cheekbone.

"None of this is fair to you," he says softly.

My eyes fill, and I grimace and pull away again. "Silver hell."

But he catches my vest and holds me there. "They don't even see what

80

they're doing to you. It's making me hate the king. *You* didn't use magic to cause harm. *You* didn't rally the Truthbringers."

Well, that chases away some of my emotion, and I can't tell if it's the slight treason—or the fact that I agree with him. "You cannot openly say that you *hate* the king."

"Sure I can." His shadowed eyes spark with defiance. "*You* should say it. You'd probably feel better."

"Jax. I don't hate him."

He uses his grip on my vest to pull himself a bit closer. "You hate him a little."

That makes me flush, because there's a kernel of truth to it. I can feel the warmth of him against me, and my belly clenches again.

I should let him go. I should stop this. Every time we're together, our moments alone all feel like a rushed prelude to my departure. Jax deserves more than that.

His fingers are twining through the lacing of my vest now, and each gentle tug sends a little flutter of fabric against my skin. I shiver and let out a breath.

His eyes skip up to find mine, and somehow he's even closer. It's taking everything I have to keep from pressing him up against the wall of this stall.

But then I remember something he said earlier, when we were standing just like this. I put my hand over his, forcing it still.

"Do you really think I have a temper?" I say.

He studies me for a moment, his expression cooling somewhat. But something about it reminds me of that protective look when we spoke of the prince. "I think you're angry."

"Angry?"

"You've been coiled up all week. It reminds me the way I used to act around my father."

81

"I'm not angry."

"Tycho."

"I'm not!" But as I say it, the denial tugs at something inside of me.

It doesn't help that Jax lets go of my vest to give me a not-so-gentle shove, right in the shoulder. "Oh, you're not? Then why do you keep looking for a fight?"

"I'm not looking for a—"

Another shove, a little harder this time.

I give him a look. "Maybe *you're* the one who's—"

He shoves me again, this time with the full force of his strength. My shoulders slam into the bars of the stall door.

Without thinking, I snarl and shove him back.

He's ready for it, though. It should be enough to knock him down, but he's grabbed hold of my vest, and it keeps him upright. For a moment, we tussle, batting at hands and straining for grip. I don't know how we've gone from embracing to crying to aggression in such a short span of time, but we *have*, and it feels dangerously good. He might not have skill, but he's strong, and he doesn't yield. When Jax slams me into the bars of the stall door again, he falls against me, losing some of his leverage. His hand presses against my shoulder to pin me there, and I seize his wrist, gripping tight, ready to grapple.

But then he just . . . stops. His other hand slips under my vest and his mouth lands below my ear.

"Shh," he whispers, and suddenly I'm caught by nothing more than his breath against my skin and the weight of his fingers along my waist.

I inhale sharply, just before his tongue burns a line right over my pulse.

I can't speak. I can't *think*. I wasn't ready for the sudden change, and my hand goes slack on his wrist.

Then his hips shift to meet mine, and it steals a ragged gasp right from my throat.

Jax presses a gentle kiss against my neck. "*We* don't have to fight."
But fighting is simpler.

The words stall in my throat. There are a thousand reasons we shouldn't be doing this, but right now, I can't think of a single one. My entire existence has centered on the feeling of his teeth capturing my ear. His fingers teasing along the band of my trousers.

Whatever your demands, I think, *I yield.*

"Jax," I gasp. "Jax."

He cuts me off with a kiss.

Despite everything, it's unexpected. After all the rough-and-tumble scuffling, I expect him to be quick, aggressive, but his hand slips up my neck, his fingers tracing the line of my jaw. The press of his lips against mine is soft. Delicate. Gentle. Sweet. *Slow.*

He pauses there, just a little, just enough. His eyes seek mine. "Yes?"

I don't have to yield. Jax never demands.

A pulse of emotion threatens to overwhelm me again, and my breathing stutters, but I nod fiercely and bury my fingers in his hair. This time, I part his lips with my own. When I taste his tongue, I nearly come undone, and then it's *my* hands on his waist, turning us, pinning him against the wall, my hips thrusting into his.

I'm gratified to earn a gasp from *him*, but then his tunic slips past my hands and my fingers find the smooth slope of his waist, and it's all I can do to keep us from ending up in the straw.

But then an equine muzzle thrusts itself against my ribs, then my shoulder, and finally blows puffs of warm air right in Jax's face.

Jax laughs softly, under his breath. "Teddy has had quite enough of this."

We break apart, and I push the horse away, but he noses at my hands. Likely hungry, and ready for us to lock up his stall for the night.

I feel flushed and off balance, nowhere near ready for that moment to have been interrupted—but there's a part of me that's glad it was.

I duck to fetch Jax's crutches, then the brushes, and we withdraw into the aisle. We stop there, side by side, as if we're *both* haunted by uncertainty.

Eventually, Jax turns to face me. "Don't make me fight you again."

He's half teasing, half serious, but I seize his wrists anyway, spinning him to fall back against my chest, trapping his arms. His crutches clatter to the ground, and I can feel his heart beating hard against me.

"I changed my mind," he says, a little breathless. "Let's do it again."

That makes me laugh. I loosen my grip, until *trapping* becomes *holding*, and Jax rests his hands over mine.

Then we're quiet again, the pressure of time weighing on both of us.

Jax turns his head, and his hair brushes my cheek. "Come back to the Shield House with me," he murmurs.

For an instant my heart leaps.

But then I consider . . . *everything*, and it falls.

Jax must feel the change in my body. His voice goes a bit cool as he says, "I suppose the King's Courier shouldn't be the subject of idle gossip on the morning he's due to leave. To say nothing of the new blacksmith."

He clearly doesn't need his hands to fight—and the worst part is that he's not even trying. "Jax."

"Is there hay in the loft?" he says. He shifts to pull free, and I let him go. "We should feed Teddy. It's late."

I swallow and nod. He's reaching for his crutches, dodging my eyes.

We keep coming to this point, and I don't know how to end up at any other.

Maybe he was right about fate.

He was definitely right about anger. I can feel it clearly now, coiled and waiting again, looking for a target. It's not him, it's not the king, it's not the scravers, it's . . . all of it.

84

"I'll climb up and throw some hay down," I say, just to break the silence. Then I turn away before I have to say anything else.

The loft is warm and dry, full of the sweet scent of alfalfa and timothy grasses. Half the space is filled with straw for bedding, too, and plenty is spread across the floor from where bales have spilled open, making for an almost plush coating underfoot that silences my footsteps. When the horses below hear me rustling with the hay, a few others nicker for their share, so I throw some into each stall.

I'm grateful for the work, the distraction. I haven't done this in years, and again, it reminds me of my time in the tourney. There are even cots in the corner, likely for stable hands to keep watch over foaling mares or sick horses. Grey and I shared a corner of the loft back at the tourney, and it's so dark up here that I could close my eyes and be fifteen again, just a boy tending horses, long before my world grew so complicated.

I was angry then, too, though I didn't know it.

Aggravated, I rip another bale open and throw hay to the horses on the other side of the stable. My movements are tight and controlled, every muscle longing for movement. Action. Release. I wish those soldiers were still here, because I'd find a sword and start swinging.

When I turn for more, Jax is ten feet behind me, and I give a little jump. He only has one crutch, and I'm somewhat amazed that he was able to navigate the ladder that leads up to the hayloft.

"Jax," I say in surprise.

He makes his way across the loft floor to me, and his crutch makes no sound through the straw. His eyes are intense, even in the darkness.

When he reaches me, he takes hold of my vest again, pulling me close. I balk, inhaling to protest, but his hand turns into a fist, holding tight.

"You once said you could fight all night," he says. "Did you mean it?"

"Yes."

"Then fight." His eyes spark with light from somewhere. "If that's all we can do, I'll fight with you all night."

It's not a threat. It's an offer, and it makes my chest clench.

"Promise?" I whisper.

Jax nods, and he steps into me again, sharing his warmth. "Always."

CHAPTER 10

JAX

Despite my vow, we don't fight.

Tycho climbs down the ladder to strip Mercy of her gear and returns with some saddle blankets thrown over one arm and the lantern swinging from the other. He lashes the lantern to a post and lowers the wick a bit, until we're surrounded by flickering shadows. There are some dusty, narrow cots in the corner, but Tycho spreads the saddle blankets over the soft piles of alfalfa near the far end of the loft, and we sprawl there instead, listening to the night. If anyone finds us here, we plan to say that Teddy seemed colicky, but we knew Master Hugh was away and we didn't want to leave the horse unattended.

We've been mostly silent, exhaustion looming, but neither of us has said a word about sleep. Not with the prospect of him leaving in a matter of hours. He's worried about leaving *me*, but somehow *I'm* supposed to watch him climb aboard his horse, knowing he'll be a potential target. I imagine a scraver ripping him right off the back of Mercy, only he'd be alone, no one to help him. Or someone like Alek lying in wait, arrows nocked, ready to fire as soon as Tycho rode into view.

But I can't seem to focus on any of that, because Tycho is propped up on one elbow, gazing down at me in the shadows. He's been winding a lock of my hair through his fingers. Over . . . and over . . . and over again.

Most of the unease has finally escaped his eyes, and I wish he could always look like this, with gold sparking in his hair and nothing but warmth between us. I want him so badly that I can feel it through every fiber of my body. I reach up and stroke a finger across his cheekbone, and he turns his head to kiss my fingertips.

I've missed *this* Tycho.

But much like when we were traveling with the soldiers, I sense that there's still a guardedness in him. It's softened now that we're alone, but I've begun to realize that it's not about me at all. It's more than just gossip or discretion, despite what he says.

He's so accomplished and capable that I always have to remind myself that Tycho's cool reserve is really just a different type of armor he wears. A different way of protecting himself when his strength and weapons aren't enough.

"You look so serious," he says. "What are you thinking?"

"I'm thinking you're beautiful." I trace a finger across his lips. "And your accent is thicker here."

He'd started to blush, but at that, he blinks. "Is it?"

I nod, then stretch languorously, because my limbs keep threatening to force me into sleep against my will.

His eyes follow my movement, filling with heat, and I watch his throat jerk as he swallows. His hand tugs on my hair, just a bit harder this time.

My own resolve isn't so strong. If he keeps doing that to my hair, I'm going to start unlacing his trousers.

"I won't be gone long," he's saying. "If I can, I'll turn back at once. I'll depart the Crystal Palace the very instant I deliver the message."

If I can. I hate that he's always beholden to someone else's whims.

I brush a thumb over his lips again. "Four days out and four days back, right?"

He nods. "Promise me you'll go to Prince Rhen if the soldiers cause problems for you."

"I will," I say breezily.

But I won't.

Tycho isn't fooled. "Master Garson, then. Promise me, Jax."

I try to ignore the tightness in my chest as I remember the soldiers who glared and muttered when I was sitting on the wagon this morning—or the ones who spit at us in the stables. But Tycho doesn't need to carry my worries with him. He's got enough of his own.

"I'm no stranger to rough travelers," I say. "And *some* of the soldiers were friendly. I rather liked Sephran and Malin. Kutter, too. He was an officer, wasn't he?" I cast my gaze at the ceiling, trying to remember. They tried to tell me, but I couldn't keep the words for all the ranks straight. I just remember the insignia on his shoulder.

"A first lieutenant," says Tycho.

"And Malin speaks some Syssalah." I think of the way he'd tease Sephran—and me too. I smile. "He knows all the profanity, anyway. But at least I won't be completely alone."

Tycho is quiet for a moment. "Well, you won't see Malin until I get back. Prince Rhen doesn't want me to travel unguarded, so he'll be making the journey with me."

"Oh." I'm glad Tycho won't be on his own, but I can't help the flicker of disappointment. It's stupid, because I hardly know Malin—but he spoke my language and he wasn't a total ass who wanted to string me up from a tree, so right now, he's practically my best friend.

"You're disappointed?"

"A little."

Tycho's eyes flick up, just a bit, and this time he gives my hair a not-quite-gentle tug. "Oh. Well. Sorry."

A new note has entered his voice, and I can't quite parse it out. When I finally do, I almost can't believe it.

I shove myself upright and grab hold of his wrist. "*Tycho.*"

He stares at me, his eyes in shadow. "What."

"Are you . . . *jealous*?"

"No."

But he is. He absolutely is. I lean in close, until my lips almost brush his and he shifts forward like he's going to meet me for a kiss.

But I draw back an inch. "*Liar*," I whisper.

He falls back on the blankets, and the straw rustles. "All right, fine." It's dark, but I could swear he's blushing. "You know I have no practice with courtship. And I'm glad they were kind. Truly. I want you to find friends here."

I can't decide if this is adorable or hilarious. Either way, I'm fully awake now. "You have no reason to be jealous. All we talked about was archery."

"Ugh." He rubs his hands over his face. "That's *worse*."

It's so unexpected that I burst out laughing. "You're jealous that they taught me about *weaponry*?"

He drags his hands down to look up at me. "Maybe."

Adorable. He's adorable. "Would now be a poor time to mention that I had an entire lesson in fletching from Kutter?"

He narrows his eyes. "Now you're teasing me. Kutter doesn't speak any Syssalah at *all*."

"I'm not! Sephran helped. Look." I pick up a few pieces of hay and blow it through my fingers, miming a breezy day. "*Wind*," I pronounce carefully in Emberish, then repeat it in Syssalah. "Yes?"

90

Tycho rises up on his elbows, watching me warily, like I'm trying to trick him. But he nods. "Yes."

I hold up a hand, measuring a distance of about an inch between my thumb and forefinger. "*Short*," I say in Emberish, then whistle and make a fast motion with my hand like an arrow. "*Good for wind*."

He stares at me.

"You want to hear more?" I grin and widen my fingers to two inches. "*Long*," I say. "*Good for—*"

"Silver hell." He grabs hold of my waist and flips me onto my back, and it's so quick and unexpected that it steals my breath—especially when he lands straddling my waist, his hands seizing my own, intertwining our fingers. I'm laughing, ready to tussle, but his mouth finds mine, and he draws at my tongue in a way that has me wanting to unlace his trousers again.

When he finally pulls away, he's a bit breathless. So am I.

"Don't you want to hear the rest of my lesson?" I tease.

He winds a hand through my hair and pulls taut, then shifts against me until I feel the full weight of his body. I inhale sharply, my teasing forgotten.

"What lesson?" he says against my ear.

"Make me forget it," I whisper, the words rough and low.

The words are hot and daring, meant to be playful, but Tycho goes still. He gazes down at me, his eyes warm and dark. For an instant, I worry that I've pushed too far, that the moment will snap again, that he'll pull away.

But Tycho gives me a nod. "As you say."

With that, his hands slide under my tunic, baring my abdomen, then my chest. The cool night air finds my skin, and it's so quick and unexpected that I suck in a breath, but then he leans down and draws my nipple right between his teeth. I cry out, arching against him, but I'm pinned.

My hands reach for him, seeking skin, but he's already moving, his weight shifting deliciously. He's straddling my thighs now, and I realize he's tugging at my tunic, pulling me upright again, dragging it over my head. I grab hold of his vest, tugging at the lacings, intending to undress him just as efficiently.

His hands close over mine, pulling them away, gently pushing me back against the blanket. It leaves him hovering over me, his brown eyes staring into mine.

"I'm supposed to be making *you* forget about fletching lengths and arrow speed," he says ruefully.

"What's an arrow?" I say.

He smiles—but then sadness flickers through his eyes. "Ah, Jax."

Oh no. I'm not losing him to this again. "Wait, I'm starting to remember. Did Kutter say that wide fletching was for—"

He dives down to kiss me, and for all his fierce strength, there's always something so . . . *tender* about the way his mouth moves against mine. He pulls at my lips and draws my tongue into his mouth like it's something he wants to savor. When he frees my wrists, I slide my hands up his jaw to twist my fingers through his hair.

But then I realize that his weight no longer pins me to the floor, and his fingers have nimbly untied the lacing at my waist. He's not usually so forward, so I'm not prepared when his hand slips fully under my trousers and his fingers close around me.

My entire body gives a jolt, and I cry out into his mouth.

He catches me somehow, which is good, because I suddenly feel like I'm falling. His free hand is tangled in my hair, and his mouth is still drawing at mine, his kisses slowing as he strokes the length of me. I might be clutching at him.

"Yes?" he whispers against my lips, his breath sweet and warm.

Yes, please, anything at all, yes. But I can't speak. I'm gasping, nodding, my world narrowed to the heat in my belly and the slow movement of his hand. By the time his lips trail a line of kisses down my chest, my veins are full of fire. When his mouth joins his hand, I have to press a fist to my lips to keep from crying out. I lose all sense of myself.

I might be whispering his name, I might be whimpering, I might be flying.

I do know I don't last long at *all*.

When I'm no longer shuddering, he crawls back up my body, tugging my trousers back, dropping a kiss on my bare shoulder, tucking himself against me.

I turn my head and stroke a hand across his cheek. His eyes are warm and dark and intent on mine, and I would lie like this forever.

But we can't. Because he's leaving. Again.

The thought enters my head without warning, and I close my eyes before he can see it register in my expression.

But then he murmurs, "You're the one that's beautiful, Jax." There's so much reverence in his tone that it makes me blush and shiver.

Tycho shifts closer, his hand splaying over the center of my bare chest. "Are you cold?"

He says it with such care, like he'd burn down the world to keep me warm. I shake my head. "I'm not cold."

The fire in my veins has turned to molten honey, and I stroke a hand across his cheek again, very aware of the hard weight of him pressed against the outside of my thigh. I reach lower, my fingers grazing the fabric of his trousers. I barely touch him and his breath hitches, so I flick my wrist and tug the laces free.

But he catches my hand, gripping my fingers in such a way that I can't tell if he's trying to slow me down or stop altogether.

The air has changed slightly, and I turn my head to look at him. His eyes are so dark and inscrutable, and I can feel his heartbeat against me, quicker than it should be.

"Yes?" I whisper.

His grip loosens, just a bit—but he doesn't answer.

It's terrifying to think that others might read his silence as consent. His loyalty, once won, seems to run so deeply that he'll sacrifice even the most wounded parts of himself, no matter what it costs him. Just like the reason he's leaving tomorrow. No one ever allows him to choose. No one ever waits for him to yield.

So *I* wait.

Eventually, he draws a heavy breath and lets go of my wrist, stroking a slow path up my bare arm. I let my hand fall against his waist, and he shifts closer to me, his lips brushing against mine.

I can still feel him pressing against my thigh, so I know the desire isn't gone—but I don't reach for him this time. He kisses me slowly, his hand gentle against my face, and I kiss him back, my lips drawing at his. Chaste. Gentle. Patient.

But there's still . . . *something*. Something unspoken, something unsaid. A weight in the air that warns me to tread carefully. When he tucks his face against my neck and rests a quiet hand over my heart, I don't move.

"No?" I whisper, but this time it's not really a question at all. I already know. It's clear.

He makes an unhappy sound. "Not *no*. Just . . ."

"Not yet?"

He hesitates, then nods against me. I kiss his forehead, then rest my hand over his, holding his palm against my heart.

His breathing slows, and the tension slips out of the air, as if he needed me to accept his hesitation. As if he couldn't relax until he knew I wouldn't push. He's so warm against me, and I feel the tug of sleep pulling at both of us. In fact, Tycho might already be there.

It takes me longer. My thoughts keep working, wound up in his hesitation and what it means. How it relates to his waiting anger. His readiness to fight.

But when he sighs against me, I realize it's the first time I've seen him relax in days. Maybe weeks. I chase the thoughts out of my head.

There will be enough time for worry later. For now, I just breathe.

We don't sleep very long. I don't know what wakes me, but the pitch-dark sky outside the hayloft doors hasn't gained a single thread of sunrise. Tycho is still curled against me, but his eyes are open and trained on the rafters overhead, glittering faintly in the dying lantern light. It makes me wonder if he really slept at all.

It almost feels like a dream when he says, "I don't hate him, Jax."

I lift my head just enough to look at him, but he doesn't move, not even to look at me.

His voice is so serious, as if he's trying to convince himself. But I felt his anger. His resentment. I've been feeling it for days. He's certainly not going to convince me.

Then he turns his head to look at me. "I do hate the soldiers, though."

A note in his voice tells me this is about more than the jealousy we teased about earlier.

Part of the reason I resent the prince is that Tycho endured so much when he was young, well before he ever came to Ironrose—and then he got caught up in a fight for a throne he had nothing to do with. He was already broken and abused long before the prince ever gave him those scars on his back. It's a vulnerability Tycho keeps hidden, buried so deeply beneath training and armor and violent skill that I'm not sure many people even know.

Tycho's eyes shift back to the rafters. "I served in the army in Syhl Shallow, and that was hard enough." He draws a sharp breath. "I never would have joined the army here. *Never.* Not after what those soldiers did to my family."

And what they did to *him*.

Suddenly, I retrace all the moments we spent on the road, every man who glared or muttered a comment. I consider the way Tycho wouldn't sleep or pulled away or kept his distance, and I reevaluate it all in a different light.

I consider the way he caught my hand, the way he pulled away tonight.

"I've been *around* them from time to time," Tycho says. "I mean— *obviously.* But I haven't been a soldier in a while. And never . . . like that. Never like we were."

No wonder he's so angry. No wonder he wants to fight. It's more than me. It's more than his conflict with the king. It's more than his orders.

It's an enemy he can't defeat. A wrong he can't right.

I frown. "I shouldn't have teased you—about the archery—"

"No—Jax. Stop." He scowls and runs a hand across his face. "This is stupid. It's not you. It's not even *them.* It's me." Now he swears. "Forget it. I hate this."

"Hush," I whisper, stroking a hand along his arm. But then I pause, reevaluating again. "Tycho, we don't . . . we don't have to lie here. I didn't mean to—"

He grabs hold of me like I'm going to drift away. "Not you, Jax. Never you."

I relax against him—but I'm not sure he does. We lie in silence again for the longest time, my fingers drifting along his forearm.

I wonder if he's ever shared any of this with anyone, or if he's kept it all trapped in his heart, allowing the pent-up emotion to escape when he couldn't confine it anymore.

I think of what I know about him, and I suspect it's mostly the latter.

"It's over now anyway," he says, and again, he sounds like he's trying to convince himself. "I likely won't have to travel with them again."

"Except for Malin."

He sighs. "It'll be fine. Just out and back."

I thread my fingers through his hair. "It's all right to hate the soldiers, Tycho." I pause. "It's all right to hate the king, too."

He flinches a little when I say that. "I don't. Truly, I don't."

"Fine. It's all right to be *angry* at him. He's taken so much from you, and I don't think he's even aware of it."

That forces him still. After a moment, he frowns. "He's *given* so much to me."

"That doesn't mean you owe him your happiness."

His frown deepens—but he says nothing. I sense that I'm pushing too hard, and I don't want to fight, especially about this.

A hint of pink appears in the sky I can see through the hayloft doors, and we both frown.

He'll have duties this morning, I'm sure. If he's due to leave by midday, he'll strap on his armor, saddle his horse, and head north for Syhl Shallow.

He'll be the King's Courier, and I'll be the blacksmith left behind. The same as before.

"The night is ending," he says, as if to confirm it.

I put a hand against his face. "Out and back," I whisper. "And then you'll be done with all your couriering."

But he won't. I know.

"I'll return as quickly as I can," he says. "And I'll give you more than a night in a hayloft. We'll ride to Silvermoon and eat too much and stay out too late and find an inn with a room to share." He twists a finger through a lock of my hair. "I swear to you, Jax."

I nod, but the words tug at me. For the first time, I consider that it's not just his happiness at stake, the way his life proceeds at the whim of the king.

It's mine, too.

But I won't burden him with that. Not on the morning he's due to leave, with threats at his back and a confrontation with the king in his future.

So I take his hand and kiss his fingertips. "Yes, my lord. I'll be waiting."

CHAPTER 11

CALLYN

When I accepted a position as lady-in-waiting for Princess Sinna Cataleha, the three-year-old daughter to Queen Lia Mara and King Grey, I envisioned days filled with quaint tea parties and reading books by the fire. I imagined lovely gowns and silken dresses for myself and my sister, our hours busied with the care for a perfect child who would have the finest instructors. We'd learn to ride, we'd learn to fight, and we'd be tutored right alongside our charge, elevated from poor bakers on the border of Syhl Shallow to ladies of the court in the Crystal Palace.

I did not expect to be crawling under beds at an hour before dawn, with cobwebs in my half-braided hair.

"Sinna!" I hiss.

A giggle echoes from out in the hallway. I sure hope Nora is out there to catch her.

I know Lord Alek and the Truthbringers might have been a threat if I'd remained in Briarlock, but when I've only gotten four hours of sleep, I begin to wonder just how *much* of a threat.

"Sinna!" I hiss again. I squirm out from under the bed where I was *sure* she was hiding, and dart into the dim hallway.

I don't see the princess, but I've discovered she has a talent for hiding in the tiniest spaces. I don't see Nora either. She's twelve, though, and usually covered in dust and cobwebs just like I am. Maybe she's under a different bed.

Another giggle echoes from the other end of the hallway, and I sprint in my bare feet. If Sinna makes it down to where the guards are stationed, news of this little adventure will *definitely* be reported to the queen.

But then I see the princess dash out from behind a tapestry, her curly red hair flying behind her, giggles echoing off the walls.

On the other side of the hallway, my sister jumps out from behind another tapestry. "I've got you!" Nora whisper-shouts—in a way that makes me think she might be enjoying this a little too much.

Sinna squeals in delight and changes course, bolting the other way, heading right for the corner that will lead to the guards.

No. No, no, no.

I drive my bare feet into the floor and all but *leap*, my arms outstretched. My arms close around the princess, who's giggling like this is the best time ever—while I just want to go back to sleep for another four hours. Nora skids to her knees beside me, ready to block. We all roll to a stop along the velvet carpeting, and I blow a lock of hair out of my mouth.

Princess Sinna lands on top of me, still giggling. She grins, her eyes bright and shining. "Let's do it again, Cally-cal."

Cally-cal. She picked that up from my sister, a nickname I've had since Nora could barely walk. Sinna calls *her* Princess Nora, as if they're both daughters of royalty and I'm tasked with looking after them together.

I'd find it all adorable if it weren't so early in the morning.

Sinna pokes at the pendant around my neck, which used to be my mother's. It's sitting in the hollow of my throat from our scuffle. But then she looks up, over my head. "Oh! Good morning, Da."

WHAT.

Beside me, Nora chokes on a gasp and scrambles to her feet. "Your Majesty."

Clouds above, we've woken the king. I fight to right myself so I'm not lying in a crumpled heap with half my hair in my face, but I have a forty-pound toddler on my chest. King Grey is probably thinking he should have locked me and Jax in the stone prison after all—or at least *me*. When I try to lift Sinna off me, she giggles again, squirming like I'm trying to tickle her. She manages to knee me right in the ribs.

Amazing. This is absolutely what I need.

"Sinna." The king's voice is quiet, but a tone of command often hides in his words. It makes people pay attention, even his wily daughter. Sinna stops giggling.

His hands appear in my line of vision, and I'm surprised to see the buttoned cuffs of a riding jacket. So he wasn't asleep after all. Before I can puzzle that out, Sinna reaches for his outstretched hands and he plucks her off me.

I scramble to my feet less gracefully than my sister, then hurry into a curtsy. I know half my hair has escaped its braid, and I don't even want to *consider* how red my face must be. My heart is hammering in my chest for a dozen reasons, and I don't have the courage to meet his eyes. "Forgive me, Your Majesty."

Nora scoots to my side and threads her fingers through mine. "Forgive *us*, Your Majesty. Were we too loud? Did we wake you?"

The king inhales like he wants to respond, but my sister is . . . well, my *sister*, and she keeps prattling.

"We could take Sinna for sweetcakes if you like," she offers brightly. "Lord Tycho told Callyn that there were sweetcakes in the kitchen every morning. That way, you could return to bed with the queen. Oh! Well. Not to imply that you were *in bed* with the—"

"*Nora.*" I give her arm a firm yank, and she gives a little *yip*, but she falls silent.

In front of us, the king is silent, so I chance a look up, but his eyes are very dark, his expression cool and unreadable. Sinna is curled against his shoulder, her tiny fingers fiddling with a buckle on his jacket, but her childish innocence doesn't steal one ounce of his severity. Actually, it makes him a bit more intimidating. Like he could put her up on his shoulders, draw his sword, and fight a war—all without thinking twice.

I swallow and jerk my eyes back down. "Sorry," I say. "I know it's early. We were trying to keep her quiet."

"You didn't wake me."

I'm not sure what to say to that. It's obvious that he was dressed, and he didn't come from their bedchambers, so he was clearly attending to . . . *something.*

In our silence, Princess Sinna keeps fiddling with his buckle and says, "Well, *I* would very much like some sweetcakes, Da."

His face softens a bit. Not quite a smile, but almost. "I'm certain you would. But I believe Mama would very much like for you to sleep a bit longer."

"I can take her back to bed," I offer, reaching out.

"I'll do it."

Oh. I lower my arms. I don't know if that's meant to be a dismissal or a rebuke—or if he's just being a father.

"Yes, Your Majesty." I offer another hasty curtsy. So does Nora, and then we step to the side so he can pass.

Maybe the king senses my sudden uncertainty, because he doesn't move. "Thank you for looking after her. I know it's a relief to the queen that you're here. There have been a lot of rumors coming from the Crystal City, and with everything that's happened, it's difficult to know what's truth and what's idle gossip." He pauses. "I'm pleased that Sinna is enjoying herself."

Sinna brightens. "Oh, I am! Princess Nora was teaching me to plait Cally-cal's hair before I made them find me. Don't you like it?"

Nora and I both snap our heads up. "I'm not really a princess," Nora whispers, as if the king doesn't know that.

But he's looking at me, his eyes flicking to my hair—which I'm now remembering is a mess of attempted braids that are half undone and probably full of dust and tangles.

I quickly shove all the loose strands behind my ears. "I told Sinna this would be the latest style at court by the end of the week."

He smiles as if he's truly amused. It brightens his whole face, and for the first time, he doesn't seem quite so fierce and unyielding. Honestly, he should smile more often.

Or maybe not, because as soon as I have the thought, I'm horrified to find myself blushing.

Luckily he's already looked away to drop a kiss on his daughter's forehead. "Come along, Sinna. I should get a few hours of sleep myself before the generals expect me on the fields."

That must mean the king hasn't been to bed yet, and it's nearly dawn. I wonder what he's been occupied with all night. It's definitely not my place to ask, but considering everything that's happened in Syhl Shallow these last few weeks, I'm definitely curious.

"Oh, and Princess Nora?" he says, just before turning away.

My sister startles, but I can tell she's delighted that the king has addressed her *directly*. She all but quivers with excitement. "Your Majesty?"

"Tycho was right. There *are* sweetcakes in the kitchen. Right now, they're probably still hot."

If it were up to me, I also wouldn't mind a few more hours of sleep, but my sister was just tempted with hot sweetcakes by the king himself. She's all but bouncing along beside me as we stride down the still-unfamiliar palace hallways, passing the occasional guard or servant.

"The king is so different from what I expected," she's saying, and she's making absolutely no effort to keep her voice down, like we're back in our bakery in Briarlock and not in the middle of the Crystal Palace. "I knew Queen Lia Mara would be beautiful, but people always say King Grey is horrible. I thought he would be ugly and old with warts everywhere—"

"Nora! Do you even know how to whisper?"

She lowers her voice. "Well. *I* thought he would have greasy hair and beady eyes, but he's really quite handsome, don't you think?"

"I suppose." I run a finger over Mother's pendant. The king *is* handsome. Quite striking, really, with those dark eyes and dark hair. In a way, it feels like a betrayal to admit it. The rumors in Syhl Shallow always painted him as a terrible man who controlled a horrible magic—magic that killed my father and hundreds of other people when they attacked the castle in an attempt to slaughter the royal family. Like my sister, I spent a long time imagining the king to be ugly and twisted, as if his outward appearance would be the sum of all the stories told about him.

When I first saw him in battle in Briarlock, I was startled to find that the king wasn't old and ugly at all. He's tall and carries himself with the bearing of a soldier, and he can't be more than twenty-five or so. If I'd crossed paths with him on the street, I would have taken him for a doting young father, possibly on leave from the army. If he'd come into the bakery, I would have been blushing at him like a fool.

But I've seen the king in blood-spattered armor, with one arrow through his shoulder and another through his thigh. I've seen him use magic to burn through his enemies to protect his family.

Just like he once did to my father.

I have to rub at my pendant again. I feel certain I made the right choice in coming here.

But sometimes I'm worried that I made the wrong one.

Nora is peering at me. "Are you still afraid of him, Cally-cal?"

I glance at her in surprise. My sister isn't usually so direct—or so insightful. But during that battle in the woods, one of the soldiers put his sword right through Nora's chest. The same magic that killed our father saved my sister's life. That changed something in both of us.

"A little," I admit.

But it's more than a little. It's so hard to reconcile that someone who's caused so much fear throughout Syhl Shallow was making me blush and telling my little sister where to find warm sweetcakes. I can't make it all fit inside my head.

I let go of the pendant, and it hangs heavy over my heart. Lord Alek once told me it was Iishellasan steel. He guessed that it was warded against magic.

But a week ago, when Nora was nearly killed, stars filled my vision. I felt sparks in my chest. Everyone thinks the queen's magic saved my sister, but . . . I wonder if it was *mine*. I wonder if my mother knew her pendant would somehow *give me* magic.

That's too terrifying to think about.

But I remember pressing a knife to my finger, watching blood well up. I remember feeling the stars and sparks again, and seeing the wound close effortlessly.

I need to stop thinking about this.

The palace halls are quiet, the stone floor cold against my bare feet.

Nora huffs at my silence. "Well, *I'm* not afraid of him anymore. He and the queen have been very kind."

"Yes, they have."

"His magic saved my life."

Also true. "I know."

She hesitates. "I think Da was wrong, Cal." She looks at me. "He shouldn't . . . he shouldn't have been here. He shouldn't have been part of the Uprising."

I look over at her in surprise. I wonder what Nora would say if she knew Jax and I were holding notes for Lord Alek and the Truthbringers—notes of treason against the king. We were doing it in exchange for silver to pay the taxes that we owed to save our homes. We didn't think it would cause any harm . . . but it did.

I nod. "You're right. Da shouldn't have been here. And we shouldn't have come with him."

Voices echo from up ahead, which isn't too uncommon since we're nearing the kitchen and the laundries, along with one of the halls that leads out to the stables and the training fields. Usually there's a good deal of commotion down here as meals are prepared, clothes and linens are laundered, and guards and soldiers come and go. It's early, but we've been hearing the low hum of chatter echoing from the kitchen as the cooks begin preparations for breakfast.

But something about *these* voices catches my attention. I can't make out who's speaking because of the echoes bouncing off the stone walls, but the tone is sharp. A bit more demanding.

I grab Nora's arm and haul her to a stop.

"Who is it?" she whispers.

"I don't know." I'm torn between curiosity keeping me right here and the urge to protect my sister by fleeing back to the royal wing. I wonder if this is related to the reason the king was awake all night.

Then the decision is made for me. At least a dozen people stride around the corner. I notice the royal guards trimmed in the gold and red of Emberfall first, but they're just ahead of two men who aren't attired in royal livery at all. They flank a third man, and once my eyes lock on his face, I forget everyone else. He's a bit windblown and travel worn, but there's no mistaking the fiery red of his hair, or the near-constant look of disdain in his blue eyes.

Lord Alek.

My heart gives a traitorous skip in my chest as if it's happy he's here, and I gasp without meaning to.

The last time I saw him, he was in my bed, whispering promises against my skin. He was convincing me that he needed my help to protect the queen. He wrapped me up in his arms and made me feel like he had followed Lord Tycho to Briarlock for *my* protection.

It was all a lie. He was only in Briarlock to help the Truthbringers lay a trap for the royal family.

I was such a fool.

The queen warned me that Alek would be escorted back to Syhl Shallow. But I thought he'd be thrown in the dungeon, locked far away from me.

I didn't expect him to march right in while Nora was dragging me to get sweetcakes.

I'm frozen against the wall as if there's any possible way he won't see us.

Maybe he won't. We're only wearing sleeping shifts, and we probably look like servants. Lord Alek isn't the type of man to pay an ounce of attention to someone beneath him. He's glaring at the queen's younger sister anyway.

I've only met Princess Nolla Verin once, but she might be the fiercest woman I've ever met. She goes by Verin to everyone outside the royal family, and she spends much of her time on the training fields with the army. Even though it's early, she's trimmed in fine black armor that's lined in silver, and she's wearing more weapons than Alek is. I wouldn't be surprised if they broke out in a fight right here.

They both sound angry enough.

"I do not care what time it is," Alek is snarling. "I do not care if the king and queen are sleeping. I have been detained long enough. I will not wait one more minute before being released from this charade. You will fetch your sister—"

"You will not order me to fetch *anything*," Verin snaps. "Most definitely not your queen. You were to return to your House, not to report directly to the palace. You will wait until you are summoned—"

"Then send a servant to fetch the king. I'm done waiting." His head jerks in my direction. "You there. Find the—"

His ice-blue eyes lock on mine, and Alek stops short so suddenly that the guards behind him skid to a halt. For a moment, we're frozen just like that, staring at each other like we've been turned to stone.

And then he breaks the silence. "Callyn," he says softly, the edge simply *gone*. There's so much emotion in his voice that it causes my heart to stumble, because I certainly wasn't expecting it. The disdain has vanished, too. "You're here." His eyes trace my dusty face, then my wildly misbraided hair, then my form. "Are you well?"

My heart gives that traitorous skip again. I inhale to answer, but I'm not even sure what I'm going to say.

I don't get a chance to find out, because my little sister launches herself away from the wall. Nora is lean and wiry from all the work we did in the barn and the bakery, but she's also strong. She smacks Alek square across the face at least three times before he gets it together to grab her arm.

"Nora!" he cries.

She switches to punches with her left hand, and when he tries to deflect, she gets him right in the throat. Alek makes a pretty horrific sound and falls back a step.

"You traitor!" she's yelling. "You tried to kill the queen! We *trusted* you!"

"Stop this!" He deflects again, and she tries to knee him in the crotch. He barely dodges that one.

"You! Hurt! My! Sister!" She grabs hold of his armor and climbs him like a tree, then digs her fingernails into the shell of his ear and *yanks*.

Alek yelps and tries to push her away, but she clings more tightly so he's only hurting himself. "Nora!" he snaps again.

The guards exchange glances, as if they're unsure whether to intervene when an unarmed child in a sleeping shift is kicking a grown man's ass.

Nora grabs hold of his hair with her other hand, twisting hard. I know this move well from when we were younger and used to squabble over chores.

"Cally-cal!" she calls. "Help me punch him!"

"I think you've got it," I say.

Alek's eyes have gone cold, and they lock on mine. "Get her off of me," he growls. "Or I'll be forced to do it myself."

Any emotion I might have felt a moment ago is gone, iced over. I've already seen my sister die once, and I'm not keen to see it again.

"Nora," I say, stepping forward. "Enough."

But the queen's sister sighs and lifts a hand, stopping me. "Oh, Alek," Verin says, her tone exasperated, like she's done with him. "You can't handle a little hair pulling?" She steps forward, plucks Nora off him like she's weightless, then sets her on the ground beside me. "Time to sheathe those claws, little cat."

Nora gasps, then stares up at her in wonder, her eyes wide.

"Come find me later this week," Verin says with a wink, "and I'll show you a few things you'll find more effective than tugging on his ear."

Nora's eyes go even wider. "Y-yes, Your Highness."

Alek steps up beside Verin, but he doesn't have eyes for me this time. He's leaning down, glaring right at my little sister. A few drops of blood run from where Nora has clawed at his face. His hair is a rumpled mess. "Yes," he says viciously. "Take your lessons. Because the next time you come at me, *little cat*, I'll make sure you—"

I punch him right in the face.

He doesn't see it coming *at all*, so I have the satisfaction of seeing him stumble back.

"Don't you threaten my sister," I say to him.

He spits blood at the ground, then straightens. For an instant, his eyes hold mine, and instead of rage, which I expect, I find something else in his expression. Something I can't quite figure out.

Much like the tone in his voice when he said, *You're here. Are you well?*

But Verin speaks, and the flicker of emotion is gone. "Alek," she says, "if you insist on remaining here, I will arrange for you to be given a set of quarters where you will be confined until the queen sees fit to visit you. If you bring down the wrath of every Royal House over the matter of a few hours, then Lia Mara will have to handle it."

He touches a finger to his lip, which is already swelling. "Fine."

The guards begin to lead him away.

Nora looks up at me. "That was amazing," she whispers.

Oh yes. Truly amazing. I want to burn myself to ash right here in the hallway.

"Do you think the sweetcakes are still warm?" Nora continues.

I'm glad her priorities are in order.

At least it gives me something else to focus on. I take her hand. "Let's go see."

When I turn, Verin is right there in front of me, and my breath catches. "Your Highness."

She smiles, but there's a hint of cunning to her expression. It's hard to believe that she and the queen are sisters. Lia Mara is full of warmth and light, all curves and gentle hands and kind words. I haven't known

110

her long, but I'm beginning to learn that she's very levelheaded, approaching every interaction with rational thought. She prioritizes peace for her people.

Verin is smaller, leaner, made of sharper edges. I've caught glimpses of her on the training fields, and she looks like she could fight a war before lunch and be ready for an evening ball by supper. When Lia Mara first offered me this position, she said that her sister would teach me to defend myself, but it hasn't been mentioned since then, and I haven't wanted to ask. Just like the king reminds me too much of what happened to my father, I often worry that the soldiers and training fields would remind me too much of what happened to my mother.

Now Verin is in front of me, and she throws a fist into her palm, then nods. "You strike well, too," she says. "When Nora comes to find me, you should join her."

CHAPTER 12

CALLYN

The following day, when little Princess Sinna is taken for her lessons, servants deliver trunks of clothes for me and Nora. With wide eyes, we watch them sort through everything. Breeches and tunics and vests, along with boots and belts and gloves—more clothes than we could wear in a week.

They're working with such a cool efficiency that I don't want to disrupt it, but this can't all be for us.

"I'm sorry," I say carefully. "What . . . what are these for?"

An older man who's hanging tunics in the wardrobe says, "By order from the queen's sister. She says you can find her in the arena when you're dressed and ready."

Well then.

I think of my mother and how she died on the battlefield. I have to rub a hand over her pendant again.

That just reminds me of Alek telling me of the pendant's origins, and I yank my hand down.

Callyn. You're here. Are you well?

His voice was so rough and startled. I wish I understood the emotion in his eyes.

But there sure wasn't any misunderstanding the threat in his voice when Nora was clawing at him. *Get her off of me or I'll be forced to do it myself.*

My knuckles still ache from punching him, and I remember the wounded look on his face. I simultaneously regret it and wish I'd done it harder.

I hate that I keep thinking about him.

Nora all but attacks the clothes when the servants are gone. She presses a pair of calfskin breeches to her cheek. "Oh, Cally-cal. Have you ever felt anything so *soft*?" She gasps and seizes a boot. "I hope they fit."

I think of every other piece of finery we've been offered since we first set foot in the palace. "They'll fit."

She's already peeling off her skirts. "Hurry. I think she's waiting. What do you think she'll teach us?"

I have no idea. Verin is terrifying in her own way. She plucked Nora off Alek as if my sister *was* a little cat.

You strike well, she said. I keep hearing the words in my head, turning them over and over like they could mean something different each time. I can't remember the last time anyone ever complimented me on any kind of *physical* prowess. My meat pies and sweetcakes, sure. Punching Alek in the face? That was more instinct.

"Come *on*," Nora urges as she throws a boot at me.

I sigh and stand to unlace my skirts.

I haven't worn trousers in years. Nora hasn't either. Even with barn chores, skirts were always more practical in the bakery: easy to mend, easy to layer in the winter, easy to stitch pockets wherever I needed them. I've never longed for anything different.

113

When we're dressed, Nora stands before a mirror, turning this way and that. She's chosen breeches the color of willow bark and a vest dyed a richer blue than I've ever seen. Black boots lace all the way to her knees. "I don't ever want to wear skirts *again*," she sighs.

I can't help staring at her. The boots make her legs look ten miles long, and the vest reveals curves that I didn't realize were beginning to appear. Somewhere along the line she's grown another few inches, too. I'm so used to her being . . . well, *Nora*, that I somehow forgot to notice that childhood was slipping away.

I blink, and my thoughts replay the moment that soldier thrust a sword through her body. I'll never be able to forget the choking sound she made. Sudden emotion grips my throat, and I step forward and wrap my arms around her.

Nora yips. "Cally-cal! What—"

But my breath hitches, and she breaks off with a sigh. She hugs me back, pressing her face into my shoulder for longer than I expect.

Eventually she whispers, "It's your monthly time, hmm?"

I jerk back. "Clouds above, Nora!"

"Is it? Please tell me it is." She sounds a bit too excited about the prospect of something that's not much of a joy. "I heard the queen's ladies talking yesterday. I think they use cotton wrapped in *silk*! You have to tell me if it's true—"

"It is not my monthly time!" I snap.

"Oh." She actually sounds disappointed.

I roll my eyes. "But I'll be sure to report back."

She straightens and looks in the mirror again, then fidgets with the end of one of her braids, which hang straight down her back. "Do you think you could help me pin them up?" She glances hopefully over her shoulder. "Like Verin does?"

There's something about it that sounds so eager and wistful all at once, the way the princess wanted to learn to plait my hair. Just like that, Nora is a girl again.

"Sure," I say. And I do.

The arena is nearly empty, which isn't a surprise, because the weather is temperate and any guards and soldiers are training out on the fields. The queen's sister is there, though she's not waiting on us. Verin is engaged in a bout of swordplay with another soldier, and their blades flash and spin in the light. The soldier is a man, easily twice her age and double her size, but Verin is quick and efficient, and she holds him off as he bears down with a strength that clearly outmatches hers.

Nora's eyes are wide. "He'll slice her in two."

"I don't think so." It's been a long time, but I remember the way our mother used to talk about swordplay. Nora was too young to learn much of anything before she died, but Mother taught me how to hold a weapon. Her first lessons were all about cleverness and skill and speed. Strength and size were really the least important.

Just as I have the thought, the man knocks the sword out of Verin's hand, and the impact sends her to the ground. When he advances, his sword is aimed for her throat.

My sister gasps, but Verin rolls between his legs, then leaps onto his back. Her dagger finds his neck before I'm even aware she drew it from the sheath at her waist.

It's my turn to suck in a breath, but he's chuckling, his hands up in surrender. "All right, Ver. You got me."

She pats him on the shoulder, then springs to the ground. "You're getting old and slow, Solt."

"Old just means I'm not dead yet." His gaze falls on us by the arena railing, and he loses the smile. "Are these the girls the queen brought back from Briarlock?"

I'm not sure how to read the note in his voice. It's not friendly, but it's not antagonistic either. There's a heaviness to it that gives me pause.

"They are," says Verin. "Callyn and Nora, this is General Solt." She pauses, and a wicked note enters her voice. "They attacked Lord Alek yesterday, so I thought maybe I'd help them with a little technique."

"I wanted to claw his eyes out," Nora volunteers.

Verin smiles. "Spend an hour with me and I'll teach you how to peel the bones out of his fingers."

"Ew!" says Nora, but she doesn't look horrified. She looks a little fascinated.

Solt's eyes are on me, though, and he approaches the arena railing. "The queen said we lost your mother during the first conflict in Emberfall. What was her name?"

It's so unexpected that I'm shocked silent, so it's Nora who says, "Mama? Her name was Adelyn."

Solt nods. "She was a captain. I remember."

That almost takes my breath away. After Da died, there weren't too many people left in Briarlock who knew our mother. She spent so much time as a soldier that most of her friends were here, in the Crystal City—or dead on the battlefield around her. I have to clear my throat. "Yes," I say. "You knew her?"

"Not well," he says, "but I knew her. She was in my brother's regiment. He would have known her better." Solt pauses. "You look just like her."

Again, I don't know how to react. My thoughts were so tangled up with worries about Alek and nerves about the queen's sister. I wasn't prepared to be confronted with memories of my mother. Maybe I should have been.

In Briarlock, our lives were wrapped up in the bakery. Mother's career as a soldier was something she did somewhere *else*. At home, she was the baker's wife, curled up in the window with a saucy romance novel. She might have taught me to hold a sword, but she also taught me how to trace pictures in the frost on the windows, or how to milk the cow in the barn out back, or how to plait my hair so it would stay in place but wouldn't give me a headache.

Here, I'm staring at a man who has memories of my mother that I'm not even a part of. Or at least . . . his brother does. "Your brother," I say. "Is he a general as well?"

"No. He died in the same battle."

He doesn't say this with any additional gravity, but I feel like I've made a misstep. I should have paid attention to his phrasing. The way he said, *She was in my brother's regiment. He would have known her better.*

"I'm sorry," I say.

"So am I. That war took a lot from us all."

This conversation reminds me of another one I had—weeks ago, with Lord Alek. He lost his mother in that same battle, where hundreds of soldiers were killed by a magical monster—crafted by the same magic the king wields. And later, as part of the same conflict, his sister was killed.

A twinge of sympathy for Alek tugs at my heart. I want to shove it away, but I can't. He may have done horrible things, but magic has done a lot of horrible things, too.

General Solt claps me on the shoulder. "I'll see if I can find anyone in the barracks who might have served with your mother. I'm sure you'd like to hear old stories."

There's a tightness in my throat, but I manage a weak smile. "That's very kind, thank you."

He nods, then looks to Verin. "I need to join Grey on the fields so we can dismiss the recruits before dinner. He's had a lot of long nights.

I'm sure he's ready." He offers me and my sister a nod. "Enjoy your lessons."

"Thank you," we say, but the first part of what he's said has lodged in my thoughts.

Grey. The king.

He's had a lot of long nights.

So maybe the morning he found us chasing Sinna wasn't the only time he didn't go to bed. I wonder what's happening with the Truth-bringers. Or maybe he and the queen have finally questioned Alek, and now they have others to arrest and detain.

The queen's sister gestures to Nora. "You first," she says.

Nora climbs under the arena railing as if she'd been promised a pile of silver topped with sweetcakes. "Yes, Your Highness."

"In here, just Verin is fine." The princess smiles. "Everything else takes too long in battle."

As they begin talking about blocks and punches, I watch General Solt stride out of the arena and into the dimming sunlight. There was no tension in his voice when he mentioned the king—despite the fact that his brother died in the same war. No bitterness, no undercurrent of anger about being forced to serve under a man who bears the same magic that caused so much tragedy. If anything, there was a note of camaraderie, something akin to true friendship.

It rattles my foundation, the way the king's comment about where to find sweetcakes left me feeling like I couldn't find the right footing.

It's like Nora said. I expected the king to be ugly and twisted. Cold, capricious, and cruel.

He's not—and even the *awareness* feels like a betrayal.

Verin and my sister grapple and punch and chase each other around the arena for an hour. Eventually, my sister is red-cheeked and breathing hard, and her braids are a little frayed. But the smile on her face is a mile wide, even though her knuckles look a little raw. She's staring up at Verin like she's found a new hero.

"That was amazing," she says between breaths.

"Come back tomorrow. We'll do a little more each day." Verin points back at the entrance to the palace. "You need to get some water. And some dinner. No need to wait on your sister. On your way, stop at the armory and tell Master Hidder that I said you need to be fitted with a weapons belt and some training blades."

I think Nora might actually take flight. "Yes, Your Highness— Verin—thank you!" But her voice trails off, because she's already sprinting away.

Verin turns to me, and I'm ready to thank her as well, because her kindness to my sister was really quite endearing. I expect her attitude to be similar with me: encouraging yet firm.

But her eyes meet mine, and there's a sharpness in her gaze. "Explain your relationship with Lord Alek."

She might as well have shot me with an arrow. "I . . . I don't have a relationship with him. I hate him."

"I heard what he said to you, and I saw the way you punched him. Why did you hit him like that?"

My cheeks warm, and I wish they would stop. "I'd hit him again if I could."

She takes a step closer to me, until the only thing between us is the narrow arena fence. Her eyes, which were so warm for Nora, are coolly picking me apart. "You still haven't answered my question."

"I was defending my sister," I say.

"Now I'm defending *mine*. Explain your relationship with him."

That warmth on my cheeks goes nowhere. "I was stupid," I say. "I fell for his lies."

"I don't know if I like the idea of someone *stupid* looking after my niece."

119

Fury swells in my chest, and my fingernails press into my palms so hard that I might be drawing blood. "Then perhaps you should address the queen regarding her choice."

Verin's eyebrows go up, and she smiles, but nothing about it is reassuring. She takes a step back, gesturing for me to follow her. "Come on."

I hesitate, but there's a part of me that hopes I'll get a chance to punch *her* now, so I follow.

I get my wish. "Strike me," she says. "The same way you struck Alek."

Fine. I'll show her a good strike. I swing a fist.

My hubris catches up with me. I should have considered the battle I witnessed when we walked in here. She blocks my arm and then shoves me in the shoulder, knocking me back a step.

"Again," she says.

I swing again. Another easy block, but this time she smacks her palm against my jaw. It's harder than a slap, quick and sudden and stinging. I stumble back, a hand to my cheek. I don't think anyone has ever hit me in the face before.

Verin is looking at me disdainfully. "That's all it takes? Again."

"How is this teaching me anything?" I demand.

"It's teaching *me* that if someone wants to kidnap the princess, all they must do is tap you on the cheek."

I grit my teeth, take a step forward, and swing again.

Another block, another smack in the face. This one is harder.

"Stop it!" I snarl.

"If you don't like it, figure out how to block," she says. "Were you and Alek lovers?" When I scowl, she keeps going. "Did he put his hand between your legs and make you his little puppet?"

I don't know what to say, but my cheeks are suddenly on *fire*.

She strides forward, and I can tell she's going to smack me again, so I dart forward and try to punch her.

120

She dodges—and her fist ends up in my stomach. I see stars and fall to my knees. At first, I can't remember how to inhale, but then I *do*, and it's awful. Breath scrapes into my lungs, and I'm dry heaving in the dust of the arena. One hand is braced against the ground, and the other is clenched across my belly. I think I'm drooling in the dirt.

"Were you lovers?" she asks again.

I can't speak yet, so I shake my head vigorously.

"Alek looked at you like a lover."

My heart stutters and I hate it. "No," I gasp. "He didn't."

"Get up."

"If I get up I'm going to kill you."

She laughs as if that's truly amusing. "You're welcome to try."

I'm embarrassed and infuriated and terrified, but I launch myself off the ground with a shout of rage. My fury makes for a good ally, because she can't account for the full force of my weight. When I tackle her, she falls back to one knee—but I'm no fighter, and she is. Verin wrestles free, and I draw back a fist to punch her in the jaw.

She's too good, too quick. She throws a strike right inside of mine. My shoulders hit the ground before I realize she's hit me square in the nose. My vision is full of spots, my eyes stinging with tears. I can taste blood. My body jolts like someone has kicked me in the belly, but I don't know which way is up, so I can't be sure.

"Nolla Verin!" a male voice snaps from a distance. I wonder if it's that general. "Enough."

I put a hand against the dirt floor, but my head is still spinning. I touch my lip, and when my fingers pull away, they're stained with red. I can't breathe through my nose at all.

My breath hitches.

Verin's voice calls to me, but it's from a distance, as if she's walking away. "Come back tomorrow," she says, the same thing she said to my sister, but now her voice is taunting. "We'll do a little more each day."

121

She leaves me alone in the arena, surrounded by the weight of pressing silence.

My entire body hurts, but my face is the worst. I don't want to touch it again, in case it's worse than I'm imagining. I get to my knees, but I brace a hand in the dirt. A drop of blood appears beside my fingers, then another, falling from my face. I squeeze my eyes shut, trying not to cry.

Footsteps crunch through the dirt of the arena, and my eyes snap open to discover a pair of boots coming to a stop in front of me. Another drop of blood falls from my face to land on the toe.

A hand backed by armored bracers appears in my vision. "Take my hand. Can you stand?"

I'm too dazed to process this, but my body is responding, my hand weakly slipping into his. Just as I'm thinking his voice can't be General Solt, I'm strongly pulled to my feet.

I find myself facing the king instead.

A needle of ice pierces my spine as shame piles onto the rest of my emotions. Did he just watch that? Everything she said was so awful. Did he *hear* it?

The king lifts a hand, reaching for my face, and I suck in a breath, thinking of his magic. I stumble back a step, and my hands are up before I realize it.

His expression doesn't change, but he goes still. "I think your nose is broken." He gestures a little. "Come here. Let me see."

That note of command is in his tone. I steel my spine and try to force my hands to lower, but it takes longer than it should. My eyes feel like they're in danger of spilling a new round of tears, but the king holds my gaze, and something about that is steadying. I don't want to cry in front of him. Especially not if he heard Verin say all those things.

After a moment, I step forward.

His fingers land on my chin, and he tilts my face up gently. My heart is pounding wildly, but I feel no flare of magic, no indication of power.

"Definitely broken," he says. "A black eye, too. Possibly both."

I swallow. My eyes feel hot again, but I beg the tears not to fall. "Maybe I deserve it."

"No. That's why I stopped her." His fingers haven't left my chin. "I can fix it." He pauses. "Or not. I know you're afraid, Callyn."

Maybe it's the sound of my name, or maybe it's the acknowledgment of the emotion, but either way, that does it. My eyes spill over. I pull away and duck my head so he won't see the tears. Being afraid feels ungrateful. "I'm sorry." I swipe at my cheek and it *hurts*, and my breath shudders again.

"Don't apologize for fear."

"She was so kind to Nora. But she hates me."

He scoffs. "She hates everyone."

The casual disdain in his tone is so unexpected that it startles a laugh out of me, but that hurts, too, and I swallow a whimper. "Your Majesty," I begin quietly. "If . . . if you think I'm a risk to the princess—I don't . . . I don't have to be here—"

"If I thought you were a risk to the princess, you *wouldn't* be here."

Oh. Right. I nod.

"Verin's actions are born of fear as well," he continues. "And possibly some self-doubt."

I look up at him in surprise.

He lifts a shoulder in a shrug. "She was unable to protect the queen herself. For that matter, neither was I." Without waiting for a response to that, he lifts a hand again. "Broken nose for weeks on end, or have you found the courage for magic?"

He's issuing a challenge, but he's leaving me with the choice. Under my vest, Mother's pendant is a heavy weight against my heart. I think of the way I pricked my finger with a knife and wonder if this pendant has already given me the ability to heal myself. Maybe it did the same for my mother—or maybe it didn't. She didn't survive the battle.

If she were standing in front of King Grey, I wish I knew what she would choose.

I know what my father would have chosen, and that almost makes me falter.

But I think of Nora's voice in the hallway this morning.

Da was wrong.

I straighten my back. "Magic," I say, and I want my voice to be strong, but it's barely a whisper.

I expect a word of acknowledgment, but the king says nothing. He touches a finger to the bridge of my nose, and at first, there's a swell of pain that takes my breath away—but it's quickly gone, and the ache begins to ease.

"When I first encountered soldiers from Syhl Shallow," he says into my silence, "they were burning a farmhouse in Emberfall." His finger traces along my cheekbone, pulling any pain out of my eye socket. "A young widow lived there with her three children, and they were planning to execute them all, with the exception of the girl, who was about seven years old. They were going to *keep* her." His eyes flick to mine, as if to see if I understand.

I do. I frown.

"I was with Prince Rhen and Princess Harper," the king continues. "We killed the men, and took the widow and her children to safety." He pauses. "The next time I encountered soldiers from Syhl Shallow, a small contingent of men attempted to burn down an inn with the occupants inside, under orders from Karis Luran—your former queen. We were able to hold the inn and chase them off. My *third* encounter was a full invasion by the Syhl Shallow army—sent with the intent to burn and destroy. I fought back. We *all* fought back." His eyes don't leave mine. "Just as anyone would defend themselves if their home were under attack."

His hand drops away, but I'm staring at him. I knew the king was from Emberfall, so it's weird that I've never considered this, but I don't think I've ever heard one single story of the war from *that* side. I've only thought of my mother and so many others dying at the hands of that monster.

I don't want to think about my mother being among officers who ordered soldiers to raze farmhouses and burn down inns.

"Less than six months later," the king says, "I was allied with Lia Mara, and I was meant to *lead* soldiers that I once faced in battle. That was not an easy transition for any of us. But despite what I'd seen with my own eyes, I quickly learned that many of the stories I had heard about Syhl Shallow were simply that—stories. And there were just as many horrible stories about Emberfall on this side of the border. We've all done terrible things, Callyn. Magic has done terrible things. But not *every* story you've heard is true." He hesitates. "There was a time when I feared it every bit as much as you do right now."

I'm not sure if I can believe that, but I nod. "Yes, Your Majesty."

He gestures behind me. "Go. I'm sure you're hungry for dinner, too."

I nod quickly, then swipe at my cheeks again, surprised when there's no pain at all. "Thank you."

"You're welcome. Oh. One more thing. When you punch, elbow *down*, not so wide. You leave yourself open." He reaches out and takes hold of my left wrist, lifting it in front of my face, tapping my forearm lightly with his fist, mimicking a punch. "And *block*."

That makes me blush. "She'll break my nose again either way."

"Jacob works with the newest recruits at dawn. You could join them in the morning when Sinna is at her morning lessons."

Jacob. The last time I met Lord Jacob, I was passionately declaring that Alek was in Briarlock to visit me. Jacob helped Jax, and he offered to help me, too—but I threw money in his face and shouted that I didn't trust him, because I'd been fooled by Alek.

Maybe he'll want a chance to break my nose, too.

I swallow thickly. I made so many mistakes. I didn't come here to be a soldier, but I'm still smarting from what Verin said about the princess being at risk in my care. They were *all* at risk because of choices that Jax and I made.

"Will she ever stop hating me?" I say quietly.

"Maybe," he says. "Call her bluff."

I blink at that. "What?"

"Don't let her scare you off. You defended the royal family in battle. You stepped in front of a crossbow to protect the queen. You and your sister risked yourselves to protect my daughter. Yes?"

His voice is intense, and I nod. "Yes."

"You're brave and capable, or you wouldn't be here." His eyes spark with challenge again. "Show up tomorrow and prove it."

CHAPTER 13

CALLYN

I show up every day. Once in the morning with Lord Jacob, and once in the afternoon with Verin. My mornings are full of drills, repetitive motions that teach me to block and punch and avoid contact. I expected Jacob to be as cold and aggressive as Verin, but he's not. He treats me with the same passive regard as the rest of the recruits—which is to say he barely talks to me at all. I don't mind, though. I can see why my mother would have liked this, how every movement is structured and planned, leaving no room for uncertainty. I've never wanted to be a soldier, but there's something settling about the drills, the routine, the way I don't need to *think*, I just need to *do*.

My afternoons with Verin, by contrast, are chaotic and full of pain.

Each day, she breaks my nose. Or a rib. Or a finger. Sometimes all three. Once she dislocates my shoulder, and it's the most painful thing I've ever experienced, and I spend three minutes sobbing into the arena dirt that I'm going to kill her.

She never stops until the king calls a halt to her abuse and heals whatever she's done.

I'm not a fan of this pattern.

At least I don't have to go to bed with broken bones or torn ligaments. The king is swift to heal the damages she causes.

But . . . sometimes I don't tell him about all of it. Sometimes I ignore a bruise or an ache or a twist in my gut, and I lie in bed at night and wonder if the magic in my mother's pendant still works.

It always does. It's slightly addictive, having this secret that no one knows, this power that undoes the damage in the arena. It's a little flicker in my gut that tells me I can endure it again and again. Like a gift from my mother. Is this something she did, too? Endured hard training to achieve her rank, secretly healing her injuries so she could come back sharper and stronger? The idea that my mother and I might have a shared bond through this secret magic always lights me with a tiny glow.

I've *needed* the glow, because for days, I've wondered if Queen Lia Mara was secretly encouraging her sister's abusive methods. I worried that she harbored all the same doubts that Verin voices every time she's slamming me into the dirt. It made for a few uncomfortable encounters where I kept my eyes down and did my best to keep Sinna engaged with her dolls or her games.

But then I'll remember what the king said. *If I thought you were a risk to the princess, you wouldn't be here.*

Surely the queen is the same. Why would they let me care for Sinna just to torment me about it?

I'm even more reassured when the queen touches a hand to my cheek one morning. "Callyn, you've looked so troubled these past few days. I must apologize that I've been so . . . distracted. Am I asking too much of you? You must tell me if Sinna isn't allowing you to get enough rest."

Clearly Verin hasn't told her what she's doing. It leaves me feeling like this is all part of a test. Like Verin is waiting for me to complain.

So I don't.

After a week, I finally earn a reprieve. I show up to a nearly deserted arena to learn that Verin has been called away by other duties. As the last of the soldiers clear out for the dinner hour, I stand in the dust and deliberate what to do. A part of me wants to go find some dinner for myself—but I worry that even *this* is a test, like someone would report to her that I'm lacking in dedication.

Though honestly, maybe I am. There's a part of me that wants to abandon this all entirely, to leave Nora to the fun *she's* having. But then I'll think of the way Verin says things like, *Your mother would be so disappointed*, and I can't quite bring myself to quit.

So in Verin's absence, I practice what I *have* learned: simple blocks and thrusts and punches that don't really seem to make any difference when Verin is pummeling me. The arena is so quiet, and I cast a glance at the fields. A few lingering soldiers are out there, and I wonder if the king is among them—and what he'd think of me working in here alone. Eventually, the soldiers move off before I can recognize any of them.

Until this moment, I didn't consider that if Queen Lia Mara doesn't know what Verin is doing, then the *king* must not have mentioned it either.

But . . . why? I try to work that through as I begin the endurance drills that Jacob makes the recruits do every morning. Now that my thoughts have a thread to follow, they want to chase it.

The more I think about it, the more I'm beginning to wonder if the king is mentioning much of anything to the queen at all.

That morning Nora and I saw Lord Alek in the hallway, the king was already awake and dressed, and I assumed that meant he'd been handling things overnight. But now that I'm training with the recruits in the morning, I see him at dawn often—never coming from the chambers he shares with the queen. Breakfast is laid out each morning, but I have yet to see them eat together. When I first arrived, I assumed that was due to the king's early duties on the training fields, but now I wonder if there's something else.

I consider the way the queen touched my cheek, when she said I looked tired.

I must apologize that I've been so ... distracted.

In thinking back, *she's* the one who looks tired. Or maybe sad.

But of course I'm not in a position to ask about her personal affairs.

I do know she was expecting a baby before she was kidnapped by the Truthbringers—but now she's not. An official statement declared that the queen lost the baby during the attack, and I've heard enough whispered outrage in the palace halls to know it's believed. The Truthbringers were supposed to target the king and his magic, and to think that they harmed the queen and caused a miscarriage is a bit unthinkable.

But I protected the queen when she was held captive in my barn. I remember her voice when she said, *There is no baby anymore.*

It might be the story they've given the people, but I don't think she lost the baby in the attack. She was dirty and bruised and anxious, but ... it didn't feel like something that had just happened. The way she said it was so final. Like something she'd accepted. It didn't feel ... *immediate.*

As much as I hate Alek, there's one thing he said that keeps sticking in my brain, rolling around with my thoughts about the queen's loss.

There are rumors that the king can't control his magic. That he's injured the queen somehow, but they're hiding it.

I wish I could go back to that night and ask him the right questions.

I'm soaked in sweat now, and I've lost track of my laps around the arena. No one is left on the fields outside, and the torches hung from the wall are beginning to dim. I'm surprised to find that I enjoyed the physical activity. If anything, it helped shake the lingering worries out of my head. If this was a test, I'm not sure I care anymore. I'll finish this round and go find Nora.

A man speaks from the shadows as I pass the far corner. "I had no idea you were so dedicated."

I'm so deep in my thoughts that shock nearly sends me sprawling, and I stumble to a stop. Lord Alek stands by the railing, dressed in shades of gray and purple, his jacket buttoned tightly across his chest. He's surely not dressed like someone who escaped from prison—but I doubt he's supposed to be *here*.

I'm breathing hard, and my heart is still pounding from the run. My eyes flick to the doorway that leads into the palace, then to the distant armory, and finally to the wide opening that leads onto the training field. All deserted. Of course there are no guards around—no one needs to guard *me*. Should I shout for help? My mouth has gone dry.

"Did I frighten you?" he says flatly. "You seem concerned."

Irritation replaces my sudden panic. "What are you doing here?"

"Fabrics and textiles are regularly delivered to the palace. Who exactly do you think oversees that?"

"You're supposed to be in prison."

He raises an eyebrow. "For what?"

Clouds above, he's such an ass. *"For treason."*

His gaze darkens. "Despite your own accusations and your sister's charming demonstration in the hallway, there is absolutely no proof that I have engaged in treason."

"You know what you did."

"What did I do?" he says. "I was held in Emberfall during the attack in Briarlock. I was at the king's side during the first events of the Royal Challenge. If I wanted to attack him, I had ample opportunity. I didn't have to do it from afar."

He wanted to kill the king. I know he did. He told me himself.

I inhale to say that, but Alek ducks under the arena railing to face me. "This attack was on the queen. I had no part in that."

My mouth clamps shut again. He's a liar. He must be. He's been a liar since the very beginning.

But . . . *this* point doesn't feel like a lie.

His loyalty to the queen has always been clear. Even when he was plotting against King Grey, it was to *protect* Queen Lia Mara.

I don't want anything he says to be true. I turn away, striding for the armory so I can put up my training weapons. "You shouldn't be here."

"Callyn." He jogs after me and catches my arm.

I whirl, my fist ready. He's better prepared than he was in the hallway, so he blocks effectively, but I must have learned *something* from my lessons, because I follow up with another strike from my left hand, and I almost get him. We tussle for a moment before he catches my wrist.

I'm glaring at him, and he's glaring right back. "*There*," he says. "Where's that spirit when you're fighting Nolla Verin?"

"You don't know anything about my *spirit*."

"I know you've let her drive you into the arena floor as if you deserve it. I know I've watched the *king*"—the disdain in his voice is clear—"heal your injuries while you whimpered. You've hardly defended yourself."

Rage swells in my chest. "You've been *watching* me?" I demand.

"I just told you that I have reasons for visiting the palace." He pauses, staring down at me. "I can't help it if I find the arena entertaining when I do."

I set my jaw. I don't want to be talking to him. "You're a traitor and a liar. Let me go."

To my surprise, he does, and we stand there facing each other. I don't know what else to say to him. He manipulated me. He *used* me. He threatened my sister. He lies about everything, and somehow makes it all sound so convincing, because even now, there are flickers in my heart that desperately want to believe him.

Alek watches my expression, then sighs. "I never lied to you, Callyn." His voice lowers a bit. "Never once."

I heard his voice like that once before, and I almost soften. I have to steel my spine. "Go away. You have no business with me."

"I have business in the palace, though. Often, in fact." He takes a step forward, and I refuse to yield ground. It puts him very close, until I can see the blue of his eyes in the dimness of the arena. His voice lowers further. "That's how I've heard the terrible things Verin says to you."

That gets me. I swallow and glance away.

Alek touches a finger to my chin and drags my gaze back. "*You* did not kidnap the queen. *You* did not endanger the princess. You did not even lure the Truthbringers to Briarlock. You protected the queen while guards and soldiers in the palace held her prisoner. Where was Verin then, hmm? It seems convenient that she publicly humiliates *you*, when it's obvious that someone with power and access had to be conspiring against the entire royal family." He pauses, his eyes blazing into mine. "Speaking of power and access, where is Verin tonight? Her own thoughts about the king have never been much of a mystery."

I suck in a breath, but he lets me go. Verin is the queen's *sister*. She has more power and access than almost anyone. All of a sudden, I don't know what to say.

I keep hearing the king's voice in my head, the way he said, *She hates everyone.*

Alek nods and takes a step back. "Someone did conspire against the queen, Callyn. But it wasn't me—and it wasn't you. It was someone *here*. Keep that in mind when you're inhaling arena dirt and begging her to stop."

I can't listen to this. I can't be in his presence one minute longer. He always twists up my thoughts and makes me feel like I don't understand anything at all.

I scowl and turn away, but this time he doesn't come after me. "You're just trying to turn me against them," I call as I duck under the arena railing. "Just like you turned me against Jax. It won't work this time."

I don't bother with the armory. I leave the weapons and armor on and shove through the doorway and into the palace hallway. Dinner must be in full swing, because the scent of roasted poultry and honeyed vegetables is overpowering. The sound of rattling dishes and cutlery from the kitchen echoes loudly. I half expect Alek to be right behind me, but the door at my back stays closed.

He probably thinks I'll keep his visit a secret. He probably thinks I won't say a word to anyone, that he took his traitorous blue eyes and looked into my soul, and now I'll go to bed dreaming of him, waiting for his next appearance so I can help him bring down all of Syhl Shallow.

But I was already stupid once. I'm not eager to do it again.

I square my shoulders and set off to find the queen.

CHAPTER 14

CALLYN

Queen Lia Mara is often busy, which is never a surprise. Her attention is in high demand, whether from advisers or courtiers or generals—or even her citizens. It's part of the reason it took me so many days to realize that she doesn't seem to be spending very much time with King Grey: she's always with someone *else*.

I suddenly wonder if that's on purpose.

I shove these thoughts out of my head. It's the worst kind of idle gossip. I'd pinch Nora's arm if she breathed one word of it to me.

Tonight, when I head for her strategy room, the guards inform me that the queen has retired early. I sigh and make a mental note to discuss Alek with her in the morning—only to find the queen in the princess's sitting rooms. She's playing a game of Wolf and Stone with Nora and little Sinna, a brightly colored array of painted tiles spread across the table between them. They haven't seen me yet, and I'm struck by the image of my sister, still in her vest and trousers, sitting with the queen, playing a children's game. A far cry from the girl in patched skirts who didn't want to fetch eggs from the barn a few weeks ago.

"Careful," she's saying to Sinna. "You don't want to give away what's under *all* your tiles. Keep some of your wolves hidden."

"But the wolves are so pretty." Sinna turns over a tile, and she's right. The game pieces are fit for a princess, each tile made from polished stone, unlike the old wooden version I used to play with Jax, and later, with Nora. On the tile in front of Sinna, the wolf's eyes are set with blue jewels, the fur painted in shades of violet and gray that might not be realistic, but is rather lovely.

The queen smiles. "I've always loved the wolves, too."

Sinna reaches out and starts turning over others. "Can I have *all* the wolves, Mama?"

"No, silly," says Nora. "Then we can't play." She patiently starts turning them all back over.

Sinna giggles and fights to flip them *back*, and my sister playfully races to keep them all in order. Half the tiles scatter onto the floor.

"Well," the queen sighs, "I suppose we can—oh! Callyn. Would you like to play?"

She looks up at me, and after the gentleness in her voice, I'm startled at the tension that seems to cling to her eyes. Her hair is usually plaited down over one shoulder, but it's loose today, a long cascade of vibrant red that hangs down her back. She's in the belted regal robes that she wears to meet with her advisers, but there's something about her stature that just seems disquieted. I can't quite put my finger on it. She doesn't look worried, she looks . . . unsettled.

Nora and the princess have fallen to their knees, giggling as the tiles clack together in their scrambling, making a colorful mess.

"I'm not entirely sure anyone is still playing," I say.

"Let's put all the animals together," Sinna says, picking through the tiles.

"I'll start with the birds," Nora says, easily changing tactics to

136

accommodate the princess. She shifts to sit cross-legged. "I like the jewels on their wings."

The queen watches them for a moment, and some of the tension slips out of her eyes. She reaches out to give one of Nora's braids a gentle tug. "Sinna is never going to have a better playmate than Princess Nora."

As soon as she says the words, she stops short, and her breath catches. It takes me a moment to understand why, and it's a moment too long. Sudden emotion slams into the room, washing over all of us. The queen obviously didn't mean to consider the baby she lost, but once the words are out of her mouth, they have an impact.

Nora looks up and offers her a smile—but it looks a little watery. Without warning, she rises up on her knees and all but throws herself at the queen to give her a hug.

"Nora!" I cry.

"Oh, Callyn, it's all right," says the queen, as if I'm the one being ridiculous, and it's completely appropriate for my sister to fling herself at royalty. She holds Nora tightly for a moment, and another pulse of emotion flickers through the room, so powerful that it almost takes my breath away. It's not just my sister's acknowledgment of her pain. It's Queen Lia Mara's grief over what she's lost, and relief over what she's found.

Then it's gone, and Nora swipes at her eyes and goes back to the tiles like nothing happened.

The queen swipes at her eyes, too, and I look away so it's not obvious.

She says, "I'll call for some tea. Callyn, would you like some? You were in the training arena late. Did you even have dinner?"

"Oh, no, I'm—"

She waves a hand. "Come sit with me while they play. I'll send for food instead. I haven't eaten yet either."

I open my mouth to decline, because her eyes are a little red-rimmed, and I almost feel like I'm intruding. But I consider that the queen was sitting down to play a children's game. I consider that she just let my sister clutch at her, how the feeling of anguish was so potent in the room.

I consider that she should be dining with the king. But she's not.

I wanted to talk to her about Alek, about his potential threats, but just now, that moment in the arena feels so far away.

I don't know what's happening, but I know she doesn't want to be alone.

I look into her tired eyes and nod. "Thank you, Your Majesty. Dinner would be lovely."

The food in the palace is always quite decadent, everything brushed with butter or laced with honey, the pastries flaking so perfectly that I sometimes long to linger in the kitchen to learn how they do it—though I have no idea if I'll ever return to my little bakery in Briarlock.

Tonight we're served tiny glistening onion tarts alongside roasted chicken that's been drizzled with an orange syrup, a combination that I never would've considered, but smells so good I can't believe I almost declined dinner. Servants offered to stay, but the queen waved them off, so we're alone again with the younger girls. Sinna has moved on to practicing braiding her doll's hair while Nora plaits hers, and they're sitting in the window of the next room, chattering like they've known each other for years.

The queen slices through a piece of chicken. "Nora is very patient with her."

"I think she's just happy to find someone who talks as much as she does." I realize how that sounds, and I quickly add, "I mean—"

"Callyn. You *must* stop worrying so much."

"Big sisters always worry."

138

A smile breaks through the tension in her expression, followed by a light laugh. "True enough." She picks up a bottle of wine and begins to pour.

The red liquid swirls to fill *both* glasses, and my eyes widen.

She meets my gaze across the table and stops before she sets the bottle down. "More?"

I have to shake myself. "Ah—no. No, Your Majesty."

She picks up her glass, then gestures for me to do the same. When I do, she taps hers against mine, and the *clink* of the crystal sings through the room. "To big sisters," she says, followed by a hearty sip.

So I guess we're drinking. I'm drinking with the queen. I echo her words and take a sip.

But then she takes another, longer swallow, and for a moment, I think she's going to drain the glass.

But she doesn't.

"Forgive me," I venture quietly, with a glance toward the girls, who are luckily oblivious. "Are you . . . all right?"

The queen meets my eyes, then nods, then sighs. "It's a fair question." She doesn't say anything more than that, which feels very deliberate. "You looked a bit harried when you arrived after your lesson with Nolla Verin. Are *you* all right?"

I hesitate, wondering if that's a loaded question—especially since Verin wasn't even there today. It makes me think of what Alek implied.

Lia Mara picks up on my hesitation and adds, "My sister can be too aggressive. If Verin is being overly harsh, tell me."

Verin has broken my nose at least five times now, but I don't say that. "No—it's fine." I hesitate again, but I was coming to tell her about Lord Alek anyway. I might as well jump in. "Lord Alek came to the arena. I . . ." I bite at my lip. "He took me by surprise. I thought he was being held for treason."

The queen frowns. "No. Verin said she discussed Lord Alek with you.

His feelings about my husband's . . . *magic* . . . are no secret, but we have absolutely no evidence to prove that he was conspiring against us. He truly was by Grey's side throughout the Royal Challenge. Even you yourself said that you believed that the king was Alek's target—not me. Is that still what you believe?"

I feel hot and cold all over. There are too many things in that statement to figure out. Verin *did* discuss Alek with me—but she didn't say he was freed. Is this another one of her tests? Did I pass or did I fail by mentioning this to the queen?

And why did the queen hesitate over the word *magic*? Or was she hesitating over *husband*? Or both? What does that mean?

Maybe I look troubled, because the queen takes another sip and says, "You can tell me your thoughts. You don't have to figure everything out on your own."

She's right. This is the whole reason I came looking for her to begin with.

I want to gulp my own wine. "It's hard to talk about Alek," I admit. "Because I feel like such a fool for trusting him."

The queen is quiet for a moment, and the only sound is the distant giggles of the girls in the next room. Lia Mara glances at them, and then back at me. "When I first became queen, Alek's older sister was one of my advisers. Ellia Maya. Their mother had been a general in the army, but like your mother, like so many others, she died in the early battles with Emberfall and that . . . that creature. But after I agreed to ally with King Grey, we attempted to stop the war with Emberfall. I thought all of my people were loyal, but Ellia Maya was caught selling information to the other side. She'd sold a weapon of Iishellasan steel to Prince Rhen, to be used against Grey." The queen pauses. "She was later killed in battle as well."

"Alek told me about his mother when we first met," I say quietly. "And about his sister." I frown, remembering the echo of loss in his voice when

140

we spoke in the bakery that night. "Did he play me for a fool right from that moment? It was one of the first things we bonded over."

The queen reaches out and puts a hand over mine. "His grief is genuine, Callyn. He lost his sister and his mother. Empathy doesn't make you a fool."

I stare back at her. "Aren't you worried that he might plot against you again?"

She draws back her hand. "In truth, I've been worried that I haven't been examining the actions of my people as clearly as I should be."

I don't know what that means. I don't know what to say.

She picks up her glass and swirls the contents, but doesn't take another sip. "I know my people are afraid, and they've been afraid for a while. Perhaps I haven't been listening." She pauses. "When Ellia Maya was killed, it was long believed that she was a traitor to Syhl Shallow—because she gave Emberfall's prince the means to kill Grey. But Alek has always steadfastly maintained that his sister was not a traitor. That her actions were taken out of loyalty to Syhl Shallow. Out of loyalty to *me*."

I can't stop staring at her.

The queen finally drains the glass. "Alek is not subtle about his distaste for Grey standing at my side, and he rather openly hates Tycho for being a part of the battle that killed Ellia Maya. He hates Emberfall, and he hates magic, and I suppose I can't blame him for either. Magic has . . . caused a lot of harm." The weight in her voice is potent.

I swallow. I had my own reasons for hating Emberfall and hating magic. I think of the pendant that hangs over my heart, and it takes everything I have to keep from touching it. I wonder what the queen would think if she knew that magic flows through *my* veins now, too. I'm afraid of the answer, so I don't ask.

Instead, I say, "He's always said that to me, too. That he was loyal to you."

She nods. "He's never wavered on that, Callyn. So I don't think you were a fool. And holding him for treason without any scrap of proof would not be viewed well by my Royal Houses. He has too many allies. This fear of magic has grown too quickly. There are already rumors of scraver attacks near the border, but I suspect that's more deceit on the part of the Truthbringers, who were upset that their plan was thwarted."

I gasp, remembering the scravers who arrived to help us in battle. One helped heal Nora's wounds when she was nearly killed. "There have been *attacks*?"

She winces. "I don't know if they're real. The Truthbringers tend to blame magic for everything. Spreading rumors that dangerous scravers have returned to Syhl Shallow would be one way to keep those fears alive. Especially since they also claim that the king uses his magic to silence his opposers. After what happened in Briarlock, the king has been interrogating citizens known to be associated with the Truthbringers, but the outcry against his actions is growing loud. Locking up Alek would make him a martyr—and I'm still not fully convinced that he was a part of *this* uprising. His loyalty seems . . . steadfast. Does that make *me* a fool?"

"No! I would never—"

"Callyn." She smiles. "Drink your wine."

I take another gulp.

Then she adds, "Tell me what he said."

"What?"

"You said he came to you in the arena tonight. Tell me what he said."

I frown. "He might be trying to trick me again."

"Maybe he is. But I'd like to know what he's saying."

I take a long, slow breath. This feels like standing at the edge of a cliff. It's one thing for Alek to trick *me*. I don't want to help him trick the queen. I bite at my lip. "He said he never lied, and that he had ample opportunity to attack the king, and there was no reason for him to be held in Emberfall." I pause. "He says he had no involvement in what happened in Briarlock, and he implied that someone was working against him *and* you."

"Does he know who?"

"No. Well—he didn't tell *me*." I hesitate.

The queen's eyes narrow. "Out with it."

"I just—" I wince. Alek is so diabolical. "He implicated your sister."

"Nolla Verin?"

"Yes."

"Hmm." She pours herself another glass of wine.

I nearly fall out of my chair at the casual way she says *Hmm*.

Then she adds, "Do you think he would tell you more?"

Now I want to drain *my* glass. "More?"

"If I arranged a private meeting, do you think Lord Alek would speak freely about his suspicions? Or do you think he would be wary?"

"I . . . have absolutely no idea."

"He is clearly drawn to you if he sought you out in the arena." Her voice softens. "And if he spoke to you about his sister and mother—if he *bonded* with you, as you said, I don't think that was a trick. He may have manipulated you in some ways, but I do think it's possible he felt a genuine connection. Would you be willing to see what else he would say?"

I almost can't believe we're having this conversation. It has gone nowhere I thought it would. "I'm not a spy, Your Majesty. He knows I hate him. I don't think I could convince him that I was there out of genuine interest."

"You misunderstand. I don't need you to be a spy. I don't *want* you to be a spy." The queen shifts her weight and leans in against the table. "Callyn, I need to protect my daughter. I cannot be at war with all of my people. If you are willing to speak with Alek, and if he is willing to be open with you, then I would ask you to listen."

143

I brace myself, and I cast a glance at the girls, then drop my voice. "But . . . what if he just blames your sister? Or what if he says that the king is a threat to you? What if he says that's why he wants him dead?"

She frowns, and a bit of that pain from earlier flickers in her eyes. But maybe she's bracing herself, too, because her voice is strong and clear. "Then I would like for you to convince Lord Alek that his queen is ready to hear everything he has to say."

CHAPTER 15

TYCHO

I set a hard pace out of Ironrose, my heart full of bitterness. I hate that I'm leaving Jax, I hate that I'm wearing this gold-and-red uniform, and I honestly hate that I have a soldier by my side.

Overhead, the sky hangs heavy with clouds that promise rain before nightfall, bringing a chill to the air. After we met in the arena this morning, Prince Rhen gave me strict orders to take shelter before dusk each day, and to not ride out until full light—which will probably stretch my four-day ride into five. It's one more point of bitterness on top of so many others, and I let Mercy have her head for a full-out gallop so I don't have to talk.

To my surprise, Malin rides flank and doesn't complain, matching my pace effortlessly, as if we've trained with each other for years instead of meeting a week ago. I really shouldn't be agitated, because he seems to be a fine soldier, and I know he was kind to Jax during our journey. He's experienced, too, with two narrow stripes on his shoulder, which makes him a second lieutenant. It's not his fault that he came up through the army on this side of the border while I fought on the other.

But I hate these colors and I hate this uniform and I hate everything about this journey.

Oh, and now it's raining.

I sigh. At first it's a gentle rain, easily ignored, but it quickly turns to a downpour, which means we need to find shelter. I travel light, but we have a ways to go, and I won't have wet tack and saddle blankets rubbing sores into the horses if I can help it.

We find a small tavern that doesn't have a stable, but it does have a low overhang where we can tether the animals. I tell Malin we should strip the gear so it can dry while we wait out the storm.

He gives me a brisk nod. "Yes, sir."

We haven't said much to each other since leaving Ironrose, but that's my fault. I glance at him over Mercy's withers as I unbuckle her breastplate. "I'm not an officer, Lieutenant. You don't have to defer to me."

"I do." He looks right back at me, his hands on his horse's bridle. "Prince Rhen gave me written orders. Until I am given a new assignment by King Grey himself, I am to report directly to you."

Oh. A small part of me is startled, because that's truly unexpected. I'm also a bit honored.

Honestly, though, I'm still too irritated to appreciate it fully. "Fine," I say. "*At ease*, then."

Malin hesitates, and his expression turns wry. "Yes, my lord."

Well, that's not really better. I sigh. "*Tycho* is fine."

Malin smiles as if he's amused by this, but he nods. I glance at the sky. Dark clouds stretch on for miles, moving in from the south, which means we might need to wait this out for hours, if not overnight. "We'll get an early dinner. If the weather breaks, we'll see if we can cover more ground before dark."

He shakes out his saddle blanket and hangs it over a post. "If the rain doesn't let up, we could ride through and change out the gear at the army outpost south of Wildthorne Valley."

146

I shake my head. "We'll wait it out."

He glances over and inhales like he's going to argue, but he must see in my face that on this point, I'm firm. He shuts his mouth and gives me a brisk nod again.

It's a solid suggestion, and one I'd expect from a soldier, but the army outposts are generally situated outside bigger towns. That means a lot of people, a lot of merchants, and . . . a lot of back-alley dealings. Scravers aren't the only thing I worry about when I ride courier. I don't follow the same paths or stay in the same inns every time, and I have safe houses in remote areas. I could make better time by swapping for a fresh horse each day, but I've heard of former couriers who were given poisoned mounts who fell ill later, leaving their rider vulnerable. So now it's me and Mercy, and we're careful about where we stop.

Then again, no one would take me for the King's Courier dressed like this. I wouldn't even be seen as a member of the nobility.

That's proven as soon as we walk into the tavern, because the barkeep gives us a narrow glance, then grunts. "Coins first. Soldiers or not, no one's pouring free ale."

Malin scoffs. "Don't worry, old man. We'll pay." Then he looks at me and drops his voice, but not very much. A teasing light sparks in his eye. "You've got money, right? If not, I think we can take him."

The barkeep grunts again.

In spite of everything, that makes me smile. "I can pay." I pull some coppers from my pouch and toss them on the counter. "Dinner for us both." My clothes are damp, so I add, "We'll sit by the fire."

The tavern isn't crowded, and no one pays passing soldiers much attention. Once we're seated, Malin pushes damp hair back from his forehead, then swipes his hands on his knees. His sharp features are keen as he takes in the room. He can't be much older than I am. Twenty-two or twenty-three at most. I consider how he teased the barkeep, or his wry look when he said *my lord*. It reminds me of how he

147

tricked Sephran into using the wrong words to say farewell to Jax. I can't decide if he's lighthearted or if he's just going to be a pain in the ass.

Then again, he's got two stripes on his shoulder, and he wouldn't have earned those if he weren't dependable.

The barkeep delivers two steins of ale to our table, and when I thank him, I realize that minutes have passed and neither of us has said a word. Malin must notice this at the same time, because he gives me a side-long glance, then unbuckles a pouch on his belt and withdraws a small deck of cards wound up in a strip of leather. He doesn't even ask if I want to play; he just shuffles and starts dealing.

Maybe I'm the one being a pain in the ass. I ruefully pick up my hand. "I'm used to making this ride alone," I say. "And I didn't expect to be sent back so quickly. I'm sorry I make a poor conversation partner."

He shrugs, then smiles, then fishes a coin out of his pocket and flips it onto the table, a clear invitation to bet. "I can take your money whether you talk or not."

Definitely lighthearted. Maybe this journey won't be *too* terrible. I fish a handful of coins out of my pouch. "As you say."

He's good at cards, which isn't a surprise. Most soldiers are. He's quick and cunning with his plays, and he does collect a few of my coins before I have the opportunity to win a few back. We relax into the rhythm of the game as the barkeep brings platters of food and the rain beats against the tavern windows.

Eventually the game or the ale or his easy manner steals most of my irritation, because I say, "You didn't mind being sent away from your regiment so soon?"

"Mind? No." He hesitates, surveying his cards, then tosses a coin on the table. "Everyone else was jealous. I thought Kutter was going to fight me for the chance."

"Really?"

"King Grey spends little time in Emberfall," he says. "And you report directly to him. A chance to serve under the king, even for a short while, isn't one to be missed."

Fascinating—though maybe it shouldn't be. I've always had access to Grey, and even as a soldier, I trained with him directly. The entire Syhl Shallow army has—for years. I never considered that soldiers here might see that differently.

With that awareness, I fixate on the first part of what he said, about how Grey doesn't spend much time here. Weeks ago, Jacob and I stopped at an inn when we were traveling, and I overheard some farmers grousing about the king and his magic, complaining that Grey spent too much time in Syhl Shallow. I didn't pay it much mind, but it's different to hear it from a soldier, and to hear it like this.

I'm so used to worrying about the Truthbringers actively plotting against the throne, but if I've learned anything in the last few years, it's that discontent and uncertainty shouldn't be left to simmer either.

"If you want to earn another stripe on your shoulder," I say, "I wouldn't tell the king to eat horseshit."

Malin grins. "That was just for Seph. He takes himself too seriously."

"You're friends?"

He nods. "Since we were recruits."

It reminds me of Jax's camaraderie with them, the way I *was* jealous. Sitting here with Malin, though, I'm realizing I wasn't jealous in a romantic way.

I was jealous of the easy rapport. The budding friendship.

My heart gives a kick, and I have to adjust my cards before anything can show on my face. The rain pours down outside. Thunder cracks hard, rattling the windows, and I sigh. We're at least two hours from my nearest safe house, so we're going to have to find an inn. I can already tell.

The door to the tavern bursts open, and a woman shouts through the doorway. "Help! Oh, help!" She's short and stocky and soaked from the rain, her gray hair hanging in drenched clumps along her back. Blood streaks the front of her dress, and she chokes on a sob. "Someone, please help me. The monster—the monster has returned! My husband—oh, please—I can't drag him any farther."

I'm already on my feet, and so is Malin. Another pair of men who were by the bar have approached, too.

"Where?" I say.

She's breathless and sobbing. "He was working in the fields. There's so much blood. Please—"

"*Where?*" I demand.

She points. "Down the hill. I couldn't—I couldn't drag him any—"

"Help her," I say to the men. I look at Malin. "We need our bows."

We fetch our gear from under the overhang, then stride into the downpour. Rain soaks through my armor almost instantly, chilling my skin. It's unnaturally cold, so I blink water out of my eyes and nock an arrow, flicking my gaze between the road and the sky. There are too many trees, too many places for something to hide.

At my side, Malin does the same, sweeping his aim in opposing directions so we cover the most angles. "Do you think it's true?" he says. "Do you think the monster has returned to Emberfall?"

"No." I remember the monster from when I was a boy—the monster that I later learned was the cursed form Prince Rhen was forced to become every season, until Princess Harper helped him break the enchantment. *That* monster is long gone. I consider the streaks of blood across the woman's dress and the freezing rain, despite the fact that it's nearly summer. "I think it's a scraver."

Just as I say the words, an inhuman screech cuts through the rain, sharp enough to make me flinch. A gray shape soars out of a tree. I don't think, I shoot. One, two, three arrows fly off my bow. Malin is doing the same.

The scraver dodges, knocking each arrow out of the air, then dives right for us.

Silver hell. I shove Malin out of the way, taking the impact fully. Scravers don't weigh as much as a human, but they make up for it in strength and claws. I'm ready for it this time, so when it tackles me to the ground, we roll. The scraver ends up on top of me, and I'm glad for the armor, because claws are already scrabbling for any bit of vulnerable skin it can find, shrieking right in my face. I cringe away, trying to dodge, but the rain has made everything slick. I can't get to my blades in time. Those fangs are going to tear out my throat before I can get a hand on the hilt of my dagger.

Malin shoots it in the head.

Then in the side of its chest.

The scraver collapses on top of me, blocking my vision. I can feel its chest heaving against me, but those were killing shots, and it won't last long. Malin kicks the scraver off me, and the creature flops to the ground, wings twitching in the rain. An arrow protrudes from its temple, the other deeply embedded in its chest.

Then it stops moving altogether.

My heart is still pounding, my breath wild in my ears. Rain finds the claw marks in my skin, and it stings. I long to call for magic to close the wounds, but Malin is right there, and Rhen was very strict.

Malin isn't breathing hard, but he stares down at me for a moment, then puts out a hand. I take it, pulling myself to my feet, and we look down at the creature. Sometimes they're clothed, but this one isn't, and he's clearly male. His skin is light gray, but there are streaks of blue along his jaw and arms, matching the blue feathers that line the underside of his wings. If he hadn't just been trying to kill me, I might think he was kind of striking. He's not wearing any weapons either, but they rarely carry any. With those claws and teeth, they hardly need them. I wonder if this is one of the scravers that helped us during the battle against the Truthbringers a week ago—but I don't think so. He's sure not going to tell me.

I cast a glance up at the sky, looking to see if more are going to attack, but the rain is warmer now, more seasonal. There's no magic in the air.

"Should we see if we can find her husband?" says Malin, and his voice is a little hollow.

I nod.

We keep arrows nocked, but no other scravers appear. It doesn't take us long to find a body at the bottom of the hill. Sparks and stars flare in my blood, because I won't avoid magic if I can save his life, but the man is already dead—and probably *was* dead before she started dragging him in her grief and terror. Claws tore him apart from neck to thigh. His skin is ashen, viscera spilling from the deepest wounds in his abdomen. Blood forms a long, terrible streak in the mud, dissolving into the earth from the rain.

I shove wet hair back from my face. We're going to have to tell her.

Jax was right. I hate soldiering.

I string the bow over my shoulder and sigh, heading back up the hill.

"Why do you think it attacked him?" says Malin.

"I don't know," I say, because I don't. That man wasn't a magesmith—which means the scravers might be attacking indiscriminately.

And this attack happened in the middle of the day. Rhen's order to stay off the road at night might not even matter. It barely kept us safe *now*.

"A lot of the soldiers wondered if those scravers followed Jax from Briarlock," Malin says, and there's no malice in his voice, but I bristle anyway.

"The scravers have nothing to do with Jax," I say. "They helped the king."

But they're attacking now.

I look up at the sky, wishing I had a way to summon Nakiis so I could ask him why this is happening. Then again, maybe he's behind it. Maybe summoning him would be the wrong choice altogether.

The rain continues to pour down. I need to make a decision here. I don't want to disobey direct orders, especially not from Rhen. I already have enough discord with Grey, and I'd rather not find it on *both* sides of the border. Whatever is happening, I might have caused it by letting Nakiis out of a cage months ago—but this is the second attack in as many days. The king needs to know. Soon.

"We'll make sure the woman has someone to look after her," I say. "Then we'll ride for the safe house on the north side of the valley. We'll head out at dawn and try to make Willminton by nightfall tomorrow."

The north side of the valley is a four- or five-hour ride in good weather, so that will put us in *well* after dark—and Willminton will mean a hard ride through twilight tomorrow, too. Malin said Rhen gave him written directives to follow my command, but I'm sure the prince also gave him the same orders he gave me: Daylight travel only. No unnecessary risks.

This will require a lot of risk.

But like before, Malin gives me a nod. "Yes, sir. I'll saddle the horses."

CHAPTER 16

CALLYN

I'm alone in a carriage, belted into the finest clothes I could find in my wardrobe, and I'm rattling over the cobblestone streets of the Crystal City on the way to visit Alek.

I wish I had weapons and armor. I feel like I need them.

Really, I wish I had my patched skirts and a cast-iron skillet from my bakery. Sometimes I can close my eyes and imagine myself back there. Usually it's when Verin is finding a new spot to leave a bruise, but just now I wish I could reverse time to that moment when Jax first dropped coins onto my table so I could tell him to give them back.

But my chest clenches. Nothing was easier then.

No one knows the real reason I'm going to see Alek. I didn't even tell Nora, and guilt is pricking at my chest. Officially, I'm only visiting his Royal House, where I've been tasked with selecting fabrics for a winter wardrobe for Princess Sinna. When I asked the queen if anyone would find it suspicious that Lord Alek wasn't bringing fabric samples to the palace, she said that obviously I would want to see the latest weaves and dyes on the loom, not something available now.

The funniest thing is that the queen said this so offhandedly, as if anything else would even be in question. As if I've *ever* had the luxury of selecting new fabric, much less choosing before it's even come off a loom. I know she wants the best for all her people, but comments like this sometimes remind me just how different our lives are.

I peek through the carriage window. Dawn sunlight sparkles on the storefronts as we pass through the city, though there's a haze in the air that warns of rain to come. The city seems vast compared to Briarlock, which was so tiny that I knew every dusty street by the time I was eight. Here, the city sprawls for miles and miles that I can see from the palace windows, shops and taverns and vendors and so many glistening paths and alleys that I could never learn them all.

I sit back against the cushion and let the scenery fly by. I wish I'd brought Nora. Her chattering is endless, but I could use a distraction.

The queen said she didn't need me to be a spy, but I feel like one all the same.

The carriage eventually rattles to a stop. Gray marble steps are all I can see through the tiny window, but then a footman swings open the carriage door. I jerk back as if he's going to physically haul me out.

But of course he doesn't. He steps back to stand at attention. "Lady Callyn," he announces.

I will never get used to that. I want to hide in the carriage for another five minutes. I smooth my damp hands on my robes. Maybe I really can just go look at fabrics and looms.

But that feels cowardly. I grit my teeth and shift forward—just as a pair of perfectly laced and polished black boots descend the staircase.

I know it's Alek before I hear his voice. "Come now, Lady Callyn," he says, the slightest emphasis on the word *lady*, "there's no need to hide in the carriage."

"I'm not hiding," I say.

But I absolutely am.

155

He reaches the bottom of the staircase just as I spur myself to step out of the vehicle, and suddenly we're standing in the early morning haze together. No matter when I see him, he always looks very fine, very elegant. I know he's a well-trained swordsman, but I have a hard time imagining him on a battlefield, just because he might get *dirty*. This morning, he's in a jacket of deep blue indigo with an intricate pattern of light blue embroidery around each button, and calfskin trousers that fit him so well they might have been stitched onto his body.

I kind of want to punch him in the throat.

"Perfectly presentable," he says. His eyes warm as they hold mine. "More so, really."

I stare right back at him boldly. "Please don't pretend to flatter me, my lord. I am only here to look at fabrics for Princess Sinna."

He smiles, and it's cunning. "I don't pretend anything with you, Callyn." He turns, extending a hand toward the staircase. "Shall we? I assumed you wouldn't have time for breakfast, so I've had some food prepared."

He's right—though it's more that I was too *nervous* to eat. But I almost falter, because this kind of generosity was unexpected.

Then I get a good look at where we're going, and all the breath rushes out of my lungs.

The building at the top of the steps is massive, gray-and-white stone stretching in all directions, with marble accents and archways everywhere. Purple flowers burst from every windowsill, and it seems there are *hundreds*. Many of the windows have tiny stained glass figures in the center, meticulous designs depicting flowers or horses or armored warriors. At each doorway, liveried guards stand at attention, and a packed dirt road seems to lead through a narrow courtyard to my right, where I spy shadows that indicate *more* outbuildings just like this one.

Lord Alek clears his throat, and I realize I'm staring, my mouth practically hanging open.

I snap it shut. "Sorry."

"Shall I give you a tour?"

I can't tell if he's serious or if he's teasing me, but knowing him, it's the latter. Something in my belly clenches tight. To think he was visiting my run-down farm in Briarlock. How it must have looked to him. What he must have thought.

I was such a fool.

I have to swallow, and it's a battle to keep a frown off my face. My thoughts have cooled altogether. "No. Thank you. Breakfast will be fine."

I don't know what he hears in my tone, but he studies me for a moment, as if he realizes that our spiteful banter is over, and he's not quite sure why. "As you say. This way."

Similarly to the palace, he has footmen and servants, people who open doors and draw out chairs and pour me a cup of tea before I even have time to think about wanting some. Everything is finely detailed in ways I would never expect, little whispers of wealth and means around every corner. Tiny stitching along the edge of each napkin, forming a perfect design that matches the mile-long tablecloth—all of which must have been embroidered by hand. Painted designs on each individual teacup, little accents of purple and gray beside the filigree. Even the stained glass that adorns this window—a flowering tree, in this room—has tiny gems set into the glass that spark the light in new directions.

In the palace, I expected extravagance. The king and queen live there. Of course they're surrounded by finery.

But . . . this is a *home*. Alek left all this to ride through Briarlock, where he saw a poor blacksmith and his best friend, the girl who owned the broken-down bakery. Once he saw how we lived, he knew we were desperate, and he used us against the king.

My chest tightens, and for a terrifying moment, I want to rip off these fine clothes and demand that he take me back so I can forget all of this.

No, I want to pour this steaming pot of tea right in his lap. Where's Nora to grab his ear when I need her?

"Callyn."

I take a glistening roll from a basket and break it in half. "What," I say flatly.

"What did I do between the carriage and this table?"

I take a small pat of butter and envision jabbing the butter knife right into his eye. "I'm afraid I don't know what you mean, my lord."

He leans in against the table. "I still don't understand how you can be so bold with me, yet cower from Verin in the arena."

"I don't cower," I snap.

"You're proving my point. Are you going to stab that bread?"

"I'm about to stab *you*."

"If you wanted to fight, you should have shown up in armor. Shall I have some brought?"

I make a frustrated sound and throw the buttered roll at him. "Don't you understand that's exactly the problem?"

He's too agile, and he snatches the bread out of the air, but not before it splatters a streak of butter across the front of his jacket. Alek sets the roll on a plate, then wipes his hands on a napkin. When he looks down at his clothes, he sighs and stands.

As he begins unbuttoning the jacket, he says, "If you want me to undress, there are more intriguing ways to achieve it."

I flush *immediately*. "We will not be doing . . . *that*."

His jacket has about a million buttons, and he's only halfway down his chest, revealing a cream-colored shirt. "Explain what you meant about *the problem*."

I hate that I can't stop looking at his hands, the way his nimble fingers are working the buttons. It's reminding me of the way those fingers felt against *me*.

I wish I could turn my brain off.

I frown at my teacup. "You said you could call for armor if we wanted to fight."

"I can. Shall we?"

"Would you stop? Don't you understand that most people can't just . . . *call* for things?"

"Yes." He's three quarters of the way down his chest now. "What does that have to do with anything?"

"It means that I resent you for what you did, Alek! You saw who we were, and you saw how we lived, and you took advantage."

I throw the words like a weapon, and I expect them to cause pain when they land, but he doesn't react. Eventually he reaches the last button of his jacket, and he shrugs free to lay it over the back of a chair. His servants have been so efficient that I'm shocked when no one appears to whisk it away. But Alek turns back his shirtsleeves, then eases into his chair once more.

"On the other side of the mountain," he says, "they believe in fate."

Clouds above, he is *infuriating*. I clench my fists. "So you're not even going to respond to my—"

"I *am*," he says. "Be patient."

I snap my mouth shut.

"I've always found it a bit fascinating," he says. "This idea that . . . that something *else* is in control. If you ask me, that belief lends itself a little too neatly to political scheming. If someone believes that fate saw fit to reward one person with power and riches, it would stand to reason that fate saw fit to punish others with loss or sickness or poverty. The people in Emberfall believe fate granted their king the throne. What do they believe about the man he took it from?" He pauses. "What do they believe about the people who suffered in their cursed country for years? Was fate punishing them? Does the king feel more righteous about his magic—magic that can cause so much *harm*? When you believe in something like fate, you could easily start to assume that your own good

159

fortune is *earned*, and someone else's bad fortune is *deserved*." He pauses. "But really, Callyn, sometimes it's all just . . . happenstance."

I'm frowning, studying him, because I have no idea what this has to do with my question to *him*.

He picks up another roll and breaks it in two, then begins to butter it. "You're right. I did see how you and Nora lived—or were you referring to you and Jax? Either way, it doesn't matter. You keep accusing me of taking advantage, but as you may recall, I did my best to improve your situation. I sent customers to your bakery. I brought you and your sister new clothes. I repaired your barn. Because I *don't* believe in fate. I'm no more to blame for my birthright than you are. I was born *here*. You were born *there*. Neither of us had anything to do with either outcome." He sets the buttered roll on a plate and slides it in front of me. "Here. You didn't get to eat your bread."

I have no idea what to say. I hate how he twists up all my thoughts and makes me doubt myself.

But I remember the scars on Jax's neck, the way he was afraid of Alek.

"You hurt *Jax*," I say. "Don't even try to deny it. You can't paint yourself as some kind of benevolent figure."

"That's your complaint? Your proof?" His eyes flash. "I would have been *just* as generous with Jax if he hadn't schemed and manipulated from the very instant Lady Karyl approached him. I would've been more trusting if he weren't spending hours with the King's Courier after we paid for his silence. I've told you before: if Jax doesn't like dangerous games, he shouldn't play."

"We were desperate!" I cry, and to my horror, my voice breaks. "Don't you understand? We were going to lose our *homes*!"

"We were *also* desperate!" he snaps. He slams a hand on the table and I jump. "It's life or death for us, too, Callyn! Just what do you think the punishment for treason is?"

I'm frozen in place, staring at him. I've never seen his anger like this,

160

but there's something very . . . very *honest* about it. Very true. His blue eyes are like icy fire, and I don't know what to say.

"It's *different*," I finally rasp out.

"No. It's not. Why is your desperation worth more? Why is it all right for Jax to demand fifty silvers for holding a note for three days—*fifty!*—all while reminding me that the King's Courier had been in Briarlock, *threatening* us with discovery—"

"That's not what Jax was doing."

"It's exactly what he was doing."

I swallow. It's *not*. Not really—but maybe we're splitting hairs too finely. Jax wasn't deliberately threatening Alek and Lady Karyl, but he was trying to get too much silver out of them. I remember worrying he was pushing too hard, that he was going to end up with a sword in his gut. He kept telling me he had nothing to lose.

And in his case, that was sadly true. I had my sister, but Jax had only a drunk, abusive father who probably would've put him in the ground if he could earn a coin for it.

"He wasn't trying to threaten you," I say to Alek, but my hands are shaking now. Everything is turned around. "He was just trying to help me. Me and Nora."

Alek's eyes are still frozen over, ice cold. "You think I live a life of callous privilege, with no regard for anyone else, despite the fact that I have tried to prove otherwise countless times." His gaze darkens. "I paid what Jax demanded because I could afford it, and it was obvious that he *was* desperate. But I've told you before that I don't like when people work for nothing more than silver. It makes them far too easy to be swayed by the highest bidder. Jax was playing both sides, and the risks were too great. I cut my losses as soon as I saw an opportunity."

I freeze, remembering. "You mean the night you came to my bakery." Alek barely knew me then. I remember how he showed up with bloodstained parchment. I drew a knife because I thought he was going to kill me—but he didn't.

"Yes. It would have been *simpler* to kill him. Easier. You certainly know I had the means, and I rather doubt anyone would've much cared. But I didn't. Because Jax is no more to blame for his birthright and upbringing than I am for mine."

I have to swallow. I hate how he takes everything I feel certain about, and he turns it on its head.

But he's right. I didn't think about it being life or death for him, too.

I inhale to tell him so, but then I consider everything else he did in Briarlock.

"But you fixed my barn," I say. "That's where you trapped the queen."

"I did *nothing* to the queen," he snaps.

I swallow. "Fine. *They.* Where *they* trapped the queen."

"As a matter of convenience, I'm sure. I didn't need to turn your barn into a prison."

Somehow we've gotten closer to the true reason for my visit, without my even intending it. This is why Queen Lia Mara sent me. To hear his warnings and learn what may be truths.

I just don't know if I can trust him. Everything he said sounds so logical. So *possible.*

Maybe that makes me the biggest fool of all.

Alek sighs. "Let me give you a different story," he says. "A different course of events."

I look up. "All right."

"Imagine if Lady Clarinas—forgive me, *Lady Karyl*—had arrived at Jax's forge, and offered him ten silvers to hold a note for another traveler who would arrive later that day. And instead of being flippant and rude and demanding twice as much, Jax accepts this *very* generous offer and holds the note. When I arrive hours later, instead of finding you both in conversation *with the King's Courier*"—his voice tightens—"I

162

find Jax right where he's supposed to be, right where he was *paid* to be: waiting in the forge. He gives me the note, I give him the coins he's due, and probably a little more, because I'm reassured by his commitment to his duty, and I want to show that loyalty will be rewarded. Imagine how the following weeks would have gone."

I inhale sharply, and he holds up a finger.

"Imagine it," he says. "Truly, before you debate with me."

I let out that breath. "Lady Karyl was rude to *him*," I say.

"From my understanding, he was short and surly from the moment she appeared at the forge." Alek gives me a look. "I've met Jax on several occasions and I have no reason to doubt her accounting."

Oh, Jax. It doesn't make her behavior acceptable, but he probably *was* short and surly.

"His entire life was miserable," I say quietly. "His father—" I stop short, because this isn't my story to tell, and I don't want to talk about Jax behind his back. His father is dead anyway. "You don't understand."

"But I *do* understand. And it doesn't matter if he had a reason for being rude. We all make choices for reasons that others don't comprehend. My point is that you continue to paint me as cruel and vicious and call me a *liar*, when I've been honest with you since the first minute I met you."

"And you truly had nothing to do with the attack on Queen Lia Mara and Princess Sinna?"

"Nothing at all."

I wait, but that's all he says. I drop my voice and say, "You know why I'm really here, Alek."

"To look at fabric samples?"

I glare at him. He stares back at me implacably.

"You know that's not really why," I say.

"Oh, I've deliberated over your motives since I first got word of your visit. But when you arrived, you rather clearly declared that you resent me. You still do. I can see it in your eyes. I'm wondering why you think I should trust *you*."

I snap back in my chair.

He studies me for a long moment, then stands to pour wine into two of the goblets on the table. It's early in the morning, so I don't reach for mine, but he sits and takes a sip from his. "See?" he says. "Much like Jax, you can't say whatever you want and then be upset when faced with the consequences of your actions."

"The queen thought you might talk to me."

"I am talking to you."

I cast a furtive glance at the doorway. "About the Truthbringers."

"Why do you keep whispering?"

I want to kick him in the shins. "Are you really not going to talk to me about anything that matters?"

"I'm going to show you some very fine fabrics that will delight the princess."

Frustration swells in my chest. "But the queen—"

"The queen will have to learn that these baseless accusations of treason have delayed my shipments and damaged my relationships among the Royal Houses. Perhaps allowing the king to treat her most upstanding citizens with suspicion and mistrust was a poor decision on her part."

"The queen is allowing the king to find out who kidnapped his *family*," I say tightly.

Alek shrugs. "Well, it wasn't me. Perhaps sending her daughter's spiteful *nanny* to negotiate for information was not the best choice."

My frustration turns into rage. "I'm not spiteful, and *you're* the one who—"

"Callyn, I'm going to have to insist that you eat breakfast at some point. I simply do not have all day."

I pick up the roll and tear a piece with my teeth. "I should've had you call for weapons, because now I'm ready to fight."

"Indeed?" He raises his voice to call for a servant.

I was one hundred percent kidding. "Wait—Alek—no, I was—"

He leans in, and the look in his eyes stops the words on my tongue. It's challenging and frightening and exhilarating all at once.

He touches a finger to my chin and holds my gaze. "Weapons, you say? Let's go."

CHAPTER 17

CALLYN

Alek has a full armory and training arena that rivals what's in the palace, because of course he does.

"Choose whatever you like," he says, indicating a wall full of swords and crossbows and knives.

I run a finger over a glistening blade, but I don't take it off the wall. "I thought you were *busy*."

"I'm never too busy for a good fight."

That's probably true. There's an edge to his voice that tells me he's going to enjoy it, too.

Verin made me feel like a fool, and then she tortured and humiliated me in the arena. Now he's going to do the exact same thing, in the exact same order. I wish I'd never come here. My mother probably *would* be disappointed in me.

The instant I have the thought, tears prick behind my eyes, and I blink them away.

"Come now," Alek prods. "Make your selection. Surely you could use the practice."

Well, that's the truth. I feel like such a failure in so many ways. I swallow past a lump in my throat. "Just show me the fabrics for Sinna. Do you have anything with butterflies?"

His eyebrows flicker into a frown.

"Or shades of green?" I add, trying to keep any tremor out of my voice. "She seems rather keen on frogs right now, and perhaps we could have a seamstress embroider a few lily pads—"

"Callyn." He studies me, his eyes searching my face.

It's life or death for us, too.

There are just too many sides here, and as usual, I have no idea who's right.

I bite the edge of my tongue, because I don't dare cry in front of him. He's the worst kind of person to bare any vulnerability in front of.

"Tell me what you really want," he says, and his voice is so soft that it draws my gaze up. The arena is full of dim sunlight that filters down from the windows overhead, and he's looking at me the way he did on that morning he arrived, when he looked concerned. When he looked like he *cared*.

I don't want to trust any of this.

I pull my hand away from the weapons. "I don't want to fight," I say, and my voice sounds hollow. I lift my chin. "It's bad enough that Verin humiliates me. I don't need you to do it, too."

He's quiet for a moment. "You truly do think so little of me, don't you."

He sounds wounded, and I have to swallow again, because I still can't tell if he's being manipulative or if he's being genuine. "How about this. I'll tell your story from *my* side."

He folds his arms. "Go ahead."

"Jax and I had *nothing*. We were both in danger of losing our homes." I can't look at him while I say all this. I trace my finger over the filigreed handle of a dagger. "I didn't know what would happen to Nora if

167

I were thrown in a debtor's prison—and I didn't want to enlist in the army for the exact same reason. So when Lady Karyl showed up with silver, Jax asked for twice as much so he could give half to me."

Alek says nothing, and I refuse to look at him now, because I won't be able to continue. I run my finger over the engraved flat side of a sword blade.

"His father was terrible. *Terrible.* Jax would work himself into the ground, and his father would spend every coin they earned on gambling and drinking. The day Jax demanded so much from you was because his father stole the little he'd managed to hide. And maybe he shouldn't have been spending so much time with Lord Tycho, but he didn't say a word about you or your notes. I know he didn't. He just—we just—" My voice breaks. "He wasn't greedy. He knew he was asking too much. But he was risking himself for me, because he was my best friend—"

Alek catches my wrist, and I gasp.

"That one is very sharp," he says, and I realize my finger was about to find the edge of the blade.

But he doesn't let go, and I don't pull away. His fingers are warm against my wrist, and I can feel the strength in his hand. I keep my eyes fixed on the wall of weapons, and the silence swells between us.

"I can't undo what happened with Jax," he finally says. "And I wouldn't even if I could. Too much was at stake."

"Too much was at stake for us, too."

"I know." His thumb runs along the inside of my wrist, and he moves a little closer. "Did you really think my intent in bringing you here was to humiliate you?"

My voice won't work, but I nod.

"Why?" he says, and the word is so simple and innocent that I have to look at him.

His expression is earnest, his eyes a little wide, as if he wants a genuine answer.

168

But I don't have an answer. Everything has gotten so tangled up and turned around, and I truly have no idea what to say to him.

"Because I keep expecting you to be cruel," I finally say, and my breath catches again. "And then you're not."

"No," he says gently. "I'm not."

The way he says that reminds me of my conversation with the queen. *Empathy doesn't make you a fool.*

"How much of it was real?" I say suddenly.

"How much of *what* was real?"

"Us. You and me." I glance at his hand on my wrist, and I feel heat bloom on my cheeks. "*This.*"

"All of it."

He says it boldly, without hesitation, and he hasn't stopped running his thumb along my skin. The movement is entrancing, stealing my thoughts. A bit of heat flickers in his eyes now, impossible to ignore. It's sparking warmth in my heart, in my belly.

But he's tricked me before, and he could trick me again.

So I say, "Prove it."

"Fine." He takes hold of my waist and presses his mouth to mine.

When I gasp, he swallows the sound, his tongue brushing my lips. I don't know if I was expecting an explanation or a story or a line of pretty lies, but his movement is so swift and gentle that I'm melting into him without realizing it. His hands are so secure, holding me against him.

That's what gets me. The *holding.* His hand splays against my back, supporting me, and I'm reminded of the night he came to the bakery, the way he held me then, too. How badly I wanted to be held, cherished, kept safe. And that's exactly what he did.

It's exactly what he's doing now.

Alek draws back a little, his chest rising and falling quickly against mine.

"Enough proof?" he whispers.

Oh, I want it to be. I want it all to be real, because there's something so comforting about being in the circle of his arms.

But I have to shake my head. "Prove it with words," I whisper.

He laughs a little ruefully and lets me go. "You really are something, Callyn."

I don't know what that means. I do know I'm already missing his warmth, and he looks a bit wounded again. But I force steel into my spine and look at him. "Can you?"

"Actually, yes. So can you. Tell me the point at which I needed to *seduce* you to gain your cooperation."

I inhale—then stop.

Alek folds his arms. "I paid you to hold a message—the same as Jax. I repaired your barn, sent customers your way, had clothes delivered—all without one moment of romantic intrigue between us. You spoke up for me to Lord Jacob of your own accord, and in fact, you jumped between our blades to stop a fight." He pauses. "Even the night we spent together, I had nothing to gain. If I recall correctly, I put *myself* at risk by sharing quite a bit about my motives."

All true.

He moves closer, and his voice drops. "Even now. What do I have to gain?"

Also true.

If I were a spy, I could probably use this. I could seduce *him*, trick him into revealing everything he knows.

But I'm not a spy. The queen even said she didn't need me to be.

That thought is striking. Is everyone else being earnest, while *I'm* the one who's all wrapped up in hidden motivations and secret intrigues? Have I been making everything more complicated than it needs to be?

I smooth down the skirts of my robes, but it's really just an excuse to look away from him. "I didn't come here for . . . *this*."

170

"I know."

I give him a look. "I didn't really come here to look at fabric either."

"I know that, too." He pauses. "I asked once before, and I'll ask again. Tell me what it is you *do* want, Callyn."

"The queen didn't send me to negotiate for information. She sent me to deliver a message. She wants you to know that she's willing to hear everything you have to say."

His blue eyes widen in surprise—then narrow. He sets his jaw and says nothing. I might as well have built a sudden wall between us.

"I know you don't have any reason to believe me," I say. "But I've spent so much time thinking you were manipulating *me*, and I don't want you to think I'm doing the same thing to you."

He regards me for a moment, then turns. "All right. Let's go look at the looms for Princess Sinna. Frogs, you said?"

I frown. "Alek." Then I scowl. "*My lord.*" I reach out to catch his hand.

He catches mine instead. "*Alek,*" he insists, his thumb brushing over mine. "Walk with me. I'll talk."

So I walk. He doesn't let go of my hand, and he leads me out of the arena.

"The queen can summon me at any time," he says, musing. "She could have said this right to my face. Why did she send you?"

That's a good question. "Maybe she thought you'd be more willing to talk to me."

"Or maybe there are people in the palace who wouldn't allow us to speak privately," he says, still musing—but that feels like a prompt.

"I don't know," I say.

"If you expect information from me, you must be willing to share your own." He pauses, his voice turning grave. "And I genuinely do worry for our queen. I've already mentioned my suspicion of Nolla Verin."

"I don't think the queen suspects her own *sister*." As I say the words, however, I remember the queen not having much of a reaction when I

171

mentioned Alek's accusation. I consider how Verin *didn't* tell the queen about the way she was treating me either.

Alek is studying me. "Verin was once the favored daughter. She was expected to claim the throne."

"She was?"

He nods. "I know you weren't at court, but surely you knew Queen Karis Luran ruled ruthlessly and encouraged brutality on the battlefield. No one expected Lia Mara to take her place."

My eyes are wide. I didn't know that—though I suppose it makes sense, considering how many times Verin has broken my bones.

I think back to the morning in the arena, when Grey used his magic to fix my face, telling me about Karis Luran's soldiers and their brutality in Emberfall. I didn't want to consider my mother being a part of that—but with this new information, I wonder if she would have been just like Verin.

Alek shrugs a little. "Verin is close with the army, too. She could have easily made sure no one prevented the queen from leaving that day—or made sure that ineffective guards would allow the kidnapping to happen."

I turn that around in my head for a while—and there's a part of me that wants to rush back to the palace. Nora has gotten to a point where she's practically idolizing Verin, and I hate the idea of my sister spending time with someone who could be conspiring against the queen.

But I can't quite make it work. "She has full access to the king and queen," I say. "Why kidnap Queen Lia Mara? There would be no need to hide them in Briarlock to lure the king out."

Alek sighs. "True. Perhaps that's a dead end. I still believe the king's magic harmed Queen Lia Mara in some way. Several of us are wondering how deep the wound goes—especially since she has been so withdrawn from the people." His voice takes on a thread of anger. "Is Grey keeping her separated from those who would be an ally?"

172

"No!" I say in surprise. Part of this conversation feels like a betrayal, and I'm surprised to find myself wanting to defend the king. "Honestly, the king and queen are barely speaking, so he wouldn't even know who she was—"

"Barely speaking!" He stops short and turns to face me.

The sudden intrigue in his voice makes me wonder if I've said more than I should. But it's not like anyone else in the palace can't see the way the king and queen are never in the same room together.

I hesitate, then nod.

Alek sighs, and I hear frustration in the sound. "Tell the queen that I could offer her sanctuary. I don't care about his magic."

I put a hand to the pendant under my robes. I can't help it.

"You too," he says. "I have artifacts here. You would be protected."

That makes me look up. "You do?"

He smiles ruefully. "Your turn."

"I genuinely don't think she's looking to escape," I say. "She wants to hear from her people. You in particular. She said you've always been loyal."

He's quiet for a moment, and I can tell those words affect him. "If she didn't summon me herself, and she gave you a false reason to come here, then she's hiding her *motives* from the king. Are they still sharing a bed?"

I flush—especially since I can name several occasions when it was clear the king hadn't been in the queen's chambers. That feels so private, so *intimate*.

"That's not my business," I finally say.

"And that's answer enough." He doesn't sound victorious about figuring it out. "Behind closed doors—are they at odds?"

"Not that I've seen. But then I'm not behind those closed doors." I think of the queen's sorrow, the way my sister leapt up to give her a hug. Maybe it's about more than just the baby she lost.

173

"You're frowning," he says.

"Because she's sad," I say quietly. "The queen seems so sad."

That affects him, too. I expect his eyes to light with frustration or anger—or maybe even calculation—but he looks just as sad as I feel.

Despite all his stories, his explanations, *that* is what finally makes me believe him.

I pull him to a stop. "You really care."

"I do," he says. "My loyalty isn't an act. My mother died to protect Syhl Shallow. So did my sister. Magic was banished years ago—and now it's sitting on a throne. If the queen needs my help, I'll give it."

"And everything you did in Briarlock—none of that was about attacking the queen?"

"No. I still haven't been able to determine who was behind it. Lady Clarinas is gone. There have been no messages at any of my usual merchants. The Truthbringers have fractured, and there are those, like me, who still want to protect the queen." A bit of anger slips into his tone. "And others who simply want to eradicate magic, no matter what the cost—even if it means destroying the entire royal family."

"And—"

"Your turn." He shifts to start walking again.

I scowl, then search my thoughts for something to share. "The queen said there are rumors of scraver attacks since what happened in Briarlock."

He nods, and he doesn't seem surprised. "I have spies on both sides of the border. I've heard these rumors. No doubt the king is sending his minions to wreak havoc and instill fear."

Spies on both sides of the border. I tuck that bit of information away to examine later. "I don't think so," I say.

That gets his attention. "Why?"

I frown and shake my head. "I was there. During the battle in Briarlock. He didn't summon them." I remember a scraver leaning over Nora,

174

lending magic to help heal her wounds. The same secret magic I have in my veins, thanks to this pendant—just like the queen gained from her rings. "The king wasn't . . . he wasn't *using* them. He wasn't commanding them. They came to help."

"They came to help—and now they're attacking?"

I falter. "I don't know for sure. But that's what I've heard."

He scoffs. "Rumors always carry a shred of fact, Callyn. A generation ago, scravers were treaty bound to stay in the ice forests of Iishellasa— and the magesmiths went there with them. If scravers are attacking our people, they're either working with the king—or they're breaking the treaty. Either way, it means nothing good for the people of Syhl Shallow. Magic was banished once, with good cause, and it should be banished again."

Magic. I touch that pendant again.

Then we turn a corner, and he leads me through a set of heavy doors, into a wide room humming with activity.

"I'll show you the newest fabrics for the princess," he says, speaking loudly over the rhythmic noise of the looms. "I have some artisans who've done some incredible work with silver thread. This way."

I suppose our discussion of intrigue is over.

But then Alek leans close. "Tell the queen what I've said." He pauses. "Including my thoughts about Verin."

I gasp and look up at him.

His voice is still quiet, his eyes blazing into mine. "I told you Verin was intended to take the throne—but Lia Mara took it," he says. "And she might hide it well, but Nolla Verin doesn't like our king any more than I do."

"Verin is the queen's sister," I say. I'm thinking of *my* sister. We might have our moments, but I can't imagine Nora plotting against me.

Maybe the queen can't imagine it either. Maybe that's how she was kidnapped at all.

Alek lifts his voice and straightens. "Once you pick the loom work you like best, you can return in three days, and we should have some fabrics ready."

It's such an abrupt shift that I nearly stumble over my words. "I— yes, my lord."

"Three days, Callyn," he says pointedly, and now I understand. "After you speak with the queen, let her know that's when you'll need to come back."

CHAPTER 18

TYCHO

It rains on and off for days.

I've made courier runs in bad weather before, and Mercy is as steady as ever, but the near-constant downpour makes the journey slow and miserable. We haven't seen any more scravers ourselves, but as we've gotten closer to the Syhl Shallow border, we've heard tavern stories of attacks by winged beasts, which isn't promising.

It's cooler this far north, especially in the mountain valleys. In sunny weather, it's pleasant, but the rain makes it hell. I've been shivering under my armor for the last day and a half, but Malin hasn't complained, so I don't either. Some of his easy nature slipped away as the long hours and driving rain wore on us both, so now he's as quiet as I am. But it's the only sign of strain. He's proven to be sharp and reliable, waking early without being called, caring for both horses without being asked, doing menial tasks like rubbing down tack or sharpening blades or fetching buckets of water. When I suggested sparring in the mornings while the horses are eating, I expected grudging acceptance, because we're both tired. But on the first morning, he was armed and ready before I was.

When the rain finally lets up, we're nearing my last safe house on Emberfall's side of the mountains, and I'm ready for a bed and a hot meal. We're less than half a day's ride from the Crystal Palace, but that's if we could go at a good clip. The mud has been keeping us at a walk, and it's late. Even the horses have lost their spirit.

But when we get to the safe house, we discover that it's burned to the ground. All that remains standing is the stone chimney.

For a long minute, I stare at the pile of charred lumber in disbelief. There's no sign of anyone, and everything left is soaked from the rain.

Malin looks at me. "When was the last time you were here?"

I think back. It's been a while. The location is remote, set well off the road in the middle of the woods. Nothing anyone would stumble upon accidentally.

"A few weeks at least." I inhale, and there's only a faint lingering odor of burnt wood. Then again, it could have happened yesterday, and the rain could have washed it all away.

Malin sniffs, obviously thinking the same thing. "There's no way to know how long ago it happened, but it doesn't seem very recent." He clucks to his horse and starts forward.

"Wait." I've been so worried about scravers that I began to forget that Truthbringers still want to kill the king. I have no idea if this is related, but I don't like the idea of someone burning down my safe house. It could have been done weeks ago—or it could have been done by someone who didn't want me to stop here *now*.

I swing down from Mercy's back. Once my feet hit the ground, I send magic into the earth, letting it stretch out and away from me. This is *seeking* magic, nothing Malin will see, and I turn in a circle, looking with my eyes while I feel with my power for anything: any people, any predators, anything that might mean us harm.

Nothing. No tracks here either.

I look up. "Ride a loop. See if you see anything." I pull my bow free, then swing back onto Mercy.

He nods. I look at the sky again. It's nearly dusk. Something about this feels deliberate in a way I don't like. The last time I was due to stop here was the first night I spent with Jax. I haven't been back since then.

Could this have been planned before the attack on the king, a way to prevent him from having anywhere safe to stop before heading to save the queen? Or could this simply be a tragic accident—completely unrelated to me and the royal family?

Malin returns to my side. "No tracks," he says. "Though they could have been washed away."

Underneath me, Mercy heaves a sigh and paws at the ground.

I run a hand through my damp hair. I'm too tired for this. "We need to find shelter for the night."

"How far are we from the guard station at the mountain pass? Can we take shelter there?"

"Under an hour," I say. But I consider how many soldiers and guards from Syhl Shallow were found to be working with the Truthbringers. Men and women I knew personally were among the traitors.

Anyone on duty at the guard station knows about this safe house. If they were plotting against the king, they would have been in a perfect position to destroy the place without anyone knowing.

If someone is planning to ambush *me*, they'd expect me to head right for the guard station.

Either way, I don't like it.

But then I look at Malin in his gold-and-red livery and realize that if someone has been waiting to trap me, I might have already ridden right past them. I always travel alone. I'm always in black trimmed with green, my armor emblazoned with the crests of both countries.

Rhen's disguise might fool more than just scravers. Right now, we just look like two soldiers from Emberfall.

"We have to go through the mountain pass," I say, "but we're not going to stop at the guard station." I swing down from Mercy's back again, but this time, I pick up a handful of wet dirt, roughing it between my hands. I run it through my damp hair, dulling the blond. Now that Syhl Shallow and Emberfall are at peace, the lookouts mostly just wave riders through from a parapet. No one should get close enough to see me closely. Even still, I add, "Trade horses with me."

Malin does me the courtesy of not looking like I'm crazy. He actually does one better: once he's on the ground, he roughs up a handful of dirt himself and rubs it into the stripe down the front of Mercy's face.

He sees me looking at him. "I heard what happened when they attacked the king," he says. "I wouldn't trust any of them right now either."

I take up the reins of his horse. "Ride point," I say. "I'll take second."

He nods. "If they stop us, what story do you want me to give them?"

That's a good question. Two soldiers traveling together isn't common, and it's late. We have no written orders to provide. As the King's Courier, I wouldn't need them. But if I don't trust them enough to reveal my identity . . .

"When we get close," I say roughly, "bind my hands. If they ask your business, tell them I was suspected to be working with the Truthbringers. Say your general ordered you to deliver me to the king. They shouldn't question it."

"What if they recognize you?"

It's a chance I'll have to take. My heart twists anyway. "There are already rumors to that effect, so the plan will work either way."

"There are?"

"I gave you a story, Lieutenant."

180

His mouth forms a line. "Yes, sir."

I swing aboard his horse. "Good. Let's go."

Half a mile out from the guard station, we stop under a copse of trees and Malin binds my wrists behind my back with a length of thin leather. This was my idea, and I didn't think it would bother me, but much like the gold-and-red livery I'm wearing, it *does*.

Malin tethers my horse's rein to the pommel of Mercy's saddle, and he leads at a walk. My shoulders are tight, my hands working at the bindings subconsciously. I may as well be a *real* captive. We're nearing full dark, and it's reminding me of the other times I've been trapped with no way to escape. The animal keeps prancing, picking up on my tension.

I need to shove the memories away. My breathing feels tight and strained, and I realize stars are flaring in my vision.

Magic. It's responding to my panic.

I hate this. I need to focus. I look at the sky, the trees. I try to center myself, the way I've done before. I'm not a child. I'm not in danger. Malin isn't my enemy.

Maybe I should just order him to untie me. Surely the guard station isn't too much of a risk.

But it is. I can feel it in my gut. And asking him to untie me would be cowardly. It would invite questions I don't want to answer.

And we're fine. *I'm* fine. This is silly.

But there's a wicked, primal part of my brain that won't stop whispering. *Maybe he wouldn't untie you, even if you ask. You're at his mercy. Maybe he's been waiting to—*

I choke these thoughts to a stop. The stars in my vision haven't gone anywhere. I take another breath, but it feels thin, like it doesn't fill my lungs. The horse sidesteps, tugging at the rein. I should murmur a soft word, but my jaw is frozen.

"So this one time," Malin says out of nowhere, "we were marching from Willminton to Silvermoon. It's a three-day walk. You know." He shrugs, and his voice is casual, like we've been in the midst of conversation for miles.

It's so startling and out of place that he might as well be speaking another language. I glance over, trying to understand what he's talking about.

He keeps going. "We weren't new recruits. Less than a year in, though. Back then, Sephran was a bit precious about his uniform, his gear. The rest of us could be in the same clothes for a week and we wouldn't care, but anytime we'd camp by a stream, there'd be Seph, washing his things."

I truly have no idea why he's telling me *any* of this, but my thoughts have abandoned some of their panic in trying to figure it out.

"I used to give him hell," Malin says. "Everyone else would be playing cards or going to sleep, and he'd be washing clothes. He'd hang his livery outside the tent to dry at night. I kept telling him an animal was going to piss on his tunic and then he'd regret it. But one day he drew early watch. He was up at the crack of dawn trying to get dressed in the dark. And you know what happened?"

Malin waits for an answer, and it takes me too long to find my voice. I sound like I'm speaking through gravel. "An animal pissed on it?"

He looks over. "Worse. His uniform was *gone.*"

That chases more of the panic away. My eyebrows go up. "What did he do?"

"He woke me in a panic, because he was due to report for duty." He grins. "I remember Kutter telling him to just wear his armor naked and see if anyone noticed. But he was desperate. First year, no one wants bad marks. I think he would have stolen ours, but like I said—most of us were *sleeping* in them."

"What happened?"

"I took his watch." Malin glances over. "So he could search for his things."

I look over and realize that most of the stars in my eyes have been banished, my pounding heart distracted away by his story. "You're a good person, Malin." And I don't just mean what he did for his friend.

"Not *too* good." He looks back, and his eyes spark with mischief. "Who do you think hid his clothes?"

That makes me laugh, and it loosens the final band of tension around my chest.

"Thank you," I say to him after a moment.

"You looked like you needed a story."

I frown. "That bad?"

"I could've sung you a song, but that might've made things worse." He nods ahead. The guard station is in view. "Should I speak to them in Syssalah or should I act like I don't speak any?"

I consider that. "Act like you don't speak any."

He nods, squares his shoulders, and looks ahead. When we near the guard station, I keep my head down like a weary prisoner, so I don't know who's on the parapet. A woman calls down in Syssalah, telling Malin to state his business, and he shouts back, "Do you have anyone who speaks Emberish?"

"I told you to state your business," she calls back in Emberish, sounding slightly annoyed by her charge.

"I'm delivering a prisoner to the king." He makes his voice equally annoyed. It's a good choice. Annoyance is the easiest thing to disregard. Two soldiers exasperated by protocol they don't want to be following.

"He is from *your* army. Why are you not taking him to Ironrose?"

I can't tell if she's just curious or if she sounds suspicious, but Malin keeps the tone of annoyance in his voice. "I'm just following orders. My

183

general told me to deliver him, so I'm doing that. He was caught carrying messages of treason for the Truthbringers."

"Wait there," she says.

Well, that's not good.

"Four archers on the parapet," Malin says under his breath.

"I know." I grit my teeth and try not to pull at the bindings around my wrists. Those stars flicker in my vision again.

After a long minute, during which Mercy starts to paw impatiently at the ground, a man calls down to us. "You're delivering a prisoner to the king?"

His Emberish is more thickly accented, and I recognize the voice immediately. Captain Sen Domo. If he comes down from the parapet, he'll know me in an instant. If I were on Mercy in my usual armor, he'd know me right now. My heart kicks.

"Yes," calls Malin. "I'm supposed to be at the Crystal Palace by nightfall."

"Then you're not going to make it, Officer. It's another five hours, and there's deep mud through the woods from the storms. You can put him in our hold and bunk here." It sounds like a reasonable offer, but then Captain Sen Domo chuckles darkly and adds, "I know a few of my soldiers wouldn't mind taking care of a traitor Truthbringer for the night."

No. That absolutely cannot happen.

I inhale sharply, but Malin reaches out and grabs hold of my bound arm and *twists*, and I'm not sure what he does, but the pain is sharp and immediate and I yelp, then growl profanity at him before I can help myself.

"I already took care of that," he calls loudly, a note of amusement in his voice. "Now I've got to tie him to the saddle to sit upright."

Both Captain Sen Domo and the female guard laugh from the parapet.

Ha. So funny.

Malin adds, "I earned a reprimand for it, though. I'm not looking to earn another one."

The captain calls, "Go ahead then. There's rocks in the mud south of Briarlock." He laughs like they're co-conspirators. "Good for dragging if your prisoner were to take a fall."

"Thank you for the advice!" Malin calls. "I'll be looking for those rocks in case his horse 'stumbles.'"

"Walk," I growl under my breath, but the horses are already striding forward. I want to speak to Malin, but I'm keenly aware that they might have lookouts among the trees, so I wait.

All the while, the distance grows, and so does my tension. I keep thinking about the threat in their voices, how they would have tortured a prisoner. Maybe they're not working with the Truthbringers after all, but I'm not sure it's good news in the other direction. I doubt Lia Mara would like it.

I wonder if they still would have done it if they'd known it was me. There *were* rumors of me working with the Truthbringers, and if I showed up bound in a uniform from Emberfall, with a soldier claiming I was guilty, that might have lent credence to them.

That could have gone very badly.

My wrists flex against the bonds involuntarily. Those sparks and stars haven't stopped flickering in my eyes, and I take a long breath. I know it was part of the act, but I don't like that Malin grabbed me.

Once we've gone a quarter mile, his voice is easy when he says, "Do you want me to drag you through the mud? Really sell it?"

He's teasing, but I'm still too tense, and my thoughts are too jangled. "No. Untie me."

Maybe he hears the urgency in my tone. He draws his dagger and slices right through. As soon as my hands are free, I rub at my wrists and shake out my shoulders.

I can feel Malin watching me, but he only says, "Are we riding on to the palace?"

"No." I finally look up. We're less than an hour from Briarlock. I might not have a safe house, but I do know of a place where *no one* would expect me to go—especially not right now. "I know where we can find shelter for the night."

CHAPTER 19

TYCHO

I tend the horses while Malin catches, then cooks, dinner. Callyn's bakery and Jax's forge will be sold in the coming months, but for now, they're both deserted and set away from the main road. The bakery is boarded closed, and it's nearer to the road anyway, so we ride on to the forge instead. The main house is also boarded up, but the forge itself is more of an open-sided shed, so we'll have shelter with the horses—and plenty of warning if anyone ventures back this way.

While Malin is cooking, I haul water from the well for the horses, then for us, then rinse the dirt from my hair. The cold is a shock to my senses, a relief and an assault all at once, and I shiver when a few drops run down my back.

I've made this trip a thousand times, but I can't remember when it's ever seemed to take so long. I don't know if it's leaving Jax, or if it's the heavy weight of everything going wrong, but every step we take seems mired in quicksand.

I flex my shoulders, my muscles aching from so much riding, my skin a bit raw from the armor. I've been mindful of saddle sores on the horses, but days in the rain haven't done much for the constant friction of my own gear. I stride across the courtyard to join Malin by the fire, and then, against my better judgment, I unbuckle my weapon belts and lay the sword and dagger in the leaves beside my bow. With swift fingers, I unbuckle the breastplate and jerk it over my head.

Malin watches me with raised eyebrows. "Yeah?"

I nod. "Go ahead."

He doesn't hesitate. He leaves his greaves and bracers in place like I did, but the heavier pieces drop in the dirt beside the fire. He roughs up his sweat-stiffened hair and goes back to the rabbits he was turning on a spit. "For a while there, I thought we were going to push on for the palace."

I thought about it, but I don't say that. "Thank you for cooking."

"Don't thank me until you try it."

"I'm hungry enough that I'd eat them raw."

That's true, but when he pulls the rabbits from the fire and I take my share, I find that the meat is tender and juicy, better than I was expecting. We eat in silence for a while, until Malin eventually says, "I didn't mean to grab you like that. I didn't want them to think they needed to detain you."

There's a careful note in his voice. Much like when he told the story about stealing Sephran's clothes, Malin is quietly perceptive. It's an underrated skill in a soldier—and a valuable skill in an officer. He said it was important to him to serve under the king, so I'll have to see if I can find an opportunity to make mention of it to Grey.

I look over. "It's all right. I'm glad we got past."

"I forgot that they torture prisoners here."

"Not anymore. The queen doesn't stand for it." But as I say the words, they sound a bit hollow. It was clear what Captain Sen Domo was offering.

"Don't they have that torture chamber? The Stone Prison, right? *Lukus Tempas?*"

"They do. But it's just a prison now." I peer at him, because now I'm curious. "How did you come to learn Syssalah?"

"My father was an army captain at the outpost near Willminton. During the first invasion, when Syhl Shallow's army was driven out of Emberfall, there were a lot of soldiers who tried to infiltrate the towns. To lie in wait for more, you know?"

I nod, but I don't really know. During the first invasion, I was barely fifteen, far south of the battles in Rillisk.

"My father would get reports and round them up," he continues. "The outpost had a small prison at the back, so he kept them there to wait for orders on what to do with them. Willminton was nearly crushed when Syhl Shallow first attacked, so my father didn't want me to join the army, but I was nineteen, and I'd already submitted my papers. I was just awaiting news on where to report. So he started giving me the worst kind of jobs you'd give a recruit. Cleaning latrines, shoveling horse manure, that kind of thing. But also feeding and tending the prisoners." Malin shrugs a little. "That part wasn't too terrible. I could tell they were afraid at first. Some of them had a lot of scars. A few were missing fingers. I remember thinking I would not be eager to join Syhl Shallow's army."

I nod. I remember hearing stories like this from when I was a recruit on *this* side of the border. "The old queen was vicious, and punished failure pretty severely."

"Eventually they would talk to me," he says. "At first, I picked up a few words here and there, and when I'd use them, they taught me more. I'm sure they were bored, but so was I, and this went on for *months*. It got to a point where we could almost have a conversation."

"And then what happened?"

"I got my first orders. I had to report for training." He looks over. "When I finally earned leave to visit my parents, the soldiers were gone. My father said they were released because we were at peace, but I have no idea if they went back to Syhl Shallow or if they found a place in Emberfall. I never saw them again."

"Wow. I'm not sure that's a very uplifting story, Malin." I pull the last piece of meat from my meal and toss the bone into the fire.

He laughs. "I didn't say it was uplifting."

"You learned a lot from the prisoners."

"It's not all from them. I've picked up more over the years. I try to practice anytime I can, especially when soldiers from the Queen's Army travel into Emberfall."

"You should have told me." I switch to Syssalah and add, "We could have been practicing this whole time."

He winces a little, then responds in kind. "I tired. Bad student. But I can try." He grins. "No more books."

I frown, not understanding. "No more books?"

He makes a frustrated sound. "Books . . . books . . . *stories*. No more stories. No words."

That makes me smile. I take pity on him and switch back to Ember-ish. "Tomorrow then." I pause. "I'm glad you speak as much as you do. It helped put Jax at ease."

I'm not sure what he hears in my voice, whether it's longing or concern or just a note of warmth, but whatever it is, Malin picks up on it. His focus sharpens and he looks over.

I lock my eyes on the fire and wish I hadn't said anything at all.

A flush crawls up my neck. I hope it's dark enough that he won't see. There's complete silence for a long moment, and I think he's going to let it go.

Of course he doesn't. "You and the blacksmith, hmm?"

That flush has climbed to my jaw. "Well."

But then I don't know what else to say.

Apparently I don't *need* to say anything else, because Malin straightens, rolling onto his knees. "I *knew* it! Silver hell, Sephran owes me ten coppers."

I snap my head up. "You *bet* on it?" I demand.

"When it's a sure thing, absolutely."

I cannot believe this. "Wait—but *how*? How did you know? We were hardly even together when we traveled."

"Please. Have you seen the way he looks at you?" Malin's face goes slack, his eyes widening, his lips parting just a bit—

"Oh, stop it." I shove him hard enough to knock him over.

He's laughing, lying in the dirt, and I smile in spite of myself.

But then his laughter cuts short, and he stares up at the darkening sky. "Tycho." He swears and scrambles for his weapons just as an ice-cold wind whips through our camp to make the fire flicker.

We haven't seen a scraver in days, but my hand is already on my breastplate.

"Malin!" I snap. "Armor first!"

But his bow is in hand, arrows pinned in his palm. He's firing at the sky just as an earsplitting screech peals across the small clearing. I've thrown my breastplate over my head, but I don't stop to buckle it. I find the shadow between the trees, wings obscuring the stars. My bow is already in my hand, and I'm shooting, too. I want to tell Malin to stop, that I'll cover him while he pulls on his own armor, but the scraver's screech suddenly goes more shrill.

Malin's eyes go wide. "We hit it!" he cries. "We hit—"

Another shriek cuts him off. The scraver crashes through branches and barely misses our fire when it lands, half in a crouch. The arrow is all the way through one muscled arm, piercing the wing behind, which now hangs crooked. Blood glistens in the firelight, the scraver's smoky gray skin seeming to absorb the shadows. His chest rises and falls rapidly, and familiar black eyes flash in my direction. Ice forms on the rocks, melting immediately in the heat from the fire.

Silver hell.

"Magesmith," says Nakiis, and my hands freeze on my bow.

Malin's don't. His next arrow snaps off the string.

"No!" I shout. "Hold!"

But the arrow drives right into Nakiis's shoulder, tearing into the wing behind. The scraver recoils from the impact, fangs bared. Bitter wind sweeps through the campsite, nearly putting out our fire altogether. The horses spook and pull at their tethers.

Malin already has another arrow nocked, but he hasn't fired. He's obeyed my order.

It doesn't matter. Or maybe it does—in the worst way. Nakiis slams right into him, claws and fangs bared. Malin doesn't even get a chance to cry out. They go skidding into the dirt, and blood erupts on his tunic as Nakiis's claws drive into his chest.

Malin never put his armor back on.

If I'm grateful to Grey for anything, it's years and years of so many drills and so much training that every possible outcome to a fight feels routine—even this one. I've got a grip on that impaled wing and a blade against Nakiis's throat before panic has even occurred to me.

"Let him go," I snap.

Nakiis does—but he turns on me. He's quick, but I have a grip on his injured wing, and it gives me leverage. Once he's off balance, I'm able to throw him to the ground. I pin him with a knee on his chest and my sword against his neck, and then I look over at Malin.

The soldier is half crumpled on his side. Blood is *everywhere*: in a spray across his tunic, in a slick across his jaw, in wide streaks in the dirt. He's not moving.

I look back down at Nakiis, and it takes everything I have not to end him right here. Ice crawls up the length of my blade, and it seems the feeling is rather mutual.

"You made a vow to me, magesmith," he growls. "Is this how you keep your promises?"

"You attacked *us*!"

"No. I did not."

I stare at him. My breath is making rapid clouds in the chilled air between us. His black eyes gleam in the firelight, and ice continues to crawl up my blade.

But he's right. We shot first.

"If you're going to save him," Nakiis says, "I would think your time grows short."

I let the scraver go. My sword drops in the dirt. I pull Malin onto his back. Nakiis didn't tear his throat out, but nearly. His teeth tore through a stretch of Malin's jaw, and claws ripped through his shoulder, down into the muscles of his chest and abdomen. I can't tell if he's breathing, and there's no time to check. I just press my hand to the injury and let the sparks and stars of my magic flare.

At first there's nothing, and I swear.

"You cannot force it," says Nakiis. His voice is quieter, as if he's drawn away. "You know this."

He's right. I do know this. But there's so much blood. I'm worried it's too late, like that first man who was torn apart.

I force myself to take a shuddering breath. To let the magic slip through my fingers. And then, to my surprise, icy wind swirls around me, Nakiis lending his magic to mine. As I watch, the skin of Malin's jaw begins to pull together, to re-form, leaving nothing but blood smeared on his skin.

I move to the tears in his chest and shoulder, and I have to draw one of my throwing blades to slice the rip in his tunic wider.

193

I should have started here. Bone glistens through the claw marks. A rib is cracked, maybe two. There's so much blood that it's soaked into the fabric underneath him.

But when I touch a hand to the deepest wound and allow my magic to flare, Malin makes a sound, his body jerking a little. His chest expands as he inhales.

"Yes," I say. "Breathe."

The next claw mark is easier, especially with Nakiis's magic swirling through the clearing to share his power. This time Malin whimpers, and his eyelids flicker. That's almost worse. His hands lift, and he tries to curl in around the pain. But the ribs straighten, the fractures healing, the skin closing. When I touch the next claw mark, his eyes snap open, and he cries out when my magic flares. He's gained some strength, and he tries to sit up, to fight me, and I actually have to pin him down. His eyes are wide, a little panicked, but there's still three clawed grooves under his rib cage, deep enough that they've nicked vital organs. Blood—and worse things—seep from them all.

I could try to coax him to settle, but I know what *I'd* listen to if I were panicking.

I harden my voice into an order. *"Lieutenant.* Be still."

He goes still at once, but he speaks through gritted teeth. "Did you kill it?"

"No. This will hurt at first. Don't move." I touch a hand to the next mark.

When the sparks and stars flicker in my vision, he hisses a breath—then lets it out slowly when the pain eases away. "Magic?"

"Yes." I hesitate, remembering how much fear exists in both countries. It seems silly to ask when the alternative was his death, but I lift my hand. "Is that all right?"

"Yes. I didn't—I didn't know you—" He hisses again as I touch the next mark.

"Very few people know," I say. I add this to the list of things the king will likely hold against me. "I'm not supposed to use it. I'd appreciate it if you kept it between us."

He nods, then cranes his neck to look out at the darkness. "You didn't kill it? Where did it—" He freezes, and his voice drops to a whisper. "Tycho. It's by the trees. Get your bow."

I glance over. Nakiis has withdrawn a good distance away, and he now sits crouched in the darkness under the trees well across the clearing. Both arrows are still driven through his arm and his wing, because one wing hangs crookedly, while the other is folded tight against his back. He's breathing hard, and I'm sure he wants to flee, but he clearly can't fly.

"Neither of you will be getting your hands on a bow, soldier," Nakiis growls, and that icy wind whips through the trees again.

Malin gasps and tries to sit up.

I sigh and push him back down. "One more."

But I look over at the scraver again. Our bows are on the ground at his feet.

I suppose I can't blame him for that.

Malin looks at me and keeps his voice low. "They can talk."

"Yes. They can." I watch my magic knit the final wound back together. "And there's no point in keeping your voice down. He'll hear anything you say." I point at where we stashed our saddlebags. "Go find some fresh clothes."

Malin sits up and rubs a hand across his jaw, as if startled to find it whole. But when he stands, he looks at the scraver, and the air thickens with hostility. He might be half coated in blood, in a shredded tunic, but he's still wearing half of his weapons.

Another cold wind rushes through, kicking up dead leaves. "Do you want me to cause an injury he *can't* heal with magic?" says Nakiis.

"Go ahead and try." Malin slips a knife out of the sheath on his bracer. "I think my odds are pretty good now."

The scraver begins to uncurl from under the tree.

The day has been too long. I step between them. *"No.* Malin. Find a new tunic."

His eyes don't leave the scraver. "I'm not leaving you alone with . . . *that."*

"I'm going to heal *his* injuries the way I healed yours, so you should."

Malin looks like I just told him I'm going to set myself on fire. "You're going to *what*?"

"He didn't attack us. We attacked *him*." I draw a heavy sigh and look across the clearing at the scraver. "And I was already in his debt, so I'm also going to see if I can make amends."

CHAPTER 20

TYCHO

The first time I met Nakiis, I was fifteen years old. He'd been shot much like this, taken down by one of Grey's soldiers. I remember finding him wounded and shaking in the dirt, afraid of Grey, worried about being bound to another magesmith if he accepted any help.

I consider how far he's pulled away from the fire, from *me*, and I don't think it's very different now. Especially since he took our bows.

He's fallen to a crouch again, and he's still breathing hard—but he's watching every move I make. The day I broke him out of that cage at the tourney, he didn't even want to leave at first. He didn't want to risk me trapping him with magic. It makes me wonder if he'll even let me help him *now*.

I take a long breath and hope I'm not going to regret this decision, then pull my breastplate back over my head. The scraver watches this, the firelight bouncing off his eyes. The knife-lined bracers go next, then I drop to a crouch to loosen my greaves. The only weapon I keep is a dagger strapped to my thigh, because I'm going to need it. I drop everything in the dirt as I walk, then lift my hands.

"This reminds me of the night we met," I say as I approach.

A cold breeze pulls through the space between us, and he uncurls to stand at his full height. Every muscle on his frame is taut. "Your soldiers shot me then, too," he says.

"They weren't my soldiers."

His eyes flick past me. "That one is."

The air hangs with something a little too close to hostility, so I stop. "It's dark. Malin doesn't know you. We've been attacked by scravers several times now."

"Several times? Where?"

"In Emberfall. Once when we were traveling with the army, and again when we were returning to Syhl Shallow."

He's quiet for a long moment. "I had nothing to do with that. It does me no good to *attack* you."

"I know."

"You should have known I was not attacking you *now*," he says. "If you cared to try, you would recognize us by the feel of our magic, magesmith."

I wonder if Grey knows that. "It's not that I don't care to *try*; it's that I don't know how."

He regards me silently, so I lift my hands again and take another step.

He pulls back toward the trees. "I will not be trapped by your magic," he growls.

I've never dealt with someone like this, someone who seems to operate solely in counterattacks and retribution. Someone who bargains for things that should be a simple kindness. I have no idea how I'm going to keep my vow to him if every interaction is going to carry this adversarial weight.

Then again, we shot him out of the sky. He took our bows so we couldn't do it again. I've never been afraid of magic, but I do know what it's like to fear soldiers.

I think of Jax and his gentle patience. "I'm not trapping you," I say quietly.

Nakiis scoffs and looks away, but he doesn't pull back any farther. Every muscle on his frame is still tense, though, his fangs slightly bared.

I come closer, though I stop when I'm within reach. He might be injured, but he could absolutely rip out my throat if he wanted to. "I can't heal you with the arrows through your body. Can I pull them?"

He draws a breath, and ice forms on the bark of every tree around us. "Yes."

I draw my dagger, and his hand whips out to catch my wrist. His grip is so tight and sudden that I feel every claw digging into my skin, and I swear.

I have to speak through clenched teeth, because it *hurts*. "I have to cut the arrowheads free first, or it'll hurt more coming out."

His grip loosens marginally, but he doesn't let me go. His black eyes hold mine for a long moment. Nakiis reminds me so much of his father sometimes that it's uncanny—but Iisak would never be wary of me.

But I'm tired and running out of patience. "Do you want me to help you or not, Nakiis?"

He lets go of my wrist. "Do it."

I take a step forward and slice the arrowheads off, and even that makes him hiss in pain. I know better than to hesitate, so I pull the arrows hard, one right after the other, and they come loose with a sickening sound. I'm glad I'm quick, because the first one earns a low growl, but the pain of the second one—the one through his shoulder and the root of his wing—chokes off the growl and makes his knees buckle.

Silver hell. I drop the arrows and catch his weight automatically. He's not *heavy*, but he's not exactly light. His claws dig into my arms as he fights to stay upright, and I feel fangs against my shoulder. I can't tell if he's broken my skin, but if he hasn't, he's a breath away from it.

"Tycho!" Malin calls, his voice sharp with concern.

"I'm fine!" I call back, just as blood begins to trickle down the outside of my arm. "Sort of," I mutter under my breath.

When I ease the scraver to his knees, Nakiis wavers a bit, so I adjust my grip to catch him under the arms. It must hurt more than he's ready for, because he hisses a breath and recoils. That's somehow worse, because he drags me onto one knee just trying to keep him upright. His claws definitely find my skin again, and I wonder if I'm going to regret dropping the armor.

Eventually, he ends up all but leaning against me, his forehead against my shoulder, one hand braced on the ground. It's like supporting a drunken soldier. I can't tell if he's going to pass out or vomit on my boots.

I should pity him, and I do, but too many things have happened in too short a span of time. Despite my vow, I still don't know if he's ultimately going to be an ally or an enemy.

The wound through his shoulder is bleeding freely, his blood a darker shade than a human's. I don't know if he's ready, but I press my hand right to it and let my power flare.

He hisses in pain again, but maybe he expected the magic. This time, he doesn't move away.

"I should have made you sit down first," I say, though I'm not sure he would have obeyed. The blood under my fingertips slows as the wound closes, and Nakiis eases more fully onto his knees, sitting back on his heels. His injured wing hangs crooked, limply dragging in the dirt.

I reach for his arm first, because it's slick with blood, but he shakes his head a bit. "The wing," he says breathlessly. "Please."

"All right." I wait to see if he's steady before I move to crouch at his back. He's facing the fire, so it's harder to see, and I have to seek the wound with my fingers. I gently spread the wing wider so it splays along the ground. I was friends with his father, but I don't remember ever touching Iisak's wings like this. The black feathers are like

200

silk, catching glints of blue and purple from the firelight. There's plenty of blood, but I don't see the arrow wound. My fingers must find it, because he growls, and every muscle in his back goes taut, his claws digging into the dirt.

"I'm sorry," I say.

He doesn't respond.

I sigh and let my magic work. After a moment, cold wind wraps around us, his own magic lending its weight to mine again.

"Could you have healed this on your own?" I eventually say.

He doesn't respond to that either, but I suspect not. He hates having me at his back; I can tell. His head is cast in my direction so he can watch both me and Malin, and his shoulders are tight, the muscles of his arms flexed and ready.

The wound eventually closes, though, and his chest expands with a slower breath. He puts a hand against the ground, sagging a little.

"Thank you," he says, and his voice is quieter, the growl gone. It's hard to resist the soothing nature of healing magic.

"You're welcome." I expected his wings to be cold, the way his magic feels, but they're warm under my fingertips. There was another arrow wound, closer to the base of his wing, and I search for it more carefully this time, my fingers moving slowly along the feathers.

"If I am to keep my vow," I say to him, "if you're going to need me to *fight at your side*, then at some point you're going to have to trust me."

"You shot me out of the sky."

I wince. "I know. But I explained why." I change tack. "Why are your scravers attacking the people of Emberfall? If that's what you expect me to do, I'm not going to be a very willing ally. I told you I'm not a mercenary."

"They are not *my* scravers." He glances at me over his shoulder, and his voice is bitter. "And I clearly need no help attacking humans."

Well. I suppose that's true.

I consider what Jax heard during the first attack. "Who is Xovaar?" I say. "Is that one of the scravers who was with you in Briarlock?"

"How do you know that name? Did he find you?"

My hand goes still, because I can't quite figure out his tone. "Almost," I say. "One of the scravers who attacked said it. They were looking for a magesmith."

Nakiis is quiet for a long moment, and then, without warning, he whips his head back toward the fire. "You will keep your distance, soldier."

I look up. Malin has crossed half the distance between us. He found a new tunic, but he didn't waste time washing any blood from his skin, and he's fully armed, ready for battle. He stops and folds his arms, his eyes hard.

"I'll stay here," he says. "But if you tear Tycho apart, I don't have magic to fix him."

"He won't tear me apart," I call back. If Nakiis wanted to kill me, he's had ample opportunity before now. "Why is Xovaar looking for a magesmith?" I say to him.

Nakiis says nothing for the longest moment. "If he finds you, he will kill you."

"I know. Trust me, the other scravers haven't been subtle about it." My hand finds the second wound, and Nakiis hisses. Malin's hand goes for his sword, and that hiss turns into another growl.

"Steady," I say, and I'm really talking to both of them. I let my magic work, but the stars and sparks in my veins seem to flicker. I haven't used this much power in a while, and I run my free hand across my forehead. Too late, I realize I'm dragging blood across my face.

I glance over again before they start another fight. "Stand down, Lieutenant." I think of what I said earlier, about making amends. "Nakiis is an ally. He saved our king during the battle against the Truthbringers.

He protected the queen and the princess. He only attacked because we were shooting at him."

His hand hesitates on his sword. "Truly?"

I nod. The arrow wound heals, and I run my fingers along the blood-soaked feathers, settling them back into place.

Before I'm done, Nakiis snaps his wings closed, jerking away from any contact. In a heartbeat of time, he's ten feet overhead, clinging to a branch. His black eyes bore into mine. I never fixed his arm, but he's clearly done.

Fine. He wants to stick to business? I can stick to business.

"Who is he?" I say. "What does he want?"

Nakiis stares back at me, but says nothing.

I sigh, then roll to my feet and move away, collecting my armor as I go. I pull the breastplate over my head and buckle it into place.

"Magesmith," he growls.

I don't stop. "My name is Tycho."

"*Tycho.*"

I bend to buckle my greaves. "What?"

Wind whips through the clearing to dust up the leaves again. The air is full of his magic, and I shiver as ice forms on the toes of my boots and the buckles of my armor.

"Listen to the magic," he says. "Hear it like a voice. Feel it like a touch."

My hands go still, and I strain to feel anything different from what I already know. At first, all I feel is magic: the ice-cold wind, the bitter-ness against my cheeks. I recognize it, but there's nothing unique. Just simple power in the air, no different from mine, no different from Grey's.

"Do not force it," Nakiis says, and the growl has eased out of his voice again.

He's right. I stop straining and close my eyes. I let the magic wrap around me. And *there*, little by little, my senses flare with different sparks from my own. I'd say they were different colors, or different sounds, but neither description quite *fits*. Different elements in the wind, little touches of Nakiis's magic brushing against mine. I couldn't explain it with words, but . . . but I can *feel* it. Like a memory. Something familiar. Something recognizable.

"Oh," I breathe. My eyes open.

He's silent for the longest moment. "You can call to it," he finally says. "With a bit of practice." He pauses. "Instead of pouring your magic into the sky without direction. I worried you were going to ground yourself like your king."

At first, I don't know what he means—but then I do. When I was riding as Malin's "prisoner," with my hands bound, my vision kept filling with sparks and stars. I was worried my magic was going to flare aimlessly.

I buckle the rest of my armor into place and stand. "It wasn't *that* much."

"I could feel your panic from miles away."

That makes me frown—because I'm thinking of the first attack on the soldiers, when I spent days with magic sparking under my skin, ready to respond to a threat that wasn't there.

Was I pouring magic into the air then, too? Did I draw the attack?

The scraver's eyes have shifted to Malin, and that growl slips into his voice again. "When I found you, this soldier kept you bound. He issued threats to drag you over the rocks. I thought he must have some leverage to keep you from using your magic to escape."

I blink. "Oh. No. Wait—"

Nakiis doesn't wait. "When he freed you, I thought you had finally used your magic to trick him—but you did not flee. I did not understand, so I followed."

I stare up at him. He stares back.

It's Malin who moves closer to me and says, "He thought you were

204

in danger." His voice turns thoughtful. Musing. He looks between me and the scraver. "He was protecting you."

"Yes," says Nakiis. "As I did before, when you were at risk in battle."

"You protected the king and queen," I say.

"No," says Nakiis. "*You* protected the king and queen."

I'm not sure what to say.

He was protecting you. And we shot him out of the sky.

No wonder he doesn't trust me.

As I think about it, his appearance in that battle wasn't even the first time. When Grey *did* ground himself with magic, Nakiis brought me water. He brought me food. He might have bargained for my help later, but he made sure I survived well before we got to that point.

My heart feels tight in my chest, and I take a long breath. "Nakiis," I say. "Forgive me. I didn't—"

"I don't want an apology." His coal-black eyes reveal nothing, and his expression doesn't flicker. "You said you intend to make amends."

That draws me up short. "I do. What do you want?"

"You swore to fight at my side. Give me more time."

Malin looks at me in surprise. "You swore to *fight at his side*?"

"I was desperate," I say. "And so was the king." I glare up at Nakiis. "But I can't offer more time unless I know *why*. You still haven't told me what you need."

"Your magic."

"Why?"

He regards me for the longest moment.

"Does it have to do with this Xovaar?" I add.

Again, no answer.

"You're going to have to tell me eventually," I say.

"Indeed," he says. "Eventually." The wind swirls up again. "You should know that the scraver attacks will continue. They will *worsen*. The others seek to cause discord with their attacks—but they are not my people."

"Are they Xovaar's people?"

His eyes narrow. "You have so little control. You would do well to keep from letting them know you are a magesmith."

"I know. That's why we're riding to warn the king." I pause as a new thought occurs to me. I might have been ordered not to use magic, but no one else has any limitations. The king is known to be a magesmith, but he's given magic-wielding rings to others: the queen, Noah, Jake . . . If *my* power drew scraver attention, if any of them use their magic, they might become a target, too. "Have there already been attacks in Syhl Shallow?"

"Yes."

Despite everything that's happened between me and Grey, my heart trips and stumbles. "Have they attacked the Crystal Palace?"

"No. I would have heard if they'd approached the king." The edge of his fangs glint in the firelight. "I do have some scravers who are still loyal to *me*."

"The ones who fought with you in Briarlock?"

"The ones who defended *you* in Briarlock. The ones *you* will defend when it comes time for me to claim my vow."

My heart keeps tripping along as I try to understand everything he's telling me. "Are you at war with these other scravers? With Xovaar?"

"Not yet." He pauses. "But your king is already besieged by those who hate magic—and it seems Xovaar has found some of them."

"The Truthbringers," I say in surprise. "They're working with a *scraver*?"

"Possibly."

If the scravers are potentially working with the Truthbringers, we need to ride for the Crystal Palace tonight after all.

"What do Xovaar and his people want?" I ask.

"The same thing the scravers wanted when the magesmiths fled

Iishellasa. They want what was taken." Without another word, he launches himself off the branch, his wings snapping open to catch an air current. Before I can blink, he's thirty feet overhead.

A moment later, his magic brushes against my senses, and it's almost shocking how it feels *familiar* now. Words find my ears, carried on the air he can control.

—*I won't be far.*

Any other time, those words would have sounded like a threat.

For the first time, they don't.

"Thank you," I whisper. I know he'll hear me.

And then he's gone from view.

I look at Malin. "We do need to ride for the Crystal Palace. The king needs to know."

He nods and turns to bank what's left of the fire. "He said they want the same thing they wanted in Iishellasa. That they want what was taken. What does that mean?"

"I don't know." I look up at the stars again, where Nakiis disappeared into the darkness. I consider the words on the air the night the scravers attacked the soldiers.

Find the magesmith.

I consider what Nakiis just told me about Xovaar.

If he finds you, he will kill you.

As I head for Mercy and pick up my gear, I try to figure out what magesmiths could have taken from the scravers when they fled Iishellasa. Something that they'd want back so badly that they'd fight for it now.

Iishellasan steel, maybe? I know it binds their magic.

The idea doesn't sit right, however. Those scravers weren't looking for steel. They were quite clearly looking for a magesmith.

But then another thought comes to me, as I consider what those

207

rings of Iishellasan steel did for *me*. As I remember what Nakiis once told me about magesmiths using rings like that to enhance their children's abilities.

I consider why scravers might be willing to work with the Truthbringers . . . and why the Truthbringers might be willing to work with them.

Maybe the scravers don't want their steel.

Maybe they want to steal the king's magic itself.

CHAPTER 21

TYCHO

We're stopped at the palace gates. I used to know most of the guards just by virtue of my position, but after what happened in Briarlock, it's clear that roles and duties have been changed. Tonight, both guards stationed there are new and unfamiliar.

Neither of them look happy to see us.

It doesn't help that we've been riding along muddy roads in pitch darkness for *hours*, and we passed midnight a good long while ago. The horses and tack are flecked with dried mud, and our armor is stained with Malin's blood. We're both still in the gold-and-red livery of Emberfall's army, and we likely look battle-worn and road weary. If it was unusual for two soldiers to be traveling across the border together, it's *definitely* unusual for them to be riding up to the palace gates in the wee hours of the night looking like . . . this.

The senior guard looks more annoyed than alarmed. From her uniform, I can tell she's a captain. When I offer my name and title, she gives me a skeptical look before turning to Malin. "And who are you?" she says sarcastically in Syssalah. "The king himself?"

He inhales sharply, but I grab his arm before he can snap back. We're not getting into a pissing match with a guard captain.

"Malin is a second lieutenant in the King's Army in Emberfall," I say. "He's been assigned to my service by Prince Rhen."

She looks between the two of us again, as if waiting for me to crack, but I stare back at her. Eventually, she says, "The King's Courier was exiled to Emberfall, so you two will have to try another story."

Exiled. Is that what they think?

Or is that what Grey said?

I draw a sharp breath myself. "I *was* in Emberfall, and Prince Rhen—"

"Look, I don't care if you think you're my mother." She points toward the city. "Move along."

Maybe we are going to have a pissing match.

"Wake General Solt," I say. "He'll verify my identity."

"I'm not waking one of *our* generals to verify a soldier from Emberfall."

"*I am not a soldier from Emberfall!*"

She looks me up and down, unfazed by my anger. "Then what are those? Stolen uniforms? You need more than that to sneak into the palace."

"Then wake the king," I snap. "If you insist on delaying me, we are prepared to go through you both."

The other guard appears in the doorway when she hears my threat, and her hand is on her weapon. At my side, Malin goes tense and alert.

But the guard captain puts up a hand. "I'll wake the general." She points. "You can wait there." She turns away, muttering something under her breath.

As we move our horses away from the gatehouse, Malin looks at me and drops his voice. "Did she just call you a stupid man?" he asks in Emberish.

I sigh. "Yes."

"I didn't follow all of that," he says. "She thinks we're lying?"

"She thinks we stole uniforms and we're trying to sneak into the palace."

"Through the main gates? How is that even *sneaking*?"

He sounds so exasperated that it makes me laugh.

Malin snorts in response. "No wonder she thinks we're stupid."

I smile. Over our days of travel, I've come to really like him. I have my close friends in the palace, people I've known for so long that they've grown into a family of sorts, but none of them have ever really felt like *peers*. Even when I was in the army here in Syhl Shallow, I never had many friends. Some of that was due to my closeness to Grey, the new king who bore magic. Some of it was due to the other soldiers' prejudice against Emberfall.

And some of it—likely *a lot of it*—was due to my past.

But maybe my growing closeness to Jax has allowed some of my instinctive barriers to fall. Maybe opening one door to trust has allowed others to unlatch, just a little.

Beneath me, Mercy paws at the cobblestones, and I murmur to her to settle. "I told the captain to wake one of the generals," I tell Malin.

"Do you think they'll make us wait long?" Malin says.

I glance at the guard house again. The remaining guard is glaring at us. They might have agreed to wake General Solt—but it's clear they still don't believe me.

"Yes," I say.

And they do. Eventually, the remaining guard sits down, still glaring at us from inside the guard house, so we dismount from the horses and lean against one of the gate pillars. Mercy's head hangs low, her muzzle pressed against my hip, blowing warm breaths against my thigh. I begin to wonder if the captain's goal is to make us wait here until dawn, just to prove a point.

I really don't want to fight my way through the palace gates.

I keep reminding myself that they're just doing their job.

"I'm going to fall asleep standing up," Malin says. "You might need to tell *me* a story."

I smile. "But I've never hidden anyone's uniform."

"Come on."

"I suppose I owe you." I rack my brain for something silly, something *clever*, but no memories are suitable. I grimace. "I was too close to the king for anyone to trust me with pranks."

Malin rolls his eyes. "Well, that sounds horrible. Anything, then. Your childhood?" he suggests. "How you found yourself here?"

Neither of those things would make a good story. My childhood certainly wasn't fun. And I found myself here after Prince Rhen flayed my back open at fifteen, chained to a wall alongside Grey. We escaped to Syhl Shallow, and I swore fealty to the future king days later. A month after that, I was a soldier myself, swallowing my fears because I didn't want to disappoint him.

Malin must watch some kind of emotion play across my face, because I'm silent, frozen against the pillar, and the teasing glint vanishes from his eyes. "Silver hell, Tycho. As soon as I earn a day of leave, we're finding a tavern, and I'm going to buy you a *drink*."

That makes me laugh, a little. I'm somewhat abashed—but rather touched, too. "All right."

He makes a disgusted sound and pushes upright, running a hand across the back of his neck. "Or maybe we should find one right now. How bad would it look if I laid out my bedroll right here?"

But finally, we hear hoofbeats from somewhere beyond the gates. "Wait," I say. "Someone is coming."

I truly hope it's more than just the guard captain who forced us to wait here, because I really might draw blades.

I peer between the bars of the gates to see if I can identify who's riding through the shadowed early morning darkness. More than one horse, for sure. It sounds like a lot—and when I finally see movement, it *looks* like a lot.

"She did wake the general," I say to Malin, and I'm surprised.

"He'll recognize you?"

"Yes, for certain." Then I notice who else is riding alongside General Solt, and my heart kicks hard against my ribs. A small part of me has been dreading this moment since the day we rode out of Ironrose, but I'm surprised to find that another part is . . . hopeful. Maybe even eager.

It reminds me of when I was younger, when I would do anything to prove myself.

Right now, I resent it.

Either way, I'm instantly wide awake. I cluck to my tired horse and draw up my reins. "Look sharp, Lieutenant. Mount up."

Malin hears the change in my voice and obeys immediately. "Who else is with them?"

"The king."

Grey is always stoic, often unreadable, and being woken at this hour doesn't change that. When he and General Solt reach the gates, the guard scrambles down from the gatehouse to open them this time. They're flanked by half a dozen members of the Royal Guard, and followed by a dozen soldiers. I'm surprised at the show of force. It's quite the imposing contingent. Malin and I wait at attention outside the gates while the guards roll them out of the way.

It leaves us facing the king across a span of twenty feet, and for a flicker of time, that familiar tension crackles between us. My chest tightens like we're on opposing sides of a battlefield, and a cool wind blows through the gates, lifting Mercy's mane and tugging at my hair.

Magic whispers on the breeze between us, brushing against my senses, and for the first time, I recognize it. *Nakiis*.

The king rides forward, but he stops at the edge of the gates. Those guards press in close, the soldiers following.

If Grey and I were alone, I'd ignore our conflict and tell him everything that's happened since we parted ways in Briarlock. Duty has always trumped emotion for us both.

But we're not alone. The moment feels too charged.

Even Malin is aware of it. I can sense his vigilance, his *readiness*.

Grey's eyes flick over us, and I watch him take in the uniform I'm wearing, the soldier at my side, and the state of our armor. Mud and blood speckle everything, and I probably still have dirt in my hair.

"Tycho," he says, and his tone carries an edge. Everyone else might hear it as a thread of anger, but I know him too well. He's *wary*.

That drives a spike into my heart. I wonder what Grey expected to find that made him bring a contingent of guards.

Whatever it is, I don't like it. That note in his voice seems to emphasize the fractured trust between us.

All I can offer is an attempt to undo it. Grey normally isn't one for extreme formality, but I swing down from Mercy, place a hand over my heart, and drop to one knee. "Your Majesty. Prince Rhen ordered me to return. I have urgent news to report."

There's absolute silence for a moment. My eyes are down, so I hear more than see the king climb down from his horse.

"Tycho," he says, and his voice is a little lower, a little quieter. "Get up."

I rise to standing, and he stops right in front of me. His expression is fierce, his eyes searching mine. There's so much tension in the air that I half expect him to order me to get back on my horse and go back where I came from.

But he just touches a hand to my shoulder. His voice is quiet. "Are you all right?"

I'm struck by his tone, or maybe the motion. Of anything, I didn't expect concern. "Yes, Your Majesty."

His eyes shift to the state of my armor before returning to mine. "Truly?"

I nod quickly. "Truly."

His hand drops away. "Rhen? Harper?"

I nod again. "They're well."

Another breeze blows through the gates, another whisper of Nakiis's magic in the air. Grey's eyes widen the slightest bit, and I know he feels it this time. He takes a step back, his eyes flicking to the star-speckled sky.

"But something has happened," he says. "Or you wouldn't be here." Any softness has vanished from his voice.

"I have a written detail from Prince Rhen," I say. "Lieutenant Malin and I can give you a full report as well." I pause, thinking of everything that's transpired. I don't even know if we can trust the guards who followed the king onto this field. "I recommend that any accounting should be done privately."

He hears the weight in my tone, and his eyes snap back to mine. "We'll return to the palace. I'll have the guards take your horses." He glances at Malin. "Lieutenant, you will follow."

Malin is on the ground in a heartbeat. "Yes, Your Majesty."

Grey glances at the sky again, but the magic in the air has fluttered away to nothing. He looks back at me. "Whatever you mean to tell me—should I dismiss these guards and soldiers, or should I be doubling the protection around the palace?"

He sounds a bit cynical, as if he might not be fully serious.

But I think of Nakiis's warnings. "The latter."

CHAPTER 22

TYCHO

In the early hours before dawn, the palace is always quiet. I expect to be brought to the royal suites, or maybe to one of the strategy rooms where the king and queen meet with advisers, but Grey leads me and Malin to the east side of the palace. This is generally where high-ranking guests reside, and nowhere near his quarters—or mine either. When we enter a set of rooms, they're vaguely familiar. It takes me a moment to remember why.

These are the rooms where we stayed when we first came to Syhl Shallow, when Grey had not yet claimed his birthright. I remember the tapestries, most of which are the same, the velvet floor coverings, the heavy wooden furniture, the stone walls. I knelt on the floor *just there* and swore fealty to him, the first person to ever do so.

I cast another glance around. The rooms look *used*, like someone has been staying here, but I don't get the sense that anyone else is present.

I don't know why Grey would bring us here.

After the way the guards flanked the king on the fields, I'm ready for them to file into the room, too, but Grey orders them into the hallway. The door swings closed behind them, leaving us alone with the king.

At my side, Malin has been silent and stoic, the perfect soldier in the king's presence. But I can feel his apprehension now—as clearly as I could feel it when Grey rode across that field. He might not know the stakes, but the tension between me and the king isn't invisible. It radiates.

Grey gives me a sidelong glance. "You're beginning to make a habit of riding up to the gates in the middle of the night and causing a panic."

He's referring to the time Lord Alek stabbed me, after I defended myself with magic. Mercy brought me back to the palace gates unconscious. A month ago, he would be teasing me with that kind of comment.

Just now, it feels like a rebuke.

"In my defense," I say, "I did tell the guard captain who I was."

"She said you threatened to fight your way through the gate."

"I was running out of options."

"You're supposed to be in Emberfall. Until I laid eyes on you, I didn't believe it myself." Grey's eyes skip down my form, taking in the uniform, the signs of battle on my armor. He wants to grill me about all of it, I can tell, and I brace myself.

But his eyes stop on Malin. The king's expression changes, turning thoughtful. Some of the aggravation slips away. I know what he's seeing: a young man who's nearing his limits.

"At ease, Lieutenant." Grey draws back one of the chairs at the table near the center of the room and drops into it, then gestures to the others. "Sit," he says to us both.

Malin glances at me, and I think he might not dare to sit if I don't do it first. If he weren't here I might have collapsed into a chair before Grey did, so I have no hesitation.

217

A pitcher of water sits on the table, and the king pours a glass for us both. Malin looks stunned, but I'm not. Despite any friction between us, Grey has always been a good leader. He's very aware of the people under his command.

It's part of the reason our conflict stings so much. Either he doesn't see me clearly at all anymore—or he does, and he doesn't like what he sees.

I can't decide which is worse.

"Drink," he says to Malin. "It looks like you've had a hard ride."

"Yes, Your Majesty." Malin obeys like it's an order, but he must have been thirsty, because after the first sip, he drains the whole glass. "Thank you."

Grey refills it, then looks between the two of us. "Tycho never rides with a companion," he says. "Why are you with him?"

I inhale to answer, but the king says, "I was asking the lieutenant."

"Prince Rhen ordered it," Malin says. "After the first scraver attack."

Grey goes still. "After the *first*. That implies there have been more."

"Yes, Your Majesty."

The king looks at me.

I look right back at him. "I told you—and your guard captain—it was urgent."

His eyes narrow a bit at my tone, but he just says, "Tell me what happened."

I do, beginning with the first attack on the ride to Ironrose and what we heard about Xovaar, and ending with us taking shelter in Briarlock, and what we learned about the other scravers from Nakiis.

"There have been rumors of attacks here, too," Grey says. "No one has mentioned scravers specifically, just monstrous creatures. Many thought they seemed too far-fetched to be believed—and I thought perhaps it was the Truthbringers stoking discord after what happened in Briarlock." He looks between the two of us. "But you are telling me that

218

we don't simply have to worry about the Truthbringers plotting against the throne, but scravers as well?"

"Scravers aren't plotting against the throne," I say. "They're plotting against magesmiths."

Grey's eyes are full of storm clouds. "Against *me*."

Against us, I think, but I don't say it.

Malin's eyes flick in my direction anyway.

The king sees it immediately. "There's more you aren't telling me."

I brace myself. "When Nakiis arrived in Briarlock, Malin was badly wounded. I used magic to heal him."

He thinks about this for a moment. "Was this the only time you've used magic since the battle in Briarlock?"

I hesitate, then shake my head. "When the first scraver attacked, it nearly killed me. It tore into Jax, too. I used magic then, too."

"So it's possible the scravers may see you as a target as well." His expression has gone cold, unreadable again, but I sense that he's angry.

I should keep my mouth shut, but I'm too tired, and the night has been too charged with emotion. "Should I have let them die instead?" I snap. "You would have done the same."

"*I* wouldn't have let Nakiis out of the cage in the first place," he says. "*I* would have followed orders."

I inhale a breath that burns like fire, and I'm not sure what I'm going to say or do, but Malin grabs hold of my forearm, his fingers pressing tight.

Fine.

"Yes, Your Majesty," I grind out.

"You're dismissed to your quarters," Grey says. "Leave me Rhen's letters. We'll discuss this further once I've had a chance to review them."

"As you say." I stand and unbuckle enough of my breastplate to pull the sleeve of letters free, and I almost fling it at him, but I have more self-control than that. I set the leather binding on the table and look at

Malin. "I'll show you to the barracks and find you space. There's a regiment from Emberfall here—"

"No," says Grey. "Find him quarters near yours. You're both to keep this to yourselves until I determine a path forward."

I stare at him, but before I can say anything, Malin grabs my forearm again.

"Thank you, Your Majesty," he says.

The king is glaring at me. I'm glaring right back.

I don't know how we've gotten right back to this point.

Malin's fingers dig into my wrist, and he all but drags me through the door, passing the royal guards stationed there.

Once we're in the hallway, some of my tension dissipates. Not all of it, though. Malin strides along beside me, but he waits until we've turned a corner before he glances back over his shoulder, and then he seems to relax.

He whistles softly through his teeth. "So . . . I should make that *two* drinks?"

"At this point, I don't think a tavern would stock enough." I glance over, then lift my arm, the one he grabbed. I have no doubt the king saw the motion, and I hope Grey doesn't hold it against him. "Thank you for the warning. I know this assignment was important to you. You didn't have to risk yourself for me."

"I wasn't going to watch you hang yourself."

I give a humorless laugh. "Anyone else would have."

He hits me in the shoulder. "No. They wouldn't." We walk through a doorway flanked by Syhl Shallow guards in green and black, and Malin's eyes narrow. "Or they *shouldn't*."

I think about this as we climb stairs and head for the opposite side of the palace. My quarters are close to the royal suites, nowhere near where we met with the king. I still can't figure out why Grey took us down to the east wing. It's not even a commonly used area of the palace.

But there were a lot of guards stationed in the hallway, which seems to indicate he's there a lot.

You're both to keep this to yourselves until I determine a path forward.

I.

Not *we.*

I've been so focused on the conflict between me and the king that I haven't considered that he might have conflict with anyone else— especially not Lia Mara.

If anything could keep me from collapsing into my bed, it's this. But it's too early to go find answers. Even Noah won't be awake yet.

We finally reach my floor, and I ask servants to ready an unused room for Malin. I show him where I'm quartered, then lead him to his own.

"You can ask the guards to call for food whenever you wake," I tell him. "I'll come find you later when I have a sense of what our orders are." I hesitate. "I'm sorry you have to be sequestered from the army for now."

He's looking around his room, which isn't very large for the palace, but it boasts a massive bed piled with blankets, a small sitting area, and a private washroom. A servant is just stoking the fire in the hearth.

Malin turns to me and says, "I really don't feel that I'm due an apology for getting a room like *this* instead of having a cot in the barracks."

I give him a tired smile and turn for the door. "Get some sleep. You know where to find me."

His voice calls me back. "Tycho." Then he winces and glances at the departing servant, as if remembering we're in the palace, and we're not two simple soldiers on the road anymore. "*My lord.*"

My smile widens, and I shake my head. "*Tycho.*"

221

He doesn't smile back. "You saved my life," he says. There's no teasing in his voice now. "That cost you something." He hesitates. "I won't forget it."

He's right, it did cost me something. But I don't care what Grey said. Faced with a dying soldier, the king *would* have done the same, as readily as he poured that glass of water. I've watched him and idolized him and trained alongside him for years. Grey shouldn't be surprised that every action I take would be a shadow of his own.

The instant I have the thought, it strikes me that maybe this is part of our conflict: maybe he sees failings in me that he truly sees as failings in *himself*.

I think of the way Malin stopped me from losing my temper. *No one* in the Syhl Shallow army would have done that for me.

For the first time, the gold-and-red livery doesn't bother me quite so much. "You're welcome, Malin." I put out a hand. "For the good of Emberfall."

Malin clasps it without hesitation. His brown eyes meet mine, and he gives me a nod. "For the good of all."

222

CHAPTER 23

JAX

I expected my first days in the forge to be hard, but they're not.

They're nearly impossible.

Master Garson seems jovial enough, but he's big and loud, and it makes me wary. The morning after Tycho leaves, he claps me on the shoulder and booms, "Master Jax! Are you well?"

I know what he's asking, and I know how to respond, but I'm overwhelmed so the words don't quickly come to mind. I nod brusquely and don't say anything—and then I completely miss what he says next, because I'm too worried he'll think I'm addled and incompetent and he'll start treating me the way my father did.

Garson must be as flustered by the language barrier as I am, because his smile falters, and he simply gives me a nod in return and leaves me alone.

Molly and Lola aren't unfriendly, but the dining room is often crowded and loud at mealtimes, and they don't have time to struggle with my words. No one else seems willing to make an effort, and there are just as many unfriendly glances as there are curious ones, so I keep to myself and eat whatever is put in front of me.

One morning Molly comes to the table with a serving platter full of small, glistening muffins that smell like lemons and honey. She places one beside each person, until she gets to me. Instead of one muffin, I get two, and she bumps my shoulder with her hip.

When I look up in surprise, she smiles. "Good . . . morning . . . Master . . . Jax."

She said the words in Emberish very slowly, with gentle emphasis, so I say them back the same way, half teasing. "Good . . . morning . . . Molly."

Her smile widens, and she says a word I don't understand, then playfully swats me on the shoulder before she moves away.

I laugh under my breath, because it reminds me of Callyn, and I'm struck by an unexpected wave of homesickness. Across the table, one of the other forge workers says, "*Hmph.*" Another man glares at me from the other side of the room, and he mutters something to Molly when she approaches his table.

I lose the smile and eat a muffin.

At least I know how to work with horses. I brought my tools from Briarlock, so I carry them with me to the forge each morning. There are nicer ones here, but I can't quite seem to let go of the few familiar things that are *mine*: tongs and pincers and a hammer I forged myself years ago, before Da was so terrible. I haven't seen any of the guards or soldiers I know, but I quickly learn that there are always armored men and women waiting, their horses stamping at flies, ready for new shoes. Some are bored, some are impatient, few are friendly.

The air is different here, too, warm and more humid, making the heat near the forges less bearable than it was in Briarlock. It rains for days before the weather turns overcast, bringing a cloying heat that's no better. The constant downpour turned everything to mud, pulling horseshoes and rusting old iron. I pin my hair in a knot like I used to, but strands stick to my neck until I really do have half a mind to cut it all off. It's only late spring, so I dread what summer will bring. By midday each day, tempers are often short, and the armored women and men are always more terse.

The worst, however, are the soldiers who clearly hate Syhl Shallow.

At first, I can't be sure of the animosity, mostly because I don't understand what they're saying. I know several Emberish terms from when Da and I used to help travelers. Words like *lost nail* or *loose shoe* or *lame*. I don't know words like *trash* or *traitor* or *scum*.

I just recognize the tone.

Especially when they do things when my back is turned, like moving my crutches or knocking my tools into the dirt. Sometimes they goose the horses when I'm filing or hammering, and the animals will kick out or stumble sideways—and I'll end up on the ground. Once I catch a hoof in the hip, and it hurts so much that I swear and tears burn in my eyes, but I'm not giving *any* of these people the satisfaction of seeing me cry.

Tycho once told me about the prejudices he faced on the other side of the border. *There are many who would hate the king, but they cannot do so openly. They can hate* me *without provocation.*

Here in Emberfall, they can clearly hate *me* just as much.

By the end of the fifth day, I'm hot and surly and muttering under my breath. The sun is finally shining, but every living creature is sweating and sticky, and biting flies seem to be everywhere. I'm also a lot slower at my tasks than I'm used to. Back in Briarlock, I had ropes and stools around the forge to make my life easier, but Master Garson doesn't understand me, and I'll set myself on fire before I ask the prince for anything. Everything seems to take twice as long as it should, and every muscle aches from compensating in ways I'm not used to. I've been so slow that I skip lunch each day to catch up, and hunger pulls at my belly on top of everything else.

It doesn't help that the heavily armored soldiers leading horses through the forge are just as sullen and snappish. If I didn't know any better, I'd think they were spoiling for a fight.

If I get one more shove in the arm or jab in the shoulder, they're going to find one.

I finish shoeing a horse, and the soldier leading it spits at the dirt in front of me.

"Asshole," I growl under my breath, making use of one of the words I've learned.

He whips around, and I have no idea what he says, but it's clear he heard me say *something*. He's twice my size and easily thirty years old, so I'm probably insane to be provoking him, but I don't care anymore.

I tilt my head and look at him like I'm confused and stupid. "Be . . . well, sir?" I say in my heavily accented Emberish.

He glares at me for a long moment, but someone calls from outside the forge, and he snorts, then spits at the ground again.

I sigh and drop onto my anvil for a moment, then run a sweaty forearm across my face. It doesn't make anything better. Surely there can't be too many more horses.

Hoofbeats clop nearby, and I sigh again, hearing another soldier's voice. Before I can attempt to translate, before I can even *look up*, an arrow pokes me right in the shoulder.

That's it. My hand whips out to grab hold, and I jerk myself upright. My free hand forms a fist, ready to swing. "Enough!" I yell.

The horse shies, its hip colliding with a post and knocking a broom to the ground. The soldier has a tight grip on the reins, so the animal settles, blowing hard, pawing at the ground. Nearby blacksmiths look over. So do some of the guards. They might not know what I said, but my anger is clear.

The freckled soldier standing there looks like he *was* smiling kindly, but his expression is settling into a frown. He lets go of the arrow and puts a hand up, his blue eyes wary. "Jax?"

Oh. My hand unclenches a little. "Sephran."

We're getting some curious glances—and some that aren't so curious. A few of the soldiers look ready for trouble, and I remember that everyone has been primed for a fight all day. Through the haze of the forge, I can see we've attracted Master Garson's attention as well, and my heart gives a little jolt.

Sephran evaluates my expression, then looks around at the others. When he speaks, his voice is easy, and he gives a self-deprecating laugh. Whatever he says disperses most of the tension. The other blacksmiths return to work, and the other guards and soldiers return to looking hot and irate.

Sephran's gaze goes to the arrow that's still clutched in my fist. He hesitates, then reaches out to take it. Sheepishly, I let go.

He taps me in the shoulder with the arrow, just like he did when he arrived. "Hello, Archer," he says slowly.

That's what he said the first time. I was just too worked up to realize it. I flush and look away. "Sorry," I manage.

He inhales as if to speak, then says, "More Emberish yet?"

"A little." I grimace and point at myself. "Slow."

He smiles. "We need Malin."

"He is with Tycho," I say, and there's a little tug in my heart when I say his name.

Sephran nods. "I know."

Of course he does. I wonder if he's heard anything about their journey, but like so many other things, I have no way to ask. This is already the longest conversation I've had in days—and what's truly pathetic is that there's a part of me that wants to beg him to stand here for an hour just because he was friendly for one minute.

But that's ridiculous. Like everyone else, he's just here with a horse that needs tending. I look down at his gelding's hooves. At least these are words I have.

"Lame?" I say, though I can already tell the nail holes look worn. "Or new shoes?"

"New shoes," he says.

I nod and reach for my tools. Sweat trickles into my eyes, and I try to ignore the persistent ache in my side. I would give anything for a stool, even one, to give me some leverage when I need to keep my balance.

I finish with one hoof, then set it down. I glance up, but Sephran is gone, and I'm alone with his horse.

I frown. None of the soldiers have ever left me alone with their horse, and a sour pinch of worry pulls at my thoughts. Maybe he's mad that I snapped. Maybe he's complaining to Garson.

Whatever. I have a job to do. I pick up the next hoof, and Sephran still doesn't return. That sour pinch of worry turns into a tug that won't leave me alone.

When I'm finishing with the third hoof, something lands in the dirt beside me with a *thunk*, and I jump, inhaling sharply. But it's just a bench, maybe four feet long, less than two feet high.

Sephran is a little breathless, his freckled cheeks red. "Do you need this?"

I stare at him, shocked. I don't know what to say.

He misunderstands my silence, because he points at the bench, then me. "You," he says more slowly. "Need? Want?"

I shake myself. "Yes. Please. Yes. I need." I don't know if I want to cry or if I want to hug him, but both options would be equally humiliating—and I feel the urge to do them all the same. I don't even know how he *knew.* "Thank you." I pause. "How?"

"From the stables," he says, which I understand, and he adds, "By the horses?"

228

That means he carried it a good distance. But it's not what I meant. I shake my head. "How . . . how to know?"

"How did I know?"

"Yes."

Sephran thinks about this for a moment, and I realize that even though I figured out how to ask the question, there's a good chance I won't understand his answer. It's easy to point at objects and ask people what they're called. I can't point at things like thoughts and memories and feelings and all the nuances that actually make up human conversation.

I have no idea how Tycho managed this when he came to Syhl Shallow.

But Sephran speaks slowly and says, "You fixed horseshoes during our ride. When we camped."

He watches me puzzle out these sentences, and I get most of it, so I nod. He points at the bench again. "You needed a bench at camp." He taps his temple. "I remember."

This is a new word, but I repeat it. "Remember." I tap my temple like he did, and search for the right words. "Think . . . of before?"

His eyes light up. "Yes! Good!"

That makes me feel like I'm six years old and I've learned to tie bootlaces for the first time, but in my heart, I'm pleased. I smile and scoff. "No need Malin."

Sephran grins. "No need Malin," he agrees.

The bells signaling the end of the day begin to ring, and I still have one hoof left. I swear under my breath and drag the bench closer to the horse. The nearby blacksmiths begin putting up their tools. There will be a mad dash to the dining room, and I'm sure the soldier mess hall is no different.

"Sorry," I say again.

Sephran shakes his head, unworried. "I have leave," he says.

Leave. I remember this word from Tycho. "Free?"

"Yes."

Still, I don't want to delay him, especially when he's been so kind. Now that I have a bench, I rasp and file and finish this hoof twice as quickly as the others. Every time I think of his simple act of kindness, my throat tightens with memories of home and longing for friendship and missing the only person I know here, and I have to tell myself to knock it off.

Then the job is done and I'm setting my tools on the ledge, and Sephran is untethering his horse.

"Thank you," I say to him, and a bit of my emotion slips into my voice.

He must notice, because he looks up, and his eyes hold mine for a moment too long. The forge is mostly empty. He's the only soldier left.

"Are you done now?" he says. "You . . . free?"

I nod. "Yes."

He pulls an arrow from his quiver again, and he holds it up. "Do you want to come shoot?" He waits to make sure I understand, then adds, "With me and Kutter?"

I'm exhausted and starving and I should probably soak in that bathtub in the Shield House for a solid hour before spending time in *anyone's* company. I have no idea *where* they're shooting, or how we'll get there. Do I need to fetch Teddy? I remember how far the archery fields are, and traveling on my crutches is never quick. It seems like a lot of conversation will need to happen, and it took us forever just to answer one question about a bench.

But none of that matters. I'm lonely and homesick and my head is already nodding. "Yes, Sephran. I want."

CHAPTER 24

JAX

I do need my horse, as well as my gear, but I have time. Sephran needs to fetch Kutter from the mess hall, and they're going to meet me in the stable yard. At least I *think* that's what our plan is, after I parsed out the important words like *need horse* and *meet here* and *half hour*. But it gives me time to fetch my bow and bracer and to swipe an apple and a warm cheese biscuit from the Shield House.

But once I'm in Teddy's stall, I'm less confident with the tack. I haven't ridden since the night Tycho showed me around the grounds, and due to the days of rain, I haven't had a lesson yet. I've only seen Master Hugh once, when he needed a tool from the forge, but the stable master finds me struggling with the girth while an endlessly patient Teddy chews at some hay. Hugh is older, well past sixty, with sun-weathered skin and a trim gray beard. He's not very tall, but he's lean and wiry.

"Sephran brought you the bench?" he says to me in heavily accented Syssalah, and it takes me by surprise. I've grown so used to everyone treating me like a complete fool that I started to forget that anyone else here actually speaks my language.

"Oh," I say. "Yes." Of course Hugh would know. Sephran said he got it from the stables. "Thank you."

"If you need," he says, "you should ask."

I nod. "I will." But I think of the soldiers knocking my tools into the dirt and I don't want to ask for anything at all.

"Recruits will ride tonight," Hugh says. "Will you return in time?"

His voice is a little stern, like I'm a schoolboy trying to skip out on lessons. "Yes," I say. "How soon?"

"Two hours."

I nod quickly.

"Good." The sternness dissipates. "You need it." Master Hugh steps into the stall beside me and unbuckles the girth, adjusting my saddle placement.

"Thank you," I say sheepishly.

He pats me on the shoulder kindly, and it's so unexpected that I'm not sure how to react. "Teddy will take care of you. Do not hurt yourself."

"All right."

He steps back like he's going to exit the stall, but then he surveys me more critically. I've left one crutch against the wall to leave my hands free, but I still have the right one. Hugh's eyes go from the crutch to the bottom of my right leg and then back to my face, and I find myself automatically bristling.

But he says, "Crutches around horses are no good. You should see the armorer. Maybe she can fashion a new foot."

I stare at him like he's speaking an entirely new language. "What?"

"Captain Ammax. I have seen her do it once or twice before. After the war." He frowns. "She does not speak Syssalah. I will ask for you. It may have been too long. But I will ask."

I shake my head, thinking of my attempts over the years to fashion something that would support my weight, wouldn't be painful, and

232

would allow me to move around the forge more efficiently than the crutches and ropes I used at home. Nothing ever worked very well—and half the time my father would snort at my efforts and toss them in the fire himself. "I've tried. Nothing stays on. It's too hard to pivot around the forge—"

"Hush." He waves a hand, *tsking*. "Let fate provide. Ammax does good work. I will ask."

Let fate provide. There are just too many surprises in this conversation.

While I'm staring at him, he moves close to me again, until we're standing side by side. "Where does your leg end? Match to mine. Show me so I can take measure."

I'm so stunned that I can't do anything but obey. He touches the same height on his own leg, measuring the distance from the ground.

"I will remember," he says.

My thoughts are so rattled that I nod and say the word back to him in Emberish. *"Remember."*

His eyes light up just like Sephran's did. "You're learning!"

I flush. Learning a lot more than I expected to.

He pats me on the shoulder again, then steps back out of the way. "Have a good ride." His expression turns stern again. "Two hours. I make soldiers muck stalls if they turn up late."

I nod. "Yes, Master Hugh."

But he's already shifted to move down the aisle, so I lead Teddy out of the stall to wait for the soldiers.

Sephran and Kutter don't come alone. Three other men arrive in the stable yard, all laden with bows and quivers and various other weapons. Between the journey here and my work in the forge, I've seen too many soldiers, and I can't remember if I've met them before. They have

233

varying skin tones, but in armor, they've all begun to look the same: short hair, broad shoulders, muscled arms.

Cool eyes when they regard me.

I'm immediately wary. I didn't realize Sephran was bringing others.

Kutter's face breaks into a smile when he draws close, though. "Jax! How do you say *hello* in Syssalah?" His smile turns mischievous, and he reaches out to knock Sephran in the shoulder, then switches languages. He carefully pronounces the words to say, "*Suck a piece of horseshit*?" and looks back at me. "Is that right?"

That bursts through my tension and makes me laugh. I can't believe he remembered the whole phrase, but then the soldiers never lacked for profanity. "Hello *and* goodbye," I say.

Sephran rolls his eyes, but he smiles. "Jax." He points to the three young men who've accompanied him and Kutter. "Trapp, Fowler, and Leo."

Trapp and Fowler exchange a glance as if they're as uncertain as I am. They must respect Sephran and Kutter, though, because when they look back at me, their expressions aren't hostile. They each lift a hand and say, "Well met."

"Well met," I echo, equally reserved.

Leo is the youngest, possibly younger than I am, because he's lacking some of the breadth and muscle of the others. He glances at Kutter, then back at me. He gives me a nod, followed by an uncertain smile. "Ah . . . *suck a piece of horse—*"

"No!" Sephran snaps. He gives a withering look at Kutter, and I have no idea what he says, but the tone sounds a lot like, *See what you've started?*

Kutter just laughs. "Let's go."

It's a few hours from sunset, so the fields surrounding Ironrose Castle are still filled with sunlight and the scents of cut grass and wildflowers. There's a breeze out here that I was missing in the forge, and days of tension slip out of my shoulders. I'd been worried that the others would want to go tearing off at a gallop, but the ground is still soft from all the rain and they seem content to amble along.

The soldiers chatter as we ride, but I've grown used to the way Ember-ish rolls over me without too much comprehension. That said, I can pick out a few phrases. They're complaining about someone I don't know, something about more hours on patrol. Then I lose the thread and the words are nonsense again.

I look at the sky, at the clouds that have shifted west, and think of Tycho. Hopefully he's reached the Crystal Palace by now. I wonder how quickly the king will allow him to return. I also wonder if there have been more scraver attacks—though the soldiers don't seem concerned. Then again, maybe that's the reason for more hours on patrol. Maybe it's selfish of me to hope Tycho might return in less than a week. He risks his life for the safety of the kingdom. I'm just . . . me.

I think of our night together in the hayloft, the way he talked about the soldiers. The way he stopped me. He doesn't talk much about what happened when he was young, but I know it weighs on him. He hides it well, but now that I know his past, I can see it in every interaction. His trust—his *loyalty*—is like a gift.

As I consider the way it's tearing him apart, I have another thought.

Maybe it's a curse.

"Jax."

I realize the others have stopped, and I was letting Teddy meander along. My cheeks flare with warmth, and I jerk the horse to a stop, then look over at Sephran. "Yeah."

He looks vaguely amused. "We're here."

We've reached the archery fields. Trapp and Fowler have dismounted, and they're already tethering the horses. Leo is definitely the young-est, and possibly the lowest in rank, because there seems to be some good-natured ribbing going on. I tether Teddy and untie my crutches, and this generates a few more exchanged glances, but at least no one is spitting at me.

Back in the woods in Briarlock, I'd created an archery course of my own, made of leather squares nailed to trees and a few rings I hung from branches. Here on the grounds of Ironrose, there are dozens of targets set at varying heights and distances along the field, from wide panels of painted wood to tiny rounds of stuffed muslin that must require impeccable aim. Some are even strung from above, bearing targets that swing in the breeze.

I don't know the rules here, whether we're to take turns or what. I'm on the outskirts of this easy soldier camaraderie. I hang back a bit, adjusting Teddy's tack, re-buckling my bracer, smoothing my thumb along my bow. Kutter shoots first, and after hearing his lesson on fletching lengths during our journey, I'm not surprised to find that he's a skilled archer, quick and accurate. Every arrow hits near the center of the target, even a smaller circle that's at least seventy yards away. He shoots four, then steps aside.

Trapp is good, too, but not quite as accurate. He hits the targets, but far from center. Fowler is accurate on anything close, but at a distance, his shots miss, and there's some teasing from the others. I try to tuck their words away, to parse them out, to understand.

Careful, you might hit the castle.

Those wildflowers had it coming.

"Yeah, yeah," Fowler says, rolling his eyes. "It's windy."

Sephran sees me looking between them, and he lifts a hand, running his fingers through the air. "Windy," he says, then blows out a breath, mimicking the wind.

I know this one, because they taught me about wind before. I tap my temple and smile. "I remember."

He grins in response. "Good."

Leo steps up next. He nocks an arrow, aiming for a closer target. Kutter speaks to him, and there's no teasing in his voice now. It's all instruction. The youngest soldier hits three targets of the four he attempts, only one skipping off the edge of a wooden plank. The others whistle and clap, and Leo waves a hand, shrugging them off, but I can tell he's pleased.

I expect Sephran to go next, but he looks at me. "Your turn," he says. "Shoot." He points at me, then mimes drawing a bow and releasing an arrow. There's a note of militaristic challenge in his voice that's similar to what I hear from Tycho.

The others are quiet now. Watching. I have no idea what Sephran said about why I was joining them, whether he truly meant it as a mark of kindness or friendship or even just plain pity, but this feels so dramatically far from my life in Briarlock that I almost falter.

But then I think of something Tycho once said to me, and it gives me courage.

What are you afraid of?

I take my spot, then drop my crutches to kneel in the grass for better stability. It *is* a bit windy, so I feel for a few arrows with short fletching from my quiver. I nock an arrow and aim for a target no one has used.

The first shot snaps hard off my bow, and I'm glad for my bracer. I haven't shot in days. The arrow strikes the target a few inches left of center. I wince and nock another, aiming farther down the range. This one hits closer to center, sticking hard. *Better.*

At my back, the soldiers are silent.

I take a slow breath. My third target is long range, but I take my time, and I'm rewarded when the arrow hits the bull's-eye. For the fourth, I choose one of the hanging panels, waving gently in the wind, easily as far as Kutter's shots. The arrow cracks right into the center.

I turn to find the soldiers staring at me. Kutter gives a low whistle and claps three times. Sephran punches me in the shoulder. "Nice shooting, Archer."

That makes me blush.

Trapp looks at Sephran. "Was he a soldier?" he asks, as if I'm not right there and can't attempt to understand these simple words. "In Syhl Shallow?"

"No," I say. I hook my bow over my shoulder, then take my crutches and push to standing. "Blacksmith."

Fowler is still staring at me, like I've tricked them all somehow. "But— but *how*?" he demands.

Lord Tycho, I want to say, but that feels too heavy, too personal. Too much of an attachment to someone who is far above my station.

Instead, I pull another arrow out of my quiver and run a finger along the fletching, then nod at Kutter and Sephran. "Short," I say, repeating their lesson from last week. I smile, then shrug. "Good in wind."

Sephran laughs. "I like you, Jax."

My blush goes nowhere. I like them, too.

CHAPTER 25

JAX

I don't return to the Shield House until late, when the sky sparkles with the first stars of the evening, and the sun is a distant memory. I expect that Molly and Lola have gone to bed, but I'm hopeful I can forage for some fruit or a few scraps left in the kitchen. After a long day in the forge, shooting with the soldiers and riding with the recruits has left me exhausted. My bow and quiver feel heavy where they crisscross my chest, and I practically lumber up the steps to the Shield House.

I don't care. My heart feels lighter for the first time in *days*.

But then I step inside and find Prince Rhen.

He's sitting with Master Garson at one of the tables, and they fall silent when I enter. Two guards stand along the wall at their backs.

They're waiting for me. I don't know how I know, but I do.

A million thoughts flash through my brain at once, and I'm frozen in place. I called that soldier an asshole, but I didn't think he heard me. Did he complain? I remember yelling at Sephran, too, how Master Garson looked over. Did the other blacksmiths say something about me? Surely none of this would be enough to involve the *prince*. But maybe it is. Am I going to lose my position?

Or . . . will it be something worse? A sudden chill grips my spine, and my fingers go slick on my crutches. I know what kinds of things Prince Rhen is capable of. People used to talk about the vicious queen in Syhl Shallow, but I've heard enough stories to doubt that things are any better here.

I know Tycho trusts this man. Maybe that should matter, but it *doesn't*. Too many years of living with my father's cruelty have hardened me, because I can't seem to *look* at Rhen without thinking of what he's done.

Even now, I can't. The image of Tycho's scars flickers in my thoughts, and a quick knife of fury slices through me.

Prince Rhen evaluates me, then speaks slowly in Syssalah. "I do not think anyone has ever looked at me with quite this combination of anger and fear."

Warmth crawls up my throat, and I glance away. I wish I could strip the emotion from my face, but it's clear that I can't.

I still haven't moved from the doorway. "Forgive me, Your Highness."

"I wasn't looking for an apology. But perhaps . . . an explanation."

Master Garson looks at him and says something, but Prince Rhen's gaze doesn't leave mine. "Garson wants to know if he should give us some privacy. Or would you rather he stay?"

I have no idea how to answer that. Every muscle in my body is so tight. My gaze flicks to the guards along the wall and then back to the men sitting at the table.

Prince Rhen watches this, and his one eye narrows. "Exactly why do you think I'm here?"

I dig my thumbnails into the crossbars of my crutches and wish I could disappear through the wall. "I don't know."

"I told Tycho I would ensure you faced few hardships while he was gone."

Like everything else, he says the words slowly, and they're so completely contrary to what I was expecting that I'm almost certain he's using the wrong ones.

Prince Rhen speaks into my silence. "So I am here to keep that promise."

"I . . . oh." I'm still not sure what to say. "Thank you. I . . . I have no hardships."

Prince Rhen looks at Master Garson and says something quietly. He must ask him to excuse us, because the other man rises and steps away from the table. He gives me a nod and a kind smile.

The prince gestures to the chair he just abandoned. "Do you care to sit?"

No. I absolutely do not.

But he's the ruler here, and I doubt that was a real question. I swing my crutches forward. The path across the dining room feels twenty miles long, and it's so quiet I can hear my breathing. Each *clop* of my crutches on the stone floor is uncomfortably loud.

By the time I sit, Master Garson returns, and to my surprise, he's brought me a small platter of food, along with a cup of chilled mead from the kitchen. The platter is full of sliced nut bread and squares of cheese and a few strips of beef, along with berries in a bowl. It's as startling as everything else since I walked in the door. I glance between him and the food, wondering if he's going to sit back down, but he moves away again.

I realize he's leaving us, possibly for good this time. "Thank you," I say in Emberish.

He pauses at the door and smiles. "You're welcome."

Then he's gone, and I'm alone with the prince. The first words he said to me are still echoing in my thoughts.

241

I do not think anyone has ever looked at me with quite this combination of anger and fear.

It makes me never want to look at him again.

"Eat," says Rhen. "You must be hungry."

I am.

But I don't.

A moment passes between us. I can still hear my own breathing. I swear I can hear his *guards* breathing.

When Rhen speaks again, his voice is quiet. "Does Garson treat you poorly?"

That makes me look up. "What? No. He speaks no Syssalah, but he's not unkind."

I say the words in a rush, and I can see in his face that I've spoken too fast, but he doesn't ask me to repeat it.

"He tells me that you skip the midday meal," Rhen says. "I wondered if there was a reason."

"The forge is very busy." And until Sephran found me a bench, I was very slow, but I don't add that. "I don't want to fall behind."

"There will never be a shortage of work," Rhen says. "Eat when you're meant to eat." He hesitates, then nudges the platter a bit closer to me. "I don't like seeing my people hungry."

There's no emphasis in his voice, but the way he says that is curious. I can't tell which part tugs at my interest the most, whether it's the way he says *my people* when pushing the food toward *me*, or if it's the fact that he thinks about his people being hungry at all.

Whatever it is, it's hard to reconcile with what I know he's done.

He's told me to eat twice now, so I take one of the berries. It explodes with sweetness in a way that's jarring when I'm feeling so bitter. I wait for him to press with more questions, but he doesn't, and tension clings to my back. If he's waiting for *me* to make conversation, he's going to wait an eternity. I take a piece of cheese.

242

Prince Rhen eventually says, "Garson told me there seemed to be an argument. With one of the soldiers."

He must mean what happened with Sephran this afternoon. I shake my head. "That . . . that was a misunderstanding."

"Would you tell me otherwise?"

I think of the soldiers who poke at the horses and knock my tools in the dirt. Would I tell the prince that half his soldiers are arrogant bastards who deserve a good fist to the gut? Would he care?

Would I want him to care?

No.

I keep my gaze on the food, rolling an almond between my fingers, and I have no idea how to answer.

My chest is so tight. I wish Tycho were here.

"Look at me."

My eyes flick up.

Prince Rhen looks back at me, and I can feel him trying to pick me apart. I have to be careful here, because the prince is a lot more savvy than a stupid soldier sweating in the heat beside the forge. He saw every emotion the instant I walked in the room, so he can probably read every emotion *now*: my resentment, my frustration, my contempt. My anxiety that I'm going to say or do the wrong thing, and it will reflect poorly on Tycho—and lead to a bad end for me.

"You haven't liked me since the moment we met," Rhen says.

The almond goes still between my fingers. My chest is caught in a vise grip, and my mouth goes dry.

His gaze has grown more coolly assessing. "For a while I thought it might be born of loyalty to Syhl Shallow, some . . ." He looks up, searching for a word. "Some *prejudice* about working in a kingdom that was once an enemy to your own. But it's not, is it?"

I should say *yes*. I should lay claim to these ideas. It would make sense, and give root to all of this emotion.

243

But it wouldn't be true, and I don't think he'd fall for it.

"No," I say.

"This is personal."

"Yes."

As soon as I say the word, as soon as I *acknowledge* it, the hostility in the air seems to flicker more openly. More honestly.

For a fraction of a second, I think I've unraveled everything, and he'll order me to leave. Worse, I'll be spending the night in chains.

To my surprise, Rhen looks genuinely intrigued. "Why?" he says quietly. "To my knowledge, I have never done anything to you."

"No, Your Highness," I say roughly. "You haven't done anything to *me*."

The instant the words leave my mouth, I wish I could take them back. Because he hears the emotion behind them. I watch them land. I see the impact.

My shoulders are tight, but the words have been spoken, and righteous fury swells in my belly. It takes everything I have not to unleash every thought in my head.

I don't like seeing my people hungry. I hate that he said it, like he cares about someone's comfort. It makes me want to throw the food at him. No, it makes me want to point an arrow at him. I want to know how he can claim to care about someone's hunger while being the same man who chained a young Tycho to a wall. I want to know how he can think about someone's *hardships*, while being the same man who ordered his guards to find some whips—

"*Hold.*"

Rhen's voice is very quiet, and I blink. He said the word in Ember-ish, and I realize one of his guards has stepped away from the wall. One of my hands is on my bow, and I didn't even realize it.

I'm breathing hard. I drop the bow on the floor, where it clatters. I have to look away. Now I really *will* end up in chains.

244

But Prince Rhen says, "I'm going to leave, Jax. Before this conversation ends in a way we'll both regret."

I can't answer. I'm biting the inside of my cheek, and I taste blood.

He stands. "I will keep my promise to Tycho. If you need anything, send word."

I force a nod.

He finally moves away. I can draw a full breath for the first time in a while. I lock my eyes on the edge of the table so I'm not tempted to shoot him again.

Prince Rhen stops by the doorway. His voice is very quiet. "This may not make a difference to you, but I hate myself for it."

I think of Tycho's strong hands, his quiet voice, his kind spirit. I think of the way he stood in the woods and gently folded my fingers around an arrow, encouraging me as I learned how to shoot—and then later, the way he dragged my father off me before the man could kill me. I think of the way his thumb brushed tears off my cheeks and how he told me of everything that had been done to him when he was a child. I think of his trust, so honest and pure. His loyalty.

How it *must* be a curse, because that's what Prince Rhen so thoughtlessly chained to a wall to torture.

"Good." My voice is tight and hard and vicious. "I hate you, too."

Prince Rhen goes still, drawing himself up, and I brace myself.

But then he seems to deflate. He gives me a nod. "Noted."

Then he's gone, and I collapse into the chair and put my face in my hands.

CHAPTER 26

CALLYN

Two days after I return from my visit with Alek, the Crystal Palace is alive with rumors. Nora and I usually have breakfast with little Sinna in her rooms, so we rarely hear much of anything before midday, but even the serving girls who deliver the food are gossiping under their breath to each other as they pour tea and spoon sliced fruit onto the delicate porcelain dishes.

"I heard they attacked the guards at the main gate," one is whispering.

"I heard that, too!" the other says in a rush. "They had to call up a full regiment to stop them!"

"What happened?" I say.

"A full regiment!" Nora exclaims. "And we didn't hear anything?"

"What's a regiment?" says Sinna.

"A group of soldiers," I say. "Here. Have a sweetcake." I move away from the table and drop my voice. "There was an attack?"

The serving girls exchange a glance. One of them says, "The rumors say two soldiers from Emberfall attacked the main gate, and that the king himself had to confront them."

Apparently we didn't drop our voices enough, because Sinna cries, "Da!" and the worry in her voice is clear.

"He's fine," says Nora. She points out the window, where the sun is shining down on the training fields. "Look, you can see him with the soldiers. Just there."

"Oh," says Sinna, her worry forgotten. She goes back to her fruit.

I frown and shoo the serving girls toward the door, but I follow them. I haven't seen the queen yet this morning, but perhaps she's dealing with whatever happened. I've been engaged to make sure Sinna is safe, however, and if there are rumors about soldiers from Emberfall attacking the palace, I want to know.

"Has anything been confirmed?" I whisper to them once we reach the door.

They exchange another glance. "Nothing yet," one says.

"The baker says it's all a bunch of gossip," says the other. "The king wouldn't be out on the fields like it's just another day if anything were wrong." She pauses. "Though I heard in the kitchen that he sent a summons for half a dozen nobles to be brought to the palace—to be questioned."

Her voice drops when she says this, and she exchanges a glance with the first. I wonder if *questioned* really means *interrogated*.

The first servant adds, "My cousin is a stable hand, and he said that the one who attacked the gates was the King's Courier in disguise."

"The King's Courier!" I exclaim, though a thread of worry stitches its way through my heart. Tycho left Briarlock with Jax a few weeks ago. "That's impossible. He was just sent to Emberfall."

"Exactly," says the second. "*And* he's a personal friend to the king." She scoffs. "Why would he be in disguise? Why would he attack the gates?"

247

"I think it's the Truthbringers," says the other. "Someone is trying to get at the queen again."

Behind us, Sinna gasps again, and I sigh, then wave the serving girls out the door. Before I turn, I paste a bright smile on my face and think of something that will distract the princess. "Sinna," I say. "Should we practice your braiding before your lessons this morning?"

Her face lights up, and I tell Nora to fetch a comb.

While we practice, I wonder when we'll see Queen Lia Mara—and whether it would be appropriate to ask for answers. When I returned from Lord Alek's, she didn't seem surprised by anything I told her. Not his attitude toward magic, not his near-accusations of her sister, not his whispered declaration that he has spies on both sides of the border. When I told her that he wanted me to return in three days with a response, she said, "Thank you, Callyn," and then nothing more than that.

So I've been wondering. Waiting. Unsure if she's going to have Alek arrested for treason against the throne—or if she's going to send me back to discover more.

And now I suppose I'm going to wonder if Truthbringers are attacking the palace, dressed up as soldiers from Emberfall.

By late afternoon, we haven't learned anything new, though the rumors are really quite spectacular. For the first time, I'm almost *eager* to go spar with Verin, because I imagine she'll at least know the truth of some of it. She might break every bone in my body, but she'll know if I need to worry about Truthbringers sneaking into the palace.

Unless she's working *with* them.

The thought smacks me in the face, and I can't even listen to Nora's prattling as we head down the palace hallways in our sparring gear. Alek's warnings about someone with power and access conspiring against the queen are suddenly whirling in my head in a new way. We turn the corner that leads away from the royal wing, and I'm so wrapped up in my thoughts that I don't see the man emerging from a room until I nearly walk right into him.

"Forgive me, my lord," I'm saying absently—but then I realize I recognize him. "Tycho!" I say in surprise. I have to catch myself. "I mean—Lord Tycho." I really need to get it together. "*My lord.*"

"Callyn," he says, and he sounds equally surprised. But then he gives me a tired smile. "I mean, *Lady* Callyn," he adds, gently teasing. His eyes shift past me to my sister. "And Lady Nora."

That makes my cheeks warm, and I'm not sure what to say. For a moment, we stare at each other. I forgot how striking he is—and I'm so shocked that he's here. It's only been a matter of weeks since I last saw him in Briarlock—if it's even been that. There's a part of me that expects to blink and discover it's not really him, like I've mistaken him for someone else.

"Just *Callyn* is fine," I tease back—just as Nora decides it's completely appropriate to launch herself forward to tackle him with a hug.

"Tycho!" she cries, like she's known him her whole life. "It *is* you! Did Jax come with you? Is Mercy here? You were so right about the sweetcakes in the morning, but Cally-cal's are better. I met your cat! But Salam is afraid of Princess Sinna, so I don't see him very often. He runs whenever—"

"Nora!" I snap, grabbing her arm to pull her off him. "You can't keep flinging yourself at people in the palace."

"It's all right," he says to me. Even his voice is tired. For the first time, I notice a bit of tension clinging to his eyes. "I'll take *this* kind of welcome any day."

There's a hint of bitterness when he says that, but before I can figure it out, he draws back to look at Nora. "Jax isn't with me, but he'll be very happy to know I got the chance to see you both. Mercy is here, though. Well, in the stables. And Salam will get used to you, I promise. Here."

He opens the door at his back, then makes a whispering *pspsps* sound. "Let's see if he comes out."

Nora gasps with delight, but I say, "We can't stay long. Verin is expecting us in the arena."

His eyes skip over our attire, as if only just realizing we're in sparring gear. "You're training with Nolla Verin?" he says.

I fight not to grimace. "Is that a surprise?"

He runs a hand over the back of his neck. "Ah . . . well, I'm not sure I'd pair Verin with a *beginner*—"

"She said she's going to teach me how to peel the bones out of Alek's *fingers*," Nora says, sounding a bit too delighted about that.

"And *that's* why," says Tycho, and Nora giggles.

I'm blushing again. I'm still too surprised to find him right in front of me.

"Come with us," Nora says. She grabs his hand. "I can show you what I've learned."

"Nora!" I say. "Honestly. Let the man *go*."

"It's fine." Tycho's eyes have actually lit up, and for a moment I think he might really join us. But then he draws back. "Next time, *Lady* Nora. I arrived with another soldier, and I should see if he's awake yet."

"Another soldier," I say, remembering the serving girls and their gossip. "From Emberfall?"

He nods. "We rode through the night. We only arrived quite early this morning."

Nora's eyes go wide. "Then it *was* you who attacked the main gates!" she exclaims.

"*What?*" he says.

I put up a hand. "There are rumors all over the palace," I say quietly, casting a glance at the end of the hallway, where two guards are stationed. "They say two soldiers from Emberfall attacked the guards at the main gate."

Tycho scowls. "The rumors here are outrageous," he says, and now he sounds aggrieved. He runs a hand back through his hair, and his strain is clear. "We just needed—" He breaks off, as if realizing perhaps he's saying too much, to two people who really have no right to confidential information. "We arrived unexpectedly, and we were held at the gate. No one attacked. There's no need for *gossip.*"

I frown. "I'm sorry."

"Once people see you," Nora says, "the rumors will stop."

That doesn't seem to improve his expression. He's quiet for a moment. "I'm sure you're right," he eventually says.

I study him, wondering what's behind the tired strain. I think of the queen and all her worries. I think of Alek and all his warnings.

Tycho probably won't tell me if I ask—but he might.

"Nora," I say. "You're always first. Go ahead so we don't keep Verin waiting. I'll be there in a moment."

"But I want to see Lord Tycho's cat—"

"Go!" I snap, giving her a pinch.

"Ouch!" she cries, but she obeys, turning away. "Come watch tomorrow, Lord Tycho," she calls behind her. "I can't wait to show you! You'll have to tell Jax!"

"I promise!" he calls back, but then she's gone, and Tycho and I are alone in the hallway together.

It's so odd to see him here—though I'm sure he feels the same about me. I remember the morning Jax blushed and admitted that he fancied the King's Courier. It was right after Alek came to my bakery the first time, offering *me* the silver he'd been promising Jax. Alek stood there and told me about his mother's death, and it was the first moment I began to trust him.

It's jarring to remember that *now*, of all times. Everything got so twisted up so fast.

"What did you want to tell me?" says Tycho, and his voice is quieter.

I blink. "What?"

"You sent Nora away. I assumed there was something."

I swallow. "I was wondering if you'd tell me why you had to ride through the night."

He studies me for a long moment.

"*Is* Jax all right?" I add.

He nods quickly. "He's well. I left him safe in Emberfall. I had to return quickly." He frowns, and for a moment, silence ticks between us. But then his eyes narrow slightly. "Wait—you said there's been gossip all day. But you're with Sinna, aren't you? The king knows why I'm here. Doesn't the queen?"

"I don't know," I say quietly. "All I've heard is that the King's Courier attacked the gates, and that the king summoned people from the Crystal City for 'questioning.'"

Tycho's tired eyes flick past me, toward the royal wing, and he sighs. "Did something happen? Between them?"

When I say nothing, his gaze returns to mine. We stare at each other in the shadows of the hallway, and suddenly the weight of untold secrets descends on both of us.

But like the moment my silence inadvertently said too much to Alek, it does the same here. Tycho frowns, and he runs a hand across his jaw. "I *knew* there had to be a reason he was down in the east wing."

"I really don't know anything," I whisper.

"You know enough." He hesitates. "Is she all right?"

"Yes," I say quickly—maybe *too* quickly, because his eyes skip over my face.

While we stand there, his orange cat comes slinking out from under his bed to wind around his ankles.

Tycho looks down and offers half a smile. "Nora will be so disappointed."

"I think your cat has more sense than she does," I say.

That makes his smile a full one. "Nora seems to be enjoying her lessons with Verin."

I snort. "More than I am," I say without thinking. Then I catch myself. "I mean—she's not—"

"Oh, I know what you mean." Now his smile turns into a grin. "She's a good sparring partner if you don't mind the bruises. When I was younger, Lia Mara tried to nudge us together, but it only took me five minutes to figure out that Nolla Verin will never be happy unless she finds someone as ruthless as she is. That is *definitely* not me."

His tone makes me smile. "I don't think it's anyone." The cat begins to wind through my own ankles, and I glance down, realizing how much time has passed. "I should go after Nora."

He nods. "I should check on my soldier."

As I move away, he calls after me. "Callyn. One thing."

I stop in the hallway and turn. "What?"

The smile is gone from his face, and his eyes are cool and analytical again. "Prince Rhen told me that Lord Alek was released to return to Syhl Shallow. Has he caused any issues for you and your sister?"

I'm glad I've moved away, because I'm able to keep any hint of surprise off my face. "No," I say, and I'm worried my voice sounds a bit breathy. I clear my throat. "No issues at all."

"For the king and queen?" he presses.

I shake my head quickly. "No. Nothing."

I hold my breath, wondering if he's going to press, but he simply nods, then lets the door fall closed, heading in the opposite direction.

As I walk, I consider what I've learned. Because he's right that the gossip is surprising. If the king and queen both knew he was here and the reason for his arrival, there likely wouldn't be gossip at all. But I felt the weight of secrets between us. He has information he's not sharing—though he obviously doesn't have to tell me. I wonder if he'd tell the queen, or if his loyalty is to King Grey.

I hate that I'm thinking about them as being on separate sides.

When I reach the arena, Verin and Nora are sparring with practice blades, and I'm shocked at how much my sister has learned in such a short time. General Solt said that I looked just like my mother, but it's Nora who *moves* like her. From a distance, she doesn't look twelve at all, and if I didn't know any better, I'd say she was one of the recruits I train with when I join Jacob in the mornings. She's quick and agile, and it's clear she loves what she's doing.

As I watch, however, Verin notices me by the railing, and something in her gaze darkens. I feel a clench in my gut, and I wish I could shake it off. It makes me think of Alek's suspicions—and now, it makes me think of what Tycho said.

Nolla Verin will never be happy unless she finds someone as ruthless as she is.

He meant it as a point of humor. But just this moment, combined with what Alek said about the former queen and the way Verin was raised to take her place, it feels like a warning.

CHAPTER 27

TYCHO

Malin doesn't answer when I knock, and I can't help the twinge of disappointment in my chest. The hall guards say he hasn't called for food yet either, so it's possible he's still sleeping. I return to my quarters to wait, though it's beginning to feel like a cell. The king's sharp censure from after we arrived has been twisting like a spike in my chest, and nothing I do will displace it. I have half a mind to retrieve Mercy from the stables and ride straight back to Ironrose.

But no. That would land me in a worse position than I'm in already.

Callyn didn't specifically say there were difficulties between the king and queen, but I'm not an idiot. I saw where the king was staying—and if rumors are flying like this, then it means he and Lia Mara might not be *speaking*. A horrible curiosity tugs at my heart—though I'm not sure where to find answers, especially if they haven't even spoken about my presence here.

Grey ordered me to keep to myself. He didn't specifically mention the queen, but if he's at odds with Lia Mara, does that mean I should keep my distance as well? What about Jake and Noah? Considering what

I've learned, I'm not sure if I should risk it—especially since I have no idea who might be working with the Truthbringers, and who might be working with Xovaar.

But I'm not one to sit idle, and it doesn't take long before I really *do* start thinking about sneaking out of here. When a knock sounds at my door near sunset, I practically leap at it.

I swing the door wide. It's not Malin. It's Noah.

He smiles when he sees me, and his brown eyes are warm. "Hey, kid. I heard you were back."

If anyone else were at my door, I'd be steadfast and cool. But Noah knows all my vulnerabilities, and everything about the past week seems to hit me at once. The hundreds of soldiers. The uniform Rhen made me wear. Malin binding my hands, and the threats at the guard station. My magic in the air. The scravers hunting magesmiths.

Nakiis.

Grey.

Jax.

My chest tightens, and when I try to breathe, it hurts to inhale.

Noah comes through the door, closing it behind him. "Hey," he says again, his voice lower.

I don't know if it's his voice or his presence or if it's just the weight of the world, but all of a sudden, I just . . . can't. I take a step forward and wrap my arms around him.

Noah catches me and hugs me back. For the longest time, I hold my breath, because I'm terrified of what will happen if I don't. But he doesn't move, and his arms don't loosen. My heart begins to slow, and eventually I can breathe.

Then I realize I'm clinging to him like a child. I draw back at once.

Noah lets me go. He never pushes. But now he's studying me.

"Forgive me," I say.

"It's all right to need a hug, Tycho."

256

I'm not sure what to say to that.

"I was worried I'd wake you," he says. "I heard you showed up just before dawn."

I shrug. "I've been awake for a while."

That sentence seems to hang between us for a moment. My thoughts are churning again, and I take another step back.

Noah watches this, but he just says, "One of the women who works in the gardens asked me to bring her a salve for a bee sting. I was going to head that way after I saw you. Do you want to walk with me?"

"Ah . . . sure."

I leave word with the hall guards so Malin will know where to find me, and then Noah and I head toward the miles of stairs and hallways that make up the Crystal Palace. After endless days of wearing weapons and armor in the rain, my body feels too light, too free. Once we step into the fresh spring air, I take what feels like the first deep breath in *days*.

"*Thaaat's* better," Noah drawls.

I cut him a glance—but he's right. "I wasn't *that* bad."

"If Jake found you first, he would've dragged you out on the fields to play with swords for a few hours. Unfortunately, I'm only good for dragging you along on medical deliveries."

"I really don't mind."

He smiles. "I know."

And just like that, the awkwardness is gone.

"Is Jake well?" I say.

"Grey woke us before dawn because he wanted Jake to go find out how many scraver attacks have happened near the city, so he's probably not in the *best* mood. But he's been well."

I wince. "Forgive me."

"Why on earth is that your fault?"

I don't have an answer for that, and we've reached the gardens anyway. A young woman tending the newly budding rosebushes curt-sies to Noah and then to me. He offers her the small jar of salve, but asks to see the swollen mound of skin on her forearm. I expect him to heal it, because he still wears a ring of Iishellasan steel, but to my surprise, he doesn't. I wonder if she's afraid. He applies a small amount of salve, and we return to the path that heads through the vibrant gardens.

"You don't need to head back to the infirmary?" I say to him.

"We'll get there eventually. I have an *apprentice* now, so I've been trying to give her some space to figure things out on her own."

My eyebrows go up. "An apprentice!"

He nods. "She's young, but she's learning." He pauses. "How are things back at Ironrose? You couldn't have been there very long."

"Barely a day," I say. "It was urgent for Grey to know."

Noah doesn't say anything to that, and I can't read his silence, so we continue walking. At the end of the gardens, there's a path that leads to the training fields, and even though I really am curious about Callyn and Nora's progress, it's very likely the king will be there. No, thank you. I turn in the opposite direction, though it leads away from the palace.

Eventually Noah says, "Jake told me that Rhen offered Jax a position at Ironrose. How is that all going?"

"Ah . . . fine." My cheeks warm a bit in the sunlight. "I was able to introduce him to Master Garson and get him settled before I left."

I remember Jax's eyes staring into mine in the early dawn light. The feel of his hands when I promised I would return as quickly as I can.

If Jake is already making inquiries about attacks, he might return with news by nightfall, and I can be on my way back to Ironrose in the morning. The thought gives my heart a little boost of hope.

Noah gently bumps me with his shoulder. "Sometimes getting information out of you is like squeezing water out of a rock. I didn't know if *that*—you and Jax—was still . . . a thing."

I smile. "Yes, Noah. It is."

"It must have been hard to leave as soon as you got there. For both of you."

Yes. It was. But I try to swallow that emotion. "He knows who I am and what I'm called to do. It's never been a secret."

"Sometimes you're gone for weeks on end. Months. That's a long time apart." He shrugs a little, and he keeps his voice easy. "A lot to ask of something new."

A bee drones over the path, and I wave it away. I don't like the band of tension that his words are adding to my chest. Because instead of remembering my promise on the morning I left, I'm thinking of another vow I made to him weeks ago.

It will not be weeks or months or never, Jax. I swear to you.

But that was different. *This* is different.

Right?

Noah sighs, and to my surprise, he sounds a little disgusted.

I whip my head around. "What?"

"I know there's a reason Rhen sent you, but sometimes I think he and Grey are lucky you don't just chuck it all and take Mercy into some town somewhere and find a job that doesn't force you to run yourself into the ground."

I stop short on the path. Noah is one of the few people who speaks so openly about the king, but everything is too tense right now.

"I'm not running myself into the ground," I say.

"You look exhausted," he says. "You look *wrecked*. And I can't remember the last time you gave me a *hug*."

I give him a look. He just raises his eyebrows and looks back at me. I frown.

"I'm just saying I'm worried about you," he says. His voice turns careful. "I was wondering if you got your heart broken."

My eyebrows go up. "Is that why you were talking about time apart?"

"Yes."

"No." I hesitate. "I mean, I didn't. I told Jax I would be back as quickly as possible." I glance his way, troubled now. "You think he'd break my heart?"

"I don't know Jax yet." Noah starts walking again, and I fall into step beside him. "But you have a hard job, kid. It would be hard on people who've been together for years."

A curl of anxiety wraps around my thoughts, and I have to shove it away. "I'll return to Ironrose as soon as Grey drafts a response to Rhen. My visit will be short. There's no cause to worry."

He hesitates, then grimaces. His voice lowers. "You mean, aside from scravers attacking, threats from the Truthbringers, and the growing rift between Grey and Lia Mara?"

If anything could distract me from these new worries about Jax, that does it. I make my voice as quiet as his. "So there's definitely a rift? I was wondering why he was sleeping in the east wing."

"Grey didn't tell you?"

"No." I frown. "But he wasn't exactly pleased with me when I arrived."

"I don't think he's pleased with anyone right now."

"What's happening?"

"A lot. He's been trying to find out who was behind the attack, and it's not going well." Noah takes a long breath and runs a hand across the back of his neck. "If you listen to the gossip, you'll hear that the Truthbringers might have the queen's ear—that she's beginning to fear magic herself."

"But . . . but she would never—"

"Careful."

We're closer to the palace now, and I fight to keep my voice down. "Lia Mara has never been afraid of Grey."

"I know. But they went through several pretty traumatic events in a row. They lost the baby, and then there was everything that happened to them in Briarlock. That's not even considering the Uprising itself. Magic has done a lot of good, but it's done a lot of terrible things, too. People are afraid." He pauses. "They might be the king and queen, but they're still human. Strip away the magic and the thrones, and she's just a young mother. He's just a young father. The Truthbringers want him dead, and they were willing to threaten the princess and the queen to achieve it. They were willing to *kill* them to achieve it. That's a lot to put on a marriage. Any marriage."

And then I rode up to the gates with another threat—all because of the king's magic.

On the night Grey told me they'd lost the baby, I remember the emotion in the air. Sinna had been missing from the palace, and stress over the event sent the queen into early labor. Grey tried to use magic to stop the baby from coming too early. He worried that his magic made things worse.

You didn't, I said to him then, but I wasn't sure.

I'm not sure now.

I think about how Noah was bringing the gardener a salve for a simple bee sting.

"The queen has magic, too," I say softly. "She used it in Briarlock."

"If she does, she hasn't admitted it," Noah says. "In fact, I think she'd deny it." He glances at me, and his brown eyes are heavy. "I'm worried she's beginning to think that his magic is making her and the princess a target."

She's not wrong. Right now, his magic *is* a target.

I consider how I waited in my quarters all afternoon, how I wondered if I was at odds with the queen. I'm not . . . but now it feels like I am. I have magic just like the king, and I brought word of a new threat.

I rub my hands over my face.

"I think they all just need time to heal," Noah says quietly. "It's only been a few weeks."

261

We've almost reached the palace doors again, so I put out a hand to stop him. Once we're inside, the press of servants and guards will be too close to speak so openly.

"Do you think people are right to be afraid of magic?" I ask him quietly.

But that's not really what I'm asking.

Do you think the queen is right to be afraid?

He takes a long breath. "I'm not sure I can give you an honest answer without feeling like I'm risking my neck."

He's never said anything like that to me. *"Noah."*

"Magic is dangerous, Tycho. I've seen him lose control. So have you. And we've all seen the damage caused in Emberfall. There's a reason Rhen was so afraid when he learned that Grey was a mage-smith." He pauses. "But magic has brought a lot of *good*, too. I've been able to heal injuries that should have meant certain death. And Emberfall isn't trapped by a curse anymore. Lia Mara's mother is no longer in power. Emberfall and Syhl Shallow are at peace. All of that came about *because* of magic. Is that worth the trade-off? I just don't know."

I don't know either.

But I consider the way the soldiers in the guard station were eager to torture a soldier from Emberfall for being a traitor, or the note in Malin's voice when he said he forgot about how Syhl Shallow keeps a torture chamber for a prison. I've spent so long with a foot in both countries that I forgot the undercurrent of animosity that still exists between them both.

We start forward again, and when the guards swing the doors open, we step out of the bright sunlight into the cool, cloaking darkness of the palace.

I think of Malin's story about the prisoners he was forced to care for, how he learned their language and formed relationships—but has no idea what happened to them. After all that, did he still see them as his enemies? Or friends?

"The alliance between Emberfall and Syhl Shallow is about more than just magic," I say to Noah.

"You're right," he says. "It's not that simple."

I have to sigh. "War never is."

By sunset, I still haven't seen the king or the queen. An edgy impatience has set up camp in my chest, and I wish I had some way to unleash it. I haven't seen Malin either, and that wicked part of my brain begins whispering that maybe he's decided it would be better to avoid me, too.

But no. I tell my stupid thoughts that he's just sleeping off the effects of soldiering in the rain for days.

When I knock, he practically flings the door open. "Has the king given you orders?" he says the instant he lays eyes on me.

"Hello to you, too, Malin."

He smiles, then glances ruefully up and around the doorframe to his room. "I wasn't sure how long we're meant to be confined to our quarters."

"We're not confined," I say. Maybe I should have fetched him sooner. "Have you eaten? I can show you to the dining hall."

"I've eaten. The guards sent for food."

"Then . . . do you care to see the palace? Or even the Crystal City? We can call for our horses."

His eyes light up a little at both suggestions, but then he glances in the direction we came from last night. "I should wait until we're summoned."

He's wary of upsetting the king. I probably should be, too. Maybe Grey *expects* us to be confined to our quarters, waiting for him to make a decision.

Then again, the first thing Malin asked about was new orders. He must be bored. I know I am. I can't stare at the walls of my room for another minute.

"Sparring?" I offer. "The training arena should be deserted right now."

Malin's eyes light up again. He doesn't move—but he *wants* to.

"I won't let you hang yourself either," I add. "The king would *never* fault a soldier for training. I promise you that."

He grins. "I'll get my gear."

The training arena is empty and dim, with a few torches lit. The back doors are still open, allowing the cool night air to swirl inside. As I thought, we have the arena to ourselves. When we begin, it feels good to move, to fight, to do something I'm capable of, instead of spending so much time worrying about things I have no control over. Malin made for a good sparring partner on the road, but he makes for an even better one now: he's well-rested and well-fed, without the promise of a long day of riding ahead of us.

Well, ahead of *him*. I'm still hopeful I'll be galloping across the border by nightfall tomorrow.

By the time we break apart from our fourth match, we're both breathing hard, and sweat is making it tough to keep a grip on my sword. It's fully dark, and attendants have lit the other torches, but we still have the arena to ourselves.

Malin sheathes his sword. "I'm beginning to regret this," he says, pushing damp hair back from his face.

"No, you're not."

"Hold that thought while I vomit on your boots."

I laugh. "So that's a *no* to a fifth round?"

"I didn't say *no*." He heaves a rough breath and swipes a forearm across his forehead, then puts a hand on the hilt of his sword. "If you go, I go. Five, six, one hundred, say the word."

He says it so lightly that he could be kidding—but I can tell he really means it. It reminds me of the way he grabbed my arm before I mouthed off to Grey, even though this assignment matters to him so much he was willing to lock himself in his room until we had new orders. *If you go, I go.*

I smile and shake out my arm, leaving my weapon in its sheath. "Let's take a minute. We don't have to get to one hundred *tonight.*"

"Oh, thank fate." Malin drops to his knees and sits back on his heels, then nods at my armor. He's caught his breath, and he says, "It's odd to face you in that, after so many days in our colors."

He means Emberfall's colors. I drop to a squat beside him, bracing my forearms on my knees. I've worn this black armor for so long that I don't remember ever giving it a second thought, but I noticed how it set me apart during our journey to Emberfall. I wonder if it's setting me apart now.

"I always feel like I've got a foot on each side of the mountain," I say.

"I can see that. A lot of people say that about the king."

The comment takes me by surprise, because I've never considered Grey feeling the same way. Maybe I look startled, because Malin shrugs and adds, "He's the king of Emberfall, but he's married to *their* queen."

And they don't want him here.

An ice-cold breeze blows through the open doors to the arena, chilling the sweat on my arms and making me shiver. The torches flicker and sputter as the air catches them. A faint trace of magic touches my senses, and I straighten to standing, snapping my head toward the doorway before I recognize the power. *Nakiis.*

Malin is already on his feet beside me. "Is it the one from the woods?"

"Nakiis. Yes." I pause. "He should keep his distance," I add, hoping the scraver will hear me. The last thing I need is anyone thinking a scraver has followed me to the palace. I look at Malin. "How did you know?"

"The cold. That happened before, too."

Just as he says it, the cool wind slips out of the arena and the magic dissipates from the air. I let out a breath of relief.

Malin is studying me. "Do you use magic?" he says. "When you fight?"

"Do you mean now?"

"I mean ever." He pauses, then casts a quick glance around, and his voice quiets, though we're still alone. "If you're allowed to say."

I shake my head. "No. I haven't had magic long, and the king gave it to me as a means of protection. So I can heal myself—or others, obviously. I can start a fire if I need to. I've never . . . I've never used it as a *weapon*. I've never used it in violence."

Though . . . I have. Once. Lord Alek pinned me against the work table at Jax's forge, his fingers pressing into my neck. He threatened to have his guards tie me down and add a few more stripes to my back. Even the memory has enough potency to steal my breath. When it happened, I let my magic flare and set his jacket on fire.

He stabbed me in the ribs in retaliation. I barely had enough magic to heal the damage.

That breeze winds through the arena again, but this time it's slower, just the tiniest flicker of magic against my senses.

Not now, Nakiis, I think. *I'm fine.*

I put a hand on the hilt of my sword. "Round five?"

Malin nods and draws. He's strong, and even though he's tiring, he fights hard. I've enjoyed the challenge of training with him this week. I block an attack that disarmed me two days ago, and his eyes flare in surprise.

"I'm learning," I grind out. I barely have time to block before he gets inside my guard.

"Me too," he says, and I smile.

As our match drags on, I become distantly aware that we're not alone in the arena any longer. A few voices echo, and shadows bounce off the walls. Some soldiers have leaned against the railing to watch. But Malin doesn't lose focus, so I don't either. Actually, his fighting changes, his strikes becoming a little more aggressive, his movements a little more precise.

That, more than anything, tells me that Grey is among the soldiers who've found their way into the training hall.

I should give Malin an opening. Let him have a win, because I know he wants to impress the king. That twisting spike in my heart won't let me. *I* don't want to fail in front of Grey either.

I redouble my own efforts, even as sweat drips into my eyes. Our swords meet over and over again, the ring of steel echoing in the arena, until his blade scrapes down the length of mine and he tries to hook my hilt to disarm me.

I hold fast, and for a moment it's a sheer battle of grappling strength. He grabs hold of my armor with his free hand, but I see it coming, and I grab hold of his before he can throw me off balance. Every muscle in my body is taut, and an equal amount of strain is reflected in Malin's eyes. We're both breathing harder than we were before. He tries for leverage, but there's none. I dig my boot into the dirt and try the same, but he doesn't move.

"Enough," calls a voice from somewhere behind me, and I was right. It is the king. "It's a draw."

I grit my teeth and tighten my grip. Malin doesn't let up either. There was a clear point where this fight stopped being entirely friendly.

Suddenly, there's an inch of give, and we tussle a little, but he's too strong. Or maybe I am. We end up locked in place again, but we're both practically panting from the effort.

Stars flicker in my blood, my magic ready and willing.

"I said *enough*," says Grey, and he's closer. "Fall back."

Fine. I let go of Malin's armor and jerk free just as he does the same. The waiting magic flitters away into nothing. We sheathe our weapons, our breathing echoing in the arena. For a moment, we're both a little agitated at the unfinished fight, but then Malin offers me his hand.

"Good match," he says with a smile.

The aggression disappears from the air as easily as the magic did. I clasp his hand in return. "Good match."

Grey glances between us. "It *was* a good match," he says, and to my surprise, his voice is mild. "You're well paired."

Malin straightens. "Thank you, Your Majesty."

I don't even look at the king. "You should have let us finish," I say, and I sound petulant. I can practically hear Malin inwardly sigh.

"I would have," Grey says. "But the Queen's Guard needs the arena."

Oh.

He continues, "Clear the space. Get some water. Tycho . . ."

I brace myself.

"When you're ready," he finishes, "come walk with me."

Well, that sounds foreboding. I set my jaw and inhale through my teeth, because I'm ready *now.*

But Malin grabs my bracer and drags me toward the railing, and he even pulls me a cup of water from the ladle and bucket stationed there.

"Drink," he says. "Cool off."

He sounds like he means that in more than one way, and he's probably right. I scowl and drink. Malin seems satisfied by my obedience, so he pulls himself a cup of water and turns to lean beside me. Half the Queen's Guard have filtered into the arena to run drills of their own, but Nolla Verin, the queen's sister, has followed them to talk to their captain.

I think of Callyn and Nora in the hallway, how Nora seemed so excited to be training with Verin, while Callyn . . . did not. It reminds

268

me of Jax's uncertainty about his new position in Emberfall. I can relate to them both. For a flicker of time, I wish I were going to be here longer than a night, because I'd offer to help Callyn. Verin comes on strong, but I know her moves, and I know what will take her by surprise.

She sees me by the railing and calls in Syssalah, "Tycho! I heard you were back. Do you have time for another match?"

"Not tonight," I call back. "Grey is waiting for me."

A light glints in her eye. "How about your soldier friend? I need to warm up a bit before I begin training."

Malin's eyebrows go up, but his eyes have lit with clear interest. "Is my Syssalah rough or is she taunting me?" he says under his breath.

I pull another cup of water. "Oh, she's definitely taunting you."

He grins. "If you spar with me," he calls back in Syssalah, "you not make training."

I choke on my water. "Malin!" I sputter.

Some of the guards inhale sharply and stare—but others chuckle knowingly. One whistles low through her teeth.

Verin laughs and strides out of the arena, the firelight from the torches glinting on her glossy black braids. "Let's take it to the fields, then, soldier."

Malin sets down his cup and looks ready to follow her. I can't decide if this is the worst idea of all time or if it's a match I wouldn't mind seeing.

"I'll just plan to collect you from the infirmary later," I say.

"So the beautiful soldier is going to try to kill me? You say that like I'll mind."

I give him a look.

"What?" He hits me lightly on the arm. "We don't *all* have a blacksmith waiting on the other side of the mountain."

My heart twists when he says that, but it makes me smile. "You don't know who she is?"

"Should I?"

I want to grin, but I notice Grey waiting for me by the doorway to the training fields, so I don't. I clap Malin on the shoulder instead. "That's Nolla Verin. Sister to the queen."

Then I turn to find my fate, leaving Malin to face his.

CHAPTER 28

TYCHO

It's fully dark when I stroll across the training fields with Grey. The Queen's Guard have begun their exercises, and swords clash in the arena behind us. Malin and Nolla Verin have disappeared into one of the groves with a torch, but I have no doubt we'll hear clashing swords from their direction, too. The breeze is stronger out here, and Nakiis's magic is in the air again. Nothing about it is a relief, because Grey would definitely not be pleased to find him here.

My shoulders are tense, waiting for him to talk, to tell me whatever Jake found so I can carry news back to Rhen. A few weeks ago, I dreaded the idea of being sent away, but now I long for it. The tension is almost unbearable. It's not *all* between me and the king, but I can't fix any of it.

But Grey doesn't give me orders. He doesn't say anything at all.

Eventually, we reach the far corner of the training fields, where it's very dark, the sounds of distant swordplay very muffled. We're closer to the soldier barracks than the palace now, and a long-buried memory comes to me. I was a recruit, and General Solt—then an army captain—caught me sneaking back after skipping drills. I hadn't been doing it maliciously; I was just hiding with Noah. But Grey found Solt cornering me and he knocked him away.

I was ashamed of the reprimand—but the more potent part of the memory is remembering how Grey had my back. Knowing he would defend me when it *mattered*.

I haven't felt that way in a while, and I don't know when I stopped.

A small fence divides the training fields from the paths to the barracks, and that's where Grey stops. He leans against the fence in the darkness.

"We're far enough from everything, Tycho." His voice is mild, and not without emotion. "Say whatever you mean to say to me."

It's not how I expected him to begin, and I fall back a step before I can stop myself. "Your Majesty—"

"Don't do that."

I close my mouth and go still. Insects sing in the trees around us.

Eventually, he's the one who speaks. "The last time we were alone, you wanted to punch me in the face. Do you still?"

That was weeks ago. I remember the burning rage in my chest when we were racing to save Lia Mara and Sinna—and I was trying to stop him from killing Jax.

But fine. If he wants to start *this* way, I will.

"A little," I say. "Are you offering again?"

"No."

"Do you want to punch *me* in the face?"

"Tycho."

"You seem like you do," I say. "I rode hard to get here. I risked my life to *warn you*, and you chastised me in front of Malin."

"You're right," he says, and his voice is a little rough. "I shouldn't have. Forgive me."

The apology takes me by surprise.

272

Maybe it's obvious, because he adds, "I mean that truly. I shouldn't have. Everything here is . . ." His eyes skip away. "Very tense."

I take a breath, because I can hear what he's not saying, and I don't want to leave the words hanging between us. "I've heard about Lia Mara," I say carefully. Despite everything, I don't want to wound him. Not with this. "That things are . . . difficult between you."

"She cares about her people. So do I, but . . ." He sighs, and sorrow flickers across his expression. "It seems *everyone* fears magic right now."

When he says the words, another breeze laden with magic swirls between us, and Grey goes rigid.

"Is that your scraver?" he says pointedly. "You told me to double the guards around the palace. If he's followed you here, it's not making anything less tense."

Your scraver. I fold my arms. "It sounds like you do want to punch me."

"Stop it. Nakiis is risking himself by drawing close to the palace." Grey says this so plainly that I know he's not just warning me. "Fears have already been stoked in the city. Archers *will* shoot him on sight. If he's seen, it would cause a panic."

"I'm not sure what you think I can do about it. He's got claws and fangs and he can tear a man apart in seconds. Short of shooting him down myself, I can't control where he goes."

The king's expression is unyielding. He says nothing, but Grey doesn't have to say the words. I hear them just the same.

You let him out of a cage to begin with.

No matter how many times he denies it, I know Grey would have done the same.

"Nakiis isn't responsible for the attacks," I say.

"How do you know? You don't know who this Xovaar is, and you have no idea who he could be working with. You have no idea what their conflict might be. Nakiis has been part of an attack on a kingdom before. Rhen tells me you don't even fully know what you've sworn to him."

I was ready to remind the king that Nakiis saved *him* in Briarlock, but those words freeze me in place.

Rhen tells me.

This feels like a betrayal. Like a trick. Prince Rhen *knew* I'd refused to tell Grey about what I traded for the scraver's assistance. When the prince asked if I trusted him enough to share the details of my conversation with Nakiis, I *did*.

My jaw is tight now.

"You swore a week of service to him?" Grey demands. "Without even knowing what he'd demand?"

"My father sold me to Worwick for five years. A week felt pretty short."

"That's not the same."

"It's exactly the same!" I snap. "I've sworn my entire *life* to you, so surely you can spare a few days."

"I didn't bring you out here to argue with you." His voice goes quiet again, and something about it tugs at me.

I sigh and run a hand over the back of my neck. "Look, I know you don't want me here. Just write your letter to Rhen or tell me whatever Jake said, and I'll be out of your way. I can be gone in an hour."

His eyebrows flicker into a frown, and he studies me in the darkness for an eternal moment. "I'm not sending you back to Ironrose, Tycho."

My heart seems to stop. The world goes still. Even the insects fall silent—or maybe that's just the roaring in my ears. The sky spins for a second and then rights itself. "*What?*"

"Why on earth are you surprised? You told me yourself that scravers are seeking magesmiths. I'm not sending you on a four-day ride *alone*—"

"Then send me back with guards!"

"So I should risk the lives of *others* because you've made yourself a target?"

274

Rage swells in me so hot and fast that I can't contain it. I stride forward and shove him in the chest so hard that he falls back a step, but he grabs hold of my wrists, and we scuffle.

"Enough!" he barks. "Stand down!"

The part of my brain that spent years as a soldier almost has me snap to attention.

The part of my brain that's colored with fury is already swinging a fist.

I nearly catch him in the jaw, but he blocks, shoving my arm wide. It leaves me open, and I don't even see him move. I just feel a blow, and then I feel the ground. Blood and dirt are bitter on my tongue, and for a wild moment, I can't breathe.

I really didn't expect him to hit me.

He caught me in the side, just under the base of my rib cage, and it takes a minute to force air into my lungs. It doesn't matter. My fingers curl into fists in the dirt, because I want to go after him again.

"Don't do this, Tycho."

Is that a warning? A threat? A plea? I can barely process the words. My heart keeps twisting, rebelling against the fact that he won't let me leave. I might as well be a prisoner. Jax went to Ironrose, and now I'm stuck *here*.

He's taken so much from you, and I don't think he's even aware of it.

Jax was right. Maybe I do hate the king.

I finally shove myself to my feet. Grey is watchful, ready for me to come at him again. We're both fully armed, and it's obvious that I'm not the only one carrying around a chest full of anger. Stars flicker in my vision, magic flaring, responding to my emotion.

Grey is watching me steadily, his eyes narrowed, and I know he senses it.

But a cool breeze whips between us, full of power. Nakiis's voice reaches my ears, carried by the magic.

—Not yet, Tycho. Not yet.

The words wrap around me like a warning and a promise, the wind swirling away as quickly as it came.

Somehow, it takes some of the tension with it. I choke out a breath and force my hands away from my weapons. My fingers unclench. When I blink again, those sparks and stars scatter. Just me and the king on the field.

The silence between us is suddenly very loud.

"I don't want to fight with you," Grey says.

"Oh, you don't?" I say, and my voice is rough.

"I'm keeping my people safe, Tycho." He's so still, so quiet. "That includes you."

"Is that what you were doing the *last* time you forced me to stay here? Keeping me safe?"

His mouth forms a line, but he says nothing.

I don't want to look at him now. "How will you send word to Rhen?"

What I really want to know is if I'll be able to send word to Jax.

"I won't," he says. "Not yet. There are many things in motion that I cannot stop, and I will not cause more alarm and unrest. You were sent to take residence in Emberfall, and then you showed up in the middle of the night. There's already enough gossip about *that*."

I scowl but keep my mouth shut.

"And if you're here," he adds tersely, "you would do well to stay out of the public eye. Definitely avoid use of your magic. As you know, things at court are . . . very uncertain right now."

I glare at him. "Stop acting like all of this is my fault," I growl. "*I* didn't break your marriage. You did."

Sudden rage flares in his eyes, and I almost regret the words. We're both a little too angry, a little too raw, and I just struck back with equal force.

276

But then I see a flicker of the true pain behind his anger, and it's as deep and potent as the moment he told me they lost the baby.

That twists at my heart in a way I don't expect, and it steals my breath. "Grey," I say. "Wait. Please. I didn't—"

"*Stop*," he says. "Stop *now*."

These words are so tight and sharp that they draw me up short. I swallow everything I want to say.

"You are relieved of your duties," he says, and his expression is as fierce as I've ever seen it. "You will remain on the palace grounds until I give you further orders. You are not to go beyond the gates, and you are not to use your magic. Am I clear?"

His voice is so cold that it almost makes me shiver. We both know what to do with violence, but this . . . this is different. I don't know if it's better or worse than when we were throwing punches.

I do know we've both been pushed far beyond our limits, and there might be no undoing any of this.

So I give him a sharp nod. "Yes, Your Majesty."

He takes a step toward me, and the starlight glints in his eyes. "And if you ever call magic to fight me, Tycho, you will not be able to walk it back."

I stare back at him. "Understood."

He turns and strides away, leaving me alone in the darkness.

CHAPTER 29

CALLYN

After I put Sinna into bed, leaving her with a stack of storybooks and an equally tired Nora, I return to the nursery to put things in order. To my surprise, I find the queen in the darkened room, standing at the window, gazing down at the fields beyond.

"Your Majesty," I say in surprise. "I can light a lantern—"

"No." She doesn't look away from the window. "When Grey first came to Syhl Shallow, I used to stand at this window and watch for him when he was with the soldiers."

I hesitate in the doorway, wondering if I should give her privacy. She's so still, her eyes locked on whatever she's watching.

I haven't seen her all day, and I think of the way Nora and I quite literally ran into Lord Tycho in the hallway earlier, how he seemed so surprised that there were rumors about his presence. It makes me wonder if *she* even knew he was here.

"Should I leave you alone?" I say quietly.

"You don't have to."

I hesitate, then join her. The training fields are mostly dark, only illuminated by random torches here and there. But as my eyes adjust to the darkness, I make out two men standing far across the fields, close to the fence line that leads to the army barracks. They're not close to any of the torches, so I can't determine who they are, but based on the heavy note in the queen's voice, I assume one is the king.

"I used to leave all the lanterns lit," she adds. "So he could see me watching."

But now the room is dark.

I bite at my lip, and I think of the moment my sister launched herself at the queen, giving her a hug in that moment of sorrow.

I can't be as forward as my sister, but I sense that same sorrow behind her words. Before I can reconsider, I reach out and take hold of the queen's hand.

She looks at me in surprise—but she grips tight. Her eyes are gleaming in the shadows.

When she finally speaks, her voice is barely more than a whisper. "He hasn't talked to me in two days."

As soon as the words are out, she presses her free hand to her mouth and stares back at the fields again. A slow tear rolls down one cheek.

I follow her gaze. Those two figures haven't moved. I can identify the king now, because he's taller, a bit more broad through the shoulders.

I knew he wasn't spending his nights in the royal chambers, but I didn't realize it had gone so far that he wasn't speaking to her.

I'm probably not the best person to offer support. They're the king and queen, and their marriage is more complex than any random romantic pairing in Briarlock.

Not that I'm any kind of expert anyway. I had a longstanding crush on my best friend, who likely feels no attraction for girls at all, and my last intimate encounter was with a man who's still plotting against the king.

But despite all the complexity of who she is, the queen's sadness is simple. She's a woman at odds with the man she loves.

Another tear follows the first.

I give her hand a gentle squeeze. "We could light a lantern now."

Her breathing hitches, but her fingers still clutch mine. "No." Her voice is still whisper-quiet. "I don't want him to know."

Then it's like she realizes she's standing here crying, with *me* of all people, because she pulls her hand away and swipes at her cheeks.

"Forgive me," she says. "I should be more composed."

"You should be whatever you want to be," I say. "You're the queen."

She laughs a little through her tears. "Well, no one expects the queen to be standing at a window, mooning over her husband."

I hesitate. "May I ask . . . ?" But then I stop.

She swipes at her cheeks again, but she doesn't stop looking out the window. "Go ahead, Callyn."

"Why two days? Did . . . did something happen?"

"I told him that fears of magic have escalated to a point where what *I* want and what *my people* want might differ."

"And he walked away?"

She begins to shake her head . . . but then she nods. "I thought . . . I thought we would find a way to move forward. But maybe there isn't one. He does not want to come between me and my people. He does not want to be the cause of conflict in Syhl Shallow. He said if his continued presence is putting me and Sinna at risk, it puts everyone at risk." Her voice breaks. "And I couldn't deny it."

Then she presses her hands to her eyes, and she's crying in earnest.

Clouds above. My heart is pounding at what she said—but I can't stand here and do nothing. I step forward and wrap my arms around her.

She grips me back, sobbing into my shoulder.

"I'm sorry," I murmur. "I'm so sorry."

280

I don't know how long I hold her, but when she finally lifts her head, she looks wrung out and raw.

I gesture to the small table where we play games with little Sinna. "Sit," I say. "Do you want me to call for tea?"

Again, she shakes her head, but then it turns into a nod. I step away to speak to one of the guards outside the nursery, and then I return to her side.

She glances at the window again. "He's gone," she whispers.

I look, and there's only one man left on the field now.

"Do you know who he was talking to?" I say.

"Tycho." Her voice is so rough. She swallows. "I haven't seen him. I didn't even know he was here until I overheard the guards—" Her voice almost breaks, but she catches herself. "Well. Once I knew the truth, Sinna begged me to go see him. And I almost did. I love him like a brother. But . . . but he's always been so close to Grey. I don't know what he'd think."

I hesitate. "I saw him in the hall earlier. I . . . I don't think he thinks anything. He seemed worried about you."

She gestures at the window and her eyes fill again. "Maybe he *was* . . . but I'm sure Grey has told him everything. He might not want to see me at all." She takes a steadying breath. "And it's quite telling that I've been given no information about whatever news he brought to the king."

My eyes are wide. "I could send word . . . ask him . . ."

"No." She shakes her head decisively. "If my people do not want me to show any favoritism for magic, I shouldn't visit with Tycho either."

I put a hand over hers again, but I feel woefully out of place here. "Should I fetch one of your advisers . . . or perhaps Verin—"

"Definitely not Nolla Verin." She snorts, and for the first time, a bit of anger slips through the tears. "My sister is *pleased*," she says. "She thinks I should tell Grey to take his army and march back to the other side of the border."

My heart stumbles when she says that. "Are you going to?" I ask, my voice hushed.

"Of course not." But there's something to the way she says it that tells me she's not quite sure. Her voice goes small again. "But I didn't expect him to withdraw from me so completely. I know he loves me. I know he loves Sinna. But I . . . I worry that he might be preparing to leave on his own."

If the king leaves, I wonder what that would do to the alliance between Emberfall and Syhl Shallow. He's the king there, and she's the queen here. But if they part ways, I have no idea what would happen. We were at war before they married. My mother *died* in that war. So did Alek's.

Is the presence of magic so terrible that the citizens of Syhl Shallow are willing to go back to *war* to get rid of it?

Or . . . maybe a war has already begun, and I simply haven't acknowledged it. I think of the terrible battle in Briarlock. Does the queen think that kind of attack will continue if the king is still here in Syhl Shallow?

Fears of magic have escalated to a point where what I *want and what* my people *want might differ.*

Yes. She does.

But Emberfall won many victories by virtue of the magic that flows through the king's veins. He might love *her*, but if the people attack, what's to stop him from using that magic against us all?

I stroke at the pendant under my tunic, wondering how much of this will turn into gossip as more and more people realize how long it's been since the king and queen were seen together.

I look at the queen, thinking of that moment in Briarlock when Tycho declared that people who'd worn the specially charmed Iishellasan rings would have access to his same magic.

"*You* have magic," I whisper to her.

She looks away. "No, I don't, Callyn."

But she does. I know she does. I watched her heal Nora in Briarlock, with a beautiful scraver lending magic to assist.

Unless . . . unless *I'm* the one who healed Nora. I've felt that same magic flow through *my* veins, and I know I didn't imagine it.

I still haven't admitted that to the queen, but it's a secret we both carry. I speak carefully. "Perhaps if the people knew magic existed in their queen, you could—"

"They'd try to kill me again." Her voice is full of iron when she says this. "They'd try even harder. They'd blame him for poisoning me with his abilities." She pauses, and her eyes bore into mine. "I have *no magic*, Callyn."

That's not a declaration. It's a warning.

I think of the king healing my injuries every time Verin is too rough, or the way he showed me how to block a punch. I think of how gentle he is with little Sinna—the same gentleness I'm sure he shows toward the queen. It's a completely different side to the man than I ever considered—and never would have *seen*, if not for everything that happened in Briarlock. I can understand why so many people hate him, because I did, too. For so long! But I know now that a lot of our fear of magic is also wrapped up in prejudice against a country that killed so many of our people.

But I try to imagine how people would respond to the *queen* if she demonstrated these same benefits. If she used *her* gentle kindness when healing the people or protecting her daughter.

Is she right? Would they try to kill her?

Or would they see the benefits of magic instead of just the harms?

Her eyes are fierce, though. On this, it's clear she won't yield.

So I nod, matching her gaze with equal intensity. "Yes, Your Majesty. I must have been mistaken."

A flicker of worry lights in her eyes. "You've said nothing to Alek about . . . about what might have happened?"

I shake my head quickly. "Nothing at all."

"Do you still trust him?"

I think of the way he pressed his mouth to mine. The way he convinced me of his innocence so easily.

I spent hours lying in bed trying to unravel his words, looking for somewhere he might have tricked me.

But there was nothing. At no point did he have to *seduce* me, as he said.

I nod. "On this, I do."

"Then go to see him tomorrow. Tell him where things stand." Another tear slides down her cheek, but her eyes are clear and sharp. Her voice has lost any hint of a tremor, and this time she reaches out to squeeze *my* hand.

It reminds me of the night I found her in my barn, when everything seemed bleak and hopeless—and she stood up to the soldiers who were threatening her and her child. Queen Lia Mara might be in distress, but she's still in control.

"Yes, Your Majesty," I say. "Should I tell him anything else?"

She nods. "Let him know his queen doesn't need sanctuary. Instead, I might need a powerful ally—and a lot sooner than I thought."

CHAPTER 30

TYCHO

I don't know how long I lie alone in the grass, but everything about my conversation with the king weighs heavily on my heart, and I don't want to move. I'm flat on my back, my hands under my head, the cool night air soaking into my bones. The sounds of distant swordplay have long since gone silent, but I have no desire to go back to the palace. The night sky presses down, the stars stretching wide overhead.

I wonder if Jax is awake in Emberfall, staring at the same sky.

He likely expects me to be on my way back now.

And I simply . . . won't return.

Again.

My throat feels tight. Jax doesn't deserve that. But . . . neither do I.

Overhead, the stars go dark, and I blink, confused for a moment. Wings beat against the stars, and a gust of cold wind blows across the training fields.

"You lie exposed," Nakiis says, and though he's nearly invisible against the night sky, the wind carries his voice right to me. "I could gut you without effort."

"Go ahead."

He soars low, and I think he's going to land in the grass beside me, but instead, he drops right onto my chest. His knees slam into my breastplate, and it knocks the wind right out of me.

I give a little cough to shock air back into my lungs. "I wasn't really serious," I grind out.

He leans down close, until his elbows settle on the ground, his claws pressing into my neck. His wings are half splayed, as if he could take flight at any second. His balance would be impressive if his knees weren't driving the edge of my armor into my shoulders.

"Ah . . . well met?" I say.

He smiles. Or at least, I *think* he does. I catch a glimpse of his fangs. The stars barely add a gleam to his black eyes.

"You've never really been afraid of what I am," he says.

He's right, in a way. I was never afraid of his father either. The scravers are fascinating and beautiful and equally terrifying—the way a wolf or a mountain lion is terrifying. Magnificent from a distance, but dangerous up close.

"I'm not afraid of you," I say. "Anyone who's ever *truly* hurt me has been human."

Nakiis looks back at me and says nothing to that. The wind rustles the feathers in his wings and whips at his hair. His skin is so dark that he could be a shadow.

"You stopped me from using magic against Grey," I add. "Thank you."

He scoffs. "You have no control yet. I would have ended up fighting your battle for you."

I stare up into those black eyes. "You really shouldn't be here. There are guards who patrol these fields. They'll shoot you if they see you."

"I can hear when they come this way."

Of course he can. "Could you let me up?"

He doesn't move.

"Or by all means," I add, "make yourself comfortable."

Nakiis seems to lean even closer. "I understand that *you* are now the one in a cage." A cold wind swirls around us, full of his magic.

"No. I'm not." But I think of everything that happened, and sudden emotion fills my throat. I press my fingers into my face and swallow, and I hate that my eyes feel damp. "Nakiis, please."

"Do you wish to flee? I could help you."

I lower my hands. "What?"

"I can see and hear the guards. I can draw their attention and mask the sounds of your departure."

My heart skips hard. I imagine it, fetching Mercy in the dead of night, sneaking past the guard station.

But I can't.

"No," I say.

"Why?"

"Because . . . because it's *treason*." I blink away my emotion. "We can't all fly away when we need to. I wish I could."

His wings flare, snapping wide to catch the wind, and his weight suddenly vanishes from my chest. I think he's going to prove my point and lose himself to the night, but he lands beside me, settling in the grass.

I sit up to face him, drawing my legs up to sit cross-legged. He's on his knees again, sitting back on his heels, his wings folded tightly. This might be the closest he's ever been without claws and fangs bared. Even when I healed his wounds, he was wound up tighter than a spring, ready to attack if I threatened him.

Now that he's not on top of me, I can see that he's wearing calfskin trousers, with a dagger belt wound around his waist, and a short blade at his left hip. A longer one is strapped to his right thigh.

"You're armed," I say in surprise. I've never seen him wear a weapon. He hardly needs them.

His eyes hold mine. "Iishellasan steel," he says evenly.

287

Meaning those weapons can cause injuries that can't be healed with magic.

"Anyone who's ever truly harmed *me* has been a magesmith," he adds.

I frown, remembering the way he usually keeps his distance. "I'm sorry. In Briarlock, when we shot you, I swear, I didn't know—"

"Tycho. I am not armed because of *you*."

I let out a breath. "Are you armed because of the king?"

He says nothing—but that says enough.

If Grey isn't happy about Nakiis being here, I *know* he wouldn't be happy about him having weapons like this. When the Truthbringers attacked in Briarlock, Grey locked away all the Iishellasan steel that we were able to find. I wonder how much more there is.

"Grey won't hurt you," I say. "I've told you that before."

"If you draw me into battle with him, I am certain he would prove you wrong."

"You really don't have to risk yourself defending me."

"So I am to watch you fall as you call magic with little skill or practice? Your vow to me goes unfulfilled because you were reckless?"

"Ah." I lean back on my hands. "You're just protecting me so I can keep up my end of our bargain."

He surveys me silently again.

"I don't believe that," I say. "When Grey burned out his magic, you brought me food and water before I ever agreed to help you."

I remember that night so clearly. Grey was unconscious. His horse was dead. Mercy was lame. I was starving and thirsty and everything was terrible. When Nakiis showed up, I thought he was going to kill me— but instead he brought me full water skins and a goose for me to roast over the fire.

"I led your horse through the woods, too," he says. "When you were in no shape to ride."

I frown. "When?"

"After you let that man stab a hole in your chest." He scoffs again. "The day after we fought in the arena. Did you never think to let your magic recover before engaging in another battle?"

For a second, I have no idea what he's talking about, and my mind is spinning. I've only been stabbed once, but Nakiis had nothing to do with it. "Are you talking about the night I fought with Alek?"

"Yes."

I realign my memories, shuffling through what happened. It was the night after I broke Nakiis out of his cage. By the time I ran into Alek, I was exhausted and my magic had been depleted. When he stabbed me, I barely survived. I remember riding out of Briarlock, dazed from blood loss, but after that, the night is a complete blank.

Grey said Mercy carried my unconscious body up to the palace gates. I was covered in snow and soaked in blood. They all thought I was dead.

All this time, I thought Mercy found her own way home.

I can't stop staring at Nakiis. Those black eyes are staring back at me implacably.

"Why?" I finally ask. "Why did you help me?"

"Do you need to ask? Why did you let me out of the cage?"

I don't know what to say. The answer seems obvious, but . . . maybe it's not.

Maybe he feels the same way. It's weird, this wary trust that's formed between us.

"If you are trapped in the palace," he eventually says, "it may be difficult for me to return. To find you when I need you."

"I won't be *trapped*," I say, though I already feel shackled by Grey's orders. I have to shake it off or I'll tell Nakiis to gut me again. "I've been ordered to stay on the grounds, but I'll be allowed to train. And I have to keep Mercy fit. There are trails into the mountains that surround the palace. If I start making regular runs with Mercy, I don't think anyone would be suspicious."

He considers this. "If you *train* alone, you must be cautious with your magic. I will find you when I can."

"I could whistle for you," I say.

He bares the edge of his fangs. "You could *whistle* for me?"

I really meant no offense, but he sounds so affronted that I smile. "Sure." I whistle low, through my teeth. "Like a dog."

He tackles me to the ground, but for the first time, it's not violent. I'm not sure it's *playful*, because his claws land over my neck again—but it's rough-and-tumble in a way that makes me think of Malin, and I laugh under my breath. My heart still aches from everything that's happened with the king and with Jax, but I'm glad to discover that Nakiis is becoming . . .

A friend? Not quite. But he's becoming *something*.

"All right, all right," I drawl. "Put your claws away. I won't whistle."

He lets me up, his claws dragging against my skin, but there's no threat to it. I brush dirt and grass out of my hair as the wind recedes, and I think about how desperately he bargained for a week of my help—after he'd been bound and tortured by a magesmith once before. How every time he's been in my presence, he's either kept his distance, or he's pinned me to the ground with fangs and claws.

I know what it's like to be desperate. I know what it's like to feel *vulnerable*.

"You didn't need to bind me with a vow," I say quietly. "If you truly need my help, I'll help you. Just tell me what it is. What you need."

Wind whips across the fields, ruffling his wings, the cold sneaking under my armor. He inhales like he's going to speak, but then his head snaps around. I follow his gaze to see shadows shifting in the distance. New torches are being lit by guards and soldiers as they change shifts and positions.

290

I drop my voice and turn back. "You should go before you're—"

But the scraver is already gone.

By the time I've disarmed and returned to my quarters, it's late, and the hall guards tell me that Malin retired over an hour ago. When I tap lightly on his door, he answers. He looks like he might have been asleep, because he's shirtless, in drawstring trousers, and his hair is a little mussed up. A line of bruises crawls up the side of his chest, and a scrape along his jaw turns into yet another bruise where it meets his cheek. He also has three long stripes across his bicep that have been stitched up with field sutures.

I wince. "Silver hell. Was it worth it?"

"Every second of it. The pain is a good distraction." I'm not sure what that means, but Malin steps back and holds open the door. "Come in."

"I don't want to disturb you—"

"You're not."

He seems a little rough-edged, and I wonder what Verin said to go along with their violent sparring. I enter the room and the door falls closed. The fire has fallen low, and only one candle is lit.

"I truly won't keep you." I hesitate, because admitting this feels like a failure, but Malin got me here, and he deserves the truth. "The king has relieved me of my duties. I thought you should know."

"I do know," he says. "The king has relieved me of mine."

That shocks me still. "Malin," I breathe.

"It's known that I arrived with you. We traveled alone for almost a week. He doesn't want more gossip or uncertainty among the ranks, especially as these scraver attacks continue."

His voice is even, but now I understand the undercurrent of agitation. He spent a week risking his life to get here, hoping for the chance to prove his worth in front of the king.

And now he's been relieved of his duties.

Because of me.

I take a long breath and run a hand back through my hair. "Forgive me. I should have—"

"Stop. You can make it up to me by asking the guards to have a tavern's worth of liquor sent up here."

I smile, a little sadly. "You don't know all the words for *drinking*?"

"Oh, I do. I just didn't want them to know I was angry."

At least this is a task I can accomplish without failure. I ask the hall guards to send for enough spirits to drown a horse twice, and they exchange a glance, but they obey. Before long, servants have brought a wide selection of wines and liquors and ales, along with a platter of bread with slabs of cheese and an arrangement of sliced fruit and sugared nuts.

Malin's eyes go wide. "Yes," he says. "You definitely did that better than I would."

"I should leave you to your . . . ah, *rest*," I say to him.

"What? No. Stay. Drink with me."

"I generally don't drink very much." A lot of that is Grey's influence, because he doesn't either. I've never wanted to disappoint him.

Malin pulls a cork free from a small brown bottle. "Want to start?"

I hesitate, but defiance curls in my chest, hot and welcome. I choose a small copper flask. "You go, I go."

"Exactly." He drinks right from the bottle, then coughs in surprise and winces. "*Whoa.* I forgot that the palace won't have cheap liquor."

I laugh and take a sip from the flask, swallowing fire.

This is probably a bad idea.

Right now, that makes it a great one. I take another, longer sip, and then I drop into one of Malin's chairs and press the cool metal of the flask to my forehead.

I'm not sending you back to Ironrose, Tycho.

You are relieved of your duties.

If you ever call magic to fight me, you will not be able to walk it back.

I tip back the flask and drain it.

Malin laughs ruefully. "Are you *sure* you don't drink very much?"

I really don't. My thoughts are already beginning to drift and loosen. "I'm definitely going to regret this tomorrow."

"Me too." He grins and takes another sip, then winces, pressing a hand to his bruised side. "I think Verin broke a rib. She said she can't wait to do it again, though—so I think she likes me."

I look up. "Want me to fix it?"

The smile slips off his face. "You're not allowed to use magic."

I put the cap back on the flask and toss it onto the table. "I've been relieved of my duties and confined to the palace grounds. What else is he going to take?" I lean forward, bracing my forearms on my knees. The world already feels a little fuzzy. "But you need to decide now, before I get too drunk. I could leave the bruises on your face, so no one would know."

He stares back at me steadily, and I know he doesn't want to disobey the king. But it's possible he's already in a place where he's not making the best decisions either. We're both a little angry, a little dejected, a little defiant.

"Silver hell," he mutters. He drains his whole bottle and swears, but then he looks back at me and holds out his stitched-up arm. "You go, I go, Tycho."

"Magic?" I say, just to be sure.

Malin gives a short nod. "Magic."

CHAPTER 31

CALLYN

I expect to sit down to breakfast with Alek again, but when I arrive, he tells me that he's called for a carriage, and if I want to talk, I need to accompany him for the morning.

At that, I balk. "The queen asked me to select fabrics today," I say, the excuse I gave little Sinna and my sister—and the same thing they'll hopefully tell anyone else who asks.

"You can certainly select them with one of my master loom workers. Unfortunately, my duties require me to be elsewhere this morning." He pauses very deliberately. "If you'd like to discuss anything *other* than fabrics, you should come along."

"I'm supposed to be with the princess," I tell him. We're standing on his opulent steps, the morning sun shining down. "I can't be gone half the day."

He shrugs. "Suit yourself." A massive violet carriage pulled by two shining horses pulls up beside the smaller one that I arrived in. Alek looks toward the top of the steps, where two servants stand by the doors.

"Navery, show Lady Callyn to the looms. Have Mistress Meah Sene display the—"

I grab his arm. "Alek."

His eyebrows go up, and I flush. I take a step back and keep my hands to myself.

"*My lord,*" I bite out. "You *know* that's not why I came."

"I do." He leans close. "And it would be in your best interest to come with me. I'll send word to the palace."

I stare into his blue eyes. I have no idea how he manages to be so challenging every time I see him.

"Fine," I say.

When we're seated in the carriage, I smooth my hands over the skirts of my robe. He takes the seat opposite me, and the driver cracks a whip.

Alek leans back into the velvet cushions of his seat, which are a deeper purple than the exterior of the carriage. Sheer lavender fabric covers the window, allowing light and air to swirl inside, though we'll be obstructed from view by anyone on the road. I'll never get used to this level of luxury, but Alek looks so natural that I almost can't imagine him anywhere else.

"Why is this in my best interest?" I say to him.

"Because I rather like this jacket and I didn't want you to throw any food at me."

I know he's kidding, but I've never met anyone who's so particular about his clothes. To his credit, I like the jacket he's wearing, too. It's a green so dark that it's almost black, with delicate light green stitching around each button—of which there seem to be a hundred.

"I can throw something else at you," I say. "Where are we going?"

His eyes are piercing. "Tell me what the queen said first."

I think of the queen standing at that window in the dark, watching the king but not wanting him to know.

She's in so much pain. I don't want anyone to cause her any more.

Alek frowns a little. "Do I need to prove myself to you every time, Callyn?"

"You won't even tell me where we're going. Do I need to prove myself to *you*?"

That startles him, but he smiles. "Very well. We're visiting one of the other Royal Houses. I'd like to introduce you to some people who may prove helpful in the future."

I go rigid against the velvet seat. "Really?"

He shrugs again, nonchalant. "Yes. I'm meeting with some of my most important customers. As you and the queen both know, I've lost quite a bit of time while dealing with the king's frivolous claims about my guilt." He pauses. "But these people are important to me for more than one reason."

I drop my voice, even though we're alone in the carriage. "So these are people who are loyal to the Tr—"

"Who are loyal to the *queen*," he says, cutting me off before I can say *Truthbringers*. "I've discovered in recent weeks that certain loyalties to Syhl Shallow may differ." He pauses. "Do you understand?"

He must mean whatever is going on among the Truthbringers that allowed some of them to splinter off and attack the queen—instead of *protecting* her. I swallow and nod.

"Good," he says. "Now tell me what you mean to tell me."

I take a deep breath. "She said she doesn't need sanctuary. She needs allies."

"Indeed. Then it is doubly beneficial that you're going with me. In fact, you should probably join me for all of my visits this week."

I consider that. "As I said, I'm supposed to be *with* the princess every day, especially in the morning. Someone will get suspicious."

"Bring Princess Sinna if you like." His eyes flick skyward. "Bring your sister, too, if she can keep her hands to herself."

"I can't bring the princess," I say. "Not without a full contingent of guards. I don't know if they'd even let me. The king has doubled the patrols around the palace."

His eyes narrow. "Why?"

"I don't know. The queen doesn't even know. But it followed the arrival of Lord Tycho."

"Tycho! The king sent him away. He's come back?"

I nod quickly. "Yesterday. Well before dawn. I only saw him briefly."

He considers this for a while as the scenery flows by the silky window covering.

Eventually, he looks back at me. "If he returned this quickly, something must have happened in Emberfall. Are you certain the queen doesn't know? Or is it that she hasn't told *you*?"

"She doesn't know." This feels so deeply personal, but I'm sure gossip is going to spread soon—if it hasn't already. "They're not speaking at all now."

He stares back at me. "The king and queen?"

I nod. "He's staying elsewhere in the palace. I only see him on the fields or in the training arena now." I hesitate. "The queen told him that she understands her people's distaste for magic, and he stopped speaking to her. She's . . . she's rather distraught."

Alek's eyes have gone cold. "Did he harm her?"

"No! At least—I don't think so." I remember her sobbing on my shoulder. "He's never . . . he's never like *that*. He's very gentle with Sinna, too. I just—" My voice breaks off. This feels like the worst kind of gossip. "I think she's hurt by his *silence*. I don't think she expected him to withdraw."

"If the king is not speaking to the queen, he should have no control of her guards *or* her army. In fact, any Emberish soldiers should be ordered to depart at once."

"No! I don't think she's—"

"Callyn, we were at *war*. If the king has become an adversary, he does not belong in the palace." He looks at the window again. "We must take action sooner than I thought."

I want to recoil, because I know what kind of *action* he's referring to. I think of the queen staring down at those fields. "She doesn't want him to be an adversary," I say quietly.

She wants her husband back.

But I don't say that. I don't think the queen would want me to.

Maybe that's part of the conflict she's feeling: duty to her country, to her *people*, against the duty she feels to the man she loves.

I wonder if my mother felt the same kind of conflict every time she walked out of the bakery to fight a war.

It's the first time I've ever looked at my mother's actions from this perspective, and I selfishly feel like she should have stayed with *us*, her family. I have to shove the thought away because it makes me feel like a terrible person.

"You said she wants *allies*," Alek is saying.

"For Syhl Shallow. Not to kill her husband."

Alek makes an exasperated sound. "You are telling me that our queen is at odds with the king of Emberfall. You said she specifically sent you to ask me for *allies*." He frowns. "I will send word to the queen that you should join me every day. We can say that I am introducing you around society so you will be better suited to take the princess on social visits. The king would likely hate it, but perhaps this will give her an opportunity to keep some secrets from *him*."

"Why?"

"Because," he says, leaning in, "it will give you an opportunity to bring messages from the queen to her most loyal supporters. And it will give them a chance to respond, without any risk of the king discovering her plans."

"What plans?" I demand.

"I know you're unfamiliar with court, but your mother was an officer in the army. You must think strategically. The king has separated himself from the queen, Callyn. Over *magic*. I'm not entirely sure if you're aware what's being said here."

Now *I'm* the one to make an exasperated sound. "What exactly do you think is being said here?"

"Queen Lia Mara may not want an adversary, but she is actively preparing for war."

As the carriage rattles along, my brain won't stop reeling from Alek's warnings. I remember the queen standing in the courtyard of my bakery in Briarlock, declaring to the soldiers who'd kidnapped her that they would regret harming her or her child. She's so vibrant. So strong. I have no doubt that if she wanted to be at war with the king, we would be.

But is Alek right? Is she preparing for that inevitability, despite her sadness? Does she genuinely feel that the people want her to drive King Grey back out of Syhl Shallow? Does she think it would require a *war* to get him to leave?

Would it?

I remember how terrifying it was when Mother had to go off into battle . . . especially since she never returned. Nolla Verin pummels me into the dirt every day, but now I imagine an Emberish soldier doing it instead. I imagine my body lying dead in the dirt somewhere near the border, another soldier eventually carrying this pendant back to my sister, telling her that *I'm* dead, too.

The thought makes my chest tighten. There's a part of me that doesn't want to set foot in the arena ever again. I want to run right back to my bakery, where the most complicated part of my day was making sure Nora didn't get lost in a saucy romance novel while the pastries burned.

But that's cowardly—and it's shoved away by another part of me that feels like I should spend every waking minute in the arena. Maybe if I were better at fighting, I wouldn't be at risk.

Then again, Mother was an exceptional soldier, and she died anyway.

I hate the track of these thoughts.

The carriage comes to a stop, and I turn away from Alek to peer through the gauzy window covering. We've come to another large manor house. This one features bricks of green and yellow, stretching so tall that I can't see the top from inside the carriage, with windows that glitter in the sunlight. We've traveled far, because the mountains don't seem quite as imposing from here. In the distance, I can hear a sharp, repetitive banging, but it's different from what used to echo from Jax's forge.

"Where are we?" I say softly.

"The Fifth House," he says. "You will meet Lady Delmetia Calo." He pauses. "You've seen her before. I recommended your bakery."

That snaps my gaze back around to him, but a footman is already drawing open the door to the carriage, and he's stepping out, offering me his hand.

I hate that I'm always off balance with him.

As we walk, the repetitive banging continues, but it's too far to figure out what it is. "What's that sound?" I say.

"Stonemasons and artisans," he says. "Delmetia's House deals with all forms of masonry and stonework. Her talent can be found all over the Crystal City."

As he says it, I realize that the bricks of the manor aren't just green and yellow, but each one is slightly carved to reveal shadows in lighter and darker colors. We're led through an archway to an outdoor garden backed by more bricks, with a path made of stones inlaid with green jewels.

Flowers bloom everywhere, along the wall, in pots along the path, in a massive spray of color along every archway. It makes for one of the most beautiful spaces I've ever seen. Two women sit at a table in the corner, surrounded by an array of pastries, and at least four glass pitchers, each one sparkling with a different-colored beverage. Six servants wait along the wall, and it seems ridiculous, because there are only four of us here—and I'm fairly certain we could all serve ourselves.

I don't belong here. I'm not a noble, I'm not a spy, I'm not a soldier. I'm better at figuring out if a merchant is trying to overcharge me for a sack of sugar than trying to determine if anyone is an ally or an enemy of the crown. I truly don't think the queen knows what she's doing, because I'm the last person she should have sent to meet with Alek.

But then one of the women stands, and I *do* recognize her as someone who visited the bakery—and more than once. She's an older woman with light brown skin and a waist-length mane of gray hair, along with a stern—though kind—expression. Her hands are full of gleaming rings, with a diamond bracelet dangling from one wrist.

"Lady Callyn," she says, with the slightest emphasis on *Lady*. "I heard you were brought to the palace, and I am pleased to see that our queen recognized your loyalty—and your bravery. I am Delmetia Calo. You may call me Della. We are glad you have chosen to visit the Fifth House." She nods to the other woman, who's easily twenty years younger, with black hair tightly tied back in a braid. "This is Firena, my companion."

I'm still stumbling over her words about loyalty and bravery, but I curtsy to them both. "Thank you," I say. "I'm honored to be here."

"You are *welcome* here. When Alek told us your mother was an army captain, we were surprised that you were left to languish on the border, without any help from the crown."

My eyes snap to Alek's. Is that what he told people? Is that why so many nobles began visiting the bakery?

He looks back at me placidly. "Callyn is very independent," he says. "Her tenacity is admirable. Or maybe it's her courage? I still haven't decided which."

Warmth floods my cheeks. Every word sounds completely sincere. *Augh*, why does he *do* this?

"I believe it's both," Della says. "You told us about the day she stepped in front of a blade for you."

My cheeks flush. I *did* do that. I'd almost forgotten.

It reminds me of the moment in the arena, after Nolla Verin had pummeled me into the dirt, when Alek asked why I have the courage to stand up to *him*, yet not the queen's sister.

Have I been letting her comments destroy my confidence? Have I been letting self-doubt ruin my fire?

Della is still talking. "I've never heard Alek talk about a young woman as much as he talks about *you*, my dear—"

"Wait—really?" My eyes flash to Alek, expecting him to brush this off, but he shrugs, denying nothing.

"*Yes*," says Della. "I'm glad our queen has seen the same courage and tenacity, if you have been assigned to assist with the young princess." Her gaze flicks to the table. "We should sit," she says. "I haven't been to court in weeks, but Alek has told me that tensions are high."

A footman is pulling out a chair for us both, but I hesitate. The queen told me to talk to Alek, but I have no idea how open she'd want me to be with someone else.

Alek reaches out a hand and squeezes mine, and I'm surprised by the warmth there. "As you mentioned," he says, "Lady Callyn is very loyal. She doesn't like to speak out of turn about the royal family."

Della smiles and nods. "I understand." She holds out a hand toward my chair. "All the same, sit. Please."

I sit. Beside me, Alek does the same. As if by some unseen signal, more servants appear. Juice and wine are poured. Sweet rolls are placed on plates beside us. Slices of cheese and fruit follow quickly.

"Thank you," I whisper. I'm the only one who acknowledges them at all.

Alek is looking across the table at Della and Firena. "Callyn may not be able to speak openly, but I can. I believe our queen is still in danger."

My back goes ramrod straight, but I keep my mouth shut.

"I thought as much," Della says. "I have received no invitations to call since the night we demanded that Lord Tycho have his magic stripped away." She pats Firena's hand. "Firena thought it was a signal of displeasure on the queen's part, but then the King's Courier was exiled to Emberfall, so we know more intrigue is afoot."

I have to clamp my mouth shut even harder.

Tycho still has magic! I want to scream. *So does the queen! So do I!*

But I can't say any of that.

"Lord Tycho has returned," Alek is saying. "Under very suspicious circumstances, too." He glances at me. "And apparently the king is not speaking to the queen, which is why our worries are prudent."

I snap my head around and stare at him.

He looks back at me implacably. "Della is loyal to the queen as well, Callyn."

Della nods. "I am. It is disturbing to think that the queen was attacked as a means of capturing the king." Her eyes flick to Alek. "I have never been involved with the Truthbringers, but many of us were alarmed at what happened when she was taken. If the king's magic has made her a target of malfeasance, then we must work to separate them. Lord Tycho was stripped of his magic and sent away, but if the king has brought him back, I am worried that the queen is in even more danger than we thought."

My eyebrows go up. "No—I don't know if that's why Tycho is back—"

"Does it matter?" she says. "The young man can access the king's magic at will, can he not?"

I hesitate. She means that Tycho can access magic with his *rings*, but I know that he's not dependent on them anymore—just like the queen isn't dependent on them anymore. But if I tell them the truth about Tycho, does that mean it would implicate the queen, too? This has all gotten so complicated.

Alek is watching me. "He can," he says.

"And I remember that day at court, when the king was interrogating you"—her lip curls—"how you indicated that Lord Tycho was the one working with these Truthbringers."

I inhale sharply, but Alek cuts me a glance.

"So the king has a magical ally," Della continues, before I can say anything.

"Yes," says Firena. "And our queen may yet be a prisoner in her own home."

I frown. "I don't know if she'd consider herself a prisoner." I shoot a dark look at Alek. "And Tycho risked himself to *save* her in Briarlock, so I don't know that he's allied with the Truthbringers."

"But it seems that the Truthbringers may have divided," says Della. "Don't you think so, Alek?"

"I do," he says. "I believed Lady Clarinas was loyal, but then she and her followers attacked the queen and her daughter. No one has seen her, but she has contacts throughout Syhl Shallow—and she was employed in the palace for a time. She could still have connections who are close to the queen."

I wonder if he means anyone in particular—and then I realize that Lady Clarinas would have known Nolla Verin. Again, I try to make that connection work in my head, but it doesn't quite fit. Maybe I only want her to be a villain because of the way she treats me.

Alek is still talking. "Perhaps Tycho did risk himself to save the queen, but it may have been due to his loyalty to the *king*."

I falter. Last night, Lia Mara said she didn't want to speak with Tycho—for that exact reason: his loyalty to King Grey.

"There have been rumors of magical attacks," says Firena. "From creatures similar to what our armies once faced in Emberfall. Could the king's magic have summoned them as well?"

"Magical *attacks*?" I exclaim.

"You remember the old stories," says Della. She glances at Alek. "What were they called? Surely you had some in your storybooks."

"Scravers," he says, and his voice is cool. He glances at me. "I've heard that they also appeared when the queen was kidnapped. You were there, Callyn. Is there truth to that rumor?"

Scravers. "Yes. But . . . but scravers *helped* the king and queen—"

"Did they? Truly? Or much like Lord Tycho, were they there at the king's summoning because *he* was in danger?"

I think back. The events in Briarlock are so muddled, because I remember the scravers appearing—but I was so focused on Nora, who had a sword thrust through her chest.

"All I know," I say evenly, "is that they helped save my sister's life." I pause. "We were trying to protect the princess, and when we wouldn't let the Truthbringers get to her, a soldier tried to kill Nora instead."

I mean to fling this like an accusation—or maybe a justification. I mean for it to explain that the scravers *did* help, and that we wouldn't have been at risk if not for the people trying to kill the king.

But Della nods sagely and reaches out to put a hand over mine. "As I said, I am glad the queen has seen your qualities, my dear. Those of you *and* your sister."

Firena nods, too. "The perfect example of why the king's magic should not remain here. Previous queens would not allow these mage-smiths to reside in Syhl Shallow, and this is exactly why. These creatures are too dangerous. This *magic* is too dangerous. If the king were not here, we would not have conflict at *all*. Your sister never would have been at risk."

That throws me for a moment.

But then I remember the king standing there on the first night he healed my wounds, telling me how things felt from *his* side, when Syhl Shallow began to attack.

I remember thinking about my mother ordering that kind of violence—before the king was even here.

"Maybe the magic is dangerous," I say, trying not to think about the flicker in my veins as I say the words. What would these women do if they knew I had the same magic running through *me*? What if they knew the queen had it?

I have no magic, Callyn.

Maybe this is my purpose here. Not to be a spy, not to drive her people to war.

Maybe my purpose is to protect the queen.

I have to swallow and square my shoulders. "I don't think the queen is willing to go to war." I take a breath. "Not again."

Della and Firena exchange a glance. "War?" says Firena. "We don't want to go to war either." She pauses. "Not yet."

I frown, wondering if I'm misunderstanding the direction of this conversation. "Then what do you want?"

"We want the king to leave." Her voice tightens. "We've all lost family to those monsters in Emberfall. We want his *magic* to leave."

Della nods, and she leans in, holding my eyes. "And if he doesn't, let our queen know we stand ready to drive him out."

306

CHAPTER 32

JAX

I should never have spoken so honestly to Prince Rhen.

This may not make a difference to you, but I hate myself for it.

Good, I said. *I hate you, too.*

The morning after he leaves, I wake up expecting to be executed. I'll be boiled alive or the skin will be flayed from my bones or I'll be set on fire for being so ungrateful. No one is waiting to drag me out of the forge, so I do my work and go to my riding lessons, but the whole while, I keep waiting for guards to show up and haul me off to prison. It's a new worry that sits on top of all the loneliness, a constant anxiety that has me jumping every time the Shield House door opens.

But days pass, and . . . nothing happens.

In fact, my days seem to improve—or at least, they're a little less terrible. My work in the forge is more efficient, thanks to the bench Sephran brought me. Most of the soldiers still hate me, but they seem to have grown bored of knocking my tools into the dirt, and instead, they ignore me. Even my nights are a little less lonely, because Master Hugh speaks to me in Syssalah—though our conversation usually consists of him shouting for me to sit up straighter or to shorten my reins.

I'm also beginning to pick up more Emberish, which takes me by surprise. Instead of words flowing over me with little comprehension, phrases have begun to come together. When a middle-aged woman in the forge walks past me, grumbling that her pincers are broken *again*, I offer a set of mine, saying, "Take. I have two." I think we're both a little shocked. But after that, some of the other forge workers are less stand-offish, and the dirty looks in the Shield House begin to dissipate.

I haven't seen Sephran or Kutter since the evening we went shooting, but I don't quite know if I should ask after them. Things might be improving in the forge, but after what happened with the prince, I've kept to myself, waiting for Tycho to return.

A week after the prince's visit, an older woman arrives at the Shield House. She strides through the door with a satchel full of books and speaks to Master Garson while everyone is getting their breakfast.

"Master Jax," he calls, and I look up from my oatmeal.

It gets everyone's attention, because aside from the night Prince Rhen was waiting for me, I haven't had a single visitor.

I set down my spoon and stand. "Master Garson?" My eyes shift to the woman. "My lady?"

The woman nods decisively and heads my way. Her hair is dark gray and twisted in two braids along the back of her head, but plenty of strands have escaped. She looks round and motherly, but her expression is stern. She's broad across the shoulders, too, and nearly as tall as I am. She drops her bag of books on the table beside my bowl.

"My name is Elayne," she says in perfect Syssalah, her accent as slight as Tycho's. I'm so startled by *that* I almost miss what she says next: "Prince Rhen has hired me to tutor you in Emberish."

After days of worrying I was going to find myself thrown off the castle ramparts, this is unexpected. And not necessarily in a good way.

I must be staring suspiciously, because she adds, "I'm very good, I assure you. I tutored the prince and princess myself."

I shake myself. "No—I mean, yes, my lady."

"I'm not a lady. You may call me Elayne." She begins pulling books from her bag. Many of them have childish pictures painted on the covers. "Can you read?"

I can't decide if she's brusque or just efficient, but I fold my arms. "Yes, I can *read.*"

"Don't be offended. I always ask. Not everyone has access to education, and there's no shame in that."

I rather doubt she asked the prince and princess, but that steals some of my vitriol. I unfold my arms.

She slides a leather-bound booklet toward me, along with a wrapped stick of kohl pencils, similar to the ones I used to keep track of projects in the workshop. "As you hear new words throughout the day, I want you to write them down if you can. We'll sit together at breakfast to go over them. Each night, I'm going to leave you a children's primer to read—" She breaks off, and I'm not sure what expression is on my face, but it must not be good. She's frowning. "Is there a problem?"

There might be. If she's been hired to spend so much time tutoring me, I'm sure it's costly.

I don't like that the prince sent her. It feels manipulative.

But my conflict with Prince Rhen isn't her fault. "I'm sorry." I look down, fidgeting with the cover on the little book. "I don't mean to be rude. This . . . this is unexpected."

She reaches out to pat my hand, and it's motherly, making me feel like a child—and I can't remember the last time *that* happened. Despite the sternness in her expression, her hand is warm, the motion kind. She reminds me a bit of Master Hugh.

"Shall we sit?" she says, and her voice is a little gentler.

I nod, and we do. Molly brings her a stein of steaming tea and a small

309

platter of breads with cheese and jam, but Elayne ignores it all. She taps the book in front of me. "Let's begin," she says. "Write down some words you've learned. Write them in both Syssalah and Emberish if you can."

I could cheat and use the words I already know from working in the forge—or simple words like *hello* and *goodbye*. Or maybe even the first words that Tycho taught me during our ride from Syhl Shallow, like *sleep* and *camp* and *stars* and *fire*.

But for some reason my thoughts summon that moment in the forge when Sephran brought me the bench, when he said he *remembered* how much I needed one.

Remember, I repeated, figuring out the word. *Think . . . of before.* Sephran looked so pleased. Then he invited me to shoot with his friends. It was the first time the constant band of tension around my chest had loosened.

Is Sephran a friend? I'm still not sure. But my heart gives a tug at the memory.

Remember. I do.

So I write that down.

It seems to be a day for visitors, because Master Hugh brings a woman to the forge in the afternoon. She's probably as old as Hugh, and she carries herself like a soldier. She has a satchel like Elayne's, but this one doesn't look burdened with books. Nothing about her looks friendly, and when her eyes skip over me in an appraising way, I try not to scowl.

But Master Hugh gives me a warm smile. "Jax. This is Captain Ammax. She brought you a foot."

I hesitate, unsure what to say. I remember Hugh told me she doesn't speak Syssalah, so I give her a nod and speak in Emberish. "Ah . . . well met, Captain."

She gives me a sharp nod in return, then speaks in rapid-fire Emberish to Hugh, and I can only pick out every fifth word. But he listens attentively, then says, "Ammax says you will need practice. Clumsy at first. Sore. Little bit longer each day."

That was a lot shorter than everything she said to him. I glance between them and raise my eyebrows. "That's all?"

He waves a hand and makes a *tsk* sound. "She was telling me about the friends she lost in the war. But you did not cause the strife. It will be fine."

"Oh." Now I understand the wary regard in her expression. She hates me like the rest of the soldiers. My hands flex on my crutches, and I want to draw back.

Master Hugh tuts and pats my shoulder. "You are a good boy, Jax. She will see. Sit. Try."

With anyone else, I always feel so prickly and uncertain. But there's something about Master Hugh that's disarming, even when my stomach is tied up in knots. I don't know if it's his voice, which is never loud, or if it's his unassuming manner. Or maybe it's simply that I can't remember a single time that anyone has ever said those words to me. *You are a good boy, Jax.*

As I sit, Captain Ammax begins pulling things from the bag. Woolen socks first, then a length of muslin. Then what looks to be a length of leather wrapped around wood. She's talking while she unravels everything, and Hugh listens, then translates.

"You'll wear two stockings," he says. "Always two! Ammax says using one will cause sores. And the muslin folds underneath. Like . . . like pillow? Do you understand?"

No, but I nod.

He continues, "She says soldiers sometimes leave the foot in the boot and then put all on together. But it's no good. Take the time, or it won't be secure. Do you understand?"

311

Still no. I'm watching her unfold the leather dubiously, but again, I nod. "Yes, Master Hugh."

Captain Ammax must see right through my nonsense because she snaps her fingers and says, "*Look. Here.*"

I bristle immediately, but then I look at the wood and leather she's unbound in her hand, and I go completely still. She's holding . . . a foot.

Sort of.

It's crudely formed and made of wood that's been sanded and stained and polished—and actually looks quite worn. No toes, just halfhearted notches where toes should probably go, and a narrow ankle with a flat base instead of a rounded heel. A bolt seems to go directly through the ankle and out the other side, but I can't quite figure out the mechanism. The wood above the ankle forms a bit of a bowl at the top, where holes have been drilled through, and a leather sheath has been attached. The laces are wider and flatter than regular bootlaces, but the sheath is high, and would reach all the way to the wearer's knee.

It's nothing like what I once tried to fashion on my own.

"Do you want to try?" says Captain Ammax more slowly, and I'm so shocked that this is for me that I don't even care that she sounds brusque.

I'm just nodding and unknotting the leg of my trousers. "Yes, Captain."

Within minutes, I've rolled the stockings into place over the end of my leg, and she's showed me how to fold the muslin inside the wooden cup to offer some cushioning. Then I lace the leather up around my calf to hold it all in place—"Tighter!" Captain Ammax orders, which Master Hugh echoes in quieter Syssalah, and then they bicker at each other in Emberish while I re-lace everything more tightly.

It's tight and snug and heavy and I just stare at it for the longest moment. In a way, it's like my thoughts can't quite process it. I haven't seen anything on the end of my leg for so long that it's weird to see anything at all there.

But a spark of hope has flared in my chest that feels so foreign I'm not entirely sure what to do with it.

Hugh breaks through my staring. "Do you have other boot?"

I frown. "No. Well, yes. At the Shield House." In the wardrobe. I think. I don't usually pay much mind to keeping track of the right-sided ones.

He waves a hand again. "No mind now. Boot should fit over leg. Tell Ammax if not."

She grunts and tells him to tell me to stand up, but I know these words, so I swallow and stand, keeping my weight on the leg I know will support me. I was right: the new foot really *is* heavy. I'm not used to the weight, and it almost drags against the ground when I shift. I somehow feel secure, but also like I'm standing on a stilt. When I drag the new foot forward a few inches, that pin in the ankle flexes, and I'm not ready for it to shift. For a terrifying second, I'm worried I'm going to stumble into the dirt, but Hugh puts out a hand. I grab hold and hop a few steps on my other leg until I'm sure I won't fall.

I swallow and frown and freeze in place. I don't want to move any farther. That spark of hope almost burns out.

Captain Ammax says something, and for the first time, her voice isn't quite as sharp. Master Hugh nods and says to me, "You must practice."

I try another shuffling step, but I'm wary and off balance—and a little embarrassed. I only move forward an inch, but again, the ankle gives a little, and I don't know how to compensate. Everything feels tight and unsteady and . . . and *wrong*.

"Slow," says Master Hugh. *"Practice."*

I take a long breath and look up. It's near the end of the day, and we've caught the attention of a few of the forge workers. When I see them watching, my cheeks burn—but Hugh scoffs at them, saying he could find more horses that need shoeing. They quickly busy themselves with

313

other tasks. But I realize that some soldiers have also come to the forge, and they're watching, too.

"Sephran," I say in surprise. The youngest soldier from the other day is with him. "Leo." The heat on my cheeks goes nowhere, and there's a part of me that wants to yank this foot off and hide it away so I can forget how awkward all this is. But I'm glad to see them, so I try to swallow my emotion. "Well met."

"Well met, Archer." Sephran pauses and glances down at the foot that's laced to my leg. "You're busy. We can come back."

He says this slowly, which I appreciate. "No! Stay. I . . . I want . . ." I fight for words, but I'm stumbling over them almost as badly as I did with the foot. It's always harder to speak their language than to understand it. "*You*," I say, pointing at him. "I want you. You stay."

Sephran smiles. "All right."

Captain Ammax looks up at them, and her voice sharpens. "If you stay, stay quiet."

Sephran and Leo lose the smiles. "Yes, Captain."

When she turns back to me, Leo looks appropriately chastised and stands at attention, but Sephran catches my gaze and rolls his eyes dramatically. I grin and have to look away before it turns into a laugh.

Leo snorts and does start to laugh, but Sephran smacks him in the arm. He snaps to attention again.

But then Captain Ammax is giving me instructions, and I have to pay attention while Hugh translates. She shows me how to adjust the muslin and the laces, and tells me to practice with my crutches so I don't fall. Before I'm ready, we're taking it all off and putting everything back in the bag.

Then the captain is gone, earning salutes from the soldiers, and I'm left with Hugh, Sephran, and Leo.

"You will practice every day," Hugh warns me in Syssalah. "Or Ammax will have my head."

I believe *that*. I give him a nod. "I promise."

Hugh glances at Sephran. "You are friends with this one?"

Friends. Maybe? I nod. "Yes."

"Good." He pats Sephran on the shoulder the same way he did to me. "Sephran is a good boy, too," he says. "Always kind to his horses."

Sephran is broad and muscled and easily stands six inches taller than Hugh—to say nothing of the fact that he's currently wearing enough armor and weapons to walk into battle. The only thing *boyish* about him is the handful of freckles across his cheeks—until he grins sheepishly, adding one more.

"Ah . . . good words?" he says in Emberish, looking to me.

It makes me blush again, and I'm not sure why. I smile and nod. "Good words."

He inhales as if to speak, then hesitates, then holds up a finger to me. He looks at Hugh and says . . . a lot.

I pick out enough phrases to understand he has leave, then something about dinner, and then I lose track. But Hugh turns to me and says, "Sephran has been on patrol with his unit, but now he has leave. He and his friends are riding to the creek to catch dinner. He invites you to join them."

My heart kicks again. I'm nodding before he's even done speaking. "Yes," I say, then repeat it in Emberish for Sephran. "Please."

Sephran grins, then mimes shooting an arrow. "Bring your bow."

When I arrive with Teddy, I expect the same small group from the evening we went shooting, but tonight there are more than a dozen men and women gathered in the courtyard. Most are soldiers, many still in armor, likely fresh off patrol like Sephran and Leo were. I remember Trapp and Fowler, and of course Kutter, but Sephran hasn't appeared yet. On the opposite side of the courtyard, I recognize two of the soldiers who've hassled me in the forge, and they're the same ones who were yelling tauts on the morning we arrived at Ironrose.

I don't know their names, but I feel the sudden weight of their attention like they've each nocked an arrow aimed for my throat. One of them is short and sandy-haired, and he leans toward the other one to say something I can't hear. The other man, a bit more swarthy with a shock of dark hair, holds my eyes and nods in response. I force myself not to flinch away from his stare.

But then one of the young women near me turns around, and to my surprise, it's Molly, the serving girl from the Shield House. She's holding the reins of a fat bay palfrey, and her eyes widen when she looks at me. She gives me a smile and a curtsy.

"Master Jax!" she says brightly.

She's so happy and guileless that I can't help smiling back. "Molly. No dinner?"

Before she can answer, the dark-haired soldier calls, "Molly, you can do better than that trash from over the mountain."

Her smile turns into a scowl, and she kicks dirt in his direction. "Like you, Niall? I don't think so."

The others around us chuckle, while Niall glowers at us both. When Molly turns back, her eyes seem hopeful that I didn't understand their exchange, but I did—and I'm sure my expression makes it clear.

She frowns. "I'm sorry," she whispers.

I shake my head. "No sorry. *You* are kind, Molly."

That brings the bright smile back to her face. "You've learned so many words! I'm glad you're coming. I didn't know you'd be here."

"Sephran . . . ah . . ." I freeze and immediately prove her wrong, because I don't know the word for *invited*. "Sephran say to come." I frown, wondering if that's right. "Yes?"

"Yes," Sephran says from behind me. "I say to come." He draws his

316

horse up alongside my own and looks across the courtyard. Leo is just behind him.

I follow his gaze. Niall is laughing with Trapp and Fowler now, but he casts another dark look our way, then leans toward them to mutter something. Those two weren't unkind when we went shooting, but they weren't friendly either. Whatever Niall says, Trapp doesn't respond, but Fowler glances my way and chuckles. After a moment, Trapp smiles, too.

I shouldn't be surprised. I saw how close-knit the soldiers were on the journey here. But an icy band encircles my chest. If Trapp and Fowler are friends with Niall, does that mean Sephran is his friend, too?

But Sephran's gaze darkens, and he sighs. "Is Niall being a jackass?"

"Yes," I say.

He grins. "Oh, you know that word, too."

I nod, but I can't smile back. I glance uncertainly at Niall again, and my stomach churns.

Molly draws up her reins and climbs aboard her horse. "Well, I will ride with you both, if you don't mind."

"*I* don't mind," Leo says, and he sounds so enthusiastic that I don't need any translation.

Sephran gives him a withering glance, but he looks back at me, and his expression is intent. The smile is gone, and his blue eyes are very serious. "Don't worry," he says. He looks pointedly at Niall and then back at me. "Stay with me and Leo. Or Kutter."

"Or me," says Molly.

Sephran smiles, but his eyes are still serious, and fixed on mine. "Do you understand? Don't worry."

My stomach feels tight again. As usual, I wish Tycho were here.

But for now, I'm glad Sephran is.

I give him a short nod and let out a breath. "I understand."

At the front of our group, Kutter gives a whistle, and we head out.

Like before, I don't really know where we're going, but after days of lessons, I feel more confident on Teddy's back, and I'm glad to have a break from the pressing heat from the forge. I'm surprised when we cross the castle grounds, pass the archery fields, and ride out past the sentry gates onto the main road. I haven't left the castle grounds since I arrived with Tycho.

There are so many people that I expect to drift along, but I really have learned more words than I realized, because I find myself picking up bits and pieces of conversation. Molly is chattering to Leo about *some* problem in the kitchen that seems to involve potatoes, but he obviously doesn't mind. He's hanging on every word she says.

Ahead of us are four soldiers who I don't recognize at all, and it seems that two of them were on patrol with Sephran's regiment, but the other two weren't. There's a conspiratorial tone to their conversation, and they're speaking in lower tones, so I can't hear everything, but I do pick out a few words.

Attack.

Scravers.

I look at Sephran. "Attack?" I say quietly, not sure if I'm meant to have heard.

He shakes his head. "Only rumors," he says. "Stories?"

"Some people say the monster has returned," Molly says.

I frown, trying to piece this together, and Leo holds up his hands and growls, "Monster?"

Molly giggles.

Sephran says, "There have been reports of monster attacks from all over Emberfall. But we didn't see anything on patrol." He taps under his eye and then points at the sky, then shakes his head. "We didn't see scravers. Just heard stories?" He lilts the phrase like a question, seeing if I understand.

I do, and I nod, but I'm already thinking of Tycho. It's been well over a week—almost two. He should be returning by now. I wonder if I would have heard this gossip earlier, if I knew enough to converse with others. I need to ask Master Hugh if he's heard anything.

I think of the scravers who attacked us in the field when we camped, and I cast a glance at the sky and wonder if we should be worried.

"Danger?" I say to Sephran.

He shakes his head and makes a big circle with his hand, indicating our group. "Many soldiers. No danger."

But I wasn't just asking about danger to *us*. "What . . . what . . ." I break off and scowl, then swear in Syssalah. This is so hard.

"Slow," he says, and his eyes are kind. "We can figure it out."

He sounds so earnest, so I take a slow breath—then realize Molly and Leo are peering at me, too. I try again. "Danger for Tycho? Malin?"

"No word yet. But there were reports of heavy rains to the north, so the going would've been—" I'm losing track of the language, and I'm sure it's obvious, because he breaks off and winces. "Sorry. Rain and mud for Mal and Tycho." He pats his horse, then points between the sky and ground. "Slow for horses. Very slow."

Oh. It hits me harder than it should. So maybe Tycho won't be back soon after all. And a slow journey might put him in more danger. I swallow any emotion before it can form.

Would anyone tell me if he were injured? Would word even reach me? He kept insisting on discretion, so maybe no one would care.

I'm just a blacksmith. I don't matter.

"Hey." Sephran gives my sleeve a tug, and I look over. "Don't worry. They're all right."

I force myself to nod, but then I realize there's a weight in his eyes, too, a gravity to the way he says that.

"Mal is my best friend," he adds. He hesitates, looking a little sheepish, and to my surprise, he blushes a little—then pats his chest, over his heart. "Best friend?"

I know this phrase, because *friend* is one of the first words I learned. It was the night we left Briarlock, and we were lying on our bedrolls, staring at the stars. I kept asking Tycho for the Emberish word for anything I could think of. I'm sure he was as exhausted as everyone else, but he was eternally patient, his voice low as he gave me the words for *sky* and *grass* and *chickens* and *bakery*, most of which I forgot.

But there were some that stuck, like *friend*, because it made me think of Callyn.

I nod to show I understand. "Sorry," I say to Sephran. "You worry, too."

"No sorry," he teases, mimicking my accent from when I said the same thing to Molly.

That makes me smile, but now I'm the one blushing sheepishly.

Sephran hesitates, and I realize he's debating what to say because a conversation is so complicated. It practically took a lifetime to tell me about the rumors and how mud and rain make travel slow.

Then his eyes light up, and he says, "Teach us some Syssalah." He quickly rolls his eyes and adds, "But real words. Not like Malin."

"Oh." My eyebrows go up. "Ah . . ."

Molly looks over. "Yes! Please!"

To my surprise, even Leo looks interested.

A burst of raucous laughter erupts near the front of our traveling party, and I don't know what about it draws my attention, but I look ahead. Niall and his friends have clearly found something hilarious, and they glance back our way.

I have no idea what they're saying, but my stomach curls into a knot. I don't want to speak Syssalah. Not right now.

But when I look back to Sephran, he's watching me, his eyes picking me apart.

I'm sure I look wary and apprehensive. My fingers twist at the reins, and my shoulders feel tight. I should have gone with my instincts and put Teddy back in the stable.

Sephran nudges his horse closer to mine, then says, "Here. I'll start." He rubs a hand over the back of his neck, then peers at me. "Ah . . . what do I remember . . . *Tahlasta mele*?"

My head snaps around in surprise. I nearly do a double take.

He laughs at my expression. "I know a *little*," he says. "From Malin."

"What did you say?" says Leo.

Sephran winces and cuts another glance my way. "Good dinner?"

He's close, but before I can say anything, Molly says, "Food! *Mele* is food. It's on the paper from Lord Tycho."

"Yes," I say.

Leo looks at me. "*Tahlasta* is 'good'?"

I have no idea how I would explain grammar, so I shake my head. "*Tahlas*—good. *Tahlasta mele*—good food."

Molly's eyes light up. "'Morning' was on the paper, too. So . . . *tahlasta dasima*? Good morning?"

She sounds so eager that it makes me smile, and an odd wave of emotion overwhelms my heart. It's like homesickness wrapped up in the sudden warmth of acceptance. I have to clear my throat so it doesn't come out in my voice. "Yes. Good morning."

This launches a round of new words that they want to know—most of which *I* don't know, but we do our best to puzzle it out. Their Ember-ish accents are so rough-edged, but I don't care. I'm sure mine is no bet-ter. The knot of tension in my belly begins to unwind.

And maybe their easygoing presence helps, because the cruel glances and raucous laughter eventually fades away, as if acceptance by a few has a ripple effect among the rest of the group.

Eventually our travel party reaches a large clearing with a wide stream, and our language lesson has to end in favor of tethering the horses and finding some food.

"*Mele*," Molly says, bumping me with her hip, and I smile.

From across the clearing, Trapp and Fowler see it, but this time they just turn away. There's no laughter, and I don't see Niall.

Good. Maybe I didn't have to worry about him at all.

I draw my bow across my chest and slip my crutches under my arms, then find Sephran beside me again, tethering his horse right next to me.

He glances across the clearing significantly, then looks back at me. His eyes hold mine, and he smiles. "*Tahlas?*"

It's so unexpected and so kind that it makes me blush. I can't help smiling back. "*Men tahlas.*"

Very good.

CHAPTER 33

JAX

I might be lucky with a bow, but clearly tracking and hunting are different skills. The soldiers are well practiced in feeding themselves, however. Rabbits and geese are prepped and roasting over a fire before half the group has even finished tending the horses. Parcels of fruit and bread and cheese and wrapped pastries are pulled from a dozen saddle bags, too, and it's so much food that I begin to think we didn't need to hunt for anything at all.

While we eat, Sephran gets drawn into a nearby conversation, and other than knowing the soldiers are grousing about a commander and complaining about their patrol duties, I can't follow much. I don't mind, though, because no one bothers me, and Sephran hangs close. When a bottle of liquor is passed around our circle, the woman next to me hands it over as if I'm part of the group. I hand the bottle to Sephran without taking a sip.

Once the sun begins to set, I think we'll head back to the castle, but the soldiers pull decks of cards and more liquor from the remaining saddlebags. Coins glint in the light as they start betting on games. Leo appears to have coaxed Molly into a game, because I hear her laugh lightly over the low conversations going on around the fires. A few of the soldiers have stripped down to their underclothes to swim, but it must be cold, because not many join them. One man gets thrown into the stream fully clothed, and I think it's part of a fight—until he emerges, laughing, splashing a handful of water at one of the others.

I hang to the side, letting their lighthearted words float over me. But as night falls, easy moods shift into something darker. Sephran tries to draw me into a card game with some of the soldiers, but I shake my head and cling to the shadows. Maybe it's my experience with a drunken father, or maybe I've spent too many days in the forge being a target, but I can't relax.

When Niall sits down to join our circle, I'm glad I'm off to the side, because it's probably too dark for him to see me. The scent of liquor is sharp on the air now, and I've heard the change in tone as games are lost and tempers rise. On the road with Prince Rhen, card games never got too spirited, but it's clear that here, with no one on duty and no commanding officers to worry about, the soldiers aren't as motivated to stay civil. I know better than anyone what happens when you combine a little bit of liquor and a little bit of anger.

Not for the first time, I wish Tycho were here.

As soon as I have the thought, shame curls into my belly. Tycho wouldn't be afraid.

Then again, Tycho is a skilled warrior, and he'd have an arsenal of weapons strapped to his body. I'm a blacksmith with a bow and a pair of crutches.

And Tycho *isn't* here, because he was sent away. As usual.

The sudden bitterness takes me by surprise, and I force myself to look around at the soldiers. I'm fine. They're fine. *This* is fine. Leo and Molly are sitting closer now, firelight flickering off their cheeks. Sephran glanced my way a few times, but it's clear that the game has reached a point of intensity, because now he's focused on the cards.

Someone shouts, and I flinch. It's the group by the water, and this time, it's *definitely* a fight—or at least the prelude to one. I don't know what they're arguing about, but I know the profanity. Two young men are on their feet, and one young woman. One of the men shoves the other, and they almost end up in the fire. Sparks flare up when they skitter away from the flames. For an instant, they have everyone's attention, and someone near me mutters under his breath. A cool breeze swirls through the clearing, and I shiver, waiting to see if someone is going to throw a punch.

But the two men storm away from each other. The woman says something mockingly, and one of the men makes a rude gesture in her direction. But they all sit back down.

The tension in my chest goes nowhere.

While everyone is distracted, I slip my crutches under my arms and head for my horse.

I half expect someone to follow me, or at least to call after me, but it's so dark that no one seems to notice. I've tethered my crutches and managed to climb aboard Teddy when I look back for Sephran again. The firelight bounces off his freckled cheeks as he studies his cards, watching his opponent for telling cues. He takes another drink from a bottle when someone passes it his way. It's clear he hasn't noticed I'm gone, and a tinge of guilt pulls at me. I don't just want to disappear.

"Hey." A man speaks from behind me. "Where are you going?"

I don't recognize the voice, but the tone is cold, and my heart gives a lurch.

The man steps out from behind another horse, and enough firelight reaches his features for me to recognize him.

Niall.

He's not alone either. That other sandy-haired soldier is just behind him. Their expressions are in shadow, and I have no idea what they intend, but I'm not an idiot.

"Home," I say. I cluck to Teddy, glad I'm on a horse and they're not.

The horse moves away at a sedate walk, but the men stride after me. "You people killed my brother," Niall says, his words slurring, making it hard to parse out what he's saying. "They killed Brinley's father, too."

My heart trips with the first spark of fear. In my forge back home, I'd deal with drunk or rowdy travelers all the time—when I wasn't dealing with my father himself. But at home, I had heavy tools and hot iron and ways to defend myself. If I got hurt, I could run to Callyn's.

Out here, I have nothing. And if I brawl with a soldier, I know two things for sure: one, it'll reflect poorly on me, which means it'll probably reflect poorly on Tycho.

Two, I'll lose.

I nudge Teddy with my heel, but he's older and slower, and part of the reason he's a steady mount is that he's *not* going to take off at a gallop. I'm not sure I could hang on even if he did.

"Hey!" Niall snaps. "I'm talking to you, blacksmith."

Well, he's talking *at* me. My brain has stopped processing what he's saying at all. I give Teddy a solid kick, and he grunts, then lumbers into a trot.

Relief blooms in my chest, but it lasts exactly one second. Niall grabs my ankle, and the other man—*Brinley?*—grabs Teddy's rein. The horse stumbles to a halt, turning a bit, and I realize they intend to drag me right off his back.

I draw back my leg and kick out hard, and I have the satisfaction of hearing Niall grunt. Good. I hope I got him in the face. His grip slackens and I draw back to kick him again.

But I forgot about Brinley. He grabs hold of my forearm and jerks *hard*.

326

That almost gets me out of the saddle. But Teddy has had enough of this nonsense, and he sidesteps to compensate for my rapidly shifting weight, nearly stepping on the drunken men who are trying to drag me off his back.

It gives me a moment of distraction, and I grab an arrow from my quiver. I can't get the bow over my shoulder fast enough, but I doubt I'd escape a hanging if I *shot* them.

Instead, I draw back my arm and whip the arrow square across Niall's face.

He shouts in surprise and falls back, swearing so loudly that we're going to draw the attention of the soldiers around the fires.

I don't wait for Brinley to retaliate. I use the momentum of my first swing to come right back around. I almost get the soldier in the neck— but he deflects, catching the arrow.

He's ready for me to tussle for it, but I let it go, slam my heel into Teddy's side, and jerk the reins to the right.

Teddy leaps forward into a brisk . . . trot.

"Please," I breathe. They're going to chase me. I know they are. Even on foot, they can chase him at a trot. *"Please."* My breathing is shaking, and I dig my heel into him again.

Then, blessedly, Teddy stretches his neck out and eases into a rolling canter. Somewhere behind me, Molly calls out my name, but I don't stop. I can't risk it.

In seconds, we're away from the stream and the campfires, and we're cantering through the pitch-black darkness of the woods. This is dangerous as hell, but so are the drunk men who were about to rip me off the back of this horse.

I have to *think*. I have to figure out what to do. My breathing is so loud that it blocks out the sound of anything else. I know the way back to the castle—I *think*—but I'm worried Niall and Brinley are getting on their own horses to give chase.

A bigger part of me is worried that other soldiers will join them to help. I whipped Niall across the face, and I have no way to explain what he was doing.

I choke back the panic before it can form. I should have followed my instincts this afternoon. Or I should have gone back to the Shield House when the sun set.

Honestly, I should have made amends with Prince Rhen instead of telling him that I *hate* him, because whatever happens here is going to come out poorly for me. I'll end up dead or beaten or berated—or even just humiliated. I have no idea how such a lighthearted evening turned into something so terrible.

A frigid wind blasts my cheeks and I shiver again. My chest clenches and my eyes sting. *Tycho. Please come back.*

But of course he's not going to appear. I might as well beg the stars for help.

And then I realize why my eyes are stinging.

The wind is cold. *Unnaturally* cold.

It's been terribly hot for days. The forge has been near unbearable in the humidity. But I draw a shaking breath and it tastes like winter.

I remember the last time this happened, the way ice formed on Tycho's armor, crystals gathering along every bit of steel.

I sit deep in the saddle and Teddy responds immediately, slowing to a walk, then a halt. My heart is beating so hard I'm practically vibrating. I can't sit here long. Niall and Brinley can't be too far behind me, and if they catch me, they'll drag me off this horse and break a dozen bones.

But I stare up, peering between the trees, looking for something. Anything.

And then I see my breath. Goose bumps spring up along my arms. A shadow crosses the sky overhead. Then another.

A wild screech splits the night, but I'm hidden by the trees. The scravers fly past, toward the stream.

Sephran. Molly. Leo. All the soldiers.

And a good number of them are drunk.

Clouds above. I jerk the bow over my shoulder and put the reins in one hand, then do my best to turn Teddy around. Maybe he can feel my panic, or maybe he suddenly realized that I don't want to plod along anymore, because he leaps into a canter so readily that I nearly lose my seat. I clutch at his mane with the reins, my other hand already slick on the bow. I'm not a good enough rider for this, so I'm not entirely sure what I'm going to do, but I remember what *one* scraver did to me and Tycho.

"Scravers!" I'm shouting. I can't remember one single word in Emberish just now, but this one needs no translation. "Sephran! Molly! Scravers!" I drive my heel against Teddy's side, and he grunts, cantering faster.

We burst out of the trees and into wide open grass—and nearly ride straight into Niall and Brinley. They're still on foot, because they were clearly too drunk—or too stupid—to realize they could have chased me on horseback. But they've found their bows, and they've made it across the clearing.

I scramble to stay on Teddy as he tries to avoid running right into them. Niall's face is bleeding from where I struck him with the arrow, a long welt ending in a stripe of blood.

I've only been gone for a minute, and I hear other soldiers still calling after them.

"Scravers!" I yell at them both, pointing at the sky. "Scravers! Scravers coming!" They speak Emberish. They need to warn everyone.

But they ignore me. Brinley is fumbling to nock an arrow on the string.

Niall already has one nocked, and he lifts the bow to aim at me. "I'll show you how these are meant to be used," he snarls.

My heart freezes. He's got a clear shot.

But ice crystals crawl down the length of his bow, glinting in the light, freezing his arrow right to the wood. He holds, frowning. "What the—"

A scraver dives out of the sky to tackle him to the ground. Blood sprays in an arc.

Brinley screams, drops his bow, and runs.

Teddy truly is the steadiest horse of all time, because he doesn't shy from the screeching creature that's raking claws across Niall's chest.

I don't think. I just drop the reins, nock an arrow, and shoot, pinning arrows in my palm the way Tycho taught me. The first arrow makes the scraver's body jerk, but the second one makes it go still, collapsing on Niall.

The soldier is breathing heavily, whimpering. He's lucky to be wearing armor, and it only got his shoulder before finding leather and steel.

"Help—help me—" he's gasping.

Another screech sounds overhead. Then a second. Soldiers are shouting from across the clearing. I hear a woman scream.

Molly. I think of her friendly smile, the way she was the first person to be kind in the Shield House.

I draw up my reins and cluck to Teddy, and he trots forward with little urging. We reach the stream in seconds. Half a dozen scravers have attacked, and it's so many. Was it like this when they attacked the regiment in the fields? I only saw the ones that attacked me and Tycho. But I remember fighting at the king's side in Briarlock, how the scravers descended from the air to assist us in battle, how we would've lost without their help.

This is like the opposite.

Or maybe it's the same. They attacked soldiers then, too.

It's too dark for me to identify their targets, but I don't take time to try. I'm already shooting before Teddy comes to a stop. Screeches erupt when I don't make killing shots, but I quickly remedy that. I grab for more arrows when my palm empties. I try not to think about the motionless soldiers who lie beneath them, or the scent of blood or the screams on the air. When we were in Briarlock, the king fought at my side, feeding me advice as we faced the advancing enemy. His words are like a litany in my brain now.

Don't forget to breathe. Take time to aim. Don't waste your arrows.

I told him I wasn't really a soldier. I'm not one now.

I hit a scraver through the wing and it screams, and the sound makes me cringe. It's the last arrow in my palm, so I reach for more.

My quiver is empty. I should've kept count.

As soon as I have the realization, the scraver leaps off the soldier and slams into me so hard that it knocks me off the horse. I crash into the ground just as claws scrape across my jaw.

Unlike the soldiers, I'm not wearing any armor.

The scraver rears back, fangs bared, eyes glinting in the moonlight. I suck in a terrified breath. It's going to tear my throat out, and Tycho won't be anywhere around to heal the damage.

A sword stabs right into the side of its rib cage, driving the scraver sideways, impaling it with enough force that it can't attack me at all. It's screaming, scrabbling for the weapon now, but Sephran grabs hold of its wing and pulls it off me. He kicks it onto the ground, pulls his sword free, and kills it with one quick thrust of his blade. After the earsplitting screeching, the silence is sudden and profound.

I stare up at Sephran, my breathing shaky. His chest is rising and falling rapidly, but he hasn't looked at me yet. He's staring at the scraver, as if waiting to make sure it's really dead. Blood is a dark streak on his cheek, but there's more of it down one arm. He's still gripping a sword in one hand and a dagger in his other, so it must not be too bad.

331

His face is all hard lines. Any sheepish kindness in his expression is gone, leaving only a fierce soldier.

He finally glances down at me, his gaze skipping over my form as if assessing damages for one quick second, before looking out and around again. I shove myself up on my elbows, realizing that there could be more.

But the screeches have stopped. The air is warm, my breath no longer clouding. The scravers are dead—or gone. Soldiers are shouting to each other. I hear a woman crying, and my heart clenches. *Molly.* But at least she's alive.

Not everyone is so lucky. Bodies are strewn everywhere. The scent of blood is still heavy in the air.

Sephran sheaths his weapons and puts out a hand, and I take it, pulling myself to standing. My heart is pounding hard, my hair spilling free from its knot. Teddy is a short distance away, my crutches still bound behind the saddle. The horse is innocently nosing at the grass beside a fallen soldier.

Beyond my horse, Niall limps into the clearing. His eyes meet mine, and he glances away without saying a word.

I saved his life. The thought is jarring.

But Sephran picks up my bow and presses it to my chest, drawing my attention back. One of the others calls his name, but he doesn't look away from me. His blue eyes are a little shadowed, a little bleak, but he gives me a grateful nod. "Nice shooting, Archer."

I take hold of the bow. The surviving soldiers are panicked and disorganized—and many are still drunk. As far as I can tell, they seem to be yelling for someone to fetch more soldiers. Healers, too, though I can't be sure. I wish I had a shred of Tycho's magic, because I see a lot of fallen bodies.

Sephran has moved away, and he's kneeling beside someone on the far side of the clearing now, checking for another survivor, but I know how vicious the scravers are. There won't be many. Even some of the horses are dead. The remaining soldiers are pale in the moonlight, looking at the sky as if trying to determine whether another attack is coming—or if it's safe to head for the castle.

They're afraid. Arguing turns to shouting. No one wants to ride out in the open.

My heart is pounding. I don't either.

But honestly, I don't want to stay here. I hop to Teddy and untether my crutches, then loop his reins around my wrist. There's no way I'm riding back without any weapons, so I start pulling arrows anywhere I see them. The ones in the scraver bodies pull free with a wet squelch, and I dip to wipe them in the grass before shoving them in my quiver.

A shadow appears at my side, and I jump a mile, nearly losing a crutch.

But it's only Molly.

"Sorry," she says, and tears glitter on her cheeks.

I stare at her. "Leo?" I ask.

She nods quickly and swipes at her face, then points. "With Kutter."

I follow her gaze and see the youngest soldier. He's quiet, but the others are still arguing, panic thick in their voices.

Molly shifts closer, and then, without warning, grabs hold of my arm. "Jax," she says, and her voice breaks. She speaks rapidly, begging for something through her tears. The only word I understand is *please*.

"Molly." I'm shaking my head. She's speaking too fast and I can't keep up.

"Please!" She clutches at my arm desperately. The bright, lively girl from the kitchen is gone. "Please, Jax."

"Molly," I say again, more gently. "Slow. Please. *Slow.*"

"Take. Me. Back. Take me. *With you.*" She draws a shuddering breath, her watery eyes level with mine. *"Please?"*

I don't know what to say. She'd be safer here, with the soldiers. I'm afraid to take *myself.*

Sephran steps out of the shadows behind her, and I look up. He must have seen me gathering arrows, because he holds out four more on his palm. He speaks slowly and clearly, his eyes holding mine. "Soldiers— stay." He pats his chest and points at the other soldiers, then looks back at me. "Need help. You go—take Molly. Yes?"

She looks up at me and nods rapidly. "Please. Please, Jax."

I don't know how to ask why the soldiers are staying—and he probably doesn't know how to tell me. I can smell the liquor on his breath, and it's possible he's not even making the best decision. Maybe there are so many wounded that they need to guard them while someone else rides for help. Maybe they're too drunk to make it back to Ironrose safely. I don't know.

I do know that it's rare for anyone to look at me the way Molly and Sephran are looking at me.

If Tycho lit a spark in my heart when he first pressed a bow into my hands, it's blazing now. I nod at Molly, then at Sephran. "Yes. I go."

Molly clutches my arm more tightly, as if I might change my mind, but Sephran steps closer and peers at me in the darkness.

Then he touches a hand to my jaw. It's so unexpected that I go still.

His fingers are warm against my skin. "Are you hurt?"

I lift a hand to my face and wince when I find the injury, because it stings. But I nod—then shake my head. "Scraver," I say. "Not hurt."

He nods solemnly, but he hasn't let go of my face, and a tiny light glints in his eye. *"Tahlas?"* he says.

No. Not good. But I give a short nod, feeling the warmth of his fingers when I move. *"Tahlas."*

He studies me for a long moment, and then his hand slips away. He claps me on the shoulder, then looks at Molly. "Come on, Mol. I'll boost you up behind him."

I'm tense for the entire ride back to Ironrose, and I keep glancing at the sky. If I were alone, I'd nudge Teddy into a canter, but keeping *myself* on his back at any kind of speed is questionable. I don't want to risk Molly. She's a warm weight at my back, her arms clutched tightly around my waist.

No one's ever clung to me like this. No one's ever looked at *me* like some kind of savior. Not even Callyn.

I can't tell if I deserve it. Before the scravers attacked, I was running away. I was running from Niall and Brinley because I couldn't fight back.

I sometimes think about the night Tycho saved me from my father's beating.

Maybe next time we should work on how to block a punch instead of shooting arrows.

But of course there wasn't a next time, because he was called away.

Molly sniffs back tears, and it draws my attention back. I shouldn't let my thoughts wander. I focus on the air, on the breaths that come out of my mouth, but it's seasonably warm again. *I'm* warm, Molly's head resting between my shoulder blades.

No scravers.

No magesmiths either. I don't know what any of it means.

The castle grounds aren't gated, but there are sentry stations set at regular intervals along the tree line. When we finally reach the sprawling fields that lead to Ironrose, the guards at the closest sentry post wave us past, but I draw Teddy to a stop.

Molly has been holding me so tightly for miles, the occasional shiver rocking her body. But I need her to talk. I can't possibly explain everything. "Molly," I say urgently. "Talk. Talk to guards."

Her breath hitches, and she lifts her head.

I put my hand over hers where it rests on my waist. "Talk," I say again, more gently. "Help Sephran. Help Leo."

"Oh," she says. "Oh, yes." She sniffs, then must gather her mettle, because she begins talking.

I watch the guards' faces shift in alarm. They begin calling orders to each other, and then one lights a torch that they use to signal another sentry station. The activity is quicker than I expected.

"Jax," Molly whispers against my shoulder. "They're going. Please. Take me to the Shield House."

I do. I tether Teddy out front, then wake Lola to help her. Lola tuts over my face when she draws close with a lantern, but I wave her away. It's just a few scratches, and I have to put Teddy away.

I expect to find the stables dark and quiet, but armored soldiers are calling for horses, and tired stable hands are running to get them saddled. They must be riding to help the others. I want to know if I should go with them, if I should help somehow, but again, I don't know how to ask, how to even *explain* that I was there.

Everyone ignores me anyway. When a breeze pulls through the aisle, I go stock-still—but it's nothing. Just the wind. I hope for Master Hugh, because I feel desperately alone, and I need to talk to someone about everything that has happened.

But it's late, and if he's here, he's helping prepare horses somewhere else. I only see soldiers and scurrying workers.

A woman barks an order near my ear, and I jump. I need to get out of the stables.

Molly must have disappeared into her room, or she's being tended by Lola, because the main room of the Shield House is empty. When I reach my quarters, the room is so quiet that the silence presses in against me. I have no way of knowing when the soldiers will return. Will anyone tell me? Can I inquire after Sephran and Leo? What about the others?

My stomach tightens when I think of the scraver swooping out of the sky to tackle Niall. I remember the spray of blood. I remember my flare of panic when I found my quiver empty, the way the scraver ripped me right off Teddy's back and flung me to the ground.

I remember Sephran saving my life.

I light my lantern and move to the washbasin in the corner of my room. It's too late to call for hot water for a bath, though I desperately need one. I doubt I'll ever sleep again. I pour water in the basin and splash it on my face, then hiss when I remember the scratches left by the scraver.

I grab for a washrag and blot the water away, then look in the mirror.

Twin scratches run down the left side of my jaw, nearly from my ear to my chin. They don't look deep enough to need stitching, but they're long. They'll probably scar, too.

I stare at the marks. If Tycho were here, they'd be gone in a heartbeat.

But he's not. They'll have to stay.

I close my eyes and take a breath. It's not fair to keep wishing for Tycho to return. To keep thinking of how things would be different if he were here.

He's not. I am.

So I dry my face, douse the lantern, and wait for morning.

CHAPTER 34

TYCHO

The day after our fight, I'm sore and hung over, so when guards rap at my door at sunrise, they're not welcome at *all*. Unfortunately, the king has issued more orders: Malin and I are to move to new quarters in the distant wing where we met on the night we arrived.

We gather our things and all but stumble down the hall.

"Is this a punishment?" Malin says, wincing every time we pass a beam of sunlight.

"Not for you," I grumble.

The new rooms are just as plush and opulent as anywhere else in the palace, but they're far from court, and far from everything. No chance of accidentally encountering the queen or the princess—or anyone else.

So I guess Grey was serious about staying out of sight.

Fine.

That spike of tension in my heart has shifted into a wedge of bitterness. I don't even go to visit Noah.

Malin and I saddle our horses and ride into the mountains twice a day: once early in the morning, before soldiers are in the stables, and again during the dinner hour, when the training fields are empty. At first, I keep our rides short, hour-long patrol loops I remember from my days as a recruit. I worry we might be watched or restricted, and I'm ready to receive a terse order from the king that we're not even allowed to do this.

But when no one questions us—or even seems to care—Malin and I spend more time in the mountains. We race along trails and spar in empty clearings and hunt for food when we're hungry. Once we even slip bottles of spirits into our saddlebags and our thoughts are loose and fuzzy by the time we return. In the absence of duty and obligation, our shared isolation begins to bond us together like brothers.

And when we're alone, I practice my magic. It's more boredom—or rebellion—than any kind of desire to gain proficiency. But I discover that the more I *use* it instead of trying to hide it, the more readily those sparks and stars flare in my blood, and the easier the magic becomes.

I don't even bother to hide it from Malin. There's no point.

At first, these bursts of power are tiny, inconsequential. I send a pulse of magic into the ground to check for other soldiers on patrol, or I start a campfire, or I cut a slice across my palm to heal it. I'm cautious, because I heard Nakiis's warnings, and I don't want to draw more scravers here.

But as days pass, my magic grows bolder, responding the instant I need it. And if I'm being honest with myself . . . I like the little burn of defiance in my chest each time I do it.

I think Malin does, too, because he's grown a little more vicious when we spar—and a lot more reckless. He tries to get inside my guard once and *misses*, and my sword cuts right into his hip before I can deflect. He swears and goes down.

I stare at him. "Mal! What were you *thinking—*"

"Silver hell, *shut up!*" He's breathing through clenched teeth, a fist pressed to the wound. "Just fix it so I can try that again."

339

Anytime we let the horses rest, we talk. He has a lot of stories, which I like. Which I *envy*. What I told him before was true: my years as a soldier weren't full of mischief and fun. No one showed up for duty hungover or spit in their commanding officer's food—at least not in front of *me*. Malin shares it all openly, and it's a new kind of trust I've never had. Most of his stories carry a warm note of camaraderie, especially when he mentions Sephran, and it makes my chest ache a bit. I've never had that kind of friendship with anyone.

Well, until now, maybe.

The instant I have the thought, I realize that my friendship with Malin has grown closer than my relationship with Jax. We've certainly spent more time together.

That's striking, and I'm not sure what it means—or if it means anything at all. I certainly don't have any romantic inclinations toward Malin, and it's *clear* he has none toward me. Every night, when we walk past the training arena on our return to the palace, he asks if I want to watch the guard drills. I don't know who he thinks he's fooling, but it's not me. He's hoping Nolla Verin will try to slice him open again.

But I remember Jax teasing me when I was jealous of the time he spent with the soldiers. I remember the pang in my chest when I realized someone else taught him about archery. I wanted him to make friends, and I genuinely hope he's making them now—but I wonder if he's finding a similar closeness with someone else, too.

It shouldn't worry me, but it does. Noah's warnings are still present in my thoughts, the way he said this time apart would strain . . . whatever we have.

The way he thought Jax might break my heart.

I think of our last night together, hiding in the hayloft. My thoughts were all wrapped up in anxiety about the soldiers for so many reasons, so I kept a distance between us.

But now, looking back, I wish I'd thrown caution to the wind. He was so beautiful in the dark shadows of the stables, his hair unbound and his eyes shining.

Come back to the Shield House with me, he whispered. I turned him down.

I'm such an idiot.

As time passes, the conversations between me and Malin turn to darker things. One day we're letting the horses walk after a long gallop, and Malin tells me more about the Syhl Shallow prisoners he had to care for, back when his father was trying to convince him not to join the army. He tells me how Emberish officers would come to question the prisoners, and he was supposed to starve them so they'd be more willing to talk. He says he could never do it. He'd go hungry and sneak them his own food.

"I was supposed to hate them," he says. "But they were already terrified. It's one thing to fight for your life in battle. It's hard to starve someone right in front of you." He shrugs, offering his horse a loose rein as we walk along the path in the sunlight. "And when they marched on us, they were just following orders. We would have done the same thing."

He's right. I think of the number of times I've pulled my sword or drawn back a bow in battle. Following orders.

The person on the other side of that violence was doing the same.

After a week, the sky turns heavy with clouds, and rain filters down through the trees. We take the horses out anyway, because the thought of being locked in the palace is worse than rain soaking through our armor. It's too muddy to risk galloping, so we're weaving between trees at a walk, heading for a small rocky clearing where one of us will probably break an ankle when we spar because we've both gotten too reckless.

I don't know what makes me think of my childhood, but I've been trapped in my memories for miles, so when Malin says, "It's your turn for a story, Tycho," I tell him what happened when I was young. How my father gambled money he didn't have, how the Emberish soldiers attacked my family. I don't quite tell him . . . *everything*, because that's too much. But I tell him enough—and I think he guesses the rest anyway.

He pushes damp hair back from his forehead and glances over at me. "No wonder you joined the army on this side."

I frown. "I told you why I joined on this side. I first came here with Grey."

"Yeah, but it's really *her* army." He scoffs. "The king joined it, too. Even now, he hardly has any of us here. It's all hers."

I'm struck by that, because until this moment, I never really thought about it that way. We *did* join the Queen's Army in the beginning, for complex political reasons. And maybe Malin is right that some of it was an unconscious rebellion against Emberfall's army on my part.

Was that true for Grey as well?

I think of the armor the king wears. Black, just like mine.

I've always avoided the Emberish army, the way Rhen avoids sparring in the arena at Ironrose.

Has Grey been avoiding *Emberfall*?

Malin is still talking. "Who could blame him? Some people still worry that the king is just biding his time until he takes revenge against his brother."

That cuts through my meandering thoughts, and I snap my head around. "Wait—really?"

"Sure. Why else would he spend this much time here? Everyone knows what Prince Rhen did to him."

I don't know what to say. My shoulders have gone tight.

Malin glances over. "You know about that, don't you? How the prince had him flogged against the castle wall? You'd have to know."

My chest feels hollow. It's weird to hear about this so casually. Just a point of gossip repeated by a soldier. I still remember everything about that night with painful acuity, from the shackles on my wrists to the torchlight flickering on the cobblestones of the courtyard.

"Ah . . . yeah," I say. "I know."

The horses plod on, and Malin shakes his head, musing. "I've heard people say that the prince strung up a little boy beside the king, but who could believe *that*? A child would never survive a—"

"Silver hell," I snap. "I wasn't a *little boy*. I was fifteen."

Malin all but jerks his horse to a halt. The sudden silence between us is so loud that it *screams*.

I keep a loose rein and Mercy continues on. My eyes are fixed on the path.

After a moment, he must realize I'm not going to stop, because his horse trots a few steps to catch up.

"Tycho," he says, and his voice is dangerously quiet.

"Forget it. It doesn't matter."

"I didn't know."

"It's not a secret. It was a long time ago."

"I should have figured it out. I knew you were close to the king, but I didn't realize—"

"It's fine."

"When they said a *child*, I never thought—"

"Would you shut up?" I growl. "I said it's *fine*."

He shuts up.

I don't have a flask of anything in my saddlebags today, but I wish I did. Somehow it's a relief that people have forgotten that *I* was a part of what happened that night—while also wildly disheartening. Like I didn't matter at all. Just a pawn in a political game.

As usual, I suppose.

Malin looks over, peering at me. "So if you were fifteen then, how old are you now?"

His voice is easy, like the last few minutes never happened, and I appreciate that. "Nineteen. I'll be twenty after the solstice."

His eyebrows go up, and he whistles through his teeth. "You *are* a child. Here I thought you were older than I am—"

I punch him in the shoulder and he laughs.

But that's enough to coax a smile out of me. "How old are *you*, old man?"

"Twenty-two." He pauses. "You must have been really young when you started as a recruit."

"It was right after we came here. The marks were still fresh on my back." I pause. "The king's too."

He's quiet for a moment. "Again: no wonder you joined the army on this side."

I frown, but maybe he's right. I remember walking with Prince Rhen in early spring, the first time we admitted our fears to each other. He confessed that the training arena carried his bad memories, while the courtyard carried mine. But it's not *just* the courtyard for me, just like I'm sure it's more than the training arena for him. These memories can be provoked in myriad ways, like that ride when Malin bound my hands, how my panic flared and made magic spark in my blood.

For the first time, I wonder what part of Ironrose carries the *king*'s bad memories. Grey is always so strong, so stoic. I've never in my life seen him as vulnerable, so it's odd to consider him in this light. But he and Prince Rhen were trapped there, tortured season after season, for what must have seemed like an eternity.

I want to find Grey and confront him.

What are you afraid of?

He used to ask me that all the time, when he was teaching me to fight. I've never asked *him* what he's afraid of.

And right now, with scravers attacking magesmiths and the Truth-bringers working so hard to remove him from the throne, I wonder.

Because, for the first time, I look at the way he's confined me here. I look at the way he's confined *himself* here. How he's isolated himself in a distant wing of the palace. How he's separated himself from the queen.

And even, I realize, how he's distanced himself from *me*.

Since I arrived here, I've been assuming Lia Mara was the one pulling away, that the growing chasm between them was from her side: a way of protecting herself and her daughter from a man whose abilities put them at risk.

But maybe that's not it—or at least, not *all* of it.

Maybe Grey also sees this magic as a torment.

Maybe, after all this time, he's afraid of *himself*.

CHAPTER 35

TYCHO

As Malin and I ride along, I'm so deep in thought that I don't realize the raindrops trickling between the trees have turned to ice. When frost forms on our reins, Malin unstraps his bow.

"Tycho," he says sharply. "Is it the one you know?"

For a moment, I'm not sure. My heart is a steady thrum in my chest, and I grab my own bow, just in case. The rain has turned to sleet around us, a cold wind sending the freezing droplets into our eyes. I shiver.

But then I recognize the *feel* of Nakiis's magic. I hang the bow back over my shoulder. "It's him."

And then, because I'm tired and annoyed and my conversation with Malin has shaken too many shadows loose in my thoughts, I put two fingers in my mouth and blow a shrill whistle.

I don't even see him coming. The black shape just suddenly *appears* between the trees, slamming into me so hard that I'm knocked off Mercy's back. There's a moment of complete weightlessness, followed by a painful meeting with the ground that rattles every bone in my body.

We go skidding ten feet through the muddy mountainside until we come to a stop against a tree.

Nakiis lands on my chest again. This time he's only got one hand on my throat. "I told you no whistling," he says.

"Trust me, I'm already regretting it." I wince and reach over my head to yank a branch out of my armor.

"Let me know if I should shoot him," calls Malin.

"Eh, probably not," I call back.

Nakiis draws back, affronted. "*Probably* not?"

"Well, you did knock me off my . . ." I begin, but my voice trails off. The scraver is bleeding from a long wound under his ribs. It looks older, because the edges are crusted with scabs that look infected, though knocking me off my horse probably reopened it.

He's bruised, too—at least, I think he is. His gray skin is mottled with darker splotches along his ribs and down one arm.

"You're hurt," I say in surprise. Rain continues trickling through the trees, but like before, Nakiis is all but pinning me to the ground. "Did someone shoot you? Let me up. I can help you."

He casts a glance at Malin, and I add, "He won't shoot you either. Tell him, Mal."

"I won't shoot," he says flatly, but it's not very convincing.

Nakiis sits back on his heels while I pull another twig out of my armor and sit up. I'm probably lucky he didn't break my neck.

Now that I can look at him fully, I notice that wound on his ribs doesn't look like an arrow strike anymore. It looks like a slice from a blade. His trousers are streaked and stained, too. They look like they've been patched and repaired in several spots. He's also missing one of the weapons he wore the last time I saw him.

I lift a hand and nod toward the slice on his chest. "Do you want me to heal it?"

"You cannot."

My eyebrows go up. "Iishellasan steel?"

"Yes."

I glance at the empty sheath along his thigh. "Did someone take it from you?"

"Xovaar."

He doesn't elaborate further, and we stare at each other in the rain for a bit. When I shift my weight, his entire frame goes tense, his wings flickering like he's ready to take flight.

"Relax," I say. "At least let me fix the bruising."

When he doesn't move further, I roll onto my knees and reach for his arm, where the worst of the bruising is. The first arrow wound from Malin is almost fully closed, but it's still swollen and hot like it's also infected. The sparks and stars flare in my blood, but like before, it's obvious when healing begins, because the tension eases out of his frame.

"What happened?" I say, as the mottled bruising begins to melt away.

He stares back at me wordlessly, and an icy wind whips between us. I shiver—then realize the magic in this one feels different from his. I let go of his arm and scrabble to get a hand on a weapon, but Nakiis slaps a hand around my wrist, his claws digging in.

"No," he says. "She is with me."

But on the path, Malin already has an arrow nocked.

Nakiis glares up at him. "If you loose that arrow, soldier, I will not leave a wound for you to heal."

"I'm not shooting!" Malin snaps. "But what was that?"

My heart is still pounding, but I stare back at Nakiis. "*She.* There's another scraver here?"

"Yes."

I cast my gaze upward, into the trees. At first, I see nothing, but it's only because I'm looking for a dark shape, a pair of night-colored wings like his. But then I spot a shimmer of purple well overhead, and I swallow.

"I see her," says Malin, and Nakiis growls.

"Put away your bow," I tell him, hoping I'm making the right choice. He does.

The scraver is too far to see much detail at all, but I remember a scraver with purple markings on her skin crouching beside little Nora when the queen helped heal her injuries.

"She was in Briarlock," I say.

"Yes."

"What's her name?"

Nakiis doesn't answer this either, but magic carries her words down to me anyway.

—*My name is Igaa, magesmith.*

"Well met," I call up to her. When my eyes return to Nakiis, I say, "She's friendlier than you are."

His eyes narrow, but he lets go of my wrist. I rest my fingertips against the broad muscle of his chest and let the magic work again.

He must have been in more pain than he was letting on, because he lets out a breath, and this time, his frame sags as the bruising disappears. I reach for the knife wound, and he shakes his head.

"Let me try," I say. "Maybe I can heal the infection."

After a moment, he nods again, and I lightly rest my fingertips over the wound. He hisses a breath, his fangs bared, but he's very still.

I wasn't really sure my magic would do anything at all, but the infection *does* begin to dissolve away, the swelling lessening.

"This looks like it's days old," I say to him. "I told you before. If you need help, you can come to me. I'll help you."

Nakiis says nothing, but from above, Igaa says, —*I told him to return to you.*

I glance up at her. "Do you know why Xovaar attacked him?"

—He knows Nakiis can identify many of the remaining mage-smiths. Xovaar's human allies do not know everyone the king has shared his magic with.

I turn that around in my head, and I look back at the injured scraver in front of me. The bruising is entirely gone, along with the arrow wound across his bicep, though that one left a scar. The knife wound is seeping blood, but the pus and infection are gone.

I don't look at any of that, though. I'm studying his face. "You're protecting me again."

Nakiis scoffs and looks away. "Someone has to. The king's magic is known, but he is surrounded by armed guards and soldiers. One could question their loyalty, but it would be hard for a small number of scravers to attack him successfully." He pauses and glances at Malin, then back to me. "*You* are not as protected."

"You said that Xovaar wants what was taken. Does that mean he's trying to reclaim magic somehow?"

He's silent for a moment, regarding me.

Igaa's voice finds me again—or maybe it finds us both.

—Trust him, Nakiis.

I snort under my breath and shift my gaze back to Nakiis. "Maybe *she's* the one who should be my friend."

"Are we friends, Tycho?"

There's a note in his voice that gives me pause. It reminds me of that moment in the tent with Rhen, when he practically asked the same thing.

Before Rhen betrayed me by telling Grey what I'd confided in him.

"I think we could be," I say.

He glances up at Igaa, then looks back at me. "You knew my father," he says. "You knew the scravers were once treaty bound to remain in the ice forests of Iishellasa."

"I know you left Iishellasa—and Iisak followed."

Nakiis nods. "The last queen of Syhl Shallow would have been within rights to punish us both for breaking the treaty. She didn't capture me, but she captured my father."

"Yes," I say. "But Grey negotiated for his freedom. And now that Lia Mara is in power, she wouldn't restrict the scravers to Iishellasa. I told you that."

"You did tell me," he agrees. "And I believed you." He glances up toward Igaa. "I returned to the ice forests with this news. Many were wary. Many did not believe it. But I convinced a small number to join me. To see." He pauses. "And we found you embroiled in a battle."

"Briarlock," I say.

"Yes."

I think of what happened in that battle, the way the scravers appeared to help—and then fled immediately. They must have been wary of Grey's magic—or Lia Mara's rule. But then the king and queen did nothing to go after them, because they wouldn't. "So those scravers who helped us in Briarlock are the ones on *your* side," I say.

"Yes." Ice forms on the bark of the trees nearby. "Xovaar was not among them. He came later, when it became clear that we could cross the Frozen River without repercussions."

—He resents the treaty, Igaa adds from above.

Nakiis nods. "We may have magic, but humans have us outnumbered. In the past, we lived in peace—and shared our magic, using Iishellasan steel. In the beginning, scravers did not realize humans would inherit the magical properties of our steel—but as I said, we were at peace. This was considered a blessing. But eventually, tensions grew among the magesmiths and the humans—and therefore among the scravers as well. When a human child died in the conflicts, the scravers were banished to Iishellasa, and the magesmiths fled Syhl Shallow. Again—the scravers meant no harm to humans, but we were treaty

351

bound to remain in the ice forests. As time went on and previous queens refused to allow us to cross the Frozen River, many scravers grew to resent the treaty. Many of us wanted to leave."

I'm studying him. "Is that why *you* left?"

"Yes." He pauses. "But I meant no harm. I sought out a magesmith, as we were once allies. I thought perhaps we could approach the queen of Syhl Shallow together." Another pause, and more ice forms around us. "But the magesmith tricked me, trapping me with her magic, using my power for her own will."

With a start, I realize what he's talking about. "Lilith," I say.

The magesmith who nearly destroyed Emberfall. Who tortured Rhen and Grey. Who provoked the war between both countries.

Nakiis nods. "Yes. I did not keep this a secret—and perhaps I should have. Many of the others refuse to risk any further strife. They have no desire to live in peace with any of you. They simply want what was taken—so it can never be taken again."

"But how?" I say—and as soon as I say the words, I *know* how.

"By killing you. Any magesmith they can find. Anywhere they sense the presence of magic. Anywhere they believe they may find a scrap of charmed steel."

I already know Nakiis himself sensed my magic in the woods, when I was traveling with Malin. And it's likely the other scravers sensed it when I was with the soldiers, too.

I think of everyone who has a ring of Iishellasan steel. Noah. Jake. Lia Mara. Princess Harper has one, but she doesn't wear it often. But there are several artifacts in the castle there, just like they have here.

As I work this through, Malin says, "But if they're only after the magic, why are they attacking innocent people?"

"The scravers know that magic is no longer welcome here. We are outnumbered. The best way for Xovaar to drive any magesmiths out of hiding is to convince more humans that magic is dangerous. On the other side of the border, that has been easy—Emberfall already has a bitter past with magic. But once Xovaar learned that the Truthbringers were also working against your king here in Syhl Shallow, he knew he would have allies on this side of the border as well."

"The Truthbringers are willing to let their own people die, just to get rid of magic?" says Malin.

"Yes," I say, realizing that they've been doing that all along. I think of Callyn in the hallway, mentioning the rumors that Grey was interrogating more citizens. I remember Alek standing in the throne room, the way he rallied enough people against *me* that Grey demanded the return of my rings that very instant. "They were willing to let the *queen* die, just to get rid of magic. They're willing to go to war. Again."

Nakiis nods. "Discontent toward the king has never been so high. A time will come when the scravers can rely on the Truthbringers to kill him—or Syhl Shallow will drive him out, and they can do it themselves. Either way, the attacks will continue until the magesmiths are revealed. I try to stop them when I can, but you saw how many of us were in Briarlock. We are few." He pauses. "They are many."

"Is this why you want my help? To stop Xovaar?"

"If it were him alone, I would not need your help. But there are hundreds who believe as he does. He is not the problem, Tycho. Now that the scravers have escaped the ice forests, they will not stop until they ensure that we cannot be trapped again."

Hundreds. Hundreds of scravers attacking people on both sides of the border, trying to eradicate magic.

All while the Truthbringers are trying to do the same thing.

As much as I hate the discord between me and Grey, I know what I need to do. "I need to tell the king."

"The king cannot help," says Nakiis.

"He has *magic*," I say sharply. "And he's had a lot more practice than me."

353

"I will not bind myself to your king," Nakiis says. "And he cannot stand against them alone."

He's said something like that before, and it makes me stop short. "Is that what you intend to do? Bind yourself to *me*?" I hesitate, trying to work it out—and I realize what he said about the magesmith Lilith. "Does it let me access your magic?"

He says nothing, and I think back to the time we met, when I was fifteen, when his father had just been killed in the battle against Lilith. I remember begging Grey to heal his wounds, and as soon as it was done, Nakiis fled.

He hasn't answered, so I move closer. "It does, doesn't it?" I say. "That's what happened before. That's how she trapped you."

Nothing.

"Please," I say desperately. I look up at Igaa, beseeching. "Please just tell me."

For a moment, neither of them speak, and the only sound is the light rain filtering through the trees.

But Nakiis finally says, "Yes. You would have access to my magic." He pauses. "Not *just* mine. All of ours."

I wait as the implications of that sink in.

"That is how Lilith was able to hold such a grip on Emberfall for so long," Nakiis adds. "Once the link is forged, it cannot be broken until one of us dies."

"So I'd have your magic forever," I say.

"Or until he kills you," Malin says.

Nakiis screeches at him, and it's so shrill that we both wince. "Or until he uses that magic to trap *me*, soldier." Ice slicks the entire length of the tree now, and I can see his fangs. "Until he realizes just how much power he has, and then *my* people suffer because of it."

Malin inhales sharply, ready to fire back, but I step forward and grab his arm.

"Stop," I say quietly. "Stop."

Because I suddenly understand. Nakiis's hesitation, his wariness, his reluctance—they all make sense.

And considering everything I've gone through, it should never have taken me this long.

I forgave Prince Rhen because I know a bit of what he endured from Lilith. I knew she tortured him, and she tortured the king—all using magic. When Prince Rhen had me chained up on that wall, I knew he was making a terrible choice to protect his people.

I never really thought about what *Nakiis* might have endured at Lilith's hands—or how that would affect him now.

He had an arrow through his wing, and he barely let me near him. He barely lets me near him *now*.

I keep my voice low, because I know he'll hear me. "I told you before," I say. "If you need my help, I'll help you. I won't steal your power. I won't trap you." I pause and glance up at Igaa. "I'll help you *and* your people."

He regards me through the rain, but the ice begins to melt.

"But you have to *let* me help you," I say. "If scravers are killing people and we could stop it, we should stop them *now*."

"*Now?* They will try to kill you, Tycho. As soon as they know. The magic will not be subtle. They will feel it, and they will attack. There are still too many of them, and far too widespread. We must bide our time."

"Then I'll tell Grey. He can call up the army, and we can—"

"There is a reason these attacks are isolated and widespread," Nakiis says. "Your army cannot march on them." He pauses. "And once you have this power, you will be more powerful than your king. If you tell him, he will not be an ally. He will lock you away where I cannot get to you."

I inhale sharply to reject the very idea of that—but I can't. "Nakiis, tell me what you want. How do we move forward from here?"

"I am not ready to lend my magic to yours. Until then, I will continue doing what I can."

"You could be killed before you're ready," I say.

At that, his frame seems to sag, and his wings droop, just a little. "Indeed," he says. "So could you."

Now it's my turn to sag. As always, my life is bound to someone else's problems. *He will lock you away where I cannot get to you.*

I want to deny it, but I can't. Grey would. He absolutely would.

But maybe I do have *one* option. I look at Nakiis. "If we have to wait, then I need you to send word to Emberfall."

"To Emberfall!" He actually sounds affronted.

"Yes. Prince Rhen's guards wouldn't let you get close to the castle, but you could get to Jax. I need you to find him and tell him why I've been detained."

He stares back at me, his eyes black and implacable.

When he says nothing, I rush on. "Please. Nakiis, *please.* I beg of you. I have no way to send word. He has no idea what's happening." To my surprise, my chest tightens, and I try to shake it off. It doesn't work. "*You* won't let me help. *Grey* won't let me leave. I know you're at risk, too. I know you're trying to stop Xovaar. Maybe I have no right to ask. But Jax is alone, and the other soldiers already think he's a target. I don't . . . I don't even know—"

I break off sharply, because I can't finish that sentence. The rain pours down, and I have to swallow.

I don't even know if he's alive.

"Tycho." The scraver's hand falls on my shoulder, his claws pressing into my skin. A whip of wind blasts around us. "I will go."

I don't have a chance to say anything in response. Before I've even realized he's agreed, before I even have time to give him a proper *message*, his wings snap wide, and he's gone.

CHAPTER 36

JAX

The morning after the scraver attack, I'm woken by clattering and voices from the kitchen, along with a faint light breaking through the gap in my curtains. I don't know how long I slept, but I'm still exhausted, so that doesn't bode well. The foot that Captain Ammax brought sits in a bag in my wardrobe, but if the kitchen is already bustling, practice will have to wait for later. When I look in the mirror, I find that the scratches on my face are an angrier red than they were last night, and I wish I'd let Lola tut over them for a few minutes. Maybe I can ask for a salve. I really need to figure out a way to ask about what happened.

Molly and Lola are in the dining room as usual, but there's a heavy weight to the air. The room goes silent when I appear.

Tension crawls across my shoulders. When the scravers attacked during our journey, everyone thought they were coming after me, that I'd drawn them somehow. Does everyone think that now? I duck my head and take my usual seat at the end of a table.

I'm prepared to wait for my food, but Molly and Lola stop what they're doing to bring my breakfast *immediately*. Lola had literally been serving rolls to someone else, but she turns away to bring some to me.

I wait for someone to protest, but no one does.

They keep staring.

Molly's expression is a bit drawn, but she gives me a crooked curtsy. She says, "*Tahlasta dasima*, Master Jax," which is really quite touching— but then her eyes fill.

I frown. "Molly." But I don't know what else to say.

She swipes her eyes and leans down to give me a kiss on the cheek, then sees the scratches on the other side of my face and gasps. She breaks off and starts speaking rapidly to Lola, and then they're both talking and staring at me—and so is everyone else. Even Master Garson comes in from the kitchen to add a few comments. They're mentioning the soldiers and the scravers, but everyone is talking too quickly.

"Please," I say. "I am . . . I cannot—" I break off and make a frustrated sound.

Luckily, Mistress Elayne, my tutor, walks through the door and into the mayhem. I completely forgot she would come at breakfast.

"Help me," I say to her desperately. "Please."

She takes stock of the situation, from Molly's tears to everyone's stares to the rapid conversation around us, and then she strides briskly across the room, taking in the scratches on my face.

"They've heard about the attack on some of the soldiers," she says plainly. "Molly says you risked your life to protect them, and then you rode through the night to get her home."

Wait. I frown. "No, I—"

But Molly cuts me off, rushing on in Emberish now that she knows she has a translator.

"Three men were killed," Elayne continues, once Molly is done speaking. "Master Garson said one of the captains told him it might have been *all* of them if you hadn't acted so quickly."

I stare at her, and then my eyes flick back to the workers who are watching this whole interaction. "It wasn't just me," I say, remembering Sephran with the sword in his hand. "We all fought them off." I glance at Molly and Lola and then at Master Garson, who's drawn closer. "Did the surviving soldiers return safely?"

Elayne repeats my question to Master Garson.

He nods, then claps me on the shoulder. Beside him, Molly says something quickly, then dashes off.

Elayne smiles, and it's kind. "She rather desperately wants to find something for your face."

I frown, though it's still stinging. "She doesn't have to."

"Ah, let the girl mother you," she says. She sets down her satchel and tells everyone else to go back to their meals, because we have to work.

It takes me a moment to realize I understood every word she said in Emberish.

Still, I say, "Today? Really?"

"*Every* day. The faster you learn, the quicker you can have these awkward conversations on your own. Did you write down any words you understood yesterday?"

Right now, the only word I can think of was Sephran calling Niall a jackass. "Ah, no."

Elayne *tsks* and pulls a book from her satchel. There's a small sketch of a calf and a lamb on the cover. "Fine. We can read."

I blink and think of the battle from last night. Blood was in the air, and soldiers were dying around me. I thought I was going to die. More than once.

I woke up this morning thinking everyone was going to hate me.

I stare at the cover, but I make no move to touch the book. I have no idea how I'm going to focus on any of this.

Elayne leans in, and her voice drops. "Sometimes it's best to just keep moving forward."

And that's enough to make me pick up the book and turn to the first page.

The forge is busier than usual. On most days, Master Garson has two or three of us shoeing horses while everyone else handles other tasks, but today, there are five. I'm not sure what's changed, but it must be related to the attack from last night. There's a different energy in the air. A nervous tension. I listen to the gossip while horses are being shod, and I'm able to piece together that more soldiers are being sent on patrol. Maybe more guards around the palace grounds, too.

For the first time, none of the soldiers are short with me. No one knocks my crutches into the dirt. No one mutters about the trash from Syhl Shallow or spits on the ground.

I hope to see someone I know, Sephran or Leo or even Kutter, but I don't. Maybe they've been ordered out on these patrols themselves.

At the end of the day, the forge has fallen quiet, and I'm ready to pack up my tools, but a young woman leads a large buckskin gelding to my spot. She's not in armor, so I don't think she's a soldier, but her arms are lightly muscled, so I'm not sure. She bears a scar across one cheek that looks like it was caused by a knife, and she's limping. She's not too much older than I am, with blue eyes and thick curls that are bound back from her face.

I have no idea who she is, but it's been a long day and I'm tired. Sweat has been stinging the claw marks on my jaw for hours now. I stoke the heat in the forge and turn my attention to the buckskin.

"New shoes?" I say automatically in Emberish. "Or lame?"

The young woman seems to startle, then looks a bit amused, then says in perfect Syssalah, "Neither, actually. I came to see you."

Now it's my turn to startle.

"I'm Harper," she says.

360

Harper. Princess Harper. Betrothed to Prince Rhen.

I'm frozen in place. I don't know what to say. I practically have to jab myself with a hot pair of tongs to force a word out of my mouth.

"Sorry," I say in Emberish, which is ridiculous, because she clearly speaks Syssalah. My thoughts won't organize, and for a moment, it's like I forget my *own* language. I have to shake myself. "I—forgive me. Your Highness."

"No, Harper is fine. I've been dying to meet you since you got here, but Tycho said you were a little overwhelmed by . . . well, *all of it*, which I can completely understand. Then Rhen told me you had words so I thought . . ." She hesitates, then winces. "Well, I thought I might be unwelcome, as well."

Her mention of Prince Rhen sends an icy chill through my heart. She's so earnest, though. Her Syssalah is effortless, too. Much better than the prince. He speaks like he's reading from a book, but she seems as fluent as Tycho.

I haven't said anything, but maybe that coolness reaches my eyes, because her expression shifts, and she's evaluating me with a bit more regard.

"So I *am* unwelcome," she says.

I cast a glance around, because guards surely followed her here, but I see none. That doesn't mean they aren't waiting out of sight. "No, Your Highness."

She watches me look for guards and she frowns. "Please. You don't have to do that. You can say whatever you want to me. Really." She pauses, evaluating me. "And . . . I know what you said to Rhen. Maybe you won't believe me, but . . . I understand why you hate him. I didn't know Tycho then, but Grey . . ." She swallows. "Grey had become one of my closest friends. I would have said that *Rhen* was one of his closest friends. When I saw what Rhen did to them—I hated him, too."

I'm frozen in place. I didn't expect her to be so forthright.

She closes her eyes and hugs her arms to her body. "I'm not going to make excuses for him. It was . . . it was terrible. It was a terrible time. But he had reasons. I don't expect you to forgive him, or to understand, but he had *reasons*."

That ice around my heart doesn't thaw. Everyone has *reasons* for the terrible things they do. I'm sure my father had reasons for drinking himself half to death and gambling away all our tax money. I'm sure Niall had reasons for coming after me last night.

But I doubt I can say any of that. I doubt it would matter. It's clear she's forgiven the prince for his actions. Nothing I say is going to change that.

I also can't stand here looking at her, because she's so ardent that it's beginning to make me feel coldhearted, and I don't like it. *The prince* is the one with a cold heart.

I thrust a fresh shoe into the forge, then bend to run a hand down her horse's foreleg. He offers me his hoof readily, and I flip the pincers in my hand to cut the nails loose.

"Wait," says the princess. "You don't have to work! I didn't come here for—"

"This one was loose anyway," I say, snapping the nails away so I can pull the shoe free. "You would've lost it within a day or two."

She's silent for a moment. "All right."

I don't say anything to that, and maybe she takes her cue from me, because after that, the only sound in the forge is the bang of my hammer. Her horse is patient and well-bred, which I'd expect, but when I set the new shoe into place, he presses his muzzle right against my shoulder, resting the full weight of his head there.

"That's very helpful," I murmur to him as I hammer each nail. "Thank you."

Harper laughs lightly, and I glance up. I've grown so used to people not having any idea what I'm saying that I forgot she would understand me.

"Do you want me to move him?" she says.

"Nah," I say. "I don't mind if the horses are happy."

"I know. Garson said you've gotten quite the reputation."

I look up fully. "What?"

"You didn't know? Garson told me you've handled most of the hardest horses, and none of them seem to faze you."

No. I didn't know. Part of me wants to scowl. I wonder if the soldiers have been sending me the worst horses on purpose, the way they've been taunting me in other ways.

"Horses never bother me," I say. "The mean ones are usually mean for a reason."

Her horse blows warm breaths against my neck, his velvet lip wriggling against my collar. I reach for my file.

"Maybe I'm unwelcome," Harper begins, "but would it be all right if . . . if I just said a few things to you?"

I don't stop rasping the file against the hoof. I really don't want to hear more about Prince Rhen and whatever his *reasons* might have been, but it's not like I can stop her. "Of course, Your Highness."

Another little laugh, but this one is under her breath, and it sounds a bit rueful. When she speaks, however, her voice is serious. "You saved a lot of people last night," she says. "But I've learned that some of the soldiers were being . . . unkind."

Unkind. That's one way to put it. I set down my file and reach for the pincers again.

"I heard you were leaving the group," she adds. "That some of them had chased you off."

I think of Niall and Brinley, how I was terrified they were going to drag me off Teddy's back and beat me to death. How they leveled arrows at my face and prepared to shoot.

I wonder how much of that they admitted—or if they just confessed to the chasing.

"But you turned back to warn them," Harper finishes.

I finally set down the horse's hoof and turn to face her. "They haven't all been unkind. And even if they have, they don't deserve to *die* for it."

She looks right back at me. "You hate Rhen, and from what I've heard, you'd have plenty of reason to hate some of the soldiers, too. You didn't have to risk yourself. I'm grateful for what you did. So is Rhen. Grey will be, too, once he hears about it."

The king. I didn't even consider that *he* would need to know about this attack, too. I wonder if that means they'll send Tycho right back when he gets here. The thought makes my chest ache.

"If there's anything you need," Harper says, "if there's anything you *want*, I hope you'll ask for it."

The only thing I really want is something I can't ask for.

"I don't want anything," I say woodenly.

She holds up a hand, and I see she has a ring like Tycho used to wear. "At the very least, I can fix your face."

I hesitate, because the scratches still burn. My eyes flick to the scar on her cheek, and I wonder what caused it.

"I won't be as fast as Tycho," she says. "I don't wear it very often because Rhen . . . well, he doesn't like it. He has a bad history with magic. But I know how. If you want."

He has a bad history with magic. I hate that it lights a spark of curiosity in my thoughts. Magic isn't feared here the way it is in Syhl Shallow. Magic is what helped them win the war.

I don't care. I shove the curiosity away. "No." I hesitate, wondering if I'm being rude. "But thank you. Your Highness."

Her eyebrows go up. "I know you're not afraid of magic."

"I . . . don't want to erase it."

Harper nods and drops her hand. For a moment, her expression is

364

a little haunted. "I understand. I don't mind my scars either. I have a friend who says they're a reminder that you survived something terrible."

The night Tycho first showed me the marks on his back, he said he'd made his peace with it and had forgiven Prince Rhen. He told me that the prince had his own scars. I've seen the patch Rhen wears over his missing eye, and the scars that peek around the edge.

I've hated the prince for so long that until this moment, I've never really considered that it probably *was* very terrible.

"Really," Harper says. "Anything." She pauses. "Even if you just want to speak Syssalah with someone who isn't going to make you read books about lambs. I'm always desperate for practice."

That startles a smile out of me, and I hate myself for it a little bit. "You speak it very well," I say.

"Thank you! I used to beg Tycho to practice for *hours*. Jake, too, when I see him." She smiles, then rolls her eyes. "Rhen is better than he seems, but he's too arrogant to risk stumbling over pronunciation."

That almost makes me laugh.

I stop myself before I do.

She notices, and sobers. "Thank you, Jax. I meant everything I said."

"Thank you, Your Highness."

"Harper."

I nod and hold out the reins to her horse. "Harper."

She takes the reins, and the buckskin presses his muzzle to her chest, but she doesn't turn away. "I just . . . I want you to know that Rhen cares for Tycho a great deal. He considers him a friend. A good friend." I stiffen, but Harper continues, "I think he worries he'll lose that friendship if he can't figure out a way to resolve things with you."

My anger swells and flares without warning. "He's *worried?*" I snap, and my voice is like the crack of a whip. "The prince doesn't deserve Tycho's friendship. He doesn't deserve his *loyalty*. Neither does the king.

Do any of you have any idea what he'd already endured? How much he'd already suffered? I will *never* resolve things with a man who could do that to him. Do you understand? *Not ever.*"

She flinches, and her breathing has gone a little rapid.

I draw back, then run a damp hand over my neck. I seem determined to find myself at the end of a rope. But I can't find the will to apologize for anything I said. I don't care if guards swarm the forge. I meant every word.

But now she looks wounded, and that steals my thunder. My anger isn't with her anyway.

"I'm sorry," I say, and my voice is rough. "I shouldn't have snapped."

"It's my own fault. I did tell you to say anything you want." Harper squares her shoulders and looks at me. "But Rhen isn't the only one who's made bad choices, Jax."

I look away. "Tycho already told me about the king and what he—"

"I'm talking about *you*."

My eyes snap back to hers.

"You were part of a plot against the king," she says. "You had *your* reasons, and I know you were desperate. But you knew who you were helping. You knew the Truthbringers hated the king. You might not have known what they were going to *do*, but you were a part of it."

I've gone stock-still.

Now it's her fury that's been unleashed. "They took the queen and the princess, Jax! Sinna is *three*, and they tried to kill her mother *right in front of her*. I heard—I heard one of them tried to cut her throat—" Her voice nearly breaks, but she catches herself.

Her emotion is so potent that I almost can't breathe. "Your Highness—"

"No. Stop." Her eyes are full of fire. "I understand why you're so angry. I do! And I know you helped save everyone in the end. But Grey is Rhen's brother. Sinna is his niece. His *family*. The only family Rhen *has*! He's allowed to hate you, too, but he doesn't. You think he doesn't deserve a friend, but he *does*. I wish you knew everything *he* endured, because if you knew what the enchantress did to him, you would never—"

"Harper." Prince Rhen's voice is quiet and sure, but he speaks from a short distance away. He's leading a large gray gelding that paws at the ground. He's trailed by guards who wait on horseback just outside the forge.

All of the other workers have gone home for the day, so the forge is cool and shadowed, and I can't read his expression from here. I have no idea how much he heard, or how long he's been standing there. Tension locks into my spine as I wait for him to react.

The princess takes a slow breath, and it's clear she's deliberating over the same thing. She finally looks over. "Rhen. I didn't mean to make you wait so long. Jax noticed Will had a loose shoe, so he offered to fix it. I can meet you in the courtyard in a minute."

He leads his horse into the forge to stop beside her. "If you're going to lecture Jax about my past," he says, his Syssalah slower than hers, "I believe I should wait right here."

There's a weight to that comment, and my fingers tighten on my forge tools.

But Harper frowns, then sighs. "Rhen. I'm sorry. That wasn't my intent."

"Ah, Harper," he says gently, and there's true warmth in his tone. "I know your heart. You don't need to explain to me." His gaze falls on me, and most of the warmth evaporates. "Jax can hate me if he desires. As you said, we're both allowed."

I wonder if that means he *does* hate me. Good. I hope he does.

But as I look back at him, I realize . . . he doesn't. There's no animosity in his expression, despite how things ended between us the last time we spoke. And now I have Harper's words rattling around in my thoughts, poking holes in all my convictions.

"You are right," Rhen adds, his gaze holding mine. "I don't deserve Tycho's friendship. Nor his loyalty. Neither does my brother."

I can hear the genuine weight in his voice. Tycho's friendship really does mean something to him—and my anger really does affect him.

That's wrapping up with what Harper said, about all the things *I* did wrong, too.

I hate that this has chipped away at the ice around my heart. I draw a long breath and scowl. "Well . . . *I* probably don't deserve his friendship either."

Harper's eyebrows go up. "So . . . does that mean you don't hate Rhen anymore?" she says hopefully. "Did I fix it?"

I inhale sharply, then stop before I can get myself in trouble. I clamp my mouth shut.

A wicked light sparks in Prince Rhen's eye. He's no fool.

"Not quite," he says. He lifts Harper's hand and kisses her knuckles, then gives me a nod. "You do have my full gratitude for your actions last night. The soldiers were very lucky you were there."

"I'm not a soldier," I say. "And it wasn't just me. I only shot a few of them."

"I saw most of the surviving soldiers when they came in. More than half were drunk. The rest of them were close to it. I heard you went through your entire quiver. Soldier or not, it rather does sound like it was *mostly* you."

I stare at him. He stares back.

Eventually, he says, "We will be taking actions to secure the castle. Patrols and guards have doubled. But as Harper mentioned, if there is anything you should need or want, I will be happy to provide."

I'd have to be staring death in the face before I'd ask him for anything at all, and I think we both know it. "Yes, Your Highness."

He turns away.

"Thank you for fixing Will's shoe," Harper says.

"Thank you for the lecture," I say, and she smiles.

"See! I fixed it a *little*," she whispers.

But I'm not smiling, and the prince takes hold of her hand as they lead the horses out of the forge.

Once they're gone, I head back to the Shield House. I pull open my wardrobe, and I find the bag with the artificial foot that Captain Ammax provided. It's lying against the armor I wore on the journey from Syhl Shallow—armor I haven't worn since, because I'm *not* a soldier.

My entire life has taught me that wishes are good for nothing: I couldn't wish for my mother back. I couldn't wish for my father to be a better man. I couldn't wish for coins to save the forge.

Now that I'm here in Emberfall, my wishes are just as pointless. I can't wish for Tycho to return, or for the scravers to be gone, or for anything to be easier.

My father used to blame me for every moment of misfortune that befell our small family. I spent so long hearing him say that I was worthless that I believed him.

But I think about everything that happened, and I consider what Prince Rhen just said.

Soldier or not, it rather does sound like it was mostly you.

I pull out the bag and I pull out the armor, then dig to find the boot I've never used.

Maybe it doesn't matter that my wishes won't come true.

Maybe instead of wishing, it's time to start *doing.*

CHAPTER 37

JAX

I fetch Teddy and head for the archery fields almost every night. Anytime Sephran and his friends have leave, they'll join me. Sephran usually brings food from the mess hall to share, and we'll eat as we ride across the grounds. I can't quite have full conversations yet, but I listen to their gossip and stories, parsing out what I can.

The soldiers tell me that there have been reports about more scraver attacks throughout Emberfall, that there are more rumors about the "monster" returning. When we shoot, there's an edge to our practice now, a pressure to be faster, more accurate—as if the soldiers are more acutely aware their lives might depend on it.

I feel that same pressure. At night, when Kutter and Sephran give Leo instruction, I listen, trying to understand as much as I can. When Sephran notices my focus, they begin to include me in their lessons, adjusting my stance, my angle, my hands. Practicing with the false foot pays off, and after a week, I can stand and shoot without needing to kneel for stability. I practice rapid firing so many times that I earn blisters on my fingers, but after four days, I can put five arrows into a distant target in less than ten seconds.

Sephran whistles, then grins and gives me a good-natured shove in the shoulder. "They should put *you* on patrol."

"I no soldier," I say. But his praise makes me blush, pleased.

The last time Tycho was gone for months, he began to feel like a dream, like someone I conjured from my imagination.

It's beginning to feel like that again. My loneliness has started to twist into something darker. Sharper. I always have to shove it away. But it clings.

One evening Sephran shows up at the forge alone, and he tells me Leo has watch duty and Kutter is on patrol. He asks if I still want to go shooting.

It's quite literally the best part of my day, so I look at him like he's crazy. "Yes," I say. "I want."

We race across the grounds, my hair whipping back from my face, the speed taking my breath away. The wild sense of freedom is still so new, so *foreign*. I sometimes think about the first moment Tycho let me ride Mercy, the way he was leading me at a sedate walk, but it felt like we were going twice as fast as I could manage on my own. Now, riding with Sephran, I feel like I'm flying.

I have bread and apples wrapped up in my saddlebag, and Sephran has dried beef strips in his, so after we shoot, we sit against a tree and share. He's also got a small flask of something that smells sharp and sweet, like cinnamon, but when he holds it my way, offering, I shake my head.

He takes a long swallow, then tilts his head and looks at me sideways. "You never drink," he says.

That's true. He and the others often have a flask of something, or a small bottle tucked away, but I never share. I shrug a little, frowning, because I hadn't realized he noticed. I don't know how to explain that I don't want to do anything that reminds me of my father.

But Sephran is patient, and I don't want to keep it a secret. He waits while I piece words together. "That drink," I say, tapping his flask, "make father sick."

A line appears between his eyebrows, and I know that's not quite the right word.

"Mean sick," I add. "*Angry* sick."

Understanding flares in his eyes. "Oh." He winces, then puts the cap back on. "Sorry."

I put out a hand to stop him. "No, Sephran. Not you."

He looks down at my hand on his wrist, then screws the lid the rest of the way on. Somehow it feels a little more purposeful. A little more intimate, in a way I can't quite define. I let my hand drop, but it makes me flush anyway. Now I wish I hadn't said anything at all. I look out at the darkening fields, because I suddenly can't meet his eyes.

He looks out at the fields, too, which is a relief. "It never makes me mean," he says, and his voice is casual. "Not Mal either." He chuckles, his voice warm with fondness for his friend. He has a lot of stories about Malin, and even though I only understand about half of them, I know Sephran misses him.

"Once we had three days of leave," he's saying. "We almost drowned ourselves in liquor in Valkins Valley. We both drew an early watch on our first day back, and he was vomiting in the bushes every time the captain stepped away."

When I frown at the word *vomiting*, Sephran mimes it, which makes me smile.

He grins. "He begged me to tie his belt to a tree to keep him upright."

"Did you?"

"Yes." He heaves an aggrieved sigh. "And while I was doing it, he vomited down my back."

372

That's so unexpected that it makes me laugh, and Sephran looks over. It's grown late, and shadows are long, darkening his eyes. "You understand so much now."

I shrug a little, but I'm pleased. "You have good stories."

He smiles, but his gaze is searching mine, and warmth crawls up my cheeks again. I turn to look toward the palace. Half a dozen windows are lit from within, and I wonder if the prince is in there, all sad and alone.

I know I am.

The thought comes from nowhere, striking with accuracy.

I feel a tug at my hair, and I turn my head in surprise. It's light but firm, and I think maybe it's a prelude to tussling or teasing, but when I inhale, Sephran's mouth lands on mine.

For an instant, I'm not sure how to react. My lips were parted, and I taste the cinnamon of the liquor before I even realize it's happening. The kiss is small and sweet and not entirely unpleasant. But then his hand winds tighter in my hair, and I remember myself. I put a hand against his shoulder, but he's already deepening the kiss, his tongue brushing mine. I try to pull back, but I'm against a tree and there's nowhere to go.

I make a sound and push against him more firmly, thinking this must all be a moment of confusion. But he grabs hold of my wrist, then pins it to the tree over my head. He's bigger than I am, and he's still in armor, giving him enough leverage to trap me there. A spark of fear lights in my gut just as his tongue thrusts into my mouth.

I wrench my head to the side, and it breaks the kiss, but Sephran makes a low sound and moves to my neck. His free hand is at my waist now, and my body automatically recoils, sucking back against the tree.

"Sephran. Stop." I jerk against his hold, then squirm away from the hand that's sliding up my waist. "*Stop.*"

He stops so abruptly that it takes me by surprise. Part of me was

373

worried he wouldn't stop at all. But he draws back and looks down at me. "Jax?"

My heart is pounding, and my hand is still trapped against the tree. He's still pinning me here.

"Let go," I say sharply.

His hands slip away at once, and he rolls back on his heels. For a moment, we just sit there staring at each other, and my heart refuses to stop racing.

"Jax." His expression turns beseeching. His voice is low. "I'm sorry. I misunderstood, all right? Do you understand me? I'm *sorry*."

"I understand you are sorry," I say darkly.

"Would you stop glaring at me?" He runs a hand across the back of his neck. "I didn't attack you! You kissed me back!"

The thought is jarring, and I freeze.

Because maybe I did. Maybe, for a fraction of a second, I allowed it to happen. Sephran is my friend, and loneliness has been clinging to me for weeks.

He speaks into my silence. "Silver hell. When you told me to stop, I stopped." He grimaces, then scowls, abashed. "But you kept looking at me, and then you put your hand on my arm, and—" He makes a frustrated sound. "I'm *sorry*, Jax. I'm sorry I got confused in the middle there. But I don't think I was confused in the beginning."

These words get a little tangled up, and I wish I couldn't figure them out, but I can. A chill of regret washes over me. I can't decide which part of this is the worst. Did I betray Tycho? Myself? Or is Sephran to blame? Have I lost one of the only friends I have here?

And if Tycho weren't constantly leaving, would *any* of this have happened?

The thought makes me feel cold inside. I've been watching for him for weeks. *Waiting* for weeks. Maybe it's not his fault, but as usual, it's not mine either. I can't decide if that makes me feel more angry—or more guilty. Either way, a flush has crawled up my neck. I turn away from Sephran and head for the horses. "I must return to the Shield House."

He follows me. "Stop. Talk to me. I want to understand. Is there someone else?"

I've reached Teddy, and the question forces me still. I put my hand against the horse's shoulder, and I remember Tycho's last night here, the way the king's orders frustrated him to the point that he fell against me, his emotion choking both of us. He was angry and resentful and miserable in his duties.

And still, he left.

"Yes," I say to Sephran. I turn and look at him. "There is Tycho."

It's the first time I've said it to *anyone*, and after so long and so much buildup, I expect a reaction.

But Sephran just sighs, and there's a rueful note to it that I can't quite figure out. "The King's Courier."

"Yes."

He scoffs and looks away. "Malin thought so, but I didn't believe it."

That gets my attention, and I frown, unsure if I understood. "Why not believe?"

"*Why?* He's been gone for *weeks*, and you haven't had word."

"You have had no word from Malin."

"Because he's a soldier. He has to follow orders. He's not an attendant to the *king*. The whole time we traveled here, Lord Tycho hardly even *looked* at you."

These words are twisting up in my gut. "He had reasons," I say.

Sephran scoffs again. "If you say so."

I scowl and turn back to the horse, then swing onto Teddy's back.

Sephran grabs the rein, then puts a hand on my boot.

My thoughts are too scrambled up, and it reminds me too much of what Niall and Brinley did. That spark of fear in my gut hasn't fully gone out. "*Let go*," I snap.

He raises his hands in surrender, but his eyes are full of righteous anger. "All right, *look*. You might hate me right now, but I know how lonely you are. I've *seen* it. Do you understand all this, Jax? Do you understand what I am saying to you?"

My jaw is set, and I look away.

But I understand every word.

"I was wrong," he says. "I shouldn't have done that. And I *am* sorry. But *you* shouldn't waste your time pining away for some asshole who dragged you away from home and left you here to wait for him."

The words take my breath away. I don't know what to say.

Sephran swears and begins to untether his own horse.

I still haven't moved.

He heaves a sigh and swings aboard, then turns his horse back toward the stables.

"Sephran," I say, and my voice sounds a bit hollow.

He whirls so quickly that it makes me think he wouldn't mind if I took it all back. But his eyes are still shadowed, and he looks at me warily.

"What?" he says.

"I not hate you." I cluck to Teddy and urge him forward.

After a moment, Sephran falls into step beside me. This time, there's a larger gap between us than there was before, and I know he's doing it deliberately.

Some of the tension in my gut won't go away, but a fraction of it eases.

"Still want to be friends?" he says.

My tongue stalls on an answer. Everything he said and did is still wound up in my thoughts, and it's going to take a while to unravel it.

Especially since some of it—maybe a lot of it—has nothing to do with him at all.

So I don't say anything, and we ride in silence for a while.

But I think about the way he put the cap back on that flask of liquor when I explained why I didn't want any. I think about the way he brought me the bench when I so desperately needed it.

I think about the fact that he stopped the instant I said his name. He apologized. He explained.

I think about the fact that he has been here, while Tycho has not.

"Yes, Sephran," I say, though I sigh. "I want."

CHAPTER 38

JAX

It's late by the time I put Teddy away and make my way back to the Shield House. I'm trying to unravel everything that happened with Sephran, and my thoughts won't stop spinning with guilt and regret.

It doesn't help that I'm exhausted. I'm sore and tired and I can't wait to fall asleep, so I can hopefully forget everything that just happened.

Then an ice-cold breeze snaps through the trees. A voice finds my ears.

—*Jax.*

I stop short on the walkway. The voice doesn't sound like a *voice*, and it's so soft that I could be imagining it. But I've already pulled my bow over my head, and my eyes search the sky.

Another cold breeze finds my skin, swirling tendrils of hair around my face. I nock an arrow without thought.

—*Lay your bow on the ground. I've brought word from Tycho.*

My heart kicks hard in my chest, and my breathing stutters. I don't know what to say. I don't know what to *do*. Is this real? Is this a trap?

But why would one of them want to trap me? Since we came to Emberfall, they've always just wanted to *kill* me.

"Where are you?" I say.

Another cold wind, stronger this time, tugging at my clothes.

—*I told you to lay your bow on the ground. I've seen you shoot.*

"Yeah, and I've seen scravers tear people apart." My breath clouds in the air as I speak, and I fight not to shiver. But my fingers tighten on the bow, and I don't let any tension out of the string. I still have nightmares of what happened in the clearing. I can still hear Molly screaming. I keep the arrow nocked and turn in a circle, my eyes searching the trees, but it's too dark.

Frost forms on the tip of my arrow, and my eyes widen. That voice takes on a tone of impatience.

—*You will lay down your bow, or I will leave. But you should know, Jax: he begged me to come.*

That hits the mark. My heart gives another tug, because it could mean so many things. I shove the arrow in my quiver, then bend to set the bow on the path. My breathing is shaking, rapid clouds forming in the darkness. I lift my hands and hope they're not about to be ripped off.

"Why did he have to beg you?" I say roughly.

—*Step into the woods. I cannot risk being seen. It was challenging enough to get this far.*

I step into the woods, and again I wish for my crutches, because I'm slow, limping heavily between the trees. "Please," I say, gazing up at the branches overhead, looking for the scraver. "Please just tell me if he's all right."

Another cold breeze swirls around me, but this time, there's no answer. I don't have any weapons other than the quiver of arrows at my back, but I feel increasingly vulnerable with each step.

"This is far enough."

I suck in a breath and turn. The scraver is standing against a tree, his gray skin and black wings blending into the shadows so effectively that I must have walked right past him. His coal-black eyes catch a faint gleam, and his hair might be as long as mine is, but it's tough to tell in the dark. He's barefoot and bare-chested, but dark leather trousers cling to his legs. It looks like he's wearing a few weapons, too, though one sheath along his thigh is empty.

I swallow hard, but my mouth has gone dry. Scravers may have come to our aid in Briarlock, but I've seen them do far more damage since then.

"There are so many guards surrounding the castle grounds that it took quite a while to determine a way in," he says. "And then I had to wait a remarkably long time for you to be alone."

I should be listening to what he's saying, but my brain won't stop focusing on the way his fangs glint in the moonlight. I can't believe Callyn and I once read stories of these creatures and found them captivating. My eyes want to stare, but every muscle in my body is taut, begging me to run.

But then he says, "Do you remember me?"

That snaps my eyes to his. At first, I want to say no, because the only ones that really live in my memories are the ones I've seen tear people apart.

But then I remember fighting at the king's side in Briarlock, watching as a scraver helped Tycho save young Princess Sinna, delivering her into the king's arms. I remember watching the same scraver yank an arrow of Iishellasan steel out of Tycho's shoulder so viciously that he vomited in the leaves.

I remember how Tycho was trapped by the bargain he made to save the king's life. A bargain that's being held against him.

Nakiis.

"You!" New worries flare in my chest, swirling with a bit of anger. I want my bow back. I'm tempted to stab him with an arrow. My fists clench and I take a step forward. "What have you done? Why isn't he back yet? Where is he—"

His hand snaps out, and he catches me by the throat. I feel the point of every single claw. I gasp and grab hold of his wrist automatically.

He steps close and seizes my waist with his other hand, fingers pressing under my ribs so tightly that it's possible he's breaking skin through my tunic. It's so surprising that I choke on my breath, and I can't break his hold.

"Do you want to see what your liver looks like on the outside of your body?" he says.

I shake my head quickly, then wince when his fingers tighten.

"Then perhaps we can start anew," he says. "Tycho asked for a favor. So here I am."

I nod, and his grip loosens just enough for me to breathe, but he doesn't let me go entirely. The air that swirls between us is so cold, but his fingers against my neck are warm. His other hand is still pressed against my side, and I can feel every single claw. My breathing is shaking, my heart pounding like a galloping horse.

"You said he begged," I say, and my voice is rough. "You said he *begged* you."

"I didn't *make* him beg. He pleaded for *you*, Jax, because he wanted you to know why he has not yet returned. He was worried you came to harm."

"Is he hurt?" I whisper.

"No. He has been detained in Syhl Shallow, and he is not allowed to send word. The king does not want to stoke panic. There are too many people working against the throne. He trusts no one."

"Detained," I say. "Why?"

"Because of the scraver attacks."

"Those have happened here, too."

"I see that." Without warning, his hand lifts from my neck, and my breath catches again. But he only touches a finger to my jaw, gently brushing along the scabs on my cheek that will certainly turn into scars. "Scraver scars are rare. Most humans don't survive."

"Many didn't."

"*You* did." His eyes hold mine, and he lets go of me altogether, taking a step back. He folds his arms and leans back against a tree. "You see why I had you lay down your bow."

I press a hand to my neck, expecting to find trickles of blood from broken skin, but there's none. I shiver, and it's not entirely from the cold in the air. "Why can't Tycho return?"

"He has enough magic in his blood that scravers can sense him. If he is attacked, a scraver would know him for a magesmith. They would kill him. But there is also growing discord within the palace, and the king worries about discontent over magic. He and Tycho argued over it, and the king refused to allow him to leave."

"So he's protecting Tycho? Or the kingdom?"

"Both? Neither?" Nakiis looks at me steadily, and he lifts one shoulder in an ambivalent shrug. "He could be protecting himself."

"Why *are* the scravers attacking?"

"The others want to root out the remaining magesmiths to destroy them. It seems the people of Syhl Shallow are determined to drive the king right out from behind his walls—and it's working. Once they do, there are scravers who will be waiting."

I swallow, thinking of the number of times I've heard people say that the monster has returned to Emberfall—right when the Truthbringers have gained a strong foothold on both sides of the mountain. King Grey and Queen Lia Mara were nearly killed over fears of the king's abilities, and it's not like these attacks will endear anyone to magic.

I study him. "Why don't *you* want to kill the magesmiths?"

"Because I have seen the ways of your wars. Xovaar and the others are shortsighted. Humans have us outnumbered. Their fear is currently directed at magic. But if we kill the magesmiths, we will have no allies when humans eventually turn on *us*."

Xovaar. I remember the name from the first attack. "Can you stop the others?"

His black eyes hold mine, and he's silent for a moment. "Not yet. There are too many of them—and they have found human allies among the Truthbringers."

I frown, turning that around in my head. "Allies? But who would—"

"I can't remain here for long, Jax. If you have a return message for Tycho, give it to me, so I can be on my way. If there have been attacks close by, I need to be swift. There are many of my kind who would harm *me* if they could. Things in Syhl Shallow are already perilous enough, and I will not leave *my* people unguarded."

For a flash of time, he sounds vulnerable, and I frown, because it's odd to hear vulnerability from a creature who casually mentioned ripping out my organs.

But if I'm understanding him correctly, Nakiis risked something to come here. All this way, just to carry a message, and to bring one back.

Tycho asked for a favor. So here I am.

Tycho would have to trust Nakiis to ask for this.

Nakiis would have to trust him to do it.

"Thank you for doing this," I say, and his eyes flick back to mine. "It's been weeks. I've been worried."

Nakiis looks startled, but his lip turns up, revealing the edge of his fangs again. "As I said. He begged me to come. He will be quite relieved to know you are alive and well." He pauses. "What message shall I bring back?"

A *message.* I don't even know what to say! What can I send through a third party?

Against my will, my thoughts summon the moment Sephran pressed his mouth to mine.

It was nothing. I stopped him.

Guilt makes my chest clench anyway.

"Tell him I can be patient," I say, and my voice has gone whisper-rough. "And when he gets back, we'll go to Silvermoon, just like he promised." I reach back and pull the length of twisted steel that holds my hair in a knot. My cheeks are hot, but it's dark, and I don't care. I hold out the pin. "Give him this. Please."

I expect him to ask why, or what it means, but he doesn't. His fingers close around the steel, he leaps into the air, and he's gone.

I'm back at the door of the Shield House before I realize the weight of everything Nakiis said. My thoughts were wrapped up in memories of Tycho and the idea of him pleading with Nakiis to send a message—and the guilt I feel over what happened.

But now I'm thinking I should have paid closer attention to everything *else.*

It seems the people of Syhl Shallow are determined to drive the king right out from behind his walls—and it's working.

Tycho would have paid attention to all of it. He's been a soldier, an *officer,* so he'd be ten thoughts ahead, knowing exactly who to warn and what to do. I'm still just a blacksmith who barely speaks the language. I certainly can't translate everything I just learned. It's after midnight, so Master Hugh has long since gone home to bed. He won't be back in the stables until morning.

I stand there at the door to the Shield House and wonder where Tycho would go, who he would tell.

But then I turn around. Across the vast grounds sits Ironrose Castle, large and dark in the moonlight.

I know *exactly* what Tycho would do. I just don't want to do it.

But I grit my teeth, steel my spine, and go to fetch my horse.

CHAPTER 39

JAX

I forget that the castle guards don't speak Syssalah until I'm there in front of them.

"I need to talk to prince," I say for the fourth time. I'm frustrated, and when that happens, I start tripping over my words. "Or princess. I need—I need say—no, I need tell *about*—" This is impossible. "They need know—"

"The prince and princess have retired for the night," says one of the guards at the steps. It's the fourth time he's said it, too. He's been the most patient, but I can tell it's wearing thin. He folds his hands together against the side of his face, miming sleep. "Asleep? Do you understand?"

"Yes, but—"

"Go back to the Shield House," says the next man. He's louder, as if I'm stupid and volume will help. "*You—*" He points at me. "Come back tomorrow." Then he makes a shooing motion toward the Shield House. Without even waiting for me to look away, he rolls his eyes and mutters something to the other guard that I can't quite catch.

I inhale sharply, because I've definitely lost *my* patience, but both guards draw themselves up, like I'm about to become a problem.

I scowl and let out that breath in a defeated sigh. "Fine," I say. "I come tomorrow." I don't know what else to do.

And maybe I didn't need to ride up to the castle in the middle of the night anyway. Maybe there's nothing urgent in the information Nakiis revealed. I draw up my reins and turn Teddy away from the castle steps.

"Jax."

Prince Rhen's voice calls me back, and I look up in surprise. He's at the top of the steps, in boots and trousers, but his shirt is only half buttoned, the sleeves pushed back. It's the most casual I've ever seen him.

"What's wrong?" he says in Syssalah.

I inhale to explain what happened, but I glance at his guards, who are standing at full attention now. Much like that moment after the first attack, I don't want to stir up gossip. The guards won't understand my Syssalah, but they'll know the word *scraver*.

Prince Rhen looks down at me. "Would you rather speak with Harper? I'll wake her if so."

He doesn't say this with a shred of anger or irritation. Not even resignation. More . . . acceptance.

I shake my head anyway. "I've received a message. I don't know how much I can say in front of your guards."

He nods. "Come inside. We can speak privately. I'll have the guards see to your horse." He glances at one of the guards and issues an order.

He says this with such assurance that I swing down from Teddy automatically, and one of the guards is leading my horse away before I consider that I'm going to have to climb fifteen steps. If I had my crutches, it wouldn't be a challenge at all, but I'm still wearing the foot, and I was tired of it hours ago.

I grit my teeth and hope I don't break my neck.

387

"If I try to help you," says the prince, "I assume you'll try to push me down the stairs."

I jerk my head up in surprise. That's so frank—and accurate—that I don't know how to respond.

"Harper would have done the same," he adds, a little ruefully. I remember the way the princess walked with a limp. Prince Rhen surprises me a second time by striding down the steps himself. He gestures to his face, his missing eye covered by the patch. "When Tycho finally convinced me to try swordplay, he offered to start slowly. He meant well, but it was infuriating. So I understand the impulse, Jax." He reaches the bottom, and we face each other in the moonlight. "My intent wasn't to challenge you. We can sit and talk right here."

I don't want these words to affect me, but they do.

And it might not have been a challenge, but it feels like one anyway.

"No, Your Highness," I say, and I put my foot on the first step.

Each one seems to take forever. I have to triple-check my balance because I'm so worried I'm going to fall, especially as we go higher. Sweat has collected between my shoulder blades, but the prince is unhurried, completely silent.

He's right, though. If he offers me a hand, I really will knock him down the stairs.

As if the thought has power, my next step lands slightly off balance, and my right knee nearly buckles. My breath catches and I put out a hand automatically.

The prince catches it.

I steady myself and scowl, pulling free at once.

Without a word, he lets go.

Once we reach the top, one of the guards draws a door open, and I follow Prince Rhen into the castle.

When we cross the threshold, I clamp my mouth shut and try not to stare. The space is larger than any room I've ever seen, and I can't stop craning my neck around, trying to see everything at once. The floors are marble, the walls lined with wood and velvet, and the ceiling stretches a mile overhead. Another staircase is at the back of the room, and I swallow, hoping I won't have to climb that, too. It's the middle of the night, so only a few candles flicker along the walls, but a massive unlit chandelier hangs high above us. I've never seen so much cut glass all in one place. It sounds like my breath is echoing.

"This way," says the prince, and that gives me a jolt. He gestures to the left, and I follow.

Our boots echo across the floor to a hallway featuring more wood paneling, more marble, and a dozen closed doors—though it eventually opens into a dim sitting room that's larger than the entire house I left behind in Briarlock. A fire must have been burning earlier, but it's gone to embers, leaving the room in shadow. The prince offered privacy, but I'm still surprised to realize that guards haven't followed, that we're completely alone here.

He glances at me lingering by the doorway, then strikes a match and lights two lanterns on the wall. Sofas and armchairs surround the hearth, while the back wall is entirely taken up by two massive windows, both cracked open to allow cool night air to flow inside. This room must have an incredible view of the grounds during the day, but just now I can only see the distant stars in the sky, and the occasional torches marking the sentry stands among the trees.

The prince is looking at me expectantly, and I realize I've been doing nothing but staring.

All of a sudden, everything I came to say feels small and unimportant. "Forgive me. I . . . I shouldn't have—"

"Jax. I know you wouldn't have come here if it wasn't important. Disarm yourself. Sit." *Disarm yourself.* No one has ever said that to me, and it takes me a moment to realize he means the bow strung over my shoulder, the quiver strapped to my back.

So I do as he says, and I lay the weapons on the floor. There's still soot on my fingers, so I hastily swipe my hands against my trousers. My hair is wild and unbound after talking to Nakiis. I don't want to touch anything, but I don't want to be rude, so I perch on the edge of a chair.

"The guards were sending me away," I say. "How did you know I was here?"

The prince glances at the open windows. "I could hear them arguing with you."

I frown. "So you *weren't* asleep."

"They thought I was." He moves to the hearth and picks up a small kettle that's nestled in among the embers. "But sleep has been hard to come by since magic began to threaten the kingdom again."

Again. I always forget that Emberfall was once terrorized by magic, that the prince in front of me paid the price. The proof is quite literally written on his face.

Prince Rhen pours from the kettle into two earthenware mugs that are situated nearby. "You said you received a message?" he prompts.

Oh, right. The whole reason I'm here. "The scraver Nakiis brought word from Tycho."

The prince straightens, studying me. "Nakiis was here? On the grounds?"

I nod. "Yes."

He's stock-still for a moment, and then his eye flicks to the window. "He made it past the guards."

"Yes."

"What did he say?"

I explain what Nakiis told me about King Grey detaining Tycho in Syhl Shallow, how they're stoking fears of magic to drive out any remaining magesmiths, including the king. I explain that Nakiis was reluctant to leave Syhl Shallow for long, that danger might be imminent. "Tycho had to beg him to bring me this news," I say. "I didn't know how much your guards would understand about a scraver being here. I didn't want to cause a panic."

He lets out a breath and offers me one of the mugs. "Here. Mulled wine."

I frown and take it. "I . . . thank you."

"I knew Tycho reached the Crystal Palace safely, but I've heard nothing since. I've been tempted to send another courier. Did Nakiis say why Grey won't let Tycho come back?"

"He said the other scravers want to kill any magesmiths they can find, so the king won't put Tycho at risk." I pause. "He also said there's growing discord within the palace."

He thinks about that for a moment. "Was the king aware Tycho was sending this message through Nakiis?"

I hesitate. Tycho wouldn't have needed to beg for a favor if he had the king's blessing. My mouth is frozen on the words, though. Admitting it feels like a betrayal.

As usual, Prince Rhen is too savvy, because his eye narrows just a bit. "Let's assume not, shall we?" He takes a sip from his cup, and he says nothing after that. He's quiet for the longest time. So long that he actually takes a second sip, a longer one.

Eventually, he sits down on the sofa across from me. When he speaks again, his voice is a bit husky. "What else did Nakiis say?"

"He was reluctant to tell me anything at all. I think he truly only came to bring me word that Tycho was safe." I remember the scraver's claws against my throat, and I shiver. "But I asked him as many questions as I could. He implied that the ones who helped us in Briarlock are small in number, and the ones now attacking want to force the magesmiths out of hiding. He said they have allies among the Truthbringers. He claimed that there are scravers who'd kill *him* if they could."

"Do you think he was telling the truth?"

I consider that. "I have no stake in any of this. He'd have no reason to lie to me."

"Nakiis was once bound by the magesmith who kept Ironrose trapped by a curse. She used the scraver's magic for her own purposes—so I've never liked that Nakiis trapped Tycho into this nebulous vow of assistance. Why does *he* need Tycho's magic?"

That's a question I failed to ask, and I frown. Suddenly, everything I've said seems inconsequential, and only a means for more questions than we started with. It's not like Prince Rhen can do anything about any of this, especially not in the middle of the night.

"I didn't think to ask him," I say. "Maybe—maybe I shouldn't have bothered you with this."

He startles at that. "No, Jax. As before, your instincts are sound. The Truthbringers were going to assassinate the royal family, and they were growing in power. Now these scravers are their allies, whether they want them or not—and I guarantee the Truthbringers have already spread rumors that the king's magic is either behind these attacks, or is failing to stop them. Citizens here already worry that the *monster* has returned. So if the attacks continue, things won't get any better on either side of the border. My brother may be facing a war from two sides now. The king may not feel secure in sending word to *me*, but this allows me to prepare support if he needs it."

A *war*. My chest clenches as I remember the destruction in Briarlock. We barely survived. I don't want to think about Tycho being stuck in a conflict on the other side of the border.

Prince Rhen glances at my mug, which is still full. "Do you not like the wine?"

I haven't even taken a sip. "Oh. I . . ." I trail off, unsure what to say. It feels odd to accept anything from him. Like I'm yielding something I don't want to yield. The mug is warm against my fingertips, and the

392

scent is inviting, like spices and berries, but I can't quite bring myself to drink it.

I set it on the small table beside my chair. "I shouldn't trouble you any longer," I say.

"You aren't troubling me. As I said, sleep is fickle." He sets his own mug on the table, then opens a drawer and withdraws a small deck of cards.

When he shuffles, I stare. If I didn't want to drink the wine, I definitely don't want to play a game.

Maybe it's written on my face, because he gives me a rueful glance. "You can still hate me and play cards, Jax. I know dice are favored in Syhl Shallow, but I'm sure Tycho has taught you *something*."

"I know a few games. I've played with the soldiers."

"You spend quite a bit of time with the soldiers," he says, and my eyes flick up.

Are the words weighted? The instant he says it, I wonder if he saw what happened with Sephran.

Prince Rhen looks to the window and adds, "You're on the archery fields often. They aren't giving you any more trouble?"

I frown, because I wasn't aware he'd known about that. I remember the way Princess Harper made a comment about how I was handling the most difficult horses. Maybe my challenges were obvious to everyone, and I only thought I was enduring it silently.

I can't decide if that's better or worse.

"No." I watch warily as he deals cards between us. "A few have become friends."

"I envy that." Before I can puzzle that out, he says, "Do you know King's Ransom?"

"Yes."

"Good."

So we play. It's the absolute last thing I expected to do with my evening. Considering Sephran tried to kiss me and I've been threatened by a scraver, that's saying something.

It's weird. Jarring. We just talked about the possibility of *war* and he discussed sending support—but now he's playing cards and sipping mulled wine like I'm a visiting noble from a neighboring city.

What did he just say?

I envy that.

Awareness clicks in my brain like the last piece of a puzzle. The prince is *lonely*.

Good. I don't care. I don't. I absolutely *do not*. He deserves it. I hope he's miserable. I have half a mind to shove these cards in his lap and dump the wine on top of them.

But then I consider the fire that had gone to embers. The fact that he was probably sitting awake in this room, alone. The scars along his cheek that the patch doesn't quite cover.

I consider that he has to be rather desperately lonely if he pulled out a deck of cards to play with *me*. In complete silence. In the middle of the night.

I bite the inside of my cheek. I really don't care. I don't.

Ugh. I hate myself, but I *do*. I'm not heartless.

Prince Rhen lays down a five of crowns, so I lay down a five of swords, and he has to draw from the pile. He runs a finger along the bottom edge as he adds it to his hand. I don't know what about it captures my attention, but it's the first time I've seen him do it.

I have a wild card in my hand, so I lay it down. It's a prince of stones, meant to capture a king if he has one, and I suspect he's just picked one up.

He looks up in surprise.

I shrug.

He holds out the king, and I slip it between my cards, and we play on.

There's a weird tension in the room that's inescapable. I was so relieved to know that Tycho is safe, and now I'm trapped in this room because I had to tell Prince Rhen that *war* might be on the horizon. That, more than anything, forces me to take a swallow of the wine. It's ridiculously good.

The hell with it. I drain the mug.

The prince smiles. "More?"

I don't smile back, but when I speak, my voice isn't cold. "No. Thank you."

He nods, and we play on.

"I do still hate you," I eventually say, as if there's any chance he wasn't sure.

"I know. I've decided that I like that you hate me."

"Why." I don't even make it a question.

It's possible my veins are humming from the wine.

"I should say, I like *why* you hate me." He pauses, surveying his cards, and then lays down a three of crowns. "It speaks to your character. It cost you something to come here tonight, but you still did it."

"It's what Tycho would have wanted me to do."

"No, I think it's a bit more than that. Tycho didn't send you a message about what the scravers are planning. You pulled that out of Nakiis yourself. You made the determination to tell me."

I don't know what to say to that. I lay down a card and continue the game.

But then I look up, realizing something I would have noticed earlier in anyone else. "Your Syssalah is better."

"Is it? Thank you."

My eyes narrow.

The prince smiles, and again, it's a little rueful. "Harper," he says, as if that explains everything, and after meeting the princess, it does. "I've had a great deal of practice. Since she met you, Harper has all but refused to speak anything else."

I turn that around in my head. "Why?"

He keeps his gaze on his cards now. "She said that if I value Tycho's friendship, I should prepare myself for this to be a conflict with every person who comes to care for him. She told me I would have to make an effort."

So he made an effort.

I hate that he's making it so hard to hate *him*.

One of the first times I met Tycho, he took me by surprise with his magic. I chased him out of Callyn's bakery, full of anger. My friend was sure I'd end up hanging from a rope, because he was a nobleman working in service to the king. To my absolute shock, he showed up a week later to apologize for causing a misunderstanding.

That same kindness and generosity is what allowed Tycho to forgive the man in front of me.

I set a card on the pile and think about Prince Rhen sitting in this room, by himself, worrying about magic, worrying about war, worrying about all the things he can't control.

Much like I was doing.

"Tycho isn't the only one who'd spar with you," I say.

"Is that your way of saying you'd like to take a shot?"

That's so honest that it shocks a laugh out of me. "No." My veins are definitely humming from the wine, and I wonder if I'm going to regret this conversation tomorrow. "But the next time you see me on the fields with the soldiers, you could join us."

Prince Rhen goes still, but then he gives me a wan smile. "A generous offer, but soldiers won't spar with me, Jax."

It sounds like he's trying not to be patronizing, and I immediately feel foolish. I've seen the way the soldiers react to the prince. I'm imagining Sephran's face if Prince Rhen actually showed up on the fields. Leo would likely have a heart attack.

Prince Rhen lays down a three of hearts.

I stare at it for a moment, as if it's not really there, and then I lay a three of swords on top of it. He's reaching for another card, but I toss down my remaining cards: the kings.

He blinks as if he's startled. "You win."

I'm annoyed that he sounds so surprised. "I've never played cards with a prince before. Forgive me if I was supposed to let *you* win."

I am *definitely* feeling the wine.

But he grins, and he looks so genuinely amused that it might be the first time I've seen a real smile on his face. "I've never played with a blacksmith before," he says. "And I'm rather glad you didn't."

I pick up my weapons and stand, because if I spend too much more time here, I'm worried I'll stop hating him altogether. Or I'll shoot him.

"Thank you for the game, Your Highness."

"Jax."

I stop before moving away.

He looks up at me. "Thank you for the offer." He pauses. "It *was* very generous. And very kind."

Any humor, any condescension, is gone from his voice. Instead, there's a hint of sorrow, and like before, I'm not entirely sure what to do with it. The cruelest part of me wants to *enjoy* it. Like I said to Harper, mean horses are usually mean for a reason. I've got my own scars, my own bruised past.

But he does, too.

I sigh and tug at the bow I've strung over my shoulder. "Can you shoot?"

Prince Rhen frowns. "Yes, of course."

Yes, of course. Clouds above, I will never get used to the casual arrogance of the nobility. But I set my jaw and nod at the darkened window. "Maybe the soldiers wouldn't spar with you, but I'll shoot with you. Next time you see us on the fields, don't sit in here and envy it. Get your horse and bring your bow."

CHAPTER 40

CALLYN

My head feels like it's full of secrets. Is something happening between the king and Tycho? He helped the queen in Briarlock—but now he's moved to another part of the palace. The queen hasn't asked to speak with him, and I know she's still not speaking to the king. *Something* has changed, however. There seem to be more guards every time I turn a corner. When I return to the Crystal Palace after my outings with Alek, I spy twice as many guards with crossbows along the roof, too. And while I was seeing King Grey when he came to visit little Sinna in the mornings, days have passed, and I've only seen him on the training fields.

Lady Delmetia Calo said they weren't planning a war, but there's so much tension here that it pricks at me anytime I walk through the halls. I've begun to look forward to my traveling with Alek, just for the chance to escape it.

But visiting the Royal Houses takes time, and I begin to miss my training, sometimes in the morning with Lord Jacob, and more often, the evening sessions with Nolla Verin. After I miss two in a row, a servant brings me a message during dinner that Verin will be waiting in the arena when I finish my meal.

My stomach clenches, and my appetite vanishes. As weird as it is to sit and sip tea with Lord Alek and all the influential people in the Crystal City, it's been rather nice to go to bed without letting someone break my nose or crack a rib first.

When I reach the arena, Verin isn't alone. She seems to be engaged in a rather tense match with a dark-haired young soldier wearing Emberfall's colors. The sound of their swords colliding rings through the space, and this battle seems more brutal than normal. I've seen her fight before, but I'm not sure I've ever seen her *sweat* before. Tendrils of hair have come loose from her braids, and they stick to her cheeks. Her opponent is relentless, his dark eyes fierce.

I've never seen Verin fight with an Emberish soldier, and it occurs to me that the ruthless nature of this battle might mean something *more*—that perhaps this is a real fight, not an exercise.

A man speaks from the shadows down near the corner, calling something in Emberish that I can't understand. To my surprise, it's Lord Tycho, and he's casually leaning against the arena railing, watching the match. I haven't seen him since the day Nora and I ran into him in the hallway.

Verin doesn't spare him a glance, but she snaps back at him in Syssalah. "I don't need your help, Tycho."

It might be the first time I've heard her sound frustrated in a fight. I shouldn't enjoy it, but I do.

I walk along the railing to where Tycho is standing, and he glances over. "Callyn," he says in surprise.

"She's going to do that to me next," I say. "I just won't be able to get up."

He winces. "That bad?"

I shrug and lean against the railing beside him to watch. "Usually."

"I've seen you on the field with the recruits a few times," he says. "You move really well. It's just a matter of time before you can do that." He nods at the battle in front of us, where the Emberish soldier deflects one of Verin's blows, then gets inside her left guard to drive a fist into the vulnerable spot at her waist, right below her armor. She falters, recoiling, and she's fast enough to get out of his way—but barely. They break apart, both breathing hard.

Tycho calls something else in Emberish, and the soldier surges forward, blade raised.

"Stop helping!" Verin snaps, and Tycho laughs under his breath.

"What did you say?" I ask him.

"I told Mal not to let her recover too long. Earlier, I told her to stop dropping her left guard. You saw she didn't listen."

His words are so casual, but they're sparking emotion in my chest, and it takes a moment for me to figure out why. For all the time I've spent in the arena or on the fields, no one has ever spoken to me with this kind of . . . solidarity before. Like I'm just another soldier. I've always been my mother's daughter, left behind to run the bakery, or Nora's big sister, left with too much responsibility. Or to hear Verin tell it, little Sinna's nanny, lacking in determination and grit.

But here's Tycho, saying things like, *You move really well* and *You saw she didn't listen*, like it's nothing.

The swords clash hard, and the Emberish soldier swears, then redoubles his attacks. Tycho winces again.

"Does he hate her?" I say.

He snorts. "Malin? No. He's practically in love with her." I make a face before I can stop myself, and Tycho bursts out laughing. "*You're* clearly not," he adds.

"Out of here!" Verin snaps. "No more distractions."

Tycho sobers, tilting his head toward the open doorway that leads to the training fields. "Come on," he says to me.

The night air is cool when we step outside, and I inhale deeply. I thought it might be easier to step away from Verin and the fight, but as soon as we're under the stars, I remember all my secrets—and all the ones Tycho surely carries as well. There's a reason the queen hasn't seen him.

As if he realizes the same thing, he says, "I probably shouldn't be alone with you. People will talk, and I'm still in enough trouble."

That takes me by surprise. "Why are you in trouble?"

He draws a long breath—then lets it out heavily. "It doesn't matter."

More secrets. I frown. "We always heard gossip around the bakery," I say, "and Jax had a fair bit from travelers through the forge, but I didn't realize it would be like this when we got here."

"Court gossip is the *worst*," he agrees. He's quiet for a moment, and when he speaks, his voice is low. "How *is* Lia Mara?"

I press my lips together, because I'm not sure how much I should say—or how much I'm *allowed* to say.

When I'm silent, he sighs. "That bad, huh?"

This is so complicated, and I hate it. I turn to face him. "Are you asking for yourself, or are you asking for the king?"

His eyebrows go up. "So it's *really* bad."

It's my turn to let out a sigh. "She's just . . . she's so sad."

"So is he."

I look at Tycho in surprise, and he shrugs a little, staring out at the night. "Not that Grey is talking to me," he adds, and there's a hint of regret to his tone. "But I've known him a long time. I can tell."

Tycho is sad, too. I can hear it in his voice. It's all so jarring to consider. The queen stood in that window and talked about Tycho being an ally to the king, but I hadn't considered that he would be seeing the king's pain, the same way I see the queen's. Alek and the nobles keep talking about *war* and threats to the queen, but they don't see this side of it.

402

I peer at him. "Why isn't he talking to you?"

For a moment, I don't think he's going to answer, that we're both going to be buried under these secrets. But he eventually turns away from the night to look at me. "I don't really know," he says, and the words are so earnest that I can tell he believes them. "I know he's mad at me for *some* of what happened." Tycho hesitates. "But the more time that passes, the more I'm beginning to think he's really just mad at *himself.* And maybe that's too painful to consider right now."

As soon as he says it, I'm struck by a memory of the king once saying something similar about Verin. How she couldn't protect the queen herself, so she was taking out her anger in other ways.

Is Verin doing the same thing? Tormenting me because she can't control anything else? Am I considering the queen's sister a potential traitor when she's really in just as much pain as they are?

Is that why the queen is entertaining the Truthbringers? Controlling something she *can*, because she regrets so much of what she can't?

"I'll tell her," I say softly, wondering if that's the right choice. "I'll tell her that he's sad."

Tycho glances at me, and I can read the concern in his eyes. "I'll tell him, too."

"Do you think it'll make a difference?"

He's quiet for a little while, considering that. "There was a time when I would've said yes. But right now . . . I don't know."

I swallow. "I don't know either."

Then we both fall silent, because we've veered too close to secrets. Somehow, I've grown to be an ally to the queen, and it's obvious that his loyalty is to the king—despite the tension I sense between them. But this silence isn't strained. It's odd to stand here with him, but comforting, too. Comforting to know I'm not the only one struggling with all the tension in the palace. And to know I'm not the only one who feels like an *outsider* while still being so tied to everyone who's in power.

"They're going to be at it for a while," Tycho says, interrupting my reverie. He nods at the doors leading to the arena, where his soldier and Verin are still trying to kill each other. "If you came to train, I'll spar with you."

"Oh!" I say in surprise. "No. I . . . I'm not very good."

"Sure you are. I've seen you."

That's said with such candor that I flush. "No, you don't—"

"Callyn." He draws his sword. "Please don't make me go back to staring at the four walls of my quarters."

I take a deep breath and hope this won't be as humiliating as when I spar with Verin.

To my surprise, it's not. It's hard—harder than I expected, even—but my time running the drills has paid off, and I'm able to deflect and parry and block a lot of his moves. When he comes at me from an angle, I see an opening, draw my dagger, and block with both weapons, trapping his blade.

His eyes light with approval. "You're better than you think you are."

The words spark a little glow in my chest. "Thank you. Maybe I just need a training partner who doesn't hate me."

His expression twists, and I see a flicker of sympathy in his eyes. "I remember what it was like when I first came here. You don't *have* to train with Verin, Callyn." He hesitates, pulling his sword free. "You can always come find me."

That's unexpected—and generous. Before I can say so, a cool wind blows across the fields to make me shiver. For an instant, I think nothing of it, but something in the breeze tugs at my awareness.

Magic.

Beside me, Tycho has gone still as well, and his attention has shifted to look out at the night. His eyes seem faraway, as if he's *listening* for something.

I don't know what he hears, but he nods toward the arena. "We shouldn't be out on the fields right now. Come on." He sheaths his sword and starts walking.

I fall into step beside him. "What is it?"

"I don't know."

We're back to secrets again. "You sound like you *do* know."

He doesn't answer until we're under cover. "There are too many rumors already, Callyn. I won't start another one." He pauses, then looks at me. "But when the air turns cold, get off the fields. It's the first sign of scravers."

That sends a chill right down my spine, but just as he says it, the cold breeze swirls away into nothing, almost as if I imagined it. The sword fight in the arena is still going on, but Verin and the Ember-ish soldier are flushed and panting. To my surprise, the soldier looks a bit victorious, and he says something taunting that makes her face twist in anger.

Then he hooks her blade with a vicious twist of his own, and yanks the sword right out of her hand. Suddenly, Verin is disarmed, and the point of his dagger lands right at the hollow of her throat.

I don't know him, but I like him already.

Verin looks ready to take his head off. She smacks his arm away and turns to fetch her fallen sword. When she straightens, her eyes find me by the railing.

"Your turn," she snaps. That chill shoots right back up my spine.

But I consider what Tycho just said about my training—and what he just offered. I consider the fact that Lia Mara said she would intervene if her sister was too rough. She expressed concern at my exhaustion.

She's never once tried to convince me to keep going.

With a start, I realize that I've been thinking the queen *expected* me to train with her sister—because I believed that my mother would have expected the same thing. But maybe all those expectations are only in my head.

"I'm already done," I say to her evenly, though my heart is pounding. "I sparred with Lord Tycho because you were busy."

"You were to train with *me*." Her eyes flick to Tycho. "And aren't you supposed to be locked in your quarters?"

Her voice is so cold it makes me flinch, but Tycho leans against the railing. "Don't pick a fight with me just because you lost to Mal."

She scowls, but her eyes return to me. "You aren't done. You have been skipping our sessions. Perhaps I should tell my sister that you're lacking in commitment and determination."

Maybe she thinks that will make me flinch, but mentioning the queen actually gives me strength—because it tells me that I've been talking to Queen Lia Mara more than Verin has.

"Go ahead. I didn't ask you to train me." My heart is still pounding, but the words come easily. "The queen didn't even ask you to train me."

Verin smirks. "Then maybe you should go back to your bakery, where you can return to making sweetcakes all day."

She says this with such disdain, and maybe among the nobility, these words would have an impact, but I've spent my whole life in a tiny town on the edge of nowhere. "Being a baker doesn't mean I'm weak," I say. "Maybe you feel like you're accomplishing something when you make me bleed in the dirt, but you're fooling yourself. You aren't solving any problems at all."

"You being powerless doesn't solve any problems at all either."

"I'm not *powerless*," I snap.

The instant I say it, sparks and stars flicker in my blood, almost taking my breath away. The torches around the arena suddenly gutter in a breeze, and Tycho looks around in surprise. His soldier friend has joined him by the railing, and he looks around, too.

"Scravers?" the soldier says, his voice low.

Tycho shakes his head.

But it wasn't scravers. Not that time. It was *me*.

I swallow. Verin is staring at me.

I snapped at the queen's sister. My magic nearly revealed itself.

Maybe it was sparring with Tycho, or maybe I've just had enough. But for once, I can't make myself care. I meant every word. If they send me back to the bakery in Briarlock, I think I really *would* be happier.

But I don't think the queen would send me back. I think she'd agree with everything I said to her sister.

"I'll train with someone else from now on," I say.

Verin steps right up to me, and for a moment, I think she's going to leave me in a pile of broken bones for someone to find in the morning. I hold my breath, bracing myself.

But then she smacks a hand on the front of my armor.

"Then go," she says. "I have no time for your insolence tonight."

I think of the way I just watched the soldier defeat her. I remember the way Tycho said, *It's just a matter of time before you can do that.*

I glance at him. "Thank you for the match," I say.

"Anytime, Callyn."

Verin's scowl deepens. But I give her a nod, then turn and go.

CALLYN

The next morning, I'm supposed to join Alek to visit the First House, headed by a man who provides precious metals to most of the wealthy people in Syhl Shallow. I should be excited to meet another potential ally to the queen, but instead, I'm full of doubts over whether I made the right choices in what I said to Tycho—and what I said to Nolla Verin. The queen said nothing about it, so I know Verin didn't make good on her threat to talk to her.

But still.

Alek, of course, notices my mood the instant he gets into the carriage.

"You look contemplative, Lady Callyn."

The driver cracks a whip, and the carriage starts rattling. Alek is in a dashing red jacket today, and I almost have to do a double take at how striking he looks. It should clash with the flame coloring of his hair, but it doesn't. I keep my eyes on the window, but I don't beat around the bush. "I told Verin I don't want to train with her anymore."

"What prompted this?"

You.

But I don't say that. It wasn't entirely him. It was the queen. It was my mother. It was my conversation with Tycho. It was my life in Briarlock.

It was me.

I smooth my skirts over my legs, but I stare out at the new scenery as we pass over the cobblestones of the Crystal City. "She was sparring with a soldier from Emberfall, so I ended up talking to Lord Tycho, and he offered to spar with me instead."

"Tycho!" He practically snarls the name. "If you get an opportunity, run him straight through."

"He's been very kind. To me *and* my sister." I hesitate. "And to Jax."

"Oh, he's been *kind* to Jax? Is that what we're calling it?"

My cheeks flush.

Alek's voice turns contemplative. "Did he say anything of interest?"

"No. He's very good at keeping secrets." I remember the way Tycho said the king wasn't speaking to him very much, and I wonder if I should share that. Our conversation felt so personal, so private, and he *was* very kind.

I can be good at keeping secrets, too.

"How did Verin take it?" Alek finally says.

"She wasn't exactly in high spirits. She said I was powerless." I sigh. "I know you hate Tycho, but at least he wasn't trying to break me into pieces. I'm sure you think I should have kept training with *her*."

"No," he says, and his voice is oddly quiet. "Actually I was thinking that it was rather brave of you to face Nolla Verin in that way—especially in front of Lord Tycho."

"It wasn't *brave*," I choke out.

"She's the queen's sister. It absolutely *was*."

"The king told me that if I wanted to prove her wrong, I should keep showing up. Now she's probably telling anyone who will listen that I'm

409

a complete failure who doesn't deserve a position in the palace." The instant I say it, I flinch a little inside. Because I didn't consider what Verin might say to my little sister when *she* shows up for training.

But Alek scoffs. "You think she's going to tell anyone that you *refused* to train with her? Her pride would never allow it."

I stare at him. "Really?"

His eyes flash. *"Absolutely."*

I roll that around in my head for a while, because I'm not sure what to do with it. I keep thinking of that moment I stood in front of Verin, when I realized that maybe all my expectations were ones I'd created for myself.

While I'm musing, a loud *crack* emits from underneath the carriage, followed by a sudden tilt and sway—and then another, more jarring one. Outside, the carriage driver is shouting, *"Whoa!"* at the horses, and we rattle to a stop. The carriage is leaning crookedly, and it's almost enough to make me fall off the bench.

My eyes snap to Alek's in alarm, but he just sighs. "It sounds like a broken axle."

A footman tugs at the door, but it seems to be stuck. Alek gives it a shove from the inside, and we climb out.

We're a fair distance outside the main part of the city, and the sun is shining down. The road is lined on both sides with trees, and the mountains backing the Crystal City seem distant, like we're miles away. I don't see any travelers coming or going. When I look at the carriage, I discover that the axle is indeed broken, with a large crack in the wheel, too. Alek's footman and driver look at each other dubiously, then at him.

"I'm sorry, my lord," says the driver. "The past rain has left the road a bit rutted."

Alek sighs again, then runs a hand across his jaw. He looks from me, to them, to the two horses, considering.

"We could walk," I offer.

Alek shakes his head. "We're on the road to Spitnare. It's almost six miles of nothing in either direction—and I'm not risking thieves." He looks to his men. "Take the horses and ride back to the city. Filcher, hire a new carriage. Adim, find someone who can repair the axle."

Filcher and Adim begin unhitching the horses, but I look at Alek. "And what will *we* be doing?"

He's unstrapping a trunk affixed to the back of the carriage, and his movements are sharp, annoyed.

"Waiting," he says.

If there's anything good about Alek's House providing textiles, it's that the trunk held several bolts of cloth. Alek spreads two of them along the grass, giving us a space to sit in the sunlight.

To my surprise, I realize this is the first time I've been completely alone with him since the night we spent together in Briarlock. No servants, no guards, nothing.

I still remember waking in bed, finding him sitting by the window, reading one of my mother's old saucy romance novels. When he first showed up, it was the dead of night. I pulled one of my mother's old swords out from under the bed to confront him. He knocked it out of my hands in *seconds.*

A sword isn't a weapon of warning, he said. *If you aren't willing to use it, you may as well put it down.*

I guess that's exactly what I did.

We've been silent since we sat down, but it's giving me too much time to think, too many opportunities for doubts to form. He even left a few feet of space between us, which is somehow surprising. A cool wind blows through the trees, stirring up dust in the road and making Alek swear when dry leaves skitter across our blanket. I turn my head to look at him, and again, I'm struck by all the red. Like a flag of warning.

411

Though bizarrely, Alek might be the only person who's been completely earnest about every word he's said since the very moment I met him.

"I thought *you* might be disappointed in me," I say quietly.

"Disappointed! Why?"

"Because you kept challenging me to be a better fighter."

He scoffs. "No, I was challenging you to stand up to her. Verin only looks for solutions at the end of a sword. You're a bit more savvy."

It's my turn to scoff. "I'm not savvy."

He laughs. "Is this the same girl who faced me with a pitchfork in her barn? The same girl who drew a knife? The same girl who grabbed her mother's sword—"

I grimace. "All of these arguments are making *me* sound like the violent one."

He looks at me, and his laughter settles into a thoughtful smile. "The same girl who still doesn't quite trust me?"

That makes me flush—because he's not wrong about that. "I don't think I trust anyone, Alek."

"Like I said." He reaches out to brush a tendril of hair from my eyes, but his hand doesn't linger. "Savvy."

The blush on my cheeks refuses to fade.

He studies me, his gaze turning a little more assessing. "And I'm glad to have you by my side for these visits. I still haven't been able to determine who was willing to risk the *queen* to get at the king." He pauses, then shrugs. "Or maybe it doesn't matter now, if Lia Mara is willing to hear us."

Despite the shrug, he's frowning, and I can tell that this bothers him. "You're worried."

He hesitates, and I realize that he's savvy, too. We both keep delicately dancing around how *much* we trust each other. But then he nods. "I am. I feel as though I was used before. I don't want to be used again."

This is striking. I hadn't considered that from his perspective—and maybe it's because I always assumed he was lying about so *much* of it.

But if he's been telling the truth all along, then he was betrayed, too.

The frown hasn't left his face. "Lord Tycho tried to point all the blame at me. It's taken some time to recover my reputation. That's part of the reason we've done so many visits." He scowls. "I've been nothing but loyal, yet I need to prove myself again and again."

I reach out and put a hand over his. "From what I've seen, no one questions your loyalty."

He snorts. "Some of that is because *you* are with me. I know the queen is sending you for her own reasons, but I'll admit that it doesn't hurt mine."

I wonder if the queen knows that. I wonder if this is part of it.

"Do you still think someone would try to hurt *her*?" I say.

"I don't know." He finally looks up from where my hand is resting on his. "But the king's magic is what makes her a target. Removing him from Syhl Shallow protects us all."

Is he right? I think the queen would agree with him.

I just don't know if *I* agree with him. The king's magic has done a lot to *protect* the queen as well. Even in the attack on the palace from the very beginning.

The wind pulls another tendril of hair across my face, and Alek reaches up to push it out of my eyes again. This time, his fingers drift across my cheek, slowly tucking the loose hair behind the shell of my ear.

He hasn't kissed me since that day we stood and looked at all his weapons. He hasn't even tried.

Tell me the point at which I needed to seduce you to gain your cooperation.

He didn't need to. And maybe he's been spending all this time proving it.

"Did you really think I'd be disappointed?" he says, and his voice is lower. Quieter.

"Yes."

"Never, Callyn."

"Not *never*."

"Truly never. Never disappointed." He twists another tendril, and his fingers slip along my jaw. "Proud."

The word makes me shiver. I can't remember the last time anyone ever said that to me. I can't remember the last time anyone but Jax even tried to look out for me.

Despite the breeze, the sunlight is so warm, and Alek is just . . . just so vibrant. I don't know if it's the dark red of his hair, or the gleaming buttons of his clothes, or the sparkling silver of the thread in his jacket. Or maybe it's just his eyes, or the sharpness of his jaw, or the slope of his mouth. Maybe it's just the fact that he might be sitting here like a spoiled nobleman, but I know he could be on his feet in an instant, fighting a battle. I can't seem to stop looking at him, especially *here*, sitting on a pile of fabric on the side of the road, the broken carriage sitting crookedly a short distance away. For an instant, I can forget the palace and the political intrigue and the potential for war. I can imagine we're just outside of Briarlock, that I'm just Callyn again, running a bakery and trying to keep my sister out of trouble.

When his finger brushes against my lower lip, my mouth opens, and his thumb finishes the motion, drifting along my teeth.

And then I don't have time to inhale, because he's kissing me.

Every time he does this, it feels like a surprise, like I have no warning. His mouth overwhelms my senses, and I'm inhaling his breath before I even realize it. When his tongue brushes mine, I feel a clenching low in my belly, and my fingers grab hold of his jacket.

His hands take hold of my waist, and then I'm captured in his arms, held against his body. The world spins, and I don't realize he's laying

414

me back until I'm just *there*, pressed into the stretch of fabric. Alek is still kissing me, his hands along my rib cage, his weight pinning me beneath him. When his hips shift, I feel *everything*, and it draws a gasp from my throat.

Alek smiles against my lips. "Did you doubt I wanted you, Callyn?"

"No, but . . ." I hesitate. "Maybe."

He sobers, regarding me. "I've wanted you since the moment you first pulled that knife."

That makes me flush. "Sometimes I think about the way you pinned me up against the wall."

His grin is back, and he kisses me, but it's slower now. He's watching me. Gauging, judging, questioning. When his hand slides up my rib cage, he's slow and cautious, every inch deliberate and purposeful.

So I take hold of his hand and press it right to my breast.

His smile widens, and his hand splays, his fingers slipping just under the edge of my corset. It makes me gasp again, but now he's more sure. He doesn't stop there, and when his hand slips fully under my corset, my gasp turns into a low sound.

He's pressed so tightly against me, but I shift my thigh, and he gives a sharp little inhale. Encouraged, I slide a hand between us, my palm seeking the warm weight between his legs.

When I find it, Alek makes a low sound himself, his eyes falling closed. "Callyn," he whispers.

"You're not the only one who can be confident," I say.

He laughs softly, canting his hips so he presses into my palm, just as his fingers stroke the sensitive bud of my breast. Alek's other hand finds my knee beneath my skirts, and I didn't even realize his fingers were seeking my skin. As his hand travels up my thigh, a fire lights in my abdomen, and my thighs shift again, opening for him.

I'm startling myself with my forwardness—but it's like sparring with Tycho and standing up to Nolla Verin has broken down my walls and

415

given me new perspective. A new sense of *control*. I want this. I want *him*. I've wanted him since the moment he looked into my eyes and whispered my name.

When his fingers brush over my undergarments, I'm all but panting into his mouth.

"Yes?" he murmurs, his mouth warm against my jaw.

I nod fiercely.

I'm ready for him to be fast and sure, his fingers sliding into me, but he's achingly slow, pulling fabric aside, drifting along my skin in a way that makes me shudder.

"Please," I whisper. I see sparks and stars in my vision, and it reminds me of the magic that flares when I need to heal myself. But I ignore them, desperate for his touch.

His hand barely moves, and it's delicate torture.

"Anyone could come along the road," he says.

It should be sobering, but it's not. I look right back into his blue eyes and grab hold of his belt. "Then stop taking so long."

That seems to light a fire in *him*, because he slips the buckle and tosses his sword belt to the side. Then he pulls away my underthings, while I'm gasping the whole time. When I take him in my hand, he makes a choked sound, inhaling deeply through his teeth. But his eyes stay open, and he looks down at me. The expression in his eyes reminds me of what he said before he kissed me.

Never disappointed. Proud.

The swell of emotion in my chest nearly brings tears to my eyes. "Please," I whisper again. "Please."

And then he's inside me, so slow, so determined. The air feels charged, my body feels charged, and each thrust makes my breath shudder. He smells like sunlight and summertime, and when he kisses my neck, I've never felt so cherished.

At some point he takes hold of my leg, the angle changing, *his* motions becoming more desperate. His hand strokes my breast, then reaches between us, seeking every delicate spot. It sends me over the edge and I cry out, stars filling my vision until I can't see anything at all. My entire existence spirals down to the warm feel of him pressing into my body, the slow, dizzying motion of his hand. When he makes a sound, it's low and guttural and makes my womb give another clench. And then it's just the weight of him on top of me, the sweet, heady scent of him, the tenderness of him kissing my cheek, my jaw, my throat. I'm ready for sweet nothings, for him to whisper promises against my skin.

Instead, he says, "Fast enough?" and I burst out laughing.

"Next time I'll keep count," I say, and he grins down at me.

"*Next time*," he murmurs, tracing a finger along my jaw, "you won't be able to keep count."

I flush. My skin is still so warm, so charged, that when a breeze drifts down the lane and finds my bare legs, it feels like ice, and I shiver. "We should make ourselves presentable."

Alek casts a glance at the road, which is still empty. "As you say." He draws back, tugging at my skirts, drawing up one of the bolts of fabric to give me some privacy. It's thoughtful and kind, and probably the *most* unexpected action from him. "I can go to the other side of the carriage," he says. "If you'd like a moment alone." He pauses. "There might be some food in the footman's carriage box, too."

"All right," I whisper.

He gives me a nod, then kisses the back of my hand, then moves away. My heart gives a clench, and I have to press a hand to my chest, just for a moment. The weight of my pendant is warm against my fingers. I know I need to get up and arrange myself, but I just watch him move.

But as Alek stands, a screech emits from somewhere deep in the trees. Before I can react, a scraver soars out of the forest. I remember Tycho's warning.

417

When the air turns cold, get off the fields. It's the first sign of scravers.

I should have been paying attention.

I watch Alek's hand immediately go for his sword—which is still lying beside me in the grass.

"No!" I shriek, but it doesn't matter. The scraver is diving right at me, claws outstretched.

Before it reaches me, Alek leaps in front of the creature. He has no armor, no weapons. The scraver slams right into him, and blood flies.

CHAPTER 42

CALLYN

My breathing is so loud, rattling in and out of my chest. Everything is so *cold*. A high-pitched whine carries over everything, and I think it's me, keening. My entire body seems to be moving in slow motion. I've grabbed Alek's sword, but I'll never be fast enough to stop the scraver. Alek's blood has sprayed everywhere, and his arm flops crookedly away from his body as the creature slashes him with its claws again.

With every pulse of my heart, I feel stars sparking through my veins. It's magic, and I know it, but it's useless. I don't know what to *do* with it.

But then I'm moving, the sword braced in my hand. Frost crawls up the length of the blade, but I don't stop.

At the last moment, the scraver turns, and the screech that pours from its throat is enough to stop me in my tracks. Alek's blood has sprayed across its chest, and I see viscera spilling from the slash marks in his abdomen.

In my moment of hesitation, the scraver leaps off him, and flies at *me*.

"*No!*" I scream—and with the sound, those sparks and stars in my blood seem to explode out of me. A rush of wind blasts from behind me, and the world goes vivid white, almost blinding. It only lasts a second, but the scraver is flung back, slamming into the ground twenty feet away.

When the light fades, the creature claws at the ground, trying to right itself. Its wings are splayed awkwardly, and one seems broken. I won't flinch this time. It shrieks again, black eyes focusing on me as I bear down with the sword.

"*Magesmith,*" it growls, claws flexing.

I don't care what else it might say, and I don't get the chance to learn. I drive that sword right into its chest, thrusting so hard that it presses into the grass underneath. The scraver is gasping, scrabbling for the weapon, but it's all the way through its body, and it can't get a grip.

I don't care. I turn and run back to Alek.

My breathing is still so loud, my heart hammering against my ribs. The vivid red of his jacket is in shreds across his chest and abdomen, and blood is everywhere.

I press my hands against his wounds, whimpering. "Please. *Please.*" But he's so still, not moving. His face has gone ashen. Blood sticks to my fingers, and I wait for those sparks and stars to flare in my blood again.

Another icy wind blows across my skin, and I snap my head up.

"I already killed one of you," I cry, and my voice breaks. "I can do it again."

For a moment, another breeze lifts my hair . . . but then it's gone.

I look back at Alek. He's still not moving.

But the bleeding has slowed. Is that my magic? Or is he simply dying?

I shift my hands, seeking further injury. I can feel the sparks and stars again, and I take a slow breath, trying to remember how it felt when I helped to heal my little sister.

And then, bit by bit, his skin begins to knit back together.

A sob of relief breaks free of my chest—and then again, when Alek's eyes open, and he inhales sharply.

I choke on my breath. "Hold still," I say, and I realize I'm crying. I shift my hands. "Please—I'm not—I'm not done—"

He makes an agonized sound, then clenches his jaw, going silent. He's breathing through his teeth, almost panting like a wounded animal.

"I'm sorry," I say, remembering how quick the king was. He surely has a lot more practice. "I'm trying to be quick."

When I shift my hands again, his eyes clench closed, but he doesn't make a sound. Every muscle on his frame is tighter than a bowstring.

But then the wounds are closed, and all that's left are the shallower scratches across his shoulder, with one along the lowest part of his jaw.

I lift my hand to reach for those, and he grabs hold of my wrist.

The motion is quick. Sharp. Almost painful. It steals my breath.

"I'm not done," I gasp. "Let me help—"

"You *are* done."

His voice is low and dark, almost a growl. At first I can't figure out why. But his blue eyes are so cold, his expression full of betrayal.

And then I get it.

It's too much, especially after everything we did *before* the scraver arrived. I swallow and glance at his hand, still holding my wrist. "Alek—"

"*Magic*, Callyn?" His breathing is almost shaking. Anger? Or fear?

"You were dying! I didn't *know*—" His grip tightens, and I gasp, then jerk against his hold. "You're hurting me."

He lets go so suddenly that I nearly fall in the road. I rub at my wrist, but he gets to his feet, glaring down at me.

"I *helped* you," I snap, climbing to my feet.

His eyes flare wide, and he takes a step back. It sends a chill right through my gut.

Because I remember the moment I did the exact same thing to the king.

For the longest time, we stand there in the sunlight, staring at each other. We're both angry. Afraid. Betrayed.

Alek runs a hand across his jaw, but he encounters the scratches and gives a sudden hiss of pain. When he speaks, his voice goes quiet. "You *lied* to me."

Another chill rolls through me. "Please," I say softly. "You must understand. I didn't know how to tell you."

"Does the king know?" he says. "Are you truly a spy for *him*?" He shakes his head, not waiting for an answer. "He summoned this creature, didn't he? You told him where we'd be. All your accusations against *me*, and I was foolish enough to—"

"I am not a spy for the king!" I cry. I'm horrified to hear my voice break. I can't believe our intimacy has turned into this. "I didn't break the carriage!"

"Then does the *queen* know?"

I draw a sharp breath—and say nothing.

His expression darkens, and he takes another step back. "She trusts you with her *child*, Callyn."

"It's not like that! Would you stop it? She's—"

"She trusts you, and you are *lying* to her." His voice is vicious.

"Please, Alek." I'm gasping now, because I'm seeing how this could play out. I didn't expect his anger, his revulsion. Is this what it's like for the king every time he uses magic?

I remember the day Jax's hand was burned in the forge. He was

422

terrified he wouldn't be able to use it for months—if it would ever heal. Lord Tycho appeared, using his magic to heal it.

Jax and I were so afraid that we chased him out of the bakery.

Yes, I think. *This is what it's like every time.*

"I love Princess Sinna," I say. "I am not a threat! Not to you, not to her, not to the *queen*. She herself—"

Alek inhales sharply, and I freeze, realizing what I was about to say.

She herself has magic.

But because I *am* loyal and I *am* trustworthy, I hold my tongue. I have to choke back a sob. "*She herself* married the king, knowing the powers of his magic. I didn't know *mine*. But I am not a threat."

He stares at me. In the grass behind him, the dead scraver has long since stopped trying to claw at the blade. Alek turns away from me and walks to the creature, then yanks his sword from the body. It gives with a sickening wet sound, and he wipes the blade in the grass.

Then he turns back to me.

The look in his eyes is enough to make *me* step back this time.

"Alek," I whisper.

Thundering hoofbeats echo along the road, and we both snap our heads around to look. There's a carriage, followed by two other men on horseback. Within seconds, they're nearly upon us. I recognize Alek's driver in the seat at the front of the carriage, and the footman is one of the men on horseback.

"My lord!" the footman cries. "We were coming to warn you! Scravers were spotted—"

He breaks off as he draws close, seeing the scraver's body near Alek's feet, the still-bloodied sword in his hand. I watch as every man's eyes shift to the bloodstained remnants of Alek's shirt and jacket, and then to me, standing over the blood spattered on the ground.

"You killed it," the footman says, drawing the horse to a halt. His

423

voice is hushed, and he looks at me again. "Lady Callyn. You were injured?"

I shake my head quickly, but I can't look away from Alek. He's still holding that sword, his eyes still locked on me.

Please, I think.

He could kill me right here, and there'd be nothing I could do about it. I swallow thickly.

Eventually, he looks at the driver. "Filcher," he says hollowly. "Return Lady Callyn to the Crystal Palace at once. Adim, remain here so the carriage can be repaired. I will take your horse and continue on to Spitnare. Lord Hashten needs to be advised."

"But, my lord—your safety—"

"I'm fine." He sheaths the sword. "Get Lady Callyn home. There are surely matters she needs to resolve."

The air feels thin and hard to breathe again, but now it's my own doing, my lungs refusing to work. "Alek—"

"*My lord*," he snaps.

His voice is so cold that my blood turns to ice. It's terrifying that I can't tell how much is anger—and how much is fear.

"Talk to the queen," he continues. "Tell her what has happened here." His eyes flash. "*Everything* that has happened."

I square my shoulders. The queen is already distancing herself from the king due to concerns about magic. Who else will Alek tell? What will this mean for me?

What will it mean for my *sister*?

But he's standing there with a sword on his hip, and he's given his footman an order. I can't run. I can't force him to take me with him.

So I give him a nod. "Yes, my lord."

And then I climb into the carriage.

434

For the entire ride back to the palace, I hug my arms to my body. Alek was so angry. So . . . *afraid*. The worst part is that I can still feel him, and my thoughts can't comprehend how we were so close, and now we're not. Every time I blink, I see his body lying crumpled beside the carriage. Then I see him standing there glaring at me, that bloodstained sword in his hand.

Not even ten minutes earlier, he was looking at me like the most precious thing in the world.

My throat is so tight, and I'm desperately trying not to cry.

I don't know what he's going to do. Is he going to tell all the other nobles? Is he sending me back to the palace in the hopes Queen Lia Mara will make an example of me?

And . . . *would* she? I know how desperately she wants to hide her own magic. She wants to prove to her people that she's on their side. Would she do something to *me* to prove that?

The thought makes me want to leap out of the carriage. But I can't leave Nora. Even if I disappeared, I have no doubt Alek would return to the palace to tell everyone what happened. I can't risk anyone going after my sister.

Could I go to the king? Would he be an ally here?

But what would I say? My visits with Alek were a secret. My *magic* is a secret.

If I thought you were a risk to the princess, you wouldn't be here.

Would he see my magic as a threat to Princess Sinna? As a threat to *him*?

I have no idea what to do.

By the time we return to the palace, I've been able to compose myself. I ask the driver to take me around to the lesser used servants' entrance on the far side of the training arena. When I press through the doors, I keep my head down, my bloodstained hands tucked in the folds of my skirts. I need to find Nora.

The hallway is so empty and I'm so singularly focused on *not* being seen that I don't realize someone is coming the other way until my shoulder slams into a man, and someone else puts out a hand to catch me before I ricochet into the wall.

I look up, finding that same young soldier in gold-and-red Ember-ish armor, which takes me by surprise—until I realize the man next to him is Lord Tycho.

"Callyn," he says in surprise. His eyes skip down my form, and I have no idea how much he can tell from my appearance, but I know he can tell *something*.

"I need to get to the queen," I say.

"What happened?"

Words stall in my throat. I don't know how much to say. I remember the queen standing at the window, talking about how the king wasn't saying anything to *her*. But surely the king should know about this attack, too, right?

My thoughts are still spinning wildly. I don't know the right answer. I don't know who I can trust.

When I say nothing, the other soldier with Tycho looks from him to me and then down at my hands, then says something in Emberish.

Tycho glances at him, then back at me. "Were you hurt? Do you need to sit—"

"No." I shake my head forcefully. "I need to get to the queen."

"Is it Sinna? Tell me what happened."

I step away from him. If Queen Lia Mara wants the king to know, she can tell him herself. "Princess Sinna is fine," I say. "This is—this is nothing to do with that. I have to—"

The other soldier steps in front of me, blocking my path. For an instant, I freeze, glaring up at him, but Tycho puts a hand on his arm.

The other man glances between us again, but after a moment, he steps aside. I hurry past them both, practically running when the hall-ways empty.

I don't pause when I get to the royal suites, because I don't want the guards there to look too closely at me either. I still have no idea what I'm going to say to the queen about any of this, and my heart won't stop pounding.

But when I arrive, I only find my sister and the little princess, again playing Wolf and Stone.

They look up in surprise when I arrive, and I tuck my hands into the skirts of my gown again.

"Cally-cal!" they cry, like they're both my little sisters. Nora is smiling brightly. "I told Sinna we could go outside once you got back." She glances at the window. "You're not as late as I thought."

My heart won't stop pounding. "Is the queen here?" I choke out.

"No," says Nora. Her voice is a little hushed, and she adds, "She said she would be in discussion with the king this morning."

I stare at her, wondering if the king and queen have grown so dis-tant that even Nora has noticed it. I have a flash of memory of that moment when she was trying on her fighting clothes, how I realized she was growing up while I wasn't paying attention.

She's noticing a lot more than I've realized.

Just now, she's peering at me more closely. "Are you unwell?" Her eyes narrow. "Is that blood—"

Princess Sinna gasps.

"No! No, of course not." I swallow and shake my head quickly. "I was—I was with one of the House lords, and the carriage hit a muddy puddle."

I'm lying. I don't know why I'm lying.

Can I interrupt the queen? I'm not even sure what I'd say.

Alek and I were attacked by a scraver, but we survived because I have magic.

427

No.

And if she's finally speaking to the king, I don't want to interrupt that at all.

Then I consider all my meetings with the Royal Houses.

Maybe the king and queen are issuing declarations of war.

I never even had a chance to tell her what Tycho said.

I move to the window where the queen looked down over the fields. I can see Tycho and that soldier now, crossing the fields, heading for the soldier barracks and the stables. Other soldiers are engaged in training exercises in the sunlight, but I don't recognize anyone else.

"Callyn?"

My sister's voice is quiet and low, right beside me. She's looking at me carefully, and she reaches out to take one of my hands. When she looks down at my fingers, I inhale sharply, ready to tell her to be *quiet*, but I don't need to.

Her own voice drops, and she doesn't mention the blood. "Are you all right?"

My throat almost closes up. I nod, then shake my head and say, "I don't know."

Nora squeezes my hand. "Go change out of these *muddy* clothes," she says. "I'll call for tea."

"And we can still go outside?" says little Sinna.

Nora looks at me, her eyes questioning.

I take a long breath. I can't interrupt the king and queen. But I do know I care about my sister, and my primary charge was to look after little Sinna.

Remembering *that* is what puts some steel back in my spine.

I look at the blue sky and the hundreds of soldiers on the training fields, then down at the sprawling, sunlit gardens.

The attack from the scraver feels so far away that I could have imagined it.

"Yes, Your Highness," I say to Princess Sinna. "Let me change, and we'll go play in the gardens."

Nora doesn't let go of my hand. She hasn't looked away from my face. *Is it safe?* she mouths.

She really has grown so much over the last year.

But I have no idea how to answer her question. I press a hand to that pendant hanging over my heart. Regardless of what Alek thinks, magic did save him, and it kept me safe. It kept my sister safe. It kept the princess safe.

And that magic is inside *me*.

So I look into my sister's eyes, and I nod.

CHAPTER 43

TYCHO

"You know," Malin is saying, "that was blood on her hands."

"I know." We're saddling horses for a midday ride into the mountains, but I keep thinking about the stains on Callyn's hands, the flecks of it on her skirts.

I need to get to the queen.

Where was she? What happened?

"Should we report it?" says Malin.

I consider that. He's really asking if we should report it to the *king*. Because even though Callyn was heading for the queen, it's grown clear that she and Grey aren't speaking to each other at *all*. I've made myself scarce around the palace, but it's obvious. Grey is always on the fields, or meeting with officers, or locked away in his rooms. As I said to Callyn, even though we don't interact, I've known him long enough, and I can feel his sorrow, as if his emotion, locked away, leaks into the air the way my magic would. There's a part of me that longs to seek him out, to undo the harm of our last conversation. The more time that passes, the more it weighs on me.

As soon as I have the thought, I scowl. He hasn't come anywhere near *me* either. And it's not like I'm hiding.

But that same tension has begun to cling to everyone and everything *else*, and it's almost like the distance between the king and queen has spread. I see it in the stables, on the fields, in the way Emberish soldiers no longer spar with those from Syhl Shallow. Even when Nolla Verin fought with Malin, there was an angry cast to it. It seems that battle lines have been drawn, and no one wants to risk crossing them.

If something has happened to Callyn, it's doubtful Grey would even hear about it.

Does that matter? I don't know. I've never battled with my own sense of duty and honor like this before, and I hate it.

I imagine striding back to the palace to look for Grey.

Then I imagine him snapping at me to get out of the public eye.

Malin is still waiting for an answer, so I make a noncommittal sound and reach for Mercy's girth, buckling it tight.

He steps around his horse to look at me. "Tycho."

I finally look at him. "Grey wasn't even on the fields when we passed," I say. "Callyn said the princess was fine. She was looking for the queen, so whatever happened, it'll be shared with Lia Mara." I pause, listening to the sound of other horses in the stable, then take a moment to cast my magic into the air, seeking . . . anything.

But I sense nothing. The rhythmic sound of soldiers running drills on the training field hasn't even stopped.

I look back at Malin. "If something major has happened, there's no sound of it."

That seems to placate him. He sighs and reaches for his horse's bridle, and then he swings aboard, and we're off.

The sun beams down on us both, and we've reached that point in the year that I'm glad for the dense tree cover, because I'm sure the soldiers on the fields are baking in their armor. Malin is quiet today, and

I'm sure he's thinking about Callyn's appearance. Guilt is nagging at me, too, refusing to be shoved away.

Why wouldn't she ask for help? Why would there be flecks of blood on her skirts? It was definitely in streaks on her hands, though it looked like she'd hastily wiped it away. I haven't seen blood like that outside of a battle, or maybe the times the scravers have—

My thoughts stall.

Scravers.

I draw up my reins and cast my eyes up to the sky.

Malin notices at once, and he does the same. "What? What is it?"

"It grew cold last night, but nothing happened. I'm wondering if there was an attack this morning—and she was involved." I cast my magic into the air again, seeking.

To my surprise, I get a flicker back.

"Nakiis," I whisper. A cool breeze pulls between the trees, lifting Mercy's mane. I've been desperate for his return, for word about Jax and what's happening at Ironrose. I brace myself, ready for him to slam into me or knock me off the horse or something equally violent, so I'm startled when Nakiis simply sails down through the trees to land directly on the path.

His sudden appearance is so unexpected that I stare at him, and it takes me a moment to find words. "You're back," I say. That wound under his ribs still hasn't healed, but it looks like he's been in another fight. Another slash bisects the muscle of one arm, and the gray of his skin is darker in places, like he's bruised. "And you're hurt again." I glance up at the trees. "Is Igaa with you?"

"No. I told her to keep her distance." He pauses. "Your castle in Emberfall is guarded as closely as you are here. It took quite a bit of effort to reach your Jax—and to return."

Your Jax. My heart thumps. I swing down from my horse to face him.

"*Jax.* Did you—is he—" I don't even know what to say. My thoughts swing wildly between concern for the creature in front of me and curiosity about what happened to Callyn and desperation for the young man I left in Emberfall. "Were you able—are you—"

"*Tycho.* Here." He pulls something small and dark out from behind one of his daggers, and for a moment, I think he's drawing a weapon. But it's a short twist of steel, simply forged, with smooth edges. "He gave me this, to give to you."

I almost ask what it is, but then I notice that a single strand of dark hair is caught around the loop in the steel.

"Oh," I breathe.

"What is it?" Malin says.

My cheeks catch fire, and I close my hand around it. "Nothing." I look back at Nakiis. "What did he say?"

"He asked me not to tear out his organs."

Sometimes I want to punch him. "Want to see how fast I can tear out yours?"

"He said he would be patient and wait for your return so you can ride to Silvermoon, just like you promised."

I take a breath. Jax is well. He's waiting. For me.

For the first time in *weeks*, my heart feels a bit lighter.

"Thank you," I say to Nakiis. I tuck the twist of steel into my pouch, then reach out a hand. "Here, I can fix your injuries."

He takes a step back. "No magic. The others will sense it, and I cannot afford for them to attack *you.*"

I stare at him, trying to puzzle that out. "The other scravers?"

He nods. "The others followed the trail of magic to the palace. They know more magesmiths have gathered here. Xovaar and the others are set to attack."

"The trail of magic? I haven't used any magic."

"Not you."

I frown. Did the king do something? The queen? Has something happened?

I turn for Mercy. "Mal. We need to warn Grey. We need—"

Nakiis reaches out and grabs my arm. His claws dig into the few inches of skin above my bracer. "I am not ready to stand against them."

"I don't care! I need to warn him!"

He shifts close. "Xovaar's scravers are here to kill all of you, Tycho. If they kill *you*, they will eventually kill me, and then they will kill what's left of my people."

I try to wrench free, but his grip is too strong. I reach for a dagger with my free hand, but Nakiis is quick, and he tackles me to the ground. Mercy spooks, and the dagger goes skittering away.

I heave against his weight, but he has my chest pinned. I can't dislodge him. I gasp against the strain, just as sparks and stars flicker in my blood.

"I have a clean shot," Malin calls.

"If you kill me," Nakiis says, "nothing changes. You both die. My people all die. There are too many of them."

My chest heaves. Magic flares in my veins, and bitter wind swirls around us. I once worried this vow might pit me against Grey.

I never thought my vow to Nakiis would prevent me from *helping* him.

The scraver looks down into my face. "You made a vow to stand beside *me*. And I will make sure you live to keep it."

I strain against his hold. There are too many angles here. Too many people who need me—and too many people to disappoint.

As usual, my choices aren't my own, and my life is bound to another.

I look up into Nakiis's black eyes. "Shoot him," I say.

Before the words are even out, ice-cold wind rushes through the trees, and Malin's shot goes wide. He swears, and sunlight glints as he draws a blade. Somewhere overhead a scraver shrieks.

I'm not the main target here, and we're wasting time. "Go," I shout to Malin. "Warn the king."

Hoofbeats echo before I'm even done speaking.

I draw a slow breath and feel the magic in my blood, trying to convince it to settle. I need to be calm. I need to think.

"Please," I say to Nakiis. "I can help him. *You* can help him. He once helped you."

Those dark eyes bore into mine. "It is bigger than that, Tycho."

I struggle under his grip, and it reminds me of the night he pinned me in the arena of the tourney. He's not heavy, but he's strong enough to trap me here all day.

"How long does he have?" I say desperately. "When will the scravers attack?"

There's a part of me that doesn't expect him to answer, but he does. His grip doesn't loosen one bit, but he leans down close, and his breath is like ice.

"Now."

CHAPTER 44

CALLYN

Nora and Sinna are chasing each other through the lush gardens in the sunlight, but I can't stop shivering. The sound of soldiers training on the fields is a dull roar in my ears. The king is probably out there somewhere, but I don't care. I can't stop thinking about everything that happened. Just a few hours ago I was sitting with Lord Alek in the grass, hearing him tell me he was *proud* of me. I was feeling the weight of him on top of me, letting myself feel loved and cherished for the first time in . . . well, I don't know if I've ever felt that way.

And now I've ruined it—in a way that's not even my fault.

A lump forms in my throat. Part of me wants to tear off this pendant and throw it under one of the flowered bushes.

Why did he let me go? Why did he send me back here? He kept that sword in his hand, and he looked ready to kill me—until his men showed up.

Will he use me against the queen?

I saved his life. With magic.

The thought is quick and sudden, and it jolts me in the spine, chasing away some of my panic and dismay.

It's quickly followed by another thought.

Ungrateful prick.

I hold on to that one, and it feels good.

Sinna comes sprinting between the bushes, Nora breathlessly trailing her. Sinna tackles me around the waist, giggling. Their happy energy makes me smile.

But then the little princess says, "Can we go inside? It's cold."

Nora shivers, hugging her arms to her body. "It *is* cold."

I frown at them, because I've been shivering for the last ten minutes, but I thought it was my panic. As I look between them, I realize our breaths are clouding.

The instant I notice it, my heart stumbles in my chest.

Just as a screech echoes overhead.

The girls gasp, whirling to look up. High above, coming from all directions, and so distant they could be birds of prey, winged creatures seem to be gathering in the sky over the training fields. A blast of frigid wind blows across the gardens, lifting my hair and making the girls shiver again.

"Cally-cal?" says Nora. "What's happening?"

Before I can answer, words carry on the wind. —*We know the mage-smiths are here.*

I think I'm the only one who can hear it, but little Sinna gasps. "mage-smiths!" she cries. "Do they want Da?"

"They helped us in Briarlock," Nora says brightly, no fear in her tone. "Maybe they're here to help your da with something—"

Another screech cuts off the rest of her sentence. The soldiers are reorganizing, training drills turning into a response to a threat.

They aren't fast enough. One of the scravers dives out of the sky to rip its claws through a soldier, tearing his arm right off his body. Another one fires an arrow, and a scraver slashes through his face.

I grab the princess and tuck her against my chest before she can see any more of this.

I don't think I'm quick enough, because she's screaming.

—*Find the magesmith!*

Nora grabs my hand and tugs, *hard.* "Come on."

Then we're sprinting through the gardens, cutting right through flowering bushes, thorns and branches grabbing at my skirts. Behind us, soldiers are shouting, screaming, dying. The screeches overhead are deafening, and it takes everything I have to keep from dropping to the ground and covering my ears.

—*Send us the magesmiths!*

I can't run fast enough. Sparks and stars are flaring in my vision, but I try to shove it away.

Instead, it seems to make me a target. The screeches in the sky are getting closer. Nearby, glass shatters overhead, shards tinkling to the ground, and I skid to a stop. A man is shouting, but only for a moment before a scraver jerks him through the window, and he falls. Nora shrieks, and I pull Sinna's face back against my shoulder. The thud of his body hitting the stone walkway is a sound I *never* want to hear again.

But we can't stop. "Run!" I say to Nora. "Go for the guards! We have to get inside!"

But when we reach the door to the palace, there are no guards waiting. When I grab the handle, the door holds fast. I suck in a breath.

They've locked the doors.

Nora starts pounding. "Let us in! *Let us in!*"

Little Sinna is crying, her fingers clutching at my shoulder so hard that her tiny fingernails must be drawing blood.

"We have the princess!" I shout, slamming my fist against the wood surface beside my sister. "Open the door!"

438

"Mama!" Sinna cries. "Da!"

A scraver shrieks behind us, and I shove Sinna into my sister's arms, turning to block both of them, my weight pressing them into the door. I'd give anything for a sword or a crossbow. Magic flickers in my veins, but I have no idea what to *do* with it. Scraver wings obscure the sun, feathers glittering in the sunlight. Claws are outstretched, fangs bared as it descends.

Nora is screaming. Maybe I am, too.

But then the door opens. We spill through the opening to go sprawling on the floor. Someone slams it closed so quickly that my skirts are caught. A crossbeam drops into place, locking it securely. A second later, the scraver crashes into the wood outside. The screeches are so loud that I scramble back, my skirts tearing free.

"Sinna." The queen's voice comes in a low rush from our right, and the crying toddler scrambles off the floor to fly into her mother's arms.

Nora and I climb to our feet to realize that we're surrounded by guards and advisers and a few other soldiers. The continued sound of screeches still carries through the walls, making me shiver. We can hear soldiers shouting outside, along with the clear sounds of people dying. Somewhere in the palace, glass shatters again.

Nora is clutching my arm. I press a hand over my pendant, then jerk it away.

"Is she all right?" a man is saying, and I realize the king is here, too.

But of course he is. The king and queen were meeting *together*. I didn't notice him because he's standing alone, off to our left.

All the guards and soldiers and servants are behind the queen.

"Yes." Her voice is hushed, and she draws back a little to look at her daughter's tearstained face before looking up at the king. "Yes, she's fine."

Glass shatters from the other direction, closer this time, and the queen gasps, clutching her daughter more tightly. Everyone looks at her, including me and my sister.

439

But Queen Lia Mara is staring past us all, her eyes fixed on the king. His dark eyes are locked on her.

One of the soldiers says, "Your Majesty. They could be breaching the palace."

Nora grips my arm more tightly. The queen doesn't speak. She doesn't even move.

Neither does the king.

"Those creatures are demanding the magesmith," says one of the advisers, her tone full of disdain—though it's undercut by fear.

"That's what will stop this," says another. "That's why they're here."

More glass shatters. There are shouts from inside the palace, and I shiver. That pendant feels like it's vibrating against my chest.

"Your Majesty, please!" says another man.

The queen doesn't move.

"Give him to them!" says a woman I recognize as Clanna Sun, one of the queen's primary advisers. She strides forward, then looks to one of the soldiers. "Take the king. Force him out."

"No!" snaps the queen.

King Grey still hasn't moved. His eyes haven't left the queen. "Whatever you want. Whatever you need." His voice is so quiet. "I will always yield for you."

"Force him out," says another adviser.

The soldiers have moved forward like they're ready to do just that.

"Da!" cries little Sinna. "No!"

Lia Mara moves forward, blocking them. "*No*," she says again. "You will not tear apart my family."

The screams in the palace are growing closer. Glass shatters again. My pendant feels so warm against my chest, and guilt and fear swell in my belly.

Because it's possible these scravers didn't come for the king.

It's possible they followed me. *Came* for me.

I need to speak up. I need to tell them. If anyone should be forced out that door, it should be me.

But my sister's hand is gripping mine so tightly, and my voice won't work.

Something slams into the door, and the resulting shriek is intense. Then again.

Every guard and soldier in the room draws a weapon.

But half of them aren't facing the door; they're facing the king.

"Give him to them," someone says, and I can't even see who speaks, because it's a chant, a plea, immediately taken up by everyone else in the room. "Force him out."

The queen's breath shakes.

But her eyes haven't left the king, and after a moment, she squares her shoulders and inhales as if to speak an order.

Before she can, he steps forward, takes her face in his hands, and kisses her.

It's only a second, but somehow also an eternity. Every ounce of emotion is potent in the room, and everyone falls silent. Even Nora gasps.

The king draws back almost immediately, then kisses little Sinna on the forehead. "Stay quiet," he says. "Listen to your mother. I'll be back."

The queen's eyes have flared wide. "Grey—"

"Stay with her," the king says, and to my shock, he's not talking to the guards or soldiers or advisers. His eyes are on *me*. *"Help her."*

"Yes, Your Majesty," I say, and my voice is barely more than a whisper.

Then he draws a weapon, and he walks through the door.

CHAPTER 45

TYCHO

The sounds of fighting in the distance are clear. Men and women are shouting, screaming, dying. I don't know how many scravers have attacked, because my attention is solely focused on the one pinning me to the ground.

I've tried calling magic to fight him, but everything I attempt is met with failure. Any fire I create is blown away by his wind. I've seen Grey repel enemies on the battlefield, but it's not a practiced skill for me—or maybe scravers are just immune. My efforts leave me panting in the dirt.

I have no idea if Malin will find the king—or if I've just sent my friend to his death.

I have no idea what the scravers will do with Grey if they find him. Will his own magic be equally useless? Will they tear him apart like they're doing to the soldiers on the battlefield?

Have they already?

I have to shove the thoughts away. They won't help me now.

In between attempts at magic, I surge at Nakiis's hold, but he barely budges.

"They're not just after the king," I snarl at him breathlessly. Desperately. "They're killing everyone."

"Those same soldiers conspire against your king, too."

"Not all of them!"

Nakiis says nothing. Down by the training fields, the scraver screams have grown louder. Something has changed—but I have no idea what.

"Grey would *help* you," I say. "He's helped you before, and he would help you now—especially if he knew what you needed."

"No. He would not." Nakiis leans down close, until I can see the glint of his fangs. "He threatened you. He trapped you here."

The words tug at my heart, leaving seeds of doubt. He's said these things before, and I remember how they felt true then, too. I consider how much time I've spent doubting Grey's friendship over the last few months. How much time I've spent regretting my loyalty.

Again, I remember the moment when I was fifteen years old and the king stood up for me to Captain Solt, how it felt to have Grey on my side.

I remember the moment I faced him on the fields a few weeks ago, when he told me I wouldn't be allowed to return to Ironrose.

I'm keeping my people safe. That includes you.

Have I been misreading his actions? Maybe we both carry so much sorrow and suffering that we're no longer seeing things the same way, but that doesn't mean Grey is working against me.

Have I been fighting an enemy that doesn't really exist? Is *he*?

Is Nakiis?

I look up into the scraver's coal-dark eyes and think of the way he said I've never really been afraid of him. I think of the way he finally trusted me enough to relax in my presence. I think of the weird truce we've formed—a truce that felt like it might be sliding dangerously close to friendship.

"If you trust me enough to help *you*," I say, "then you have to trust me enough to help *him*."

He says nothing. His grip doesn't loosen one bit.

"And if you trap me here," I add, "with the intention of forcing me to work for you, then you are no better than the people you're afraid of."

That gets a reaction. I can feel the jolt in his body. But he still doesn't loosen his grip.

"He let my father die," he says.

"No," I say. "He didn't. I swear to you, he didn't. He did everything he could to save him. And your father's last words were begging Grey to find *you*. To help *you*. And that's exactly what he did." I take a breath, listening to the screams from the distant fields. Even if Grey isn't out there, Malin is. Other soldiers are. "Nakiis, *please*. I owe the king my life. Let me help him."

Nakiis stares down at me.

And then, without a word, he snaps his wings wide. He launches himself into the trees, leaving me alone on the path.

Mercy spooked and bolted a while ago, so I have to run. My boots are loud on the path, my breathing clouding as I draw closer to the training fields. Magic is in the air everywhere, so many different threads that I couldn't even begin to count. The distant cries from falling soldiers and screeching scravers echo through the woods. It's even louder than when Jax and I were attacked with the traveling party. There must be dozens of the creatures in the sky—if not more. As the trees begin to thin, their wings flicker against the sun in every direction, though they seem to be narrowing to a point.

When I near the training barracks at the base of the mountain, soldiers are running in the opposite direction, fleeing into the mountains.

"Stop!" I shout at them. "We have to help the king!"

They blow past me, one of them colliding with my shoulder sharply.

Some of them have blood streaming from open wounds. But none of them stop.

A younger soldier stumbles as he runs past me, and I grab hold of his armor, recognizing the single mark on his shoulder that signifies him as a recruit.

"The king!" I snap as other soldiers stream past us. "We have to help—"

"They want a magesmith," he gasps. "So we're letting them have him."

I stare at him, sure I couldn't have heard that correctly. "What?"

He jerks at my hold. "General's orders. We're to run—"

Another soldier sees that I'm holding the recruit in place, and he knocks him free. "Come on!" he snaps.

They bolt away toward the trees. My blood goes ice cold.

They want a magesmith.

So we're letting them have him.

General's orders.

I dig my boots into the turf and run again. As I near the training fields, I begin to pass bodies, every one lying in a pool of blood, most bearing claw marks that sliced armor free to find the flesh below.

But there, just past the gardens, I see a man in black with a sword in one hand, and a dagger in the other. He's driving scravers away, one at a time, though he must have magic, because they can't all descend on him at once.

Grey.

A few Emberish soldiers must have tried to defend him, but they lie in crumpled heaps of gold and red all over the battlefield. My heart drops as I think of Malin—just as I notice a soldier tucked in a stone alcove of the garden, arrows firing wildly.

Before I can squint to see if it's Malin, a screech overhead draws my focus. I barely have time to draw a blade and swing before the scraver swipes for my throat. I see blue feathers and a flash of fangs, and then it's bleeding and falling to the ground.

I keep running, but another dives from above. Sparks and stars glitter in my vision, but I spin and stab and this one falls, too. Another one attacks at my back, and claws latch into my armor. I don't think I'll be able to spin in time, but I hear the *thwick* of an arrow, and the scraver jerks, falling away.

I shoot my gaze toward that stone alcove. Definitely Malin.

I don't have time for relief. A light-winged scraver is diving for Grey, and his back is open, unguarded. Malin is shooting away a scraver that's aiming for him, and the king's sword is busy driving away a scraver that's attacked from the front.

I slip a throwing knife out of my bracer, and it spins free of my hand. I don't even wait to see it land, I just throw another. One goes into the light-winged scraver's back, and I lose track of the other.

It doesn't matter. The scraver falls to the ground behind the king, shrieking.

Grey whirls, and he doesn't hesitate. He thrusts his blade into the creature, a killing blow.

His eyes are already lifting, questioning, seeking, and they settle on me.

"Tycho!" he calls, pulling his blade free. "Get to cover."

"You're *welcome*," I say, jerking another knife out of my bracer to throw it. "Right shoulder. *Now.*"

He spins without looking, blade already arcing, blood spraying when he makes contact.

It gives me time to reach him, and another *thwick* sounds from above. The scraver shrieks are nearly deafening, but I draw my sword and shout over them.

"I've got your back," I say—and that's all I have time for, because more descend, and my entire being dissolves into nothing more than a fight

446

for my life—and his. We barely speak, but we don't need to. Much like the way I could feel his anguish, I've trained by his side for years. When he says, "*Left,*" I don't need to look, I just stab. When I say, "Drop," I don't wait for him to move; I just swing my sword because I know Grey will get out of the way.

This is nothing like the time I fought Nakiis in the arena. That was *one* scraver, and I don't think he was trying to kill me. Here, I can feel Grey's magic in the air, but I can feel theirs, too, and there are so very many of them. The air is biting cold and hard to breathe, and frost keeps forming on my blade. Every time I kill one, it seems that another appears.

They call taunts now, too, words that find our ears by virtue of their magic on the wind.

—*Prepare to die, magesmiths.*

—*We followed you here.*

—*You will no longer control us.*

Grey says nothing, but I can feel him weakening. I am, too. Every time the scravers draw blood, we heal the damage, but we've been fighting for so long. I can't remember the last time I heard Malin snap an arrow. The scravers are gaining ground, and our magic begins to tremble. I can hear his breathing, a bit ragged, and I'm sure mine matches. I remember the night we galloped hard to ride for Lia Mara and Sinna, how he burned out his magic. He collapsed, unconscious.

If that happens now, we're both dead.

Just as I think it, a scraver slams into him—which sends Grey crashing into me. We all go down in a tangle of armor, weapons, and wings. The scraver's fangs brush against my face, and Grey cries out.

But then I hear a blade pierce flesh, and the scraver slides sideways.

Malin stands over us, his breathing ragged. His face slick with blood from a wound over his eye, but a sword is in his hands.

Grey and I scramble free. We're both speckled with blood—our own, as well as from the dying creatures that surround us.

447

A dozen more remain high in the air, but these aren't attacking—yet. I don't recognize any of them, but a male scraver at the center has deep rust-colored skin, with vibrant red-and-purple wings.

Words find our ears.

—Your magic won't last much longer.

I'm panting like I've sprinted a mile, and so is Grey. The air is still so cold, and our breath makes quick clouds. A deep wound across my left shoulder is burning. When I try to send magic to heal it, my vision flickers dangerously.

"Why aren't they attacking?" says Malin.

"They're assessing how much longer we can last," Grey says bitterly. He glances at us. "You should get under—"

"If you tell me to get under cover again," I say, "I really am going to punch you." I look past him, at the sky, and frown. "I thought Nakiis and his scravers might help."

If Nakiis is anywhere nearby, he'll hear me. But if he is, he doesn't respond.

Overhead, the red-and-purple scraver seems to smile. A blast of ice-cold wind tears across the field.

—Nakiis won't face us, he says.

"Are you Xovaar?" I call. "You don't have to do this. You don't have to—"

—We do have to do this. You took our magic. And we want it back.

Then he dives, and there's no time for thought. There's no time for anything. I just brace for the attack.

CHAPTER 46

CALLYN

The guards and advisers keep trying to convince the queen to withdraw deeper into the palace, but she refuses. Nora has taken little Sinna into the corner, and now they're curled up behind a series of guards while my sister braids the princess's hair. I can hear Nora telling the same silly stories I once told *her*, and if the world weren't falling apart around us, it might make me smile.

The queen has moved a bit down the hallway, to where a slit in the stone wall allows for a bit of view of the training fields beyond, but we can't see much. I followed her over here, the king's final order still echoing in my ears.

Stay with her. Help her.

Not the guards, not the advisers. Not even the queen's sister.

Me.

I don't know how to do that. I don't even know if I'm the right *person* to do that.

The queen hasn't said a word since the king walked through the door, and her eyes haven't left that narrow slit in the wall. He's barely visible, and we only catch occasional glimpses when he steps into view. I can tell from the shadowed movements that he's not alone, but I can't tell who's with him. The screeching from the scravers is loud and intense, but at least the sound of breaking glass has ceased.

I wonder if the king's final words to *her* are echoing in her thoughts, too.

Whatever you want. Whatever you need. I will always yield for you.

She inhaled to give an order, but he cut her off with a kiss. Was she going to send *him* out? Or was she going to send the *guards* out?

Did he spare her the choice, or did he make it for her?

It makes me think of Alek, the way he stood there with a sword in his hand, looking at me like I'd betrayed him—but then he sent me back to the palace, unharmed. He left it up to me to tell the queen.

A mercy? Or a warning?

Did *he* yield for *me*?

My heart thumps, and I press a hand over my chest, my fingers falling against the pendant. It feels warm against my skin, and I feel those sparks and stars in my veins, just like when I healed Alek.

The queen gasps, and I look, and it seems that the fighting has slowed—or maybe there just aren't enough fighters left. To my surprise, she grabs hold of my hand.

"What's happening?" I say, my voice barely more than a whisper.

"His magic is waning, I think." Her breath almost hitches, but she catches herself, and slowly exhales. "The scravers are able to get closer."

I want to ask how long his magic will last—but I don't think I want the answer.

"Is he sacrificing himself for my people?" says the queen, and her voice is so quiet and broken that I can't tell if she's asking me or if she's asking *herself*.

But then she turns to look at me. "Am I supposed to allow this?"

My breath catches, because much like the king's final order to me, this is so unexpected.

But all of a sudden, the last few months snap into new focus. The way the queen called for dinner and poured glasses of wine for *me*. The way she stood at that window and talked about her husband.

The way she stayed in my bakery, for *days*, instead of returning to the palace.

The way I haven't seen her with one single *friend* in the entire time I've been here.

Her people might hate the king and his magic, but *she* doesn't.

Emotion wells up in my gut. I didn't see the full scope of the conflict here. I didn't realize.

Her eyes have filled, and when I blink, I realize mine have, too.

"We can help them," I whisper to her. "We can. I . . . I have—"

But I can't finish that sentence, or maybe my words are lost to the air.

Either way, it doesn't matter, because the queen has gripped tight to my hand, and she's opening the door.

I'm not prepared for the cold or the wind. Every flower in the garden is frosted over and wilting. The stone walls of the palace have a thin layer of frost, every piece of metalwork glinting with ice. Threads of blood have turned to ice everywhere, in streaks on the field, along the pennants strung below the windows, on the armor of fallen soldiers.

But there, just between the gardens and the training fields, the king is fighting scravers, practically hand-to-hand. Lord Tycho and that other soldier are by his side. A large scraver with red-and-purple feathers seems to be the worst of the aggressors, because his movements are quicker than lightning, and he darts away, moving in to swipe with claws. The air is humming, and it takes me a moment to realize it must be magic. Is it the scravers? The king? Lord Tycho?

"Do you feel it?" says the queen.

"Yes," I breathe. The pendant at my chest seems to be vibrating, and I press my hand over it.

The hum in the air goes stronger, until it presses in against me, and I can barely breathe.

That red-and-purple scraver lifts his head, and he looks right at me and the queen.

My heart seems to stop. Panic floods my chest, those sparks and stars threatening to overtake my vision. We're unarmed. We have nothing.

But we have magic.

—*Magesmith*, says the scraver.

Without warning, he leaps away from the king, and aims directly at us.

Light explodes in my eyes. For an instant, the world goes completely silent, or maybe that hum of magic just swells to a volume that drowns out everything else. It's more than what happened when I defended Alek. I don't know if this is my magic, or if it's the queen, or even if it's the king—just that it overwhelms every sense I have. Maybe it's all of us. I don't feel the cold, I don't feel the wind, I don't feel the impact. I just see blinding, vivid white, and it seems to go on for an eternity.

And then it ends, snapping away so hard that I'm thrown back against the palace wall. The queen strikes the stone beside me.

When I blink, I realize the scraver has been thrown back—and far, too. At least a hundred feet. They all have, because the king and the other men have found their feet, and they're now standing with us, weapons drawn, ready to defend.

The scravers are rising from the field. My breath catches, because I still don't know what happened.

But a shriek echoes from overhead, and the ones remaining on the field look up. The red-and-purple one shrieks right back at them, and I think maybe more have arrived to lend their strength to the attack. But then his wings snap wide, and he launches into the sky. The others quickly follow.

But a voice drifts back to us as the cold wind swirls away, ice melting almost as quickly as it formed.

—*We know where to find you, magesmith.*

The queen sucks in a breath and looks up at the king—but something in my gut warns that the scraver was talking to *me.*

King Grey is looking at the queen. "Lia Mara. Are you well? Is Sinna—"

"Sinna is fine," she says in a rush, talking over him. She grabs his hands, looking at the stripes of blood on his forearms. "Grey—Grey, you're hurt—we need—"

"I'm fine." He takes hold of her hands and presses them between his own. "Lia Mara. I'm *fine.*"

She looks at their hands, and that seems to settle her. "I heard him. They'll come back."

The king's face is grim, and he glances at the door to the palace. "And this will embolden the Truthbringers."

Queen Lia Mara pulls a hand out from between his, and she presses it to his cheek. "We'll stand against them," she whispers.

I expect him to lean in and kiss her, the way he did earlier—but he doesn't. A muscle in his jaw twitches, and something about it makes my gut clench.

But he looks to me. "The queen and I must check the wounded. Return to Sinna, Callyn."

I glance at the queen, and she nods.

"Yes, Your Majesty," I say. And then I turn for the door, ready to do my duty.

CHAPTER 47

TYCHO

After the conflict in Briarlock, Jax and I worked with Grey to strip fallen soldiers of their weapons and armor. It's grim, gruesome work, and I should probably do it now, too.

But he heads off onto the training fields with Lia Mara, and something in the air tells me not to follow, so I don't. I grab Malin's sleeve when it looks like he's about to.

"Let them go," I say.

Off to our right, Callyn is about to go through the door back into the palace.

I turn to look at her. "Callyn."

She pauses with her hand on the latch, and she hesitates before looking at me.

"Did you know?" I say. "Did you know they were coming?"

She swallows—but says nothing.

"Is that why you were looking for the queen?" I press.

"I didn't know," she says quietly. "I didn't . . . I didn't know they'd follow me here."

"But you knew *something*."

She almost falters, but then she glances after the king and queen and squares her shoulders. "My loyalty is to the queen. Yours is to the king. If she wants to share the information with you, she will."

Then she pushes through the door and back into the palace.

I draw a heavy breath, then run a hand across my face, only to realize that I'm dragging dirt and blood and sweat into my eyes.

"Did you kill your scraver?" Malin says. "Is that how you got free?"

Nakiis. I frown. The world has grown so complicated. "No," I say. I look up at the sky, trying to cast my magic into the air, but I'm tired and weak, and it trembles like an overused muscle. "I thought he might help me."

If the scraver is anywhere near, he'll hear me—and I expect him to respond.

He doesn't.

I can't decide what that means. Did he *try*, and was he hurt? Was he *killed*? Or did he simply hide, the way he tried to keep me out of the fray?

If that's the case, it's disappointing. Though maybe I should have expected it. Since the moment I left Ironrose, nothing has gone the way I hoped. I glance out at Grey and Lia Mara, wondering if they might be on a path toward resolution.

Though I'm not sure what they're going to do about Syhl Shallow. When those scravers attacked Grey, no one stayed to fight at his side. They all fled.

I remember one of the soldiers saying that a general ordered it. I wonder which one.

Fears of magic have grown so deep, and there might be no undoing it.

"Come on," I say to Malin. "Let's find the horses."

He falls into step beside me. "What do you think is going to happen?"

Malin is asking about the state of things in Syhl Shallow. Or maybe he's asking about the army, and what his next orders might be. Hell, maybe he's talking about the scravers and Xovaar's vow to return.

But I'm thinking about Callyn, and what she said about her loyalty—and mine. I'm thinking about the way I made it back to Ironrose, just to be sent away.

I'm thinking about the way Nakiis trapped me with a vow—a vow I made to save someone else's life.

I'm thinking about the way my life has always been tied to someone else's problems, someone else's needs, someone else's desires.

Grey and Lia Mara walked out across the field. Together. Alone.

We'll stand against them, the queen said.

And the king didn't reply.

I swallow hard, and glance out across the field toward Grey. Maybe they're not on a path toward resolution at all.

But if he wouldn't let me leave before, he's definitely not going to let me leave now.

A familiar spike of tension and discontent buries itself in my spine, and I look back at Malin. "Time will tell."

By nightfall, I still haven't returned to the palace. The queen ordered her surviving soldiers back to the training fields, so I know the dead have been carried away, the bodies stripped of valuable gear, the signs of death and devastation pushed out. It's late now, and the soldiers have headed to the barracks. Even Malin claimed exhaustion and went to his quarters hours ago.

But I'm in the stable, leaning against the doorway to Mercy's stall, watching her nose through a pile of hay. There's dried blood in my hair and the marks of battle on every inch of my armor, but I can't bring myself to leave. It's quiet and dark and I'm alone with the safe smells of alfalfa and horse sweat, and it reminds me of when I was fifteen, working at the tourney with Grey. The world was uncertain and terrible then, too, but at least I had a safe place to hide.

A boot scrapes in the aisle, and I look up, expecting one of the sol diers out for the nightly check. I only have a lone lantern lit, so shadows are everywhere, and it takes me a long moment to realize that the man might be in armor, but it's not just a soldier.

It's the king.

"Grey," I say in surprise.

"I've been looking for you." He inhales like he's about to say something important, but then he draws close, his eyes skipping up and down my form. "Have you not yet returned to the palace?"

"No," I say.

"Why not?"

The answer to that is too complicated, and I hesitate, then glance away, fixing my gaze on the far wall. The air seems to pulse with the ongoing tension between us. I might understand him better, but nothing has been resolved. I know how much he still blames me for. I know how much he asks of me.

I know how our last conversation ended.

Perhaps Grey can feel it too, because he doesn't press for an answer.

Eventually, he says, "I assume you are still hoping to return to Ironrose."

I snort and keep my eyes on the wall. "Is that an offer?"

"Yes."

I snap my head around. His dark eyes are shadowed in the dim light, but he looks right back at me, and I realize he's serious.

But I'm being stupid. Of course he's going to send me back to Ironrose. He'll have to send word to Rhen about what happened—just like Rhen had to tell *him*.

"Yes, Your Majesty," I say at once. "If you have a letter prepared, I can leave immediately—"

"Tycho."

His voice is so low, so rough, heavy with words unsaid. It draws me up short.

"What?" I say.

"It's not . . . I don't . . ." He sighs and looks away, but only for a second. When he glances back, his voice is as rough and low as before. "I'm leaving the Crystal Palace. And if you would not be opposed, I'd like to go with you."

My heart stumbles to a stop, and I'm not sure how to make it start beating again. I don't even know what to say. I'm staring at him, speechless.

"They came after *me*," he says. "And it's not just the scravers—it's the Truthbringers, too. They're in the army, in the city, in the—" He breaks off and swears, then runs a hand across the back of his neck, agitated. "I can't keep making my family a target. They'll be safer if I'm not here."

I stare at him. "They won't. You can't leave. You *can't*—"

"I can't risk this again, Tycho. I can't. They almost breached the palace. They almost—" He breaks off, and draws a slow breath. "It's not just the scravers. They all want me dead. They've all proven they're willing to go through my family to make that happen. I can't fight everyone. Not from all sides. Not like this. As far as the Truthbringers are concerned, I'm the only one with magic. If I leave, the magic leaves with me."

These words are as quiet as everything else he's said, but these carry the weight of anguish. I inhale to protest, because I know he doesn't want to do this. But before I can say a word, he swears sharply.

"Forget it," he says roughly, turning away. "I won't argue with you again. If you would prefer to ride alone, then—"

I put a hand against his shoulder and stop him. His frame is tight, his expression a mask of tense shadows.

"Grey," I say. "Of course you can ride with me."

He looks down at my hand against his shoulder, and for an eternal moment, I feel like he might crumple—and I'll catch him. But then he takes a breath, and the emotion is gone.

"I am not announcing my departure," he says evenly. "From a political standpoint, the queen will state that I am returning to Emberfall for the time being. Jake will remain to facilitate the departure of any remaining Emberish forces over the next few days, and he and Noah will return with them."

I stare at him. He's not just leaving, he's *leaving*. We all are.

This is possibly more shocking than the attack this afternoon.

I let my hand drop from his shoulder. "What about Sinna?"

The words are spoken softly, gently, but Grey jerks like he's taken a blow anyway.

"I told her that I am needed in Emberfall, and I will see her as soon as I can."

"And the—"

"Tycho. *Stop*." He cuts me off, putting a hand on *my* shoulder. "*Please.* I need—"

His voice breaks off. I hold my breath, waiting. We're standing so close, and the weight in his hand is potent. There's so much emotion in the air, so much urgency in his eyes. It's not quite desperation. It's something darker, more needy. It reminds me of the very first time he offered me his trust, the night I discovered he was the heir to the throne. In this moment, we're not a king and his servant, we're not a soldier and his commander. He's just Grey, and I'm just Tycho.

Only I'm not fifteen anymore. I don't need him to protect me anymore. I don't need to hide.

Maybe what he needs is someone to protect *him*.

I look right back at his dark eyes. "Tell me what you need," I say quietly. "I'll do it."

"Fetch your things. Tell no one." A pause, and his rough voice almost breaks again. "No guards, no soldiers. I don't trust anyone here. I'm a target, and I need to be gone."

I give him a sharp nod. "As you say. Saddle Mercy for me. I'll be back in half an hour."

He nods in return and lets me go.

But I stop before I push through the stable doors into the night air. "If you're not bringing Jake, we should bring Malin."

Grey inhales to object, so I add, "You're still the king. It shouldn't just be you and me."

He sighs and reaches for a tack closet, and I can tell he wants to refuse even this. But he says, "You trust him?"

"With my life."

"All right. But no one else." Then he turns back to the horse.

I watch him move for a second, sorrow seeming to fill every movement. I understand why he's leaving. I understand all of it. But we survived a terrible battle. He's the king of Emberfall, but he's making a sacrifice to protect *this* country—while returning to lead his own.

I'm sure he knows that, but I wonder if this feels like running. Like *yielding*.

Even though it's not.

"Your Majesty," I say, and maybe he can hear the serious note in my tone, because he stops short and turns to look at me.

"For the good of Emberfall," I say.

He goes still. Straightens. Some of the tragic emotion eases out of the air. "Thank you, Tycho." For the first time since he walked into the stable, his voice is strong and clear. "For the good of all."

I give him a final nod, clap a hand against the door, and then I'm gone.

CHAPTER 48

TYCHO

It's odd to travel with Grey and Malin at the same time. Tense in a way I didn't expect, though I probably should have. All three of us donned gold-and-red livery for the journey, with no rank markings aside from the lieutenant stripes on Malin's sleeve. We left in the middle of the night, leading the horses through a servant's passage, riding in silence through the Crystal City until we found the darkened paths through the woods that led to Briarlock and the border. I thought Grey might talk, or outline a plan of action, but he pressed us into a gallop, and we didn't stop until we reached the mountain pass a few hours before dawn.

Once there, he told Malin to take point and report that we've been sent to fetch supporting regiments due to the scraver attacks. Still eager to prove himself to the king, Malin gave an even better performance than when he had my hands bound. When we were waved through, Malin clucked to his horse and said, "Let's go."

Beside him, Grey gave him a sharp nod and said, "Yes, sir," and I thought Malin might fall off his horse. Later that night, he whispered to me, "Seph is never going to believe *that*."

Once we were through the pass, Grey pushed the pace again, and it feels like we've barely stopped to eat or sleep for three days. No safe houses, no taverns, no people—at all. We sleep in shifts, riding long into the night. Grey doesn't say much, so I don't either, and I can see Malin weighing the silence, wondering if he should be the one to break it. The king's sorrow is a weight that's followed us for miles, almost smothering us all. Malin might not know the details, but even he can sense it.

And it's obvious that Grey has parted from his wife, his family. That this isn't a normal journey for the king.

It's obvious that this wasn't planned—or at least not planned *well*.

On our final morning, we're only four or five hours away from Ironrose, but Grey calls for a halt anyway. I'm full of adrenaline, longing to press on despite my exhaustion, but he's the king, so I tether Mercy and strip her gear while Grey draws his bow to find us breakfast.

So I guess we're resting for a while. I sigh.

I'm sure my annoyance is obvious, because every movement is sharp and agitated as I gather wood and strike flint to start a fire.

"*Hey*," says Malin, followed by a short whistle under his breath. He's stripping his own horse's gear, but he gives a quick glance in the direction the king went. A warning.

I roll my eyes at him and strike the flint even harder.

Grey steps out of the brush with two hares hanging from his hand. "Did you just roll your eyes at an officer, Tycho?"

His voice is light, and I'm a little shocked, because I can't remember the last time I heard anything close to levity from him. There's a part of me that wonders if I heard him wrong, like maybe he genuinely meant that.

My hand goes still on the flint, and I glance over. "Yeah," I say, trying to make my voice equally light—though I probably just sound flippant. "I sure did."

He drops a saddle blanket in the brush beside me, and then he drops himself right on top of it. He draws a dagger to skin one of the hares. "We don't know the state of things at Ironrose. If scravers lie in wait, we should be prepared—and rested."

He's right, though we haven't seen scravers since we fought Xovaar on the training fields. We might have killed dozens of them, but there are dozens left. Possibly more.

And I still haven't seen Nakiis. No magic, no screeches in the air. Nothing.

Grey's warning steals some of my ire, though, and I slow my strikes. This time, fire catches, lighting the kindling. I drop back to sit crosslegged in the brush beside him, and I take the other hare.

Malin's still by the horses, and he glances at us, clearly deliberating whether to join us—or give us space.

He's done that every time we stop, and there's never a clear answer. There's not one now.

Grey has been so cloaked by his own heartache that I don't even think he's noticed, but he glances up. "Sit, Lieutenant."

Malin does. "Yes, Your Majesty."

The king frowns a bit, but I don't know what about that is displeasing. We all fall back into silence.

So I guess the levity was short-lived—if it existed at all.

The king's hare is done first, of course, but I'm not far behind. We put them on a stick over the fire, and when they're done, we all eat in silence.

I wish I knew how to fix this. Then again, I couldn't fix the conflict between us *before*, so maybe I'm not the right person to say anything at all.

But I think of that brief moment of levity. Grey and I have always been quiet, always trapped by worries that we silently bear. When we worked together in the tourney, there was never any tension between us, but we could go for *hours* without speaking.

Maybe he's as wound up in his own thoughts as I am, and he doesn't know how to unravel them any better than I do.

"Malin." I jerk my head toward Grey. "This time the king needs a good story."

Malin lets out a breath, then shoots me a rueful glance. "Ah . . . give me a second to think of one that won't get my rank stripped."

Grey's eyebrows have gone up a little, and he pulls some meat off the bone. "I rather think I'd like to hear one of those."

Malin looks a little strangled, and it makes me smile. "Grey is never privy to soldier pranks and mischief, either," I say.

"Not as the king," Grey says. "As a guardsman, I was privy to *plenty*."

Now my eyebrows go up. "Maybe you should tell a story, then."

His eyes light with memories, but just for a second—and then, somehow his sorrow returns, storm clouds rolling over his expression. He glances south, then tosses an empty bone into the fire. "It was a different life, Tycho. I was a different man."

My mouth forms a line, and I stare into the fire.

"Wow." Malin gives an aggrieved sigh, then runs a hand back through his hair. "All right. I have one. When I was a recruit, we had one captain who was a real prick. Nothing was ever done right, could never be satisfied. That kind of officer. He'd order you to stand out in the rain for hours on end, just because he could." He hesitates, glancing at the king, and I can tell he's already worried he said too much.

"What did you do?" says Grey.

Malin lets a breath out through his teeth and glances back at me.

"You go, I go," I say. "Finish this story, and I'll tell him how drunk we got that night he confined us to the palace."

Grey snorts. "As if I don't know."

Malin mutters, "Silver hell." But he must decide the risk isn't too great, because he continues, "One of my friends suggested that we should swap the captain's boots when he was sleeping. So we did. Every night. Sometimes they were a little too small, sometimes a little too big. For *weeks*." He pauses, and a grin escapes as he's caught by his own story. "Once they were so big that he tripped over his own feet when we were running drills. He went face-first into the mud. Another time they were too tight, and we heard him complaining to one of the other captains that he needed to go to the infirmary because his feet kept swelling."

"He didn't figure it out?" I say.

Malin shakes his head and bites a piece of meat from a bone. "Never."

"Who's your friend?" says the king.

Malin looks strangled again. "Ah . . . I don't remember."

That makes Grey smile. "You're loyal, Lieutenant. I like that."

Malin seems struck by that.

"I guess you don't need to rip that stripe off your sleeve just yet," I say, teasing.

"Indeed," says Grey. "Maybe you need another one."

At that, Malin goes still. Completely frozen, as if he's not sure if he heard that correctly.

So I clap him on the shoulder and grin. "See? Aren't you glad you didn't tell the king to suck on a piece of horseshit?"

Malin chokes on his food. "Damn. Where's *my* loyal friend?"

Grey smiles. "I sense there's another story there." But then he looks at me, and his expression sobers. "Tycho *is* a loyal friend." He pauses to throw another bone in the fire. "Better than I deserve."

Now it's my turn to be struck. I don't know what to say to that.

"That's not true," I finally say, but my voice is a bit rough.

"It is." He's quiet for a long moment. "When Rhen and I were trapped by the curse," he says slowly, "it was eternal. All of my friends were killed, my family, *his* family . . ." His voice trails off bitterly. "The curse took everything, and I couldn't stop it. But then I watched as he failed to break it. Again. And again. And again." He pauses. "At some point, I began to

465

lose faith that he *could*. But still, I was loyal, despite all his failures. I was probably loyal far longer than he deserved. Right up until the moment he chained us on that wall."

Malin's gaze flicks between us, but he's silent.

So am I. Every muscle in my frame is tense.

"It's not your fault what Rhen did," I say, and my voice is a rough rasp.

"It's my fault that I didn't yield, to spare you. And I often wonder if the reason you don't hate Rhen is because if you did, you'd have to hate me, too."

That makes me flinch, but I say nothing. He's never said anything like this to me. We've never talked about that moment. Not even once.

Grey continues, "I know your loyalty is steadfast. You've proven it countless times, and you're proving it even now. But much like my brother, I forgot that true loyalty is *earned*, not owed. I forgot that true friendship requires sacrifice—from both sides. And so I know I've lost your trust, the way Rhen once lost mine."

My breath catches, but my eyes are locked on the fire, my jaw clenched.

"I see your loyalty, Tycho. I see your sacrifice. When it comes to your trust, when it comes to your friendship, I swear to you. I will do my best to earn it back."

I finally turn my head and look at him. For a flash of time, I'm fifteen again, staring up at him after he figured out how to use magic to heal the worst of my wounds. I remember thinking he was the bravest man I'd ever met, knowing I could trust him to protect me from any threat—until he did one better and taught me how to protect *myself*.

And just like when I was fifteen, I roll up on my knees and throw my arms around his neck. "You never lost it."

"I did. A little." He hugs me back, and again, I can feel the weight of his sorrow, the sheer emotion he's carrying with him back to Ember-fall. He won't be able to carry it all alone, I know.

But his voice is lighter when he says, "Though I do prefer this to you punching me."

I draw back to sit on my knees again. "I'm sure I'll get a chance to do that later."

He laughs, and I'm startled to realize that I don't think I've heard him laugh in . . . in *months*.

Maybe we both need to earn back our trust and friendship. A little.

Grey nods toward Mercy. "Take your horse," he says. "I know you're eager. We'll follow by sundown."

I freeze in place. "What?"

He glances across the fire at Malin. "I'm sure the lieutenant can escort me the rest of the way. Tell Rhen what's happened so he's prepared, and have him send out a small contingent of guards by late afternoon so we can arrive quietly."

I'm already on my feet, throwing Mercy's saddle on her back. But then I hesitate. "You said you were worried about scravers."

"I am," he says, and that's not encouraging. "But you're the King's Courier, aren't you?"

I realize this is what he meant about earning back my trust, so I stop protesting and swing aboard to draw up the reins. "Yes, Your Majesty."

"It's open ground from here. Ride fast. Watch your back. And—"

I don't hear the rest. I'm already gone.

CHAPTER 49

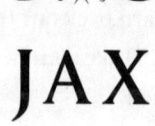

JAX

I've been watching the horizon for weeks, but there's been no sign of Tycho. It's clear that the prince is still preparing for battle, because the forge is endlessly busy, and some nights I'm not done before dark. Sephran still comes when he's off duty, and we still go shooting, but our friendship feels tentative and uncertain. He's never alone anymore, and I'm not sure how to undo the undercurrent of . . . *something* between us. Maybe it's just a matter of time—especially since he keeps showing up.

Like today. I'm finishing my last horse for the day when Sephran arrives in the forge. He's alone for the first time since that night. When I have work to complete, he and his friends usually sit on the bench and entertain me with soldier gossip. Today, however, he's quiet. Watchful. Pensive.

I don't mind, because I have no idea what to say to him, especially since we're alone. So I swallow my worries, and I hammer and file and rasp while he sits there, waiting.

Eventually, however, the horse is done, and neither of us has said a word. Nearby, the remaining forge workers are already packing away their tools.

So I do the same thing, and I don't look at him.

Sephran doesn't move from the bench. But when I reach past him to stack my file with the pincers, he takes hold of my arm. "Jax."

I freeze and look at him. He's done that a thousand times before, grabbing my arm or poking me in the shoulder or giving my hair a tug. Every touch is different now, laced with intent that I might be imagining—but I know I'm not.

As if he can tell, he lets go, his hand slipping away. "I haven't told anyone," he says. His voice is low, a little tormented. "And for what it's worth, I'm still sorry."

"I know," I say, because I do.

He stares up at me, and the silence thickens between us.

But then his gaze shifts, and he looks past me. He swears under his breath, then shoves himself to stand at attention.

I think an officer has come to the forge, and I inwardly swear myself, because I'm the only worker left. But when I turn, it's not an officer at all. It's Tycho.

It's so unexpected, and I nearly do a double take. He's windblown and ragged like he rode hard to get here, his eyes shadowed with exhaustion. Instead of his usual black armor, he's dressed in the same livery as Sephran, all gold and red, not a speck of green or black anywhere. No marks of Syhl Shallow at all. He's dusty and dirty and he looks like he hasn't slept in a week.

And despite all of it, he's still the most beautiful man I've ever seen. My heart gives a hard thump to find him right in front of me. "Tycho," I say, and my voice is hushed. Then I catch myself, remembering where we are. "My lord."

He shakes his head. "Tycho. Always Tycho."

My heart gives another tug, and I take a step toward him—but then I remember why Sephran is behind me, and I nearly falter. "You are here."

"I'm here," Tycho says. His eyes are searching mine, skipping over my face, to my hair, and then down my body. "Jax," he breathes. "You . . . you've changed so much."

"I have changed?"

"Yeah. You're—you're *walking*." His eyes snap back to mine. "And you're speaking Emberish!"

That makes me flush. "Not well. Not yet."

Sephran gives me a gentle shove from behind. "Pretty well."

Once, it would've made me smile. Today, it makes me stiffen.

"Welcome home," he's saying to Tycho. "Did Malin return with you?"

Tycho nods. "He's a few hours behind, traveling with the king. They'll arrive by sundown, but the king sent me ahead."

Sephran claps me on the shoulder. "I'll find you later, Jax. I'll need to report to the barracks if the king is returning." Before I can respond, he's past Tycho, heading away. But he stops to look back at me.

He left you, he mouths.

I stiffen further, and it steals my ability to speak for a moment. But it doesn't matter, because he's already moved away. I watch his back as he goes.

"Jax."

My eyes snap back to Tycho's, and I have to shake off . . . whatever this is.

He's frowning at me. "What's wrong?" he says. When I don't answer immediately, he shakes *himself* and says it again in Syssalah.

It's so rare for me to hear it so fluently here, and I'm struck by a wave of homesickness I haven't felt in weeks. Some of the tension slips out of my body.

"Nothing," I say, and it's such a relief to speak my own language. "Nothing." I take another step forward, because I want to throw my

470

arms around him and never let go. But then I remember everything he said the night before he left, and I stop myself.

Discretion.

I have to fight not to scowl. He's right here in front of me. I should be leaping with joy.

"The king has returned?" I say. Suddenly, my heart pounds as I realize what this could mean. "With the royal family? Is Callyn here, too?" I desperately long for my friend. I could tell her about what happened with Sephran. I could ask for her advice.

Tycho shakes his head. "Just the king." His voice goes quiet. "Many changes are coming. I have so much to tell you." But his eyes are still searching my face, and they stop on the scars along my jaw.

"There was a scraver attack," I say.

His eyes flare a little, and he lifts a hand as if to press it to my cheek. He stops, though, hesitating. "May I?"

My heart thumps again, and I nod.

When his hand lands against my face, I want to lean into it and close my eyes. I want to fall against him and inhale his scent.

But then I remember everything that's happened since he left, and a wave of regret washes through me. Before I realize what I'm doing, I turn my face away.

His eyes flicker with concern, and he lets go. "I'm sorry, Jax," he says softly. "I'm so very sorry it was so long."

"It wasn't your fault," I say.

He grimaces. "Every time we're apart, I feel as though we need to begin again when I return."

That makes my gut clench—because I feel the same way.

But then he lifts a hand to brush a tendril of hair out of my eyes, and the familiarity of it nearly makes me shiver.

"Want to go shooting?" I say. "I've gotten rather good."

He smiles, his eyes lighting with familiar challenge. "I wouldn't mind

471

seeing *that*—but I've been in this armor for four days, and I desperately need a bath and some sleep."

Tycho says this like maybe it's a prelude to his departure—but he doesn't move, and I don't either.

"I've missed you so much," he whispers. This time when he lifts a hand, I don't wait for him to ask. I just catch his wrist and bring it to my face. I close my eyes, lean into the weight of his palm, and inhale.

Then my eyes snap open. "You really do need a bath," I whisper.

He laughs and playfully shoves me away. But I catch his arm, and we tussle, just for a moment.

His eyes flare as he yields, letting me grip his forearm to pull him closer.

"You're stronger, too," he says, surprised.

"I know."

His eyebrows go up. "And not at *all* cocky about it."

That makes me laugh. Clouds above, I missed him, too. I stare into Tycho's brown eyes, and suddenly it feels like no time has passed at all.

But with that feeling comes the memory of our last night together, the way we had to hide.

He left you, Sephran said.

Regret twists in my gut again.

"You know," I say, "I have my own rooms in the Shield House. A bed and a bath and everything."

I don't mean for the words to come out like a challenge, but they do. They *are*. It's not quite an invitation, but my meaning is clear, and I watch a flare of interest spark in his eyes, just like when I mentioned shooting.

When the smile fades from his face, I expect him to refuse. He probably *has* to refuse, if he returned with the king. He has duties, I'm sure. And of course there's *discretion* to think of.

But Tycho shifts a step closer, until we could share breath. "A bath and a bed?" he says. "You should have said something sooner." His voice has gone quiet and low, speaking right to my core. "Is that an invitation, Master Jax?"

His brown eyes are gold in the fading sunlight, and I can't look away from his mouth. I swallow, my strength forgotten. I could melt into a puddle right here. "Yes, it is, Lord Tycho."

He smiles. "Then lead the way."

CHAPTER 50

CALLYN

The king has been gone for a week.

In public, the queen is steadfast and kind, issuing orders to have the damaged parts of the palace rebuilt, meeting with soldiers and advisers, making plans to look forward to no magic in Syhl Shallow. No scravers have attacked. None have even been *seen*. Heralds ride through the city to declare that the king has returned to Emberfall to rule, that magic has departed Syhl Shallow.

In private, I see the queen's sorrow.

I know she worries about the traitors who are still surely among the army on this side of the border. I've heard Verin vow to find out which generals gave the order to abandon their duties and leave the field, but I still don't quite trust her—especially when days pass and none of the soldiers have admitted to any wrongdoing.

But the queen doesn't seem pressed to discover who might have been working against her. Maybe she feels as though they were *all* working against her. I remember the way her advisers were ready to send the king out alone, the way King Grey took her face in his hands and swore to yield for her. The way he made a choice—so she wouldn't have to.

Some evenings we sit together, watching Nora play games with little Sinna, but her grief is obvious. Her regret is obvious. She loves her husband, but she fears for her people. She fears what his magic would *do* to her people.

All the while, I think of the magic in my veins.

I think of the magic in *hers*.

The king's magic was failing. So was Tycho's. We both stopped the scravers—me and the queen.

But she doesn't say a word, so I don't either.

I begin to think that perhaps our magic will fade, that no one will ever know. That perhaps her sacrifice will work, and any threats will be on the other side of the border.

Just as this hope settles in my chest, Lord Alek appears to meet with the queen. Privately.

I am not asked to join them, and I sit and fret the whole time. I can only imagine what he's telling her. If my magic is known to the people, will the queen send me to Emberfall, too? Will she lock me away in the dungeon? Will I be hanged for possessing magic? I spend the entire time listening to Nora and Sinna bicker about the prettiest tiles of their game, and the whole time I wait for guards to come drag me off to the stone prison.

But when the queen returns, she looks at my face in surprise. "Callyn, you look like you've seen a ghost."

"Is he still here?" I gasp. "Lord Alek?"

"Of course. He said he would like to speak with you."

"What . . . what did he tell you?"

I have no right to ask, but I can't help myself. Her eyebrows pinch together. "He simply wished to give me a list of which Houses have reasserted their loyalty. Did you expect something else?"

475

"No," I say, shaking my head rapidly. "Nothing."

"He's waiting in the salon."

I pinch myself. I need to get it together.

When I arrive in the salon, he looks the way he always looks—which is to say he's buttoned into perfect attire, every thread exactly where it should be. His red hair is vibrant in the sunlight streaming through the windows, and when he looks at me, his expression is bored.

That feels like a slap in the face.

"I've told the queen that considering the king's absence, your services to me are no longer required." His voice is flat. Cold. "I should not have kept you away from your duties with the young princess as long as I did."

"Oh," I say, surprised.

But then I don't know what else to say.

I blink and I remember him above me, and I have to take a slow breath. "I wish you well then, my lord." My voice almost breaks, startling me, and I have to turn for the door.

"Callyn," he says.

I put a hand over my chest, because there's a note in his voice that reminds me of everything he said. It reminds me of that moment in the hallway.

Callyn. Are you well?

It chases back my tears, just a little. I hate how desperately I want to hear that note in his voice again. To know he cares.

I look over my shoulder. "Alek?" I whisper.

"It was real," he says softly, and for a flicker of time, I see betrayal in his eyes. I see regret. Then it's smoothed over, and his expression is as cold as ever. "But I know what you did. I know what you are." His eyes bore into mine. "I know the secrets you've kept. As I said, I am merciful and fair, and I don't want any harm to come to you or your sister. But if magic remains in the palace, it will."

I swallow. This is worse than a slap. It's a punch to the gut.

"You don't know anything," I snap.

"I do." He draws close, his blue eyes piercing. "So find a way to leave Syhl Shallow, or I will tell the queen."

I raise my chin. "What if I tell her myself?"

"She will drive you out the way she drove her husband out."

"No. She won't."

His eyebrows go up. "Are you implying the queen is still harboring magic in the palace, Callyn? That she is lying to her people?"

"No!"

"Don't you realize that if magic remains," he says, "those scravers will return?"

My heartbeat stutters in my chest. "The scravers are gone," I say. "The king's magic chased them away."

Alek's gaze narrows. "I think we both know it was more than the king's magic that chased them away. Just as it was more than the king's magic that drew them here."

"The king is gone," I say. "The queen is safe."

"She *will be* safe," he says. "You know my loyalty is to the queen. Again, I would not have harm come to you or your sister . . . but if you force my hand, I will."

"What are you telling me, Alek?"

"I am telling you to leave Syhl Shallow." Again, just for a moment, that flicker of regret and betrayal flashes through his eyes. He blinks and it's gone. "Leave, or I will rally my supporters, and we will get rid of the magic ourselves."

With that, he turns his back, and I'm alone.

ACKNOWLEDGMENTS

Here we go. I always say I'm going to make this short, but now I've set a precedent.

As always, I am so incredibly grateful to my husband, Michael. You've had my back since the day I told you I wanted to do this, and I will never forget it. Publishing is such a roller coaster, and I'm truly glad that we're hanging on for dear life together. Thank you for everything, baby. I love you so much.

Mary Kate Castellani is my incredible editor at Bloomsbury, and this book took a *tremendous* amount of work. (Truly. You guys have no idea.) Mary Kate, it means so much to me that you never let me get away with anything, and I appreciate every minute you spend helping me make my stories the best they can be.

Suzie Townsend of New Leaf Literary is my phenomenal agent. Suzie, I am so grateful for your guidance, especially when things get tricky and complicated. I am so incredibly lucky to have you, Olivia Coleman, and the entire team at New Leaf Literary on my side. Thank you all so much for everything.

The team at Bloomsbury is so incredibly dedicated with every single book! Huge thanks to Kei Nakatsuka, Lily Yengle, Erica Barmash, Faye Bi, Phoebe Dyer, Beth Eller, Kathleen Morandini, Valentina Rice, Diane Aronson, Jeanette Levy, Donna Mark, Hannah Bowe, Laura

Phillips, Nicholas Church, Katie Ager, Emily Marples, Josephine Blaquiere, Barney Duly, Jennifer Choi, Andrew Nguyễn and every single person at Bloomsbury who has a hand in making my books a success.

Huge thanks to my amazing Street Team! If you're a part of it, thank YOU. It means so much to me to know that there are *thousands* of you interested in my books, and I will never forget everything you've done to spread the word about my stories. Thank you all so very much.

Huge debts of gratitude go to Melody Wukitch, Sarah Rifield, Jodi Picoult, Jodi Meadows, Amie Kaufman, Beth Revis, Alexa Donne, Erin Bowman, Nicki Prau Preto, Susan Dennard, Tanaz Bhathena, Stephanie Garber, Isabel Ibañez, Bradley Spoon, Reba Gordon, and Amalie Howard, because I honestly don't know how I would get through the day without your support. I am so grateful to have you all in my life.

This book was rewritten about a billion times (not really) (okay maybe really), and I am deeply appreciative to the friends who offered to give me fresh eyes on each subsequent manuscript. Tremendous thanks to Jodi Picoult, Reba Gordon, Sarah Rifield, Jodi Meadows, and Max Walker.

Tremendous thanks to readers, bloggers, librarians, artists, and booksellers all over social media who take the time to post, review, tweet, share, and mention my books. I owe my career to people being so passionate about my characters that they can't help but talk about them. Thank you all.

And many thanks go to YOU! Yes, you. If you're holding this book in your hands, I am honored that you took the time to invite my characters into your heart.

Finally, tremendous love and thanks to my boys. You love each other so very, very much, and I am so incredibly lucky to be your mom.

Devour the breathtaking first novel in the
DEFY THE NIGHT
series

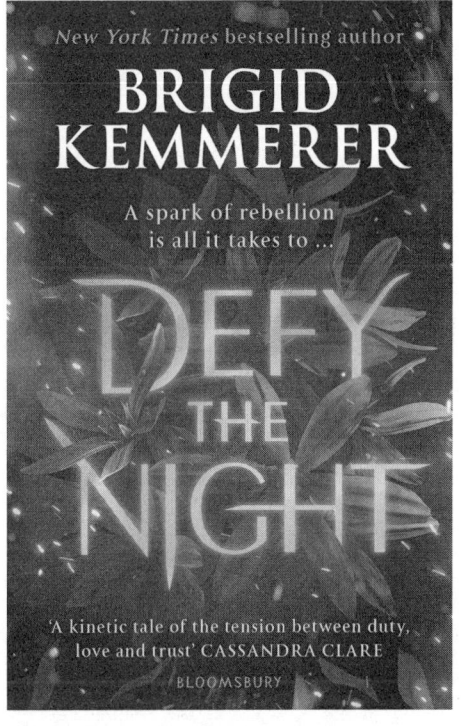

'A kinetic tale of the tension
between duty, love and trust'
Cassandra Clare

Devour the breathtaking first novel in the
CURSEBREAKER
series

'Absolutely spellbinding ... An
intensely original retelling'
Stephanie Garber

ABOUT THE AUTHOR

Brigid Kemmerer is the *New York Times* bestselling author of the Defy the Night series and the Cursebreaker series, which includes *A Curse So Dark and Lonely, A Heart So Fierce and Broken* and *A Vow So Bold and Deadly*. She has also written the contemporary young adult romances *Call It What You Want, More Than We Can Tell* and *Letters to the Lost*. She lives with her family near Annapolis, Maryland.

brigidkemmerer.com
@BrigidKemmerer